BATTLE IN THE BADLANDS

Marcus opened communication with his com officer, Ki-Lynn. "Where the hell are the reserves? I wanted them to close up with us ten minutes ago. This *Orion* is taking me a bite at a time."

"The enemy slipped their second lance of light-mediums in behind us," Ki-Lynn said, sounding unflappable as ever. "Reserves have reported two *Blackjack* 'Mechs causing trouble with Streak-variant short-range missile systems."

Marcus checked the nightmare that had settled over his tactical screen. The passages were so narrow and the rock thick enough to shield magscan that he had only a rough idea of where any of his men were. Half had been forced out the far northern side of the maze, up onto a plateau—part of an area known as The Fringes. These Fringes might still offer the Angels some basic cover, but beyond them were some flat desert plains. From what Marcus could tell, maybe only four of the Angels remained in this tight area of the badlands.

The battle raged all around him—and it was far out of his control. . . .

DOUBLE-BLIND

BATTLETECH®

DOUBLE-BLIND

Loren L. Coleman

A ROC BOOK

ROC
Published by the Penguin Group
Penguin Books USA Inc., 375 Hudson Street,
New York, New York 10014 U.S.A.
Penguin Books Ltd, 27 Wrights Lane,
London W8 5TZ, England
Penguin Books Australia Ltd, Ringwood,
Victoria, Australia
Penguin Books Canada Ltd, 10 Alcorn Avenue,
Toronto, Ontario, Canada M4V 3B2
Penguin Books (N.Z.) Ltd, 182-190 Wairau Road,
Auckland 10, New Zealand

Penguin Books Ltd, Registered Offices:
Harmondsworth, Middlesex, England

First published by Roc, an imprint of Dutton Signet,
a division of Penguin Books USA Inc.

First Printing, April, 1997
10 9 8 7 6 5 4 3 2 1

Series Editor: Donna Ippolito
Cover art by Les Dorscheid
Mechanical Drawings: Duane Loose and the FASA art department

 REGISTERED TRADEMARK—MARCA REGISTRADA

BATTLETECH, FASA, and the distinctive BATTLETECH and FASA logos are trademarks of the FASA Corporation, 1100 W. Cermak, Suite B305, Chicago, IL 60608.

Printed in the United States of America

To my lovely wife,
Heather Joy Coleman.
For believing.

Acknowledgments

The author would like to identify the following people who conspired to make this happen.

Jim LeMonds, for starting the ride. My parents, for all their support along the way. Everyone in the Orlando Gaming Group who got me involved in "those games," with a special note to Ray Sainze. A lot of people back in aft reactor berthing, U. S. S. *Theodore Roosevelt* CVN-71, who were repeatedly subjected to the noise of my fly-wheel printer and allowed me to live.

Jonathan Bond, for helping me make first contact with those in the business. The Eugene Professional Writer's Workshop, for beating me into submission, especially Dean Wesley Smith and Kristine Kathryn Rusch, who took pity on me and taught me a lot. Christopher Kubasik and Doug Tabb for giving me those first few breaks and Greg Gordon, for his all assistance in learning the game-writing field.

The wonderful people at FASA who had made this all happen. Bryan Nystul, a very patient man, and Sam Lewis, who arranged my intro to Bryan over the phone. Donna Ippolito, who took a chance with me and then helped me make this a better novel.

My wife, Heather Joy, for believing in me, and my sons, Talon LaRon and Conner Rhys, for giving up time on their favorite living jungle gym.

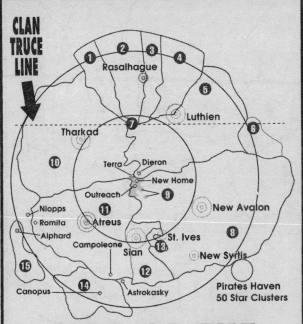

CLAN TRUCE LINE

Rasalhague
Luthien
Tharkad
Terra • Dieron
New Home
Outreach
Niopps
Romita
Alphard
Atreus
Campoleone
Sian
St. Ives
New Avalon
New Syrtis
Canopus
Astrokasky
Pirates Haven
50 Star Clusters

MAP OF THE INNER SPHERE

1 • Jade Falcon/Steel Viper, 2 • Wolf Clan, 3 • Ghost Bear,
4 • Smoke Jaguars/Nova Cats, 5 • Draconis Combine,
6 • Outworlds Alliance, 7 • Free Rasalhague Republic,
8 • Federated Commonwealth, 9 • Chaos March,
10 • Lyran Alliance, 11 • Free Worlds League,
12 • Capellan Confederation, 13 • St. Ives Compact
14 • Magistracy of Canopus, 15 • Marion Hegemony

Map Compiled by COMSTAR.
From information provided by the COMSTAR EXPLORER SERVICE
and the STAR LEAGUE ARCHIVES on Terra.

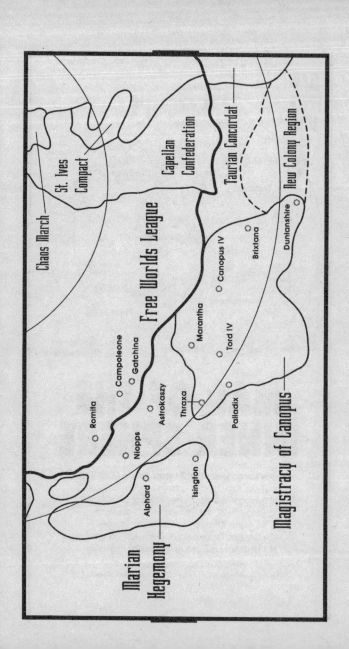

BOOK I

All warfare is based on deception.
> —Sun Tzu, *The Art of War*

The actual events of war are secondary. It is how those events are perceived that occupies most of a ruler's time and effort.
> Sun-Tzu Liao,
> journal entry, 5 August 3051, Outreach

Prologue

Word of Blake Warehouse
Harrisburg, Gibson
Principality of Gibson, Free Worlds League
15 October 3057

Precentor Demona Aziz stepped into the doorway of the dimly lit room, an office tucked into a corner of a huge warehouse, one of several the Word of Blake organization maintained on the planet Gibson. Though the rest of the place was stacked almost to capacity with crates, barrels, and pallets of supplies, the cramped aisles smelling of dust and the diesel fumes of cargo-loaders, the office itself was spotlessly clean. The undecorated plaster walls were painted off-white, and the room was sparsely furnished with several folding metal chairs, a desk holding a small lamp that was the room's only source of light, and a white-noise generator to guarantee the privacy of any conversation.

The office window, which looked out onto a pile of crates rising almost to the ceiling, rattled as the entire floor vibrated at regularly spaced intervals. Everyone present recognized the sound as the monstrous footsteps of the ten-meter-tall BattleMech that routinely patrolled Harrisburg's warehouse district. Upon arriving, Demona had recognized the huge war machine as one of the new *Grand Crusader*s, its bulky frame reminding her of a squat, well-muscled wrestler. The combination of deadly intent and new technology recalled to her some words of the Blessed Blake, who had taught that "those who fight to preserve technology and knowledge are the grandest crusaders of all."

Jerome Blake. Sainted founder of the ComStar Order, the semi-religious organization that had taken upon itself the task of preserving both knowledge and technology against the apocalypse of "dark times," as prophesied by the Blake. For nearly three centuries, its members had patiently bided their time, tending the hyperpulse generators—the only means of timely communication between stars—for the Great Houses of the Inner Sphere.

As the Blessed Blake had foreseen, the vast expanse of worlds colonized and inhabited by the sons and daughters of Terra had fallen into chaos and despair during those centuries of warfare, a long dark night from which Com-Star would light the path back to civilization. In recent times ComStar had tried to hasten this moment by intentionally sowing chaos, the quicker to give birth to the new order. Blake's will be done—ComStar would be the salvation of the Inner Sphere.

But ComStar had forsworn that sacred duty six years ago when the traitors Anastasius Focht and Sharilar Mori assassinated Primus Waterly and taken control of Com-Star, shamelessly announcing their intention to reform the Blessed Order into a secular organization that would freely share the technical secrets it had closely guarded for centuries. Even more upsetting was that so many members of the Order were willing to follow them into this heresy.

But not all. Demona Aziz stepped into the room, leaving someone else to close the door. Such manipulative little gestures came naturally to her, this one a subtle reminder of who held the power. A half dozen members of the Word of Blake's Toyama faction sat or stood about the office, most pulling their white robes tighter about them to ward off the warehouse's chill. Demona let her gold-embroidered hood fall back over the raised shoulders of her own formal robes, ignoring the cool touch of the air against her cheeks.

Her anger would keep her warm.

The man seated behind the desk rose even as she heard

the quick snick of the door being closed behind her. He folded back his own hood, exposing chiseled features that took on a foreboding look in the dim light. Stepping to one side, he gestured to his chair. "Precentor," he said, nodding respectfully in greeting.

Demona shook her head, disturbing a few long, wild strands of dark hair. "I will stand, Cameron."

She had been three weeks in arriving here from Atreus, capital of the Free Worlds League. Cooped up in the tight confines of a DropShip, ferrying from one JumpShip to another in order to traverse those many light years. Being out of communication with the Inner Sphere for so long, Demona felt as if she'd been deprived of a substance, a drug vital to her existence, and was only now receiving it again. So she would allow demi-Precentor Cameron St. Jamais to keep his seat, and he would feel that much more important. Good. He was a powerful man in his own right, and Demona would need such supporters. It was for similar reasons that she put up with his theatrics—these remote meeting places, the dim lighting, the white-noise generator. She would even have been willing to bet he'd purposely turned down the warehouse thermostat to heighten the drama.

But Demona Aziz also understood the need for secrecy, perhaps better than anyone in the Toyama. She had the most to gain, and therefore also the most to lose.

When the traitors Focht and Mori seized the reins of ComStar it had been Demona Aziz, Precentor of Atreus and member of ComStar's First Circuit, who had first stood against them. She could still recall her rage and feelings of betrayal as the two heretics initiated their reforms. The ComStar Order had stood for almost three centuries, keeping communications open among the thousands of worlds of the five Great Houses that divided the starry reaches of the Inner Sphere like slices of a vast interstellar pie. To listen to Focht and Mori rant on about reform, abandoning the very premises that were the foundation of ComStar . . .

Aziz had fled to Atreus, there to gain the support of Captain-General Thomas Marik, ruler of the Free Worlds League. It was she who had led the righteous to a new home. She who first organized resistance to the "reformed" ComStar. She who brought into existence the Word of Blake, an organization religiously devoted to the founding principles of ComStar, as set down so long ago by the sainted Jerome Blake.

And it was she who had then been betrayed again, passed over for leadership as Thomas Marik and high-ranking members of the new organization supported Precentor Blane as spokesman for Word of Blake. Demona knew with what political coin Blane had made that purchase. Hadn't it been Blane who'd first suggested naming Thomas Marik their new leader, their Primus-in-exile? Meanwhile Demona found herself relegated to leading the Toyama, a mere minority faction within the very organization she had birthed.

For more than five years now she had worked to regain her position of prominence, confident in her divine right to lead the Word of Blake toward its destiny. The Toyama still numbered among the smaller factions, but now carried political weight surpassed only by Blane's True Believers. And inside the Toyama were powerful men and women who could do more than talk and negotiate. They could accomplish things.

Demi-Precentor Cameron St. Jamais numbered among these. He led the ultra-radical 6th of June movement, a splinter group within the Toyama that took its name from the date Primus Myndo Waterly was murdered by the traitors Focht and Mori. The 6th of June now called for the assassination of every Great House leader within the Inner Sphere. This would surely plunge known space and its people into chaos, from which the Word of Blake would lead the way back to order. Though St. Jamais' methods were yet to be tested, such convictions gave him, and by association Demona, a powerful voice. So if small doses of ego-stroking and a tolerance for his theatrics were the price to pay, Demona would accommodate him. Yes, she knew the value of secrecy, and she understood the value and mechanics of loyalty even better.

St. Jamais understood the latter as well, and remained standing as Demona turned to face each Toyama member in turn. "There is no easy way to cushion the blow that has been struck at us," she began, keeping her voice low but unable to conceal the tremor of rage. "Blane"—she pronounced his name as the vilest curse—"in his ultimate wisdom has decided that the Toyama are not to be used in retaking Terra."

All six Toyama members began to voice their angry protests, those who'd been seated leaping to their feet. Only Demona and St. Jamais remained calm. She had spent her fury in private, during the first few days of travel to Gibson, and St. Jamais never allowed himself emotional outbursts.

Terra, the birthplace of humanity, had been under the direct control of ComStar for almost three centuries. Taking it from the heretics would be the test of Word of Blake's faith. *Of our divine right.* Preparations for Operation Odysseus had been in the works for some two years now, with the Toyama instrumental in several areas. The idea for the whole plan had, in fact, come from Demona Aziz herself—the insertion of a Word of Blake regiment onto Terra under false identity.

Demona looked to St. Jamais, who met her stare with a steely intensity. Against his dark skin the whites of his eyes almost seemed to glow eerily in the light of the desk lamp. She could sense the crouched presence within him, waiting for a direction to leap. *I will give you what you long for,* she promised silently.

At her nod, St. Jamais brought his hand down flat on the desk with a resounding slam. His simple order of "Enough!" stilled the buzz of complaints, which trailed off with somebody's final, "He can't do that."

"He *has* done it," Demona said, again turning slowly about the room to let them all see the calm but commanding mask she wore. "By not permitting us to participate in the actual battle for Terra he deprives us of the recognition we deserve."

A soft voice spoke up from Demona's left, one she recognized as that of demi-Precentor Jillian Adams. "Perhaps they will fail without us. We could cite that as a demonstration of Blane's ineptitude."

Demona shook her head firmly. "I have graciously donated two companies of the Toyama's assault

BattleMechs to Precentor Blane, to replace any of lighter design or questionable repair. I have also provided him with our latest intelligence reports concerning the Com-Star presence on Terra."

Demi-Precentor St. Jamais leaned forward, hands resting on the desk. "Why?"

It was not a challenge, but a simple desire for more information. Demona felt reaffirmed in her choice of lieutenants for the mission to come. "Word of Blake *must* succeed, with or without us. It must also prove to the whole Inner Sphere that we are a power to be reckoned with. I will not undermine its strength in order to improve our internal position."

"Then we must increase our strength by other means," St. Jamais said calmly. "To rival the support Blane will enjoy after retaking Terra."

"That and more," Demona agreed. "Once Terra has been regained, Blane plans to initiate aggressive diplomatic efforts to establish relations with the independent worlds surrounding it. At the very least he hopes to form a buffer zone with these worlds. It will also show him as a peace-maker, a powerful symbolic gesture that will cost him nothing and gain him much. I believe he has every chance of succeeding, and will then use the additional power base to declare himself Primus."

Amid another outburst from the others, St. Jamais took the news well. If Demona hadn't been watching, she might have missed the slight narrowing of the eyes and the faraway look that showed him lost in thought for but a few seconds before his gaze shifted carefully back to her. *Yes, Cameron*, she thought. *The Primacy is never far from your thoughts either, is it? You are young still, but you are learning.* She offered him a thin smile, her gaze steady. *You may hold that office one day, for your ambition might drive you the distance, but only when I am done with it.*

St. Jamais was first to regain full composure, quieting the others and then holding the floor by sheer force of will. "Perhaps Precentor Blane has grown too important in his own eyes, as have other Inner Sphere leaders."

Demona recognized the barely veiled suggestion, but

she had already rejected the idea of loosing the 6th of June against Blane. "Absolutely not. Such practices are reserved for use outside our Blessed Order."

Demona allowed them all a moment of reflection before continuing. "Precentor Blane has not been so obvious as to keep the Toyama away without some pretext, no matter how contrived. He thinks he is much too clever for that."

She smiled to herself at the thought. "Blane claims he is too occupied with planning and mobilizing our forces for Operation Odysseus to oversee other important agendas." She let her eyes travel over every face in the group. "And so he has asked me to oversee another of his schemes: engineering a full alliance between the Magistracy of Canopus and the Taurian Concordat."

She paused to let the others take this in. The Concordat and the Magistracy were two of the more powerful states of the Periphery, that distant region of space beyond the borders of the Inner Sphere. Emma Centrella, Magestrix of Canopus, had already negotiated a limited alliance with the neighboring Concordat. But everyone in this room knew more than they would ever tell about how that particular event had come to pass.

"Blane even cited 'current hostilities between the Magistracy and the Marian Hegemony' as a possible area of exploitation," she added, her smile growing broader.

Precentor Raymond Gabriel managed a dry chuckle, despite all the dire news. "The man is a fool. Word of Blake would welcome the creation of a new state in the Periphery to rival a Successor House, but Blane must think that mere fortune and prayer will drop into his lap every tool he needs to accomplish it. We could smuggle weapons on his personal ship underneath his own bed and he would never know it."

"But the man is not a fool, Precentor," St. Jamais said quietly. "Would that we were so fortunate. We have merely been blessed with circumstances that would seem a natural progression from past events."

Demona Aziz listened silently, noting that as usual St. Jamais held the stronger position. The Marian Hegemony, another of the states in that region of the Periphery, was

ruled by Caesar Sean O'Reilly and lay rimward of House
Marik's Free Worlds League. It butted up against the
Magistracy of Canopus, which separated the Marian
Hegemony and the Taurian Concordat with a body of star
systems only two hundred and fifty light years across.
The Toyama had been smuggling weapons and new technology into the Marian Hegemony for nearly four years,
encouraging O'Reilly to maintain a hostile attitude
toward Canopus. It was that action which had driven
Emma Centrella into an alliance with the Taurian Concordat. For the past year, O'Reilly had been increasing his
raids on Canopus border worlds with great success. This
could only serve to drive Canopus closer to the Taurian
Concordat. But there was more to it than that.

"There's more to it," she said, voicing her last thought
aloud. "Right now, the Marian Hegemony is ready to
cooperate with us in almost any effort. I say we step up
the pressure on Canopus. Our supply lines are already in
place and we control the key officials. Demi-Precentor
Adams, could we double or even triple the flow of weapons and material through Astrokaszy?"

"Double, at least," Adams said. "Perhaps triple, though
that would risk exposing our involvement."

Demona nodded. "Then we double it for now. Blane
would like a full alliance bordering on a merger between
Canopus and the Taurians within a year's time. I think we
can cut that in half. Controlling the creation of the
alliance will gain the Toyama the influence we seek. Then
we allow the Word of Blake's assistance to the Marian
Hegemony be discovered."

"And Blane takes the blame," Precentor Gabriel finished. "Very nice."

"Not quite." Demona Aziz smiled thinly. "We are
already set up to implicate either the Capellan Confederation or the Free Worlds League. I say we let Thomas
Marik absorb the damage. His reputation for noble ideal-
ism will be destroyed, and that too will bleed over onto
Blane, who is his biggest supporter." *And I gain a measure of revenge in the name of the Blessed Blake.*

"But we still prepare for both," St. Jamais said. "Yes?"

Demona hesitated for a moment and then nodded. "Yes.

So far Sun-Tzu Liao has been fairly predictable, but we should remain ready to drive a wedge between him and Thomas should he step out of line. 'Preparation is always the key to victory.' Thus said the sainted Blake."

Silence greeted Demona's last words as the group considered the power they would hold over the Word of Blake. In the distance, Demona could just make out the heavy footfalls of the patrolling BattleMech as the shock waves came up through her own feet.

I shook the Inner Sphere in such a way when giving birth to the Word of Blake, she thought. *They* may credit *it to Blane or even Thomas Marik, but it was I. This time I shall wake them with a thunderous overture to the rise of the Toyama.* She glanced at St. Jamais, who seemed lost again in his own thoughts. *And when I have finally taken my place as Primus, the whole of the Inner Sphere might well turn to me as the only great leader still left.*

1

Ceruman Plateau, Ashentine Mountains
New Home
Chaos March
17 March 3058

Two klicks shy of where the southern edge of the Ceruman Plateau butted up against the near-vertical rise of the Ashentine Mountains, a long-abandoned industrial complex was the scene of the latest battle for the planet of New Home. Thunderous explosions of missiles and the crackling discharges of big energy weapons had already broken the early-morning stillness, but the mists of dawn still covered the area, swirling around the mammoth legs of the BattleMechs.

Near the center of the complex a *Warhammer* painted the brown and gray of mountain camouflage stalked the mist-covered grounds between derelict factories and abandoned warehouses. Its arms, which ended in the large bore of PPC barrels instead of hands, tracked left and then right. Painted onto the *Hammer*'s lower-left leg, where the armor plating ran smooth from knee joint to ankle, was a rough-looking angel with white and dirty-gray feathered wings, a five o'clock shadow, and carrying a gyroslug rifle.

Not the sort of design to promote belief in the Almighty unless a person thought of Heaven in terms of an armed camp.

Sweat trickled down the face of Marcus GioAvanti, commander of the mercenary company known as Avanti's Angels, stinging his eyes and leaving a salty taste on his lips. The air inside the *Hammer*'s cockpit was hot, dry, and stifling, made bearable only by the cooling vest that kept his body temperature down. The growing faintness of missile and energy fire told him just how deep the battle had swept into the complex. *Doesn't matter,* Marcus thought. He blinked hard to clear his vision, then searched his head's-up display for the enemy *JagerMech* he'd lost among the low hills that surrounded the widely spaced buildings. The HUD compressed a full 360 degrees of scanning into only 120 degrees of vision, projecting the tactical imagery in a band across the upper portion of his cockpit window. Learning to read it properly was one of the trickier skills a 'Mech pilot had to master. But that *Jag* was almost certainly the enemy commander's BattleMech. Defeating him would go a long way toward winning the battle, so Marcus doggedly pursued his quarry, trusting his people to handle themselves.

As it was, the enemy 'Mech found him first as Marcus moved the *Warhammer* through the rubble-strewn area of what had once been a large warehouse. The 65-ton *JagerMech* suddenly appeared from around a building farther ahead, its blocky torso and the large, barrel-like appendages that were its arms letting Marcus' computer identify it immediately. Its autocannon arms spat out fifty-centimeter depleted-uranium slugs that hammered away at the right leg and torso of Marcus' *Warhammer,* making the 'Mech stumble as it moved through the loose rubble.

Trying to keep almost 70 tons of upright metal in balance is no small feat. Marcus tightened his grip on the *Hammer*'s control sticks, their neoleather covering wicking away the sweat from his palms as he fought to keep the huge war machine on its feet. While he moved the 'Mech's arms to provide a stabilizing shift in weight, his neuro-helmet fed signals from his brain—based on Marcus' own equilibrium—straight into the BattleMech's huge gyro-scope and myomer musculature.

This time it worked, and Marcus managed to find solid purchase within the loose rubble long enough to trigger the particle projection cannons that were the arms of his own 'Mech. Two azure beams stabbed out at the *Jager-Mech,* one grazing the left leg and the other boring deep into an already-damaged right arm. Armor melted and poured to the ground in streams of molten steel. Then the *Jag*'s right arm suddenly dropped, a blackened, ruined shell swinging loosely from its shoulder-mount hinge. Deprived of a major weapon and rocking under the loss of two tons of armor, the enemy 'Mech staggered his machine back around the building.

Marcus cleared the field of rubble and paused to check his tactical display. As far as he could tell from the collection of colored dots and lines, his entire unit was still intact and in position according to plan. He swallowed dryly, trying to coax life back into his parched throat, then drew in a steadying breath. The heavy, rancid scent of sweat left an ache in his upper sinuses, which he merely ignored as he spoke into his helmet mike.

"General announcement," he called out, giving Ki-Lynn a second to patch him into the unit's open channel. Ki-Lynn Tanaga functioned as his comm officer, screening all non-essential communications between Marcus and his company. She was also particularly adept at breaking enemy communications, which was why Marcus was sure he faced the enemy's commander in the *JagerMech.*

"Archangel to the flock," Marcus continued, bringing his *Warhammer* up to a steady walking pace of 40 kph. "Press them now! Prometheus element, light up the sky." Even as he gave the order, Marcus coaxed the *Warhammer* up toward its top speed of 65 kph. The

JagerMech had yet to reappear on either side of the building, so Marcus held weapons ready and moved straight in. The cockpit swayed lightly from side to side as the huge machine's colossal gait ate up the distance, each step sending a small tremor up through the machine and its pilot.

Then a bright, reddish-orange flash of light blossomed far off to Marcus' right, turning the normal amber glow of his instrument panel a sickly pink. He heard the deep bass roar of a large explosion at about the same moment the tremors hit, though at this distance it threw only the smallest hitch into the *Warhammer*'s normal step. A column of fire roiled up into the sky, quickly turning an oily black as it smeared a dark scar against the blue.

That's it, he thought, and smiled grimly as he plowed the *Warhammer* straight into the wall of the building.

Six short months ago, New Home and a few dozen worlds like it had been under the peaceful rule of the Federated Commonwealth—the mighty Inner Sphere state formed nearly thirty years earlier by a marriage between House Davion and House Steiner. For two decades it had seemed that little could stand against the Steiner-Davions, the first major alliance since the fall of the Star League three centuries before. Many hoped—and others feared— that it heralded a return to grander times, when the whole Inner Sphere had been united under the single government of the Star League. And that might actually have come to pass if not for the Clan invasion, a debacle from which the Inner Sphere was still trying to recover.

Only six months ago, the Free Worlds League and the Capellan Confederation had formed an alliance of their own to attack the FedCom region known as the Sarna March, retaking worlds they'd lost to the Federated Commonwealth twenty-five years before and inciting rebellion on dozens of others.

Then came what some thought might be the final death blow, when Katrina Steiner-Davion made off with the Steiner half of the Federated Commonwealth—renaming it the Lyran Alliance. In just a few short weeks Prince Victor Davion lost several decades worth of political ground, with a large region of disputed space suddenly emerging as a kind of interstellar no-man's-land in what had once been the very heart of his realm. More than fifty settled worlds were suddenly set free, many of them claimed by no less than three of the great powers of the Inner Sphere.

Half of these, worlds that had originally belonged to House Liao before the Davions took them, reverted their allegiance to Liao. Capellan Chancellor Sun-Tzu Liao had yet to consolidate his position, either unable or unwilling to stretch his military resources so far. Still, these worlds remained under his political influence, and for the garrison price of three or four BattleMech regiments, the Capellan Confederation could reclaim almost sixty light years' worth of space.

The other half, another globular area of space roughly sixty light years in diameter and sitting in the very center of the Inner Sphere, became known as the Chaos March. It was so named because no one government held sway and the various worlds were now involved in Byzantine power struggles, with as many as three or four different sides vying in some cases. And always, the tantalizing carrot of independent rule dangled in front of them.

Most of these worlds craved that independence, a few going so far as to establish minor alliances with neighboring systems, while the Great House leaders refused to relinquish their own claims. This meant a lot of job opportunities for smaller mercenary units such as the Angels, but also a greater involvement in the politics of the situation as well as serious potential for betrayal. There was no way to really tell which side held the most power at any given moment—your ally today easily stabbing you in the back tomorrow.

Of which the Angels had already had a serious taste.

The unit had just come off a contract on Arboris where the Farmers Freedom Army had hired them to harass Capellan Confederation forces on the planet. Someone somewhere must have decided to recoup some of the expenses of hiring a company of BattleMechs. After two months of successful hit-and-fade tactics against the Ishara Grenadiers, the FFA literally sold the Angels' position to Grenadier commander Choung Vong. The Angels barely made it off Arboris—their losses cutting deeply into their strength. They lost two warriors and three of their BattleMechs, with the rest of the company severely mauled. Bringing themselves back up to even near-full strength had cost the Angels every last C-bill in the company coffers as well as most of the mercenaries' personal funds.

With the operating expenses necessary to support a military unit threatening to drive the Angels into dissolution, Marcus had jumped at Baron Shienzé's offer of a contract to help New Home maintain its recently won independence. The fee would barely pay bills from two months back, but it did include better salvage rights than the Angels had seen for some time. Not enough to bring them back to full strength after expenses, but maybe enough to help them on their way.

So with one eye on the future and another warily regarding their new employer, the Angels had come to the aid of New Home.

The planet was making its bid for freedom, supported by the Thirtieth Lyran Guards, who had decided not to accept Katrina Steiner's invitation to return to the Lyran Alliance. The New Home Regulars, a faction of the Zhanzheng de guang terrorist group supported by Sun-Tzu Liao, had been waging a fairly successful guerrilla war against the Thirtieth for several months. With the decision not to accept Katrina's offer, the Thirtieth lost its chief source of supply and could not afford to risk resources in an extended campaign. So it fell to the Angels to locate and destroy several remote bases in an attempt to cripple the resistance efforts of the New Home Regulars.

A job for which Avanti's Angels were especially suited.

The Angels specialized in a blitzkrieg-style of warfare. Infiltration, extraction, raiding—any situation calling for a hit-hard-and-fade-fast approach. It was a philosophy of combat fostered by the two years of hell that had been the Clan invasion.

Many historians dated the fall of the Star League from the moment of General Aleksandr Kerensky's exodus in

2784, when he summoned more than eighty percent of the Star League Defense Force and fled the Inner Sphere before his troops could be drawn into what would come to be known as the Succession Wars. Nearly three hundred years later, Kerensky's heirs returned as the greatest threat the Inner Sphere had ever faced. The Angels had been a part of House Kurita's DCMS forces then, a six-BattleMech ad hoc unit created to provide regular units any amount of extra resistance against the Clans. The unofficial term was *sacrificial offering,* as Marcus always put it, the Angels always drawing rear-guard duty to allow line regiments precious moments to escape.

Whether augmenting DCMS regular forces or standing alone, the Angels took a beating in almost every stand against the Clans. Marcus saw too many good warriors fall, some of them friends, men and women losing their lives over a patch of ground that was soon scorched black by weapons or churned up under the giant feet or heavy treads of war machines. But the Angels survived, grafting to themselves the orphans of lost battles and other shattered units. Technicians and infantry. 'Mech pilots with their own machines or numbering among the Dispossessed. Their survival potential drew the stragglers in, just as their experience of being on the run taught them superior—even elite—tactics in small-unit engagements, not to mention special skills such has how to salvage on the fly.

That early sense of growth was fleeting, however, as the next battle would promptly claim its price in lives and equipment. Those years of almost constant combat and change bred into the Angels their nomadic lifestyle, as well as their belief that the offense held all the advantages. The mercenaries avoided defensive engagements and they never accepted garrison duty. Marcus himself would never again allow too much importance to settle on any one thing. Not a place, person, or battle. *Keep the initiative, and you can dictate the battle.*

A lesson he was applying in the Angels' current situation.

The New Home Regulars' Ceruman base camp contained their chief stockpile of supplies. Guarding it was a strengthened company of BattleMechs and a battalion of conventional infantry, while Marcus had landed on New Home with only a bare company—one of his 'Mechs currently down for repair—and one light hovercraft. Eleven against sixteen—not the best odds, until Marcus decided to tip the balance. *Take away what is important in the base to the New Home Regulars, and their will to defend it lessens that much more.* Marcus' plan called for elimination of the New Home Regulars' supplies of weapons and material. That was what his order to Prometheus element had been all about. The area around their ordnance stockpile was now lit with the afterglow of the explosion and the fires leaping up among the buildings.

His *Warhammer* erupted from the far side of the building amid a final shower of rubble and timbers. The enemy *JagerMech* stood less than thirty meters off, turned slightly away from Marcus as it faced the direction from which the explosion had come. Marcus floated the gold targeting cross hairs over the enemy 'Mech even as it began to react to his presence. The primary triggers on both control sticks were configured to fire either all left-side or all right-side weapons. Marcus pulled back on both, treating the *JagerMech* to one of the most destructive light shows an Inner Sphere BattleMech could deliver.

A bit of a cheat, though, to call it fully Inner Sphere. From their times against the Clans, the Angels had managed to salvage a small array of Clan-tech weapons and other equipment. While they had never retrieved a functional OmniMech—the dreaded Clan version of a BattleMech—they did stockpile a half-dozen Clan PPCs, some lasers, and even a Gauss rifle. It gave the Angels a slight edge where others didn't expect it, and now two of those PPCs delivered half again as much punch as their Inner Sphere cousins.

The twin beams of blue-white lightning streaked out to slam into the *JagerMech*'s torso, boiling away armor and then cutting away at the foamed-titanium skeleton beneath. Two medium lasers also stabbed at the enemy machine, one missing high over the right shoulder and the other clipping the left arm. The torso-mounted machine gun rattled a hail of bullets off the *JagerMech*'s head, doing little damage but no doubt adding to the enemy commander's dismay. Last to strike were the six missiles of the *Warhammer*'s SRM pack, rising on trails of fire and smoke to swarm across the scant thirty meters between the two machines in a matter of seconds. One missile exploded between the machine's colossal legs, tearing up a large chunk of the ground that rained over the area in a black cascade. Two missiles slammed into the BattleMech's upper right thigh, and the remaining three flew straight into the cavity bored out by the PPCs.

The heat scale indicator jumped from green straight into the high red zone as the fusion engine that was the heart of a BattleMech spiked to match the power demands. Temperature in the cockpit soared, momentarily overloading the cooling vest and making Marcus' vision swim as he slapped at the override switch to prevent automatic shutdown of his machine. His eyes burned from the sweat pouring down his face, and he gasped for oxygen as the first few breaths of the hot air smothered him.

When Marcus was able to concentrate a few long seconds later, the *JagerMech* was already falling. Large chunks of metal poured from the hole in its side. Pieces of its gyro, Marcus thought. It landed on its ruined right arm, crumpling the arm beneath its massive bulk. It finally came to rest face downward and sprawled out as if a puppet master had cut the strings to a giant marionette. Unable to control his machine, the enemy commander powered down all weapons and popped his cockpit hatch in a gesture of surrender.

That has to do it, Marcus thought, beginning to regain a measure of his breath. His cooling vest was cold against his chest, but the rest of him felt utterly broiled. *Even if the explosion wasn't enough, this should be.*

Even as Marcus was opening a commline to Ki-Lynn, he was already hearing the reports of his lance commanders as Ki passed them along. The bulk of the New Home Regulars were in full flight. Charlene Boske, the Angels' executive officer, reported a full role call. Thomas Faber's *Marauder* was the worst damaged, with one arm destroyed. He learned also that the infantry had abandoned their hardened

positions and were fleeing in an assortment of old vehicles.
Charlene ordered one stopped and secured as battle spoils:
a 5-ton Savannah Master hovercraft similar to the one the
Angels already owned.

Plus the burned-out shell of a *Wolverine* and a crushed
Locust, as reported through Ki-Lynn by other Angels.
Plus a half-scrapped *JagerMech,* Marcus added silently to
the list.

And a warehouse full of enough munitions and supplies
to repair the Angels' machines and possibly get the *Jager-
Mech* back on its feet. Marcus smiled to himself. Charlene
and Vincent Foley, the two members of Prometheus element, had set off a blast all right, but not in the ordnance
warehouse. The Angels were loathe to destroy supplies
that could be taken instead, especially when the detonation of a few large aviation fuel tanks would suffice.

"Clean-up time, everyone," Marcus said as the reports
trailed off. "Cordon off the warehouse. We don't want
any retreating Regular to realize what happened." He
called off the names of the four most junior Mech-
Warriors. "I want a two-Mech element pursuing the most-
rearward stragglers, but only to keep them moving along.
I repeat, let the Regulars run."

The Angels had a solid victory, and there was no need
to risk a life or a BattleMech in a hard pursuit. Such a loss
would hurt the Angels far more than another salvaged
enemy 'Mech would help them. "First team to set up
watch at a quarter-klick. Second element to break pursuit
and establish patrol at half a klick. Everyone else stay
buttoned up until the ground forces sweep the place
clean."

Marcus watched through his viewport as the enemy
commander climbed from his ruined machine and threw
his helmet to the ground. "Paula, get your *Wasp* over here
and take charge of guarding our prisoner." Marcus hated
to hand over another MechWarrior for what was sure to
be confinement, but the Baron was paying the bills and he
wanted any prisoners he could get. Marcus comforted
himself with the thought that the enemy commander
would be repatriated to the Capellan Confederation once
this was all over.

He switched his commline over to the general frequencies again to listen in on some of the chatter among his Angels. Although their DropShip, the *Heaven Sent,* had yet to touch down, they were already feeling the post-mission decompression. He switched back to his direct channel with Ki-Lynn and left them to it. There'd been little enough rest this last month, and with their coffers still low the unit would be jumping back into the fire soon enough. They deserved whatever brief respite he could give them.

Who knew when the next Angel would fall.

2

Shienzé Stronghold
Bastille, New Home
Chaos March
19 March 3058

Charlene Boske walked out to where the Angels had gathered outside the walls of the Shienzé Stronghold for the post-mission debrief. She wore shorts and T-shirt, normal MechWarrior attire in the stifling confines of a 'Mech cockpit but now worn merely to enjoy the lazy warmth of the afternoon sun. Her long blonde hair hung down her back in a thick cord, exposing the pale skin of her neck and shoulders. A cool breeze intermittently blew in from the west, off a large inland sea, carrying the hint of moisture and salt and adding to the pleasantness of the afternoon.

Pleasant, Charlene, thought, until the Angels learned of their next assignment.

As executive officer, she usually handled contract agreements with the aid of Jase Torgensson, a Free Rasalhague Republic native and one of the most resourceful men she'd ever met. Even the way he'd joined the Angels

had been impressive. Having learned of their mission to
raid behind Clan Ghost Bear lines on his homeworld of
Utrecht, he'd offered his services if he would be allowed
to extract his family. He'd even brought with him one of
the Combine's rare C³ computers that allowed 'Mechs to
share targeting system information, a feat he put down to
clerical oversight at his last command. Jase now operated
as the Angels' chief scout and was a fine assault 'Mech
pilot to boot.

For this mission, however, he'd been left back on the
world of Outreach, the center of almost all mercenary
hiring activity in the Inner Sphere. The Angels were still
in a precarious position financially, and Marcus knew
they needed to have another assignment lined up. Jase had
lent his *BattleMaster* to one of the two dispossessed
MechWarriors currently on the Angels' roster, and he'd
remained behind on Outreach with the Angels' other
DropShip, the unit's dependents, and most of their technical support staff. The *Head of a Pin*, or *Pinhead* as it
was affectionately known, was an ancient *Fortress* Class
ship held together with not much more than promises and
the skill of a few really good techs. Safe enough as long
as it stayed out of combat, the *Pinhead* normally carried
the Angels' dependents and support personnel from station to station. That Jase had been left on Outreach to
negotiate a new contract without her sat all right with
Charlene. What had bothered her was that Marcus was the
only one who knew anything about it and he still had said
not a word about it to her or the others.

And now she knew why. The reason was in an HPG
message that had just been delivered and which she was at
this moment carrying to Marcus.

Just ahead and towering a good eight to ten meters
above her were four of the heaviest 'Mechs owned by the
Angels. They stood in a tightly spaced row, their
backs to the thick, gray walls of steel-reinforced ferrocrete that framed Baron Shienzé's large stronghold. She
had ordered them placed there as a courtesy to the baron.
The rest of the Angels' BattleMechs were racked into
their places in the 'Mech bay of the *Heaven Sent,* the

Union class DropShip grounded not a hundred meters behind her.

The Angels sat or stood around the feet of Thomas Faber's *Marauder,* the last 'Mech in line. Faber was perched up on the giant foot of his machine like some improbably massive, dark-skinned sprite, dressed only in cooling shorts and looking placid enough as he lay back to soak up the warmth of the day. Charlene thought of the rumors that Faber had formerly been an Elemental, one of the genetically bred Clan infantry. The black man was almost tall enough, and the way he seemed to live only for combat was as obsessive as that of any Clansman. Charlene knew that Marcus had checked out Faber's past, right back to his birth in the Dieron District of the Draconis Combine, but sometimes she couldn't help but wonder.

The eight-meter-high walls of the Shienzé stronghold cast a shadow that cooled the area around the *Marauder*'s feet. Sitting in the shady half of one of them, Brent Karsskhov leaned back, stealing glances at Charlene whenever he thought she wasn't looking. The other Angels also seemed to prefer protection from New Home's G-type sun, most of them spread out and reclining here and there in whatever shade could be found around the 'Mech, but Paula Jacobs had spread out a blanket and oiled herself up to take in the deep heat of the day.

Charlene might have smiled at that sight, if not for the message she carried to Marcus.

Marcus GioAvanti lounged just within the area of shade. Shoulder-length dark blonde hair framed a still-youthful face, though Charlene could see where the burdens of command had begun to etch lines around his faded blue eyes and across his forehead. In red jeans and black T-shirt he could have been merely another member of the company, except for the way the Angels had unconsciously arranged themselves around him to make Marcus the center of the group. The light, honey-coconut smell of Paula's tanning lotion drifted up to Charlene, and she wondered if Paula's near-naked posing almost directly in front of Marcus was another of her many unsuccessful attempts to attract the commander's attention. Marcus cared for his people well, but he let very few ever get close to him. Charlene thought that must be a lonely way to live, and counted it as the one flaw in her commanding officer.

" 'Bout time, Charlie," Marcus said, making a show of studying a non-existent chronometer on his wrist. A few of the more senior Angels chuckled outright, though she noted that all junior personnel appropriately hid their smiles.

Charlene stepped into the shade to hand him the message, a folded sheet stamped with ComStar's spiked-starburst insignia. Everyone knew it must be from Torgensson on Outreach, and some couldn't help but shift around as anticipation worked on their nerves.

While Marcus read, Charlene stepped back into the warmth of the sun. As the Angels' executive officer, running such meetings usually fell to her. If she wanted an informal meeting outside, she'd have one. With the text of the message haunting her, she knew she'd better enjoy it while she could.

"First of all," she began, "Baron Shienzé has expressed his appreciation for our work. The commander of the Thirtieth Lyran Guards, Dolores Whitman, also expresses her satisfaction, though she still bargained hard for some of those supplies we liberated from the Regulars."

Technicians and some of the more savvy MechWarriors nodded. As mercenaries the Angels well understood the difference between professional courtesy and business. "What supplies we didn't keep for ourselves," Charlene continued, "we cashed out to the Baron. That clears the projected costs of repairing our own machines and maybe the *JagerMech*."

What it did not cover—which Charlene didn't have to say because everyone knew—was one more month of back debts the Angels would be forced to float on the credit they'd built up over the past several years. And then there were the normal operating expenses. As of tomorrow, the unit would begin to accrue more debt as they fueled their ships, paid administrative fees, and ordered supplies not recovered from the warehouse. All this didn't take into account that once again there would be no personal monies distributed. As a unit the Angels were better off, but still under the onus of Arboris. From the way some of them watched Marcus as he continued to study the message, Charlene could tell they were hoping Torgensson had come through for them.

Charlene decided to lighten the atmosphere, and turned to some special notes she and Marcus had taken during the raid.

"Ki," she said, looking around and finding the small Oriental woman kneeling placidly off to Marcus' right. Like Faber, Ki-Lynn Tanaga was a native of the Draconis Combine. Where Thomas had come up from the lowest class and could never have hoped to rise higher in the Combine's rigid social structure, Ki's family was of more fortunate station. Marcus and Charlene knew Ki-Lynn had joined the Angels to escape the destiny her family would have liked to buy for her. She had become a passable MechWarrior, but possessed a rare talent for communications, which made her an invaluable asset. "Good work breaking the House Regulars' comm channels," Charlene praised her. "If we hadn't been able to identify and distract their commander, our little trick might not have worked."

Dressed in a traditional silk kimono despite the heat, Ki-Lynn shrugged lightly. "They made it easy," she said, her voice soft and with a humility typical of her Combine upbringing. "They used the same general code I'd broken before. It was just a matter of finding the correct frequencies." She paused almost imperceptibly before continuing. "They also used the same specific code words to identify the different elements of their company, much as we do."

Ki-Lynn's comment almost slipped past Charlene's attention. *Much as we do,* she repeated mentally as she suddenly realized the significance, and reminded herself to pay more attention to Ki's seemingly offhand comments. The people of the Combine often practiced the fine art of indirection to their talk. "See me from now on before any mission. We're going to start changing our designations along with our codes. What we can do to others, they could do to us."

"Faber," Charlene called out, glancing back over her

shoulder. "Battle ROMs show that your targeting was up in the eightieth percentile. You missed only one PPC shot and a few laser salvos. Nice gunnery."

Faber remained nearly motionless in his repose. She almost thought he hadn't heard her until he mumbled, *"itashimashite."* Charlene knew enough Japanese to recognize a sloppy "you're welcome."

"You also soaked up the most damage, again, going point-blank against 'Mechs you should be hitting from long range. It cost you an arm this time."

"Itashimashite," the big man said again, but he nodded once to let her know the message was understood. Not that Charlene expected him to change his style. In her mind, Faber defied the statistical odds. He'd had more 'Mechs shot out from under him, most by catastrophic damage, than anyone she'd ever heard of. Yet he always walked away from the wreckage and always gave out better than he got.

Charlene waited then as Marcus finished reading, folded the sheet back up, and stuck it into a pocket.

"Thanks, Charlene," he said, taking charge of the meeting. She gave him a friendly nod, then walked over and slumped to the ground next to Brent Karsskhov, who nearly jumped up out of nervousness. She smiled as she too leaned back against the *Marauder*'s big foot. Though she was sitting in the sun-warmed portion, she found the scent of lubricating grease more pleasant than Paula's tanning lotion.

Charlene enjoyed the nervous tension she caused in Brent. He was the newest member of the unit, picked up on Arboris after he quit the FFA in protest over their treatment of the Angels. Everyone knew that Brent had a jones for her, but was nervous about approaching his new XO. Charlene found the situation both amusing and frustrating, but had resolved to wait until Brent got over it on his own. When Paula squirmed around in the pretense of stretching, she was glad Brent paid her less attention than did Marcus.

"All right, everyone," Marcus said, sitting up now. "Baron Shienzé has invited us to a dinner this evening. It's a reception for some Word of Blake reps who the

Baron invited here to discuss New Home's need for military supply. So it's dress clothing or—for those of you who still have them—dress uniforms."

That last was greeted with a chorus of groans and booing, some good-natured and some real. Marcus let it play out until one of the Angels jokingly suggested they strip the sheets off their beds and all go in white robes in honor of Word of Blake. With a wave of one hand, Marcus cut off the chants of, "Toga, toga."

"Dress clothing and/or uniforms," he repeated. "Attendance is mandatory except for those on duty. No switching. Exceptions will be made only for technicians who'd rather be working." That received claps from Yuri Petrovka, the Angels' chief tech, and his subordinates. "The Word of Blake reps are to be treated with courtesy and respect."

Marcus looked to the left and right, as if to make sure everyone was paying attention, but Charlene thought that last order would be hard to stomach. In her opinion, the Word of Blake people were everything bad in ComStar come back to haunt the Inner Sphere.

"Word of Blake is here to stay, people," Marcus continued. "We don't upset a potential employer, even if we don't agree with their politics." He paused. "*Especially* if we don't agree with their politics."

Vince Foley sat picking lint off his cowboy hat. "So, tell us again why you insulted the Capellan ambassador on Outreach last year?"

Foley's tone sounded a bit too innocent for the question to be serious, but Charlene decided to take it as such anyway and answered for Marcus. "He made it a personal matter. That wasn't politics, it was"—she paused to consider her words—"an exercise in restraint of courtesy."

That drew a smile from Marcus, which made it worth the effort in Charlene's book. "I don't expect much trouble from the Blakists," he said. "Now that they've taken Terra away from ComStar, they've been busy trying to build good relations with their new neighbors here in the Chaos March. We don't upset that. They were one of the few organizations hiring small mercenary groups when we were last on Outreach, and like ComStar they've got access to Star League-era equipment. So we do not raze the JumpShip, so to speak."

"That isn't who hired us, is it?" Brent Karsskhov leaned forward, doubt clouding his features. "I mean, that message—it was from Torgensson? We got hired?"

Marcus nodded solemnly. "Yes, the message was from Torgensson on Outreach. Good news," he called out in general. "We've got a new employer."

There were claps and whistles of relief at that news. Even Paula sat up to pay closer attention. Charlene heard a deep bass whisper float down from above her—a few lines from one of the ear-splitting songs Faber always played in his cockpit during battle. Only Ki-Lynn also seemed to notice something odd about Marcus. Charlene saw the other woman's dark eyes flick to her for a second before returning to their commander.

Marcus waited until silence fell again. "Jase has gone on ahead via commercial transport to look things over, make contacts. The *Pinhead* and the rest of our people are on the way here to rendezvous with us. A JumpShip will be here in three days, and be ready to jump us out in about a week, so time is short. We bail out of the Baron's party at midnight and burn for the zenith jump point, which means the *Heaven Sent*'s got to be loaded and ready to go in three hours."

Charlene watched Marcus climb to his feet, and pushed herself up off the ground as well, giving Brent's shoulder a reassuring squeeze as she did.

"Commander," Paula Jacobs called out, reaching over to tug at his pants leg. "Where are we headed?"

Marcus shrugged, as if their destination wasn't that important. "The Magistracy of Canopus," he said matter-of-factly. "We're heading out into the Periphery."

Glancing from face to face, Charlene read the sudden flashes of concern—the same worry she'd begun to feel from the moment she'd read that message. The Periphery had long been a dumping ground for broken units and a place to which mercenaries crept off until their finances—or lack of them—either improved or got the better of them. It was hard to make a name for oneself out there, so far from where the real action was, and the leaders of Periphery realms could be notoriously capricious.

Vince Foley was the first to speak, shocked straight out of his exaggerated cowboy drawl. "Wasn't there anything else? I mean, we aren't that bad off, are we?"

"We need the work," Marcus said, avoiding the question. "They wanted a unit with our kind of expertise and were willing to pay well for it. Enough to slash away at our back debts and bring our finances back up to where they were before Arboris. And we'll have the chance to get everyone outfitted again."

Charlene knew that meant heavy salvage, which would be appreciated by the two Angels who were Dispossessed. But nothing ever came free. If some Periphery state was willing to pay out good money and generous salvage, the job wasn't likely to be an easy one. The Magistracy must be desperate. "You know the mission then?" she asked.

Marcus nodded. "Most of you know enough about the Periphery to have heard that the Marian Hegemony's gotten pretty aggressive of late. Not only have they stepped up their raids on Canopus worlds, but they've somehow gotten their hands on new technology and 'Mech designs.

"Our job is to locate the line of supply to the Hegemony, disrupt it, and report back to Emma Centrella on the identity of the supplier and the location of any equipment caches we aren't able to capture ourselves. With any luck, Jase will have solved the first problem for us by the time we get out there." Marcus shrugged. "That's it."

"That's it?" Vince asked, incredulous. "One company against a supply depot garrison force? Probably something between a battalion and a full regiment? That's enough. More than enough."

"Anybody wanting a leave of absence?" Marcus asked softly, glancing around. Charlene saw the worry still showing on the faces of several people, who quickly flushed with embarrassment as their commander's gaze moved from face to face. If nothing else, they'd learned to trust him.

"Well," Faber said, swinging down to the ground and landing lightly on his big frame, "think I'll go rack the

Mary Dear." He walked over to the retractable ladder that would take him up to the cockpit of his *Marauder,* the 'Mech which he'd baptized with such an unlikely nickname. "Sounds like we're done here."

Without further comment, Marcus walked off too, headed toward the DropShip. Charlene watched him go. She was glad the Angels would have work and a chance to rebuild, but she couldn't help wondering what Marcus had gotten them into this time.

3

Shienzé Stronghold
Bastille, New Home
Chaos March
19 March 3058

Marcus' restraint lasted only until dessert.

It wasn't anything Precentor Sandra Schofield said or did. In fact, Schofield was the very soul of politeness from the first moment Baron Shienzé introduced her to Marcus. That had been over appetizers. The Precentor and her aide, demi-Precentor Ryan Hughes, had arrived late.

Baron Shienzé had tapped his knife against his wine glass for attention. The piercing chime cut through the murmur of a score of conversations, commanding silence down the impressive length of the formal dining hall. The table had places for two hundred, and its setting rivaled the many tales Marcus had ever heard about the royal dining halls of New Avalon or Tharkad. Crystal with the Shienzé family crest cut into the base just below the stem. Fine china and gleaming silverware, each piece engraved with a stylized "S" and picked out in gold leaf. The baron claimed the set dated back to the days when New Home had been part of the Terran Hegemony, one of the six states that made up the legendary Star League. The Hegemony, along with the Star League, had dissolved some three hundred years before.

The meal proceeded in eight courses. Servants attired in formal wear, one for every four guests, kept plates heaped and glasses full. Marcus couldn't begin to estimate what the whole thing might have cost, but the extravagance was impressive even though he was sure it was more for the benefit of Word of Blake than his mercenary crew. The Blakists and their rigid adherence to the old ComStar secrecy and fanaticism annoyed Marcus, but he also understood why Baron Shienzé might be courting them. The Baron needed a firm source of supply if he was to continue to defend his world, and the Word of Blake now controlled the production of weapons and everything else on Terra. Besides, the festive atmosphere had done much to dissipate his people's concern over assignment in the Periphery, at least for the evening, and that in itself was welcome.

The high-pitched peal caught Marcus with a mouthful of some delicious local fowl, the slivers of meat roasted in a honey sauce and spiced with something hot enough to make his eyes water and his mouth burn. He swallowed the morsel quickly, then drowned the fiery aftertaste with a heavy draught of dry white wine.

"Ladies and gentlemen," the baron called out as the white-robed pair were led to the head of the table. "May I present Precentor Sandra Schofield and her aide Ryan Hughes. Precentor, these are the Avanti's Angels, the mercenary company who has just completed a successful contract for us here on New Home. And this"—he gestured to Marcus, who had stood up automatically—"is Marcus GioAvanti, their commander." Introductions complete, the baron ordered fresh plates brought for the new arrivals.

Demi-Precentor Hughes went straight to his place at the table, two seats down from the baron and next to Charlene Boské. Sandra Schofield took a moment to greet Marcus personally before taking her place at the baron's immediate right.

"Commandante GioAvanti," she said, changing his

rank into the Italian equivalent and adding the correct accent to his family name. She offered her hand formally.

Marcus' eyes widened in surprise, not altogether pleasant. He'd been born to a wealthy mercantile family that had kept alive its Italian heritage. It was a part of his life he had turned away from. Far from being flattered that the Word of Blake precentor would know his family's dialect, Marcus was put on his guard.

Still, old habits died hard. Coming to strict attention, Marcus clicked his boot heels together smartly as he bent over the precentor's hand. In less formal circumstances he would have brushed the hand lightly with his lips, but as she was the guest of honor he maintained proper decorum. *"Il piacere é mio,* Signorina Schofield," he returned. *The pleasure is mine.*

The precentor's smile was easy and full of warmth. "I have been informed of your recent successes, Commander. It seems appropriate that your Angels should herald the true beginning of New Home's move to independence."

"You are very kind," Marcus told her, executing a simpler bow this time. *And very smooth,* he thought.

The rest of the dinner went on in much the same way, with Precentor Schofield charming everyone around her. She could instantly put someone at ease, and not once did she mouth any quasi-mystical phrase by the oh-so-sainted Jerome Blake. Marcus watched as even Charlene Boske fell under her sway as Schofield inquired and commented with great interest on Charlene's Federated Suns background. Baron Shienzé too was utterly captivated, forgetting his food and drink as Schofield also drew him in with a knowledge of New Home and its former place among the worlds of the ancient Terran Hegemony.

"It's true," she said, setting down her fork and letting her gaze travel the faces of those nearest her. "New Home was famous as a place of culture and refinement. The arts flourished here and several of the Star League's greatest statesmen came from this world."

"Ah, yes," the Baron Shienzé said with obvious pride.

Marcus dredged up what he could remember about the long-gone Terran Hegemony. That it was one of the ring of worlds that surrounded and was governed from Terra. That it had been founded by the McKennas and later ruled by their cousins, the Camerons. That it had been Ian Cameron who had forged the alliances that ultimately formed the Star League back in the 2600s, uniting the far-flung worlds colonized by humanity under a single government. Then near the end of the twenty-eighth century, the Star League came apart at the seams, and the worlds of the Terra Hegemony were eventually absorbed by the five remaining Houses. He couldn't recall any specifics concerning New Home, but then his school-day memories were certainly no match for the precentor's apparent studied knowledge.

Sandra Schofield nodded to the baron, and her earnest expression turned to one of sorrow like the slow fall of a dying leaf. "New Home was also the first to suffer the ravages of the Succession Wars," she said slowly as if not wanting to shatter the image she'd built. "The Successor Lords saw to that, as each wanted to claim such an important symbolic prize."

Marcus felt a kind of warm flush spread over his face and head, and the dull roar of multiple conversations muted as the Precentor's words echoed within his mind. Warning bells were going off, though he couldn't put his finger on why. He only knew that Precentor Schofield was a dangerous person, for all her charm and poise.

"A symbolic prize?" he asked, sipping at the sweet wine the servants had just begun to pour them. "Like Word of Blake retaking Terra from ComStar?" Marcus was sure no one else caught the slight narrowing of Schofield's eyes, but then he'd been watching specifically for just such a reaction."

"I wouldn't compare the two things at all," Schofield returned, voice steady. "Terra is the rightful home of Word of Blake, just as New Home is the rightful home of the Shienzé line. We seek to claim no more territory, only to continue to protect technology from the ravages of war." She shrugged and turned up her palms in a gesture of harmlessness. Marcus could almost hear her saying, *Look, nothing up my sleeve.* "Surely that is a just cause."

Baron Shienzé was quick to agree, as were several

members of the Angels who were near enough to be involved in the conversation. Charlene flashed Marcus a warning glance that told him she was beginning to sense something amiss as well.

Marcus merely shrugged and nodded with a smile, as if he had no interest in disputing the Precentor's words. He took another bite of his dinner, pretending to savor the spicy flavors and pungent aroma of the sauce. In truth, the food had lost much of its taste. He wasn't sure what game the Word of Blake was playing, but his own cautionary words came back to haunt him. *The Angels don't need to make enemies here.* He and his mercenary company had come to New Home to do a job, been paid for services rendered, and now the hour approached for them to leave the place for another destination hundreds of light years distant. They couldn't afford to get involved in politics, and soon New Home would be just a memory. He forced down another bite and tried to convince himself of that. *The Angels don't get involved unless they're paid to.* That was a motto he could live with.

Until dessert.

"So, Baron Shienzé," Precentor Schofield was saying, "I understand that New Home is also suffering under attacks by the Bryant Regulars."

The baron frowned, his almond-shaped eyes nearly disappearing as he considered the problem. "The Bryant Raiders, you mean. Yes, this Viscount Dvensky has virtually seized Bryant for himself and seems determined to expand his domain by attacking his neighbors. Our problems with the New Home Regulars have given him plenty of opportunities to raid us when our backs are turned." He glanced at Marcus with a friendly, almost conspiratorial smile. "But maybe Dvensky won't be so anxious to hit us from now on," he said. "The Thirtieth Guards are predicting a fast clean-up ever since we put the fear of God into the Regulars."

Marcus did not miss the fact that Baron Shienzé eliminated the word *Lyran* from the Thirtieth *Lyran* Guards, and he was sure the precentor must have noticed it too.

Precentor Schofield sipped at the dessert wine they'd

been served. "So you believe the Bryant Regulars won't be back?"

"I doubt we will be so fortunate." The baron spread his hands. "New Home is Bryant's closest neighbor by only a few light years. Dvensky's bound to keep harassing us. But once we put down the New Home Regulars for good, the Thirtieth will be freed up to mount more effective defenses."

The precentor looked doubtful, the slightest frown creasing her pale skin. "I've heard that the Bryant Raiders have struck even as far away as Carver V and Caph."

Marcus rolled the sweet liqueur around in his mouth, noticing but not enjoying its fruity flavor and scent. *What's your game, Precentor?* Even without a star chart, he knew the worlds of Carver and Caph were at least thirty light years from the planet Bryant. *Trying to make the Bryant Raiders look expansionist by adding a few more light years to their raids?*

Shienzé nodded. "And Procyon," he added, naming a world on the far side of New Home from Bryant. "When your Precentor Blane visited New Home last month, he mentioned that Viscount Dvensky had refused to receive him at all. He and his people are a most disreputable lot."

"I had not heard of their attacks on Procyon." Schofield sounded slightly worried. "Someone should really put a stop to their barbaric activity."

Marcus set his glass down on the table with deliberate slowness. "When one independent world attacks another, you call it barbaric, Precentor. When Word of Blake attacks ComStar, you call it policy."

The conversation Charlene had struck up with demi-Precentor Hughes broke off as both turned sharply to Precentor Schofield for her reaction.

Schofield only smiled. "Eloquently put, Commander. I consider myself chastened." The precentor raised her glass slightly to Marcus as if about to toast him, then paused dramatically. "Perhaps here lies your answer, Baron Shienzé. Why not hire these able mercenaries to put a stop to the Bryant Regulars, much as they did the New Home Regulars?"

The baron shook his head emphatically. "Hiring

mercenaries to help establish peace on my own world is a far cry from hiring them to attack another world. My neighbors would suddenly look at New Home as a potential aggressor, and I prefer to get along with them when possible."

"There is much wisdom in that, Baron." Schofield nodded sagely. "I know Epsilon Indi suffered fewer raids after signing a mutual assistance pact with Epsilon Eridani. As you say, the peaceful solution."

The baron's eyes widened. "Epsilon Indi has won its independence? I'd heard that they were still beset by the Capellans."

She nodded. "Yes, of course, but ever since Duke Abraham signed the mutual assistance agreement, the raiders have concentrated their attacks against the Capellan forces. Epsilon Eridani is a powerful force when it comes to trade, and even Count Dvensky is wary of upsetting them."

"I had not heard of this," the baron said, voice thoughtful. "I understand that Precentor Blane planned to visit Epsilon Eridani after leaving here, to propose a formal non-aggression pact and see about opening up better trade relations. If New Home is beginning to see the end of our trouble with the Regulars, perhaps we should be thinking about making similar arrangements."

The precentor raised a delicate eyebrow. "Indeed? I will be on New Home for the better part of a week, Baron, after which I travel to Carver V to join Precentor Blane and then on to the Epsilon worlds. I would be honored to carry a message to him."

Marcus grinned broadly. "Most convenient, eh, Baron?" He kept his tone light, but Charlene's frown reminded him of his own earlier advice.

The precentor turned it to her advantage, however, by quickly agreeing. "Very convenient." She favored Baron Shienzé with a warm smile. "Precentor Blane mediated the pact between the Epsilon worlds. The leaders of Epsilon Eridani would consider your initiatives with greater seriousness if he were to endorse it."

Marcus tried to convince himself that he was over-reacting, that Precentor Schofield was sincere in making a simple offer of assistance. *Am I merely letting my dislike for Word of Blake influence my thinking?* Schofield herself had been nothing but cordial, but then maybe that was the problem. She was so smooth, almost too perfect as she ingratiated herself with Baron Shienzé.

Marcus leaned forward to attract her full attention. "Why would Precentor Blane waste so much time away from Terra? You'd think he'd be needed there now more than ever."

Sandra Schofield offered him another palms-up shrug. "The Word of Blake does not forget its roots, Commander. Once we were ComStar, and thus we remain a logical choice for such arbitration. Mediators should be neutral parties, with no personal ambitions."

Marcus smiled thinly, a dry chuckle escaped him even as he ignored Charlene's glare. "Everyone has ambitions, Precentor. Only the methods differ."

4

Shienzé Stronghold
Bastille, New Home
Chaos March
20 March 3058

New Home's moons hung at opposite ends of the velvet sky, two smiling crescents that seemed to share a private joke as they watched the Angels complete the loading of the *Heaven Sent*. And those grins suddenly looked exceptionally cruel to Marcus, as if the universe knew some joke on him.

But such gloomy thoughts were cut short by the approach of Baron Shienzé, trailing a small retinue of soldiers. With a casual wave the baron halted the soldiers at a respectful distance and went alone the rest of the way toward Marcus. He extended his hand and gave Marcus' a strong handshake. "You have done New Home a great service, Commander GioAvanti. I will not forget it."

Marcus nodded, but was still troubled by the way Precentor Schofield seemed to manipulate Shienzé at the reception. Marcus was only able to keep his comments to himself after Charlene finally kicked him under the table. "You have a nice world here, Baron. I hope you keep it."

Shienzé nodded. "The Bryant Raiders or Word of Blake notwithstanding," he said, with surprising good cheer. When Marcus merely stared at him, dumbfounded, the baron laughed rich and full. "Don't let the gray hairs fool you, Commandante," he said, stumbling over the Italian. "I can recognize a hidden agenda."

"Don't trust either of them, Baron," Marcus said quietly, resting one hand on the other man's shoulder. "Keep a firm grip on New Home and tell the rest to go to blazes."

"A nice thought, but not practical." The baron glanced up into the sky, and Marcus wonder if he too sensed the Cheshire grinning of the two moons. "Every star up there is a reminder that there will always be others who wish to take away what we have," he murmured. "The Chaos March is aptly named, but it will not remain so forever. The Successor Houses have not forgotten us. And the Clans are still there."

Marcus felt a slight shudder, and his eyes flicked instinctively to the heavens as if the mere mention of the word *Clans* might summon them.

"Besides," the baron said, returning to his earlier point, "I prefer to get along with my neighbors."

Noticing Charlene standing at the ramp's head, waiting to button up the DropShip, Marcus offered his hand again to the baron. "If you ever need us, you know where we'll be." *The Periphery,* he thought with another shudder. Not one of the places most mercenaries wanted to work, but these were hard times and he had a unit to maintain.

"On Outreach," Baron Shienzé said kindly, clasping Marcus' hand with both of his. "I will always expect to find your Angels through the Hiring Hall on Outreach."

Marcus saluted, then turned and moved up the ramp, grateful for the vote of confidence. The baron had an instinctive knack for handling people. He used neither cheap flattery nor condescension with those of lesser rank, but honestly sought to bolster those who also strengthened him. *And that, Baron, is why men will follow you.*

From the ramp's head, Marcus glanced back to watch Shienzé returning toward the gates of his stronghold. In the distance he could see the BattleMechs that had brought Precentor Schofield and her aide to the Baron's hold. The giant machines stood waiting silently outside the gates, with a squad of troops guarding the base of each. It was an ominous sight, Marcus thought—almost as if the Blakist 'Mechs stood silent vigil over their own stronghold, not that of their host.

It was the last thing he saw before finally entering the DropShip, and Marcus told himself that he had to leave New Home's problems to the Baron and his people. The Angels had enough worries of their own.

5

DropShip **Head of a Pin**
Nadir Recharge Station, New Home System
Chaos March
27 March 3058

Marcus cursed fluently as the myomer bundle twisted in his grip, then again at Yuri Petrovka, who laughed.

The *Heaven Sent* had rendezvoused with the Canopus JumpShip *Bacchus* three hours ago, locking into the docking collar right next to the *Head of a Pin*. With the *Heaven Sent* coming off New Home time and the rest of the DropShip-JumpShip contingent set to some Magistracy clock, Marcus suddenly found it to be four o'clock in the morning. With several hours to kill before he could meet the Canopian representative, he had grabbed his chief technician and hauled him off to the *Fortress* Class DropShip's Number Two 'Mech bay and Marcus' project.

The BattleMech occupying their attention was a *Caesar,* a machine Marcus had been trying to restore for six months, even before the ill-fated Arboris contract. Standing on back-canted legs that ended in talon-like feet, the *Caesar*'s relationship to the *Marauder* design was obvious. Its upper-torso design spoke of the 'Mech's ties to the Capellan *Cataphract,* with forward-thrust, wedge-shaped cockpit and a large torso-mounted weapon. But the *Caesar* had an air about it unlike either design, a calm but deadly attitude that stood out in its sleek silhouette.

Currently, though, the 70-ton machine looked ravaged, its right arm still unattached and armor stripped off from head to feet to allow access at even the most remote location.

The huge bay stood empty save for the *Caesar* and numerous spare BattleMech parts. The only other people around were two astechs in the adjacent 'Mech stall who labored to modify an internal chassis arm to fit Faber's damaged *Marauder.* Noticing the occasional hiss of a cutting torch or flash of an electric welder was as far as Marcus let his attention wander.

Petrovka was diverting enough.

The myomer bundle Marcus was struggling with dangled from the 'Mech's hip actuator, falling in a long, dull-gray rope that threaded its way through a maze of internal supports and other, smaller bundles. Every meter or so a thin metal ring bound the fibers together in a tight grip to prevent Marcus from fouling their weave as he wrestled the bundle into place. On the advice of Petrovka, he had also attached support wires to each ring, keeping strain off the actuator until the entire bundle was installed.

"We have managed to repair the Jenner's gyro," Petrovka told him, referring to the one Angel 'Mech that had been crippled before the final raid on New Home. Marcus had wriggled into a small cave formed by a sheet of leg armor and some of the smaller myomer bundles, trying to wrestle the *Caesar*'s artificial muscle into its last guide. Petrovka bent over to speak down into the tangle of metal, fibers, and Marcus. "She up and runnin' perfect wit'in a week."

Marcus jumped as Petrovka's strong voice and sharp accent echoed inside the narrow confines of his crawl space. He misjudged the distance needed to get the bundle of fibers over the metal fork of the guide, smashing his fingers against the upright. The heavy gloves he wore prevented skinned knuckles, but his numb fingers would make another try impossible for a moment. Sliding out from the crawl space, he sat back against the Battle-Mech's ankle and gazed up at Petrovka.

Yuri Petrovka was an older, robust-looking man from Valil'yevskly, a Free Worlds League planet originally settled by a large Russian contingent back in the early days of Terran expansion. His red-brown hair and beard were shot through with gray, and he wore both trimmed very short. His accent seemed to get worse over the years instead of better.

"How's the *JagerMech*?" Marcus asked, flexing his hand to get feeling back in it.

The elder man shrugged. "I think I bring that one back from grave as well," he said, then grimaced. "Though I not sure what to do about right arm. You ruined the thing, an' there was no replacement in warehouse."

"Any chance on adapting one from another 'Mech?"

"I think not." Petrovka rubbed one hand against the side of his face. "But maybe I build one from scratch."

An electric spark left a blue-black ghost image hovering in Marcus' vision. He blinked it away as the acrid stench of hot metal drifted over to supplant the normal scent of grease. "I better try this again," he said, starting to climb back up into the space. "You think they'd have a tool to make this a bit easier."

"They do," Petrovka said, grinning.

Hovering at the opening, Marcus looked back at the other man. "Then how come I haven't been using one?"

Petrovka's grin widened. "Because you might put kink in fibers unless I help, and you wanted to do all work yourself."

Marcus made a gun with his fingers and pretended to shoot himself in the head, then dove back up into the crawlspace. He managed to get the artificial muscle into its guide on the first try this time, and then set to work fastening the bundle's end into one of the ankle supports. It took the better part of an hour, with Petrovka's running dialogue pausing only for breaths and the first warning alert that the ship was about to jump to a new star. The myomer bundle finally installed, Marcus removed the two lowermost support wires and the retaining rings.

He hadn't really noticed Petrovka's sudden quiet, having tuned the technician out except for the occasional question, until he heard a muffled feminine voice ask, "Commander GioAvanti?"

A gentle kick at his feet and a, "Hey, Marc," brought him sliding out from inside the *Caesar*.

Marcus came to his feet, peeling the heavy gloves off his hands. His visitor almost matched him in height. She wore a turquoise tunic and trousers, accented by black gloves and knee-high leather boots. Silver piping chased the cuffs and down the sides of the trousers. Her dark wavy hair was pulled back tight into a ponytail that fell all the way down her back. Spiked collars fastened around her left wrist and ankle lent a menacing air to the dress uniform of the Magistracy Armed Forces, but the easy way she carried herself would have been enough to tell Marcus she was more than just a political appointee. "Commander Ryan?" he asked.

She nodded. "Jericho Ryan, First Canopian Cuirassiers. I'm your liaison to the Magistracy."

Torgensson's message had told Marcus that a liaison officer would join up with them—and of course a female one—though he hadn't expected it to be a Mech-Warrior. And she probably wasn't expecting to meet a grease monkey. He glanced down at his tattered coveralls, stained with the red grease myomer bundles came packed in. "Sorry I'm not really dressed to receive you, Commander."

"Looks like you've been busy," she said, giving the *Caesar* an appraising glance. "And please, make it Jericho. We're going to be together for awhile."

"Marcus then. Or Marc. This is my chief technician,

Yuri Petrovka." He nodded to the tech. "He's supervising me on this project."

Petrovka smiled a greeting. "Looks like we won't be doin' much more right now. 'Scuse me, please, I go back to *Heaven Sent*." He shuffled off, gathering up the two astechs with a grunt as he passed by.

"I came down early and your exec on the *Heaven Sent* said you'd been over here all night."

Marcus smiled. "We're still on New Home time. To us, this is late afternoon."

"I hadn't thought of that," Jericho admitted. Marcus stepped up onto a small gantry that gave him better access to the *Caesar*'s knee and began to remove more of the temporary support wires. Jericho studied the work. "Wait a minute," she said in warning. "You've got a quarter-twist in that bundle." After a slight pause, she caught herself. "But then, you would have had to redesign the end attachment in order for it to lift, so you know that. But why?"

"*Caesar*s often have a slight bow-legged gait," Marcus explained through clenched teeth as he wrestled with the restraining clip. "Yuri showed me how to put the twist in there so when the myomer bundle contracts—"

"It pulls the leg inward and gets rid of the problem," Jericho finished for him. "Slick." Another glance over the 'Mech. "Those aren't standard weapons, either," she said, fishing for information and not trying to hide it.

"Clan tech," Marcus admitted. "Both the right-torso Gauss rifle and the hand-held PPC that will be attached along with the right arm. That gives me back four tons to play with. This 'Mech will carry an extra ton of armor when I'm done with it, an extra double heat sink, and instead of four medium pulse lasers, I can mount five. The three forward-firing are also Clan, giving me better reach."

"You've got a lot of these Clan weapons?"

"Not as many as you might be thinking now. A grand total of one Gauss, four PPCs, two large lasers, and maybe eight mediums. The reason so many are mounted in the *Caesar* is because it takes so long to adapt them to

Inner Sphere designs. The *Caesar* is the only 'Mech that
has had the downtime for experimenting."

She nodded. "I don't remember a *Caesar* in the TO&E
Victor Torgensson discussed with me."

"You wouldn't. This 'Mech isn't functional." Marcus
stepped back to look up at the giant machine. "It needs a
General Motors 280 Extralight engine. We haven't been
able to pick one up yet."

A hint of puzzlement underlay Jericho's voice. "Torgensson mentioned the trouble you had on Arboris. If the
Angels were so worried about finances, why didn't you
sell it? Even three-quarters complete, that 'Mech has to be
worth a tidy sum."

Marcus turned and regarded her coolly. "Because,
Commander, I had two warriors without a 'Mech after
that fiasco. And the Angels take care of a Dispossessed
warrior before anything else."

"I understand," Jericho said with a nod. Her shiver at
the word *dispossessed* told Marcus that perhaps she did.
To a MechWarrior, not having a BattleMech was a worse
fear than dying in battle. "With a small company, the loss
of a single machine would be devastating."

"Only partly," he explained, his voice a touch warmer.
"You should have seen our unit history." At her nod, he
continued. "The Angels often take in orphans from the
battlefields where we've fought. When we get a new warrior, he's often dispossessed or his machine is shot up so
bad he might as well be. All of us have been in that condition at one point in our lives, so we try to take care of
them as soon as possible." He turned back to work. "The
Angels watch out for their own."

He pulled at the fiber bundle, trying to reach an awkwardly placed support wire, but some remaining packing
grease kept making his hands slip. He hoped he hadn't
spoken so sharply that he'd begun the mission by torquing
off the representative of his employer. She probably
thought him pompous or just plain rude.

A single, quiet footstep on the gantry behind was all the
warning Marcus got before another pair of arms joined
him in the *Caesar*'s leg. It was Jericho Ryan grasping the
myomer bundle with the heavy gloves Marcus had dis-

carded earlier. She gave the bundle an expert twist, providing him access to the wire. "Sometimes," she said through clenched teeth, "it doesn't hurt to ask for a little help."

Marcus removed the wire and then stepped back as she released the myomer bundle. "Thanks," he said. "And I'm sorry if I sounded like I was giving you a lecture."

"No need to apologize." Jericho removed the gloves and offered them back. "I understand. You've got to watch out for your people because no one else will. That includes my government."

He nodded. "It does come down to that," he said carefully.

"No one hires mercenaries and then expects their loyalty to anything but the contract." She watched him with unblinking blue eyes. "Especially when they're being hired to perform work too dangerous to risk regular forces, and probably being underpaid at that."

Marcus couldn't help the thin smile that crept across his face. "If we were on Canopus, I'd have to say that such a blunt attitude wouldn't sit too well with your government."

Jericho shrugged and grinned back. "Maybe that's why they sent me away, Commander."

That brought a laugh from Marcus, and suddenly the Periphery didn't seem so far to travel after all. He glanced up at the *Caesar*'s empty shoulder socket. "Know anything about shoulder actuators?"

6

Word of Blake HPG Station
Ausapolis, Campoleone
Rim Commonality
Free Worlds League
29 March 3058

Precentor Demona Aziz nodded a dismissal to the white-cloaked adept who had escorted her from the spaceport straight to this private conference room in the hyperpulse generator station in the Free Worlds city of Ausapolis. With seats for eight people, the conference table was made from the beautiful black ginja wood she knew to be one of Campoleone's few exports. The lighting had been dialed up to only three-quarters intensity, muting the room to a soft glow. The holographic projection screen dominating the far wall displayed a thrust-down broadsword, its hilt decorated with the old ComStar starburst insignia now surrounded by six concentric rings. The Word of Blake logo glowed seductively in the room's muted lighting.

Demi-Precentor St. Jamais already stood there waiting, hands tucked into the wide sleeves of his robe. He gave her a courteous bow of the head. "The peace of Blake be with you, Precentor," he said reverently. "It is good to see you again."

She returned the greeting with solemn voice, as always drawing strength from the reminder that it was Jerome Blake's sacred vision of the future that guided her path.

Demona moved to the chair just to the left of the table's head. "Let us be comfortable," she said, seating herself. She pushed her hood back, letting her dark hair spill down her back, then leaned forward so that her elbows rested lightly on the table and she could clasp her hands before her in a posture of pious dignity.

St. Jamais went to the chair directly across from her, seating himself with the slow grace Demona might expect in a more formal setting. He regarded her with impenetrable brown eyes and the barest touch of a smile.

You did that so easily, she thought, *without even the slightest glance toward the chair at the table's head. Are you as respectful of my position as you seem, St. Jamais, or is this more of your carefully calculated mask?* Demona narrowed her eyes, gaze hardening, as if she would plumb the depths of his soul. *How loyal are you?*

"I am moving the control of our operations from Gibson to this world," she said without further preamble, the "our" referring to the Toyama as a whole. "Precentor Blane would prefer me on the Magistracy capital of Canopus, devoting my full attention to creating an alliance between them and the Taurians. I managed to divert him from that idea with a promise to remain close by here on Campoleone so that I would be immediately available should our representative to the Magistracy request my personal aid."

While the planet Gibson's central location in the Free Worlds League did make for better coordination of various Toyama operations, it was too far away from what was considered—at least by Blane—to be the Toyama'a chief project. But Campoleone, riding the border separating the Free Worlds League from the Periphery, was as close to this operation as Demona ever planned to get. *Always leave a way out.* As long as she remained within the Inner Sphere, relying on St. Jamais and his 6th of June movement, she would be isolated from blame if the operation somehow went bad. Any blame would fall squarely on St. Jamais.

"Demi-Precentor Nicholas is one of my best operatives," St. Jamais said, his face clouding over. "She is quite capable of handling the minor affairs of a Periphery court, and ready to *remove*"—he stressed the word so there would be no doubt of its meaning—"Magestrix Centrella whenever we wish."

And you are worried that I shall usurp your power out here, Demona added silently. She needed St. Jamais and his 6th of June movement, but despised the thought that she might have to purchase his loyalty with concessions. *I did promise him command, though, and my arrival on Campoleone does threaten that.*

Dropping her gaze, she saw her reflection in the highly polished finish of the wooden tabletop. It cast back a dark caricature, turning her blue eyes into sinister black orbs and blanketing her entire face in warping shadow. But holding her gaze there for a moment, she also noted the fine wood grain that spoke of a strong natural order beneath the illusions of the reflections. It made Demona recall some words of the Blessed Blake that the way must be ". . . led by those with the vision to see past illusion and the depth of commitment to carry through on our chosen course."

I am such a person, she thought, regaining her composure. *It is my destiny to help fulfill Jerome Blake's prophecy. St. Jamais will see this, or he is not the aide I require for the times ahead.* She placed her hands flat on the table's cool surface and sat with head high and back straight. The depth of her convictions warmed her, and she matched his troubled expression with one of calm strength.

"Events sometimes conspire to direct our course, Cameron," she began, her voice pitched low and gentle, almost seductive. "I *will* remain on Campoleone, Blake's will be done. From here I can direct Toyama efforts in the Free Worlds League and the Capellan Confederation, as well as monitor the Periphery situation."

Demona waited for his reaction, never once breaking eye contact. A slight tensing made her wonder for the briefest moment if he might actually draw a weapon against her despite their shared convictions and the intimate relations they'd known back on Gibson. But then his brown eyes softened and broke from hers as he nodded.

"You're right, of course, Demona. You are not to blame for the interference of Precentor Blane."

Now that he had once again acknowledged her power, it was time to rebuild his confidence in their alliance. "Be not cast down, Cameron. Your time approaches." His eyes came back up, hardening with a fanatic's zeal as he read into her words. "Now why don't you brief me on *your* Periphery operation?" she said.

Leaning back in his chair and tucking his hands back into the sleeves of his robes, St. Jamais smiled. "The movement of weapons and other military supplies into the Marian Hegemony is proceeding smoothly. I eliminated the secondary route demi-Precentor Adams had established through the Marik world of Romita. Everything now comes through Campoleone and then proceeds on to Astrokaszy."

Demona nodded. Astrokaszy was a barbaric desert world just beyond Free Worlds League space. Only a single jump from Campoleone, it sat directly between the Magistracy of Canopus and the Marian Hegemony. Hostile, savage, and rife with corruption, Astrokaszy was still everything people used to fear about the Periphery. It also made an excellent distribution point for the secret flow of weapons into the Hegemony. It was a double-blind, concealing any connection between the Hegemony and the Word of Blake activities on Campoleone. *Just as Cameron and his 6th of June group protect me and the rest of the Toyama should this fail.*

"Caesar Sean O'Reilly is very pleased with the increased flow of supplies," St. Jamais continued, "and actually untied those tight purse strings of his to award us with a bonus shipment of germanium along with our regular payment."

Demona raised an eyebrow. A twitch at one corner of her mouth gave a brief sign of her pleasure at that news. Germanium was a critical element in the production of a jump drive, the device that allowed a starship to make its instantaneous leaps between stars. Every power within the Inner Sphere—and without, she amended thinking of the Clans—needed the elusive element. And by a stroke of cosmic fortune, Alphard of the Marian Hegemony was blessed with a bountiful supply. If Word of Blake could become the dispenser of that supply . . . "And our hints at establishing a production facility on Alphard?" she asked.

"Well, of course, O'Reilly would like to possess the ability to produce the newer technologies himself," St. Jamais said, his voice revealing a rare hesitancy. "But he is not about to give Word of Blake the exclusive rights to purchase his germanium."

Demona frowned as she thought on possible ways to deal with Caesar Sean O'Reilly. Then she dismissed that line of thought with a wave of her hand. "No matter. Yet. O'Reilly will see the wisdom of accepting our offer, especially once his strengthened army suddenly becomes a threat to nearby portions of the Free Worlds League, and Thomas Marik begins to eye him with greater suspicion. For now, just work to keep O'Reilly's lust for more worlds in check. We want the Magistracy to feel harassed and vulnerable enough that they start to rely more on the Treaty of Taurus. But if the Marian Hegemony begins to conquer worlds, the Canopians might rally even without Taurian support. And that would strengthen their independence instead of making them inclined to form an alliance."

St. Jamais smiled. "Not to worry. Caesar O'Reilly makes the perfect cat's paw. He knows that he gains more through access to the higher technology we give him than what he might win through conquering any Magistracy border world. Besides, he could always use the improved army we're helping him to build for conquests at a later date."

Demona brushed a hand idly along the table as if discussing nothing more than routine business. "So what has the Caesar done with his new toys?"

St. Jamais drew in a deep breath as if considering the best presentation. "Hegemony raids against the Magistracy of Canopus have accelerated to the point of constantly threatening six Magistracy worlds, in a line from Thraxa to Marantha," he finally said, "and also including Palladix and Tarol IV. Those are the worlds closest to the border, as if the attacks are being staged out of the Hegemony world of Islington."

"Good choices. And the Magistracy Armed Forces?"

"The MAF are beginning to heavily garrison these worlds, but with little headway. We provide the Hegemony with accurate intelligence on where garrison forces are located, which lets the raiders avoid them every time. Also, the raiders don't limit themselves to military targets, which forces the garrison units to spread thinner."

"They're not attacking civilians," Demona said, her mouth suddenly dry and a warm flush spreading along the base of her neck. Mass destruction leveled against a civilian population violated the accords of modern warfare, as set down in the Ares Conventions some two centuries before. The Conventions had made war more humane, but also a continual fact of life in the centuries since. It would bring unwanted attention to the area if St. Jamais allowed such flagrant violations as the massacre of civilians.

The demi-Precentor's quick shake of the head calmed her fear. "Of course not. I would never authorize widespread slaughter." He paused. "But the raiders *can* target support facilities such as power stations and transportation centers, as well as the supply depots for large commercial enterprises. Such attacks raise the level of dissatisfaction among the world population, which in turn puts more pressure on the government and Canopus itself."

The explanation made sound tactical sense, but Demona also read a special significance in his pause. *Widespread slaughter, as opposed to single murders?* She swallowed against the dryness of her throat and adjusted her robes to cover her lapse of self-control. "Who have you *sanctioned*?" she asked, using his preferred euphemism for assassination.

"The planetary governors of Gambilon, Palladix, and Marantha," St. Jamais said with a grim smile. "I have full reports prepared on each world. My BattleMech forces dropped under the guise of Hegemony raiders to hit military supply depots while a 6th of June team infiltrated and disposed of the governors. Analysis of follow-up raids conducted by actual Hegemony forces show a marked decrease in garrison efficiency, ranging from ten to twenty-five percent, due to lack of coordination and a reluctance to commit to battle. In the case of Gambilon, it took the accession of the ranking regimental commander and her declaration of martial law to restore adequate defenses." His smile turned colder. "I am interested to see how her *sanction* will affect the garrison troops' performance."

Demona carefully stifled the anger building within her, smothering it with the same determination that let her meet with Precentor Blane and suffer his subtle disapprobation. *I should have known St. Jamais would try something like this. Still, I can't argue with success.* Her anger in check, she considered what he was saying and found herself more interested in the results than upset over the methods. "And the outcome of your raids?" she asked, her tone even and noncommittal.

"More successful than the Hegemony efforts by an average of thirty percent. I've lost only five warriors, all bodies recovered, and ten BattleMechs, eight recovered and seven of those repaired and back in service." The words came out in a rapid stream, allowing St. Jamais to hold the floor and justify all his actions before Demona could protest. "The other two 'Mechs suffered complete loss of containment in the fusion reactor. Not much left of them." Another pause. "Of course, all identifying marks had been removed beforehand."

Demona nodded, as if his actions were in keeping with her own plans. A new thought did occur to her, though. "Have you performed an analysis of the level of improved technology being acquired by Canopus in the form of salvage?"

Again, he was ready with his answer. "All taken into account. With the limits we place on technology flowing into the Marian Hegemony, Canopus can salvage little that they couldn't purchase from the Free Worlds League in the form of field-upgrade packages—a small supply of raw construction material or the odd extra-light engine notwithstanding. And, analysis clearly shows the damage done in the average raid exceeds their average salvage recovery by over two hundred percent. It's a losing effort on their part."

"Has there been no official response from Canopus on the assassinations?"

"Demi-Precentor Nicholas reported a small quarrel among Emma Centrella and two of her daughters, which is apparently as far as it went. One daughter argued for public condemnation and the other counseled caution, with the Magestrix still undecided. Emma Centrella is leery about going public with her outrage, since the Hegemony could dredge up the assassination attempt against Caesar O'Reilly back in 3056."

Demona reached into one of her robe's deep pockets and removed a small datadisk. "I have other news as well. The warning that came down from demi-Precentor Nicholas has been validated. Canopus is indeed hiring mercenaries to bear the brunt of the fighting."

The frown that settled over St. Jamais' face was dark and foreboding. "That is not welcome news. I had hoped the Jeffrey Calderon would finally honor the Magestrix' request for Taurian forces to assist in border defense."

"What's the problem? The Treaty of Taurus provides for just such mutual assistance."

St. Jamais shook his head. "Apparently the treaty is not as binding as we'd hoped. From what my sources have gathered, Calderon doesn't want to put the entire breadth of the Magistracy of Canopus between his troops and home. He's offered to relieve the Magistracy Armed Forces on worlds bordering his own realm to free up MAF troops for reassignment to the far Magistracy border. But Emma Centrella balked. If she handed over the protection of those worlds to Calderon, he might be tempted to simply annex a large portion of her realm, or even form the initial staging area for a thrust directly at Canopus IV."

Demona exhaled in a drawn-out sigh. "Is there any way to break through this barrier of distrust and paranoia?" Seeing the wild light shining in the eyes of St. Jamais, she quickly amended her question. "Without the use of the 6th of June's particular talents?"

A shrug. "Only by continuing on with our current endeavors and hoping to sway either Emma Centrella or Jeffrey Calderon toward a more trustful position. I do know that Emma's eldest daughter, Danai Centrella, believes the Concordat should forget about trying to help from the Taurians and simply attack the Marian Hegemony directly. Her position in the Royal Guards makes her believe Canopus can handle its own problems. Danai is also the current favorite to succeed her mother as ruler of the Magistracy."

"No assassinations, Cameron." Demona caught and held his gaze, again testing the limits of his loyalty to her. When he finally nodded, she continued in an authoritative tone. "Keep your people in place, but for now we give the Hegemony border conflict time to work. Your job is to keep that conflict fresh and threatening in the minds of the Canopians."

She waited until he again gave her a gesture of his assent, then threw him a bone. "You may continue your raids disguised as Hegemony troops. I am bringing up a second Level III BattleMech unit of the Toyama from Gibson. Those will be enough to guard our interests here on Campoleone. The other Level III unit is released into your command and can travel with you to Astrokaszy."

The demi-Precentor blinked his surprise. "Astrokaszy?"

Demona nodded. "The man we're dealing with there— what's his name?"

"Caliph Shervanis. The closest thing they have to a ruler."

"Him. Keep a rein on Shervanis and make sure the false evidence is in place to implicate either Thomas Marik or Sun-Tzu Liao, depending on what we eventually need. Safeguard our distribution point, and be ready to burn all bridges behind you. Also, I trust that from there you can strike at areas considered too risky for actual Hegemony raiders."

She pushed the datadisk across the table, pausing at the halfway point and letting her hand rest over it. "This is the data we've gathered on the mercenary units being deployed to the border. It includes unit histories, where available, and even general terms of their contracts as gleaned from message traffic by Toyama members. There are many gaps in both due to time restraints, but I have people working on it."

St. Jamais reached out to accept the disk, but Demona caught his hand in hers and held it. With expression stern and voice harder, she continued. "Avoid the mercenaries when at all possible, and crush them when not. Let the Magistracy see them as an additional expense that neither deters the raids nor provides an adequate defense."

St. Jamais gave her hand a warm and reassuring squeeze. "Blake's will be done," he intoned, then let his eyes soften as he smiled an invitation.

Demona allowed her own sternness to melt away as she smiled back assent, noting the immediate effect it had on St. Jamais. *Is this a weakness I detect on your part, Cameron? Can it be used to control you?* "Keep control of the Periphery," she said, permitting an uncharacteristic warmth to seep into her voice. "I depend on you."

Cameron St. Jamais used one hand to take the disk from her and pocket it, while the other kept the familiar contact with hers. "Not to worry, Demona. A handful of mercenaries won't make the difference, and I doubt we'll ever see much more than that.

"There just aren't that many in the Inner Sphere who concern themselves with the affairs of the Periphery."

7

Celestial Palace
Sian
Sian Commonality, Capellan Confederation
30 March 3058

The office smelled lightly of sandalwood incense and wood polish. It was a comfortable room, with soft charcoal sketches hung on the walls and a small aquarium set into one corner. Rosewood gleamed darkly in the room's subdued lighting, its cherry-glow trimming shelves, french doors opening onto a small balcony, and the desk.

Sun-Tzu Liao hesitated in the doorway, almost as though he thought to see Candace Liao, his aunt and ruler of the St. Ives Compact, seated behind that desk. The memory of her visit was seven years old. That night Candace had murdered his mother, Romano, then-Chancellor of the Capellan Confederation. That night Sun-Tzu ascended to the Celestial Throne.

This is an evening for old memories, he thought.

One such memory had disturbed him this evening, rousing him from his bedchamber before he could sleep. To sleep would risk the memory invading his mind in the form of a dream, and Sun-Tzu hated dreams. He loathed the half-formed thoughts they represented. His younger sister, Kali, attached great spiritual significance to such things, but then she rushed to attach great spiritual significance to anything that appealed to her pseudo-religious mania.

Sun-Tzu believed that dreams were a subconscious analysis of events, nothing more. And any old memory, dredged up from the depths of his normally well-ordered mind, could only be of similar nature. Able to recognize this, he could analyze it for its true significance. He always allowed himself time, refusing any rush to judgment that his sister or their mother before them might have made. Sun-Tzu knew he could not afford the luxury of hasty decisions.

His long robes whispered of heavy silk, and his slippers offered only the softest footfall against the hardwood floors as he entered the room and shut the door behind him. He crossed over to the aquarium, studiously ignoring the desk. It was an exercise in patience, like any one of several routines he performed throughout a given day. *All good things come to those who wait.*

Bending over to peer into the clear waters of the aquarium, Sun-Tzu felt as much as heard the low hum of the pump. Inside, near a small yellow patch of long grasses, a flame-orange Chinese Battling Fish cruised gracefully. Its overly large fins were tinged with just the slightest touch of violet. A beautiful creature, its hostility matched only by another male Battling Fish placed in with it. Sun-Tzu reached into a ceramic pot kept on a nearby shelf, and withdrew a pinch of food. When he lifted the aquarium's top, the dull odor of much-recycled water momentarily overrode the sandalwood scent. As he sprinkled the food across the waters, one of the fish rose on strong cuts of its tail, nipping gracefully at the surface to swallow large portions of the food. "That's right, Kai. Put on your little show."

Sun-Tzu smiled thinly. Kai Allard-Liao, his cousin and son to Candace Liao, was one of the greatest threats to his position as Chancellor of the Confederation. In spite of Kai's self-proclaimed lack of interest in the Celestial Throne, he was heir to the St. Ives Compact and had recently taken over leadership of the Free Capella movement. He ran it more like a charitable enterprise than a resistance movement, but Sun-Tzu was all too aware of the power base it gave his cousin. Not to mention the backing Kai received from Victor Davion, Prince of the Federated Commonwealth. Though good old Victor had more than enough to keep him busy at the moment, what with the Chaos March and his sister Katrina making off with half his realm.

As for the St. Ives Compact, nestled between the Capellan Confederation and the much larger Federated Suns, the region of space had originally belonged to the Capellans. Sun-Tzu now considered it a knife poised at his back, since Victor Davion could pour troops through the small state and be halfway to Sian before news ever reached his ears.

Naming his little pet after Kai was not intended to belittle his cousin, though that was an added bonus. No, it was to remind Sun-Tzu of the dangerous resemblance. Kai was a deadly warrior, one who could move through either political or military circles with an enviable ease. And the fish's wide, unblinking eyes reminded Sun-Tzu that every move he made from the Celestial Throne was observed by Kai's steady gaze.

His private smile faltering, Sun-Tzu stood and crossed to his desk in a few unhurried strides. He still did not seat himself. Instead he walked slowly around the desk, tracing one of his long fingernails along the rosewood trim.

Gone was the antiquated monitor that had once dominated the desk, now replaced with a screen set flush into the desktop. At the moment the screen displayed the Draconis Combine, but would eventually cycle through star maps of each of the Great Houses and then a full map of the Inner Sphere. The wood surface surrounding the screen was waxed and polished to a perfect finish. Sun-Tzu demanded that it be kept so, a fitting monument to the past. This had been Justin Allard's desk, as this had been Justin Allard's office.

Sun-Tzu had vowed to have the office destroyed the day he rose to the Celestial Throne. Too much treachery had been hatched here against House Liao. Justin Allard, known then as Justin Xiang, had crippled the Confederation's military efforts from this very office—leaving the Confederation near-defenseless in the onslaught of the Fourth Succession War. More than a hundred occupied worlds were lost to Hanse Davion and the newly formed Federated Commonwealth, nearly half the Capellan realm. Allard escaped with Candace Liao, the two of them later resurfacing in the seceded St. Ives Compact. Sun-Tzu had not yet been born, but he recalled his mother's description of what that war had done to Maximilian Liao, her father and his grandfather. Allard's treachery had changed old Liao into a feeble-minded weakling, the broken shell of a man who had ruled billions.

Another old memory.

But Sun-Tzu had changed his mind. Instead of having the office destroyed, he'd renovated it for his own use. He would not be ruled by superstition. It was from this desk that one short year ago he had helped coordinate the offensive that won back for the Capellan Confederation many worlds lost in the Fourth Succession War, plus a few dozen others under a cloak of Capellan influence that he hoped to strengthen. He might have gone further had Thomas Marik not refused to continue the war once he'd achieved his own goals, but Sun-Tzu was wise enough to know when to accept a winning hand. The decision to support Thomas's truce was also made at this desk. As with so much in his personal life, many things in this room served more than one purpose. It reminded Sun-Tzu to be wary of both appearances and complacency, and also that all victories must be guarded.

The memory that had drawn him to his office so late in the evening had to do partly with the latter thought. Though the Capellan Confederation had taken back some planets lost to the Davions in the Fourth Succession War, the greater portion still remained as fledgling independent worlds in the area known as the Chaos March. Some were reluctant to accept House Liao rule again, while the hated Sarna Supremacy represented a threat from within his own borders. Sun-Tzu had to admit that he simply did not have the military strength to retake *and hold* these worlds. Yet.

An almost audible click sounded within his mind as another piece of the puzzle slipped into place. *Yes,* he thought, nodding to the empty room, *it all could fit quite well.*

The old memory was of his mother Romano, who had ruled the Capellan Confederation for more than twenty years before him. Sun-Tzu had been a child—seven, perhaps eight years of age—and found his mother in a briefing room watching holovids of the 3030 invasion of the Capellan Confederation. He had already learned to avoid his mother when she was preoccupied, her uncertain temper able to transform without notice into driving rage. She'd noticed him, though, and called him to her. Sitting in her lap, Romano's strong arms wrapped tightly about him, Sun-Tzu's thoughts cycled between fear over what his mother might do to him and fascination as he watched the holovids of the war.

He hadn't understood fully back then, but he did now. The Duchy of Andurien had tried to secede from the Free Worlds League in 3030. Believing the Capellan Confederation weakened because of Maximilian Liao's insanity, the Anduriens had allied themselves with the Magistracy of Canopus in the Periphery to invade the Confederation. Romano Liao led the Capellan military against them, fueled by her fanatic devotion to the state and her hatred of anything that threatened it, driving them completely back by 3035.

With her son on her lap, Romano had pointed out to him some valiant stands made by the invaders, even as the Capellan forces routed them. "Such disorganized states could not hope to win, but what courage they show in their deaths," she'd said, almost in admiration. "If only they could be harnessed and driven at our enemies."

Sun-Tzu had never forgotten that rare moment of intimacy or his mother's idea that a Periphery state could someday hold a balance of power. Wild beasts broken to a leash could still turn on their masters. But if they were handled properly, given the right prey to bring down, they could be partially tamed.

Sun-Tzu looked down at the screen, now displaying a map of the Capellan Confederation. A few taps against the touch-sensitive screen and the image was joined by the Taurian Concordat and the Magistracy of Canopus, the two Periphery states lying just outside the Confederation's rimward borders. The combined area of the two Periphery realms was almost half again as large as his own. They looked very much like the head of a hammer, while his Capellan Confederation was the handle for wielding it.

But where to begin? Political relations with the Taurian Concordat could only be described as frosty at best, and Sun-Tzu's ambassador to Canopus IV had recently been expelled for his arrogant behavior toward Magestrix Emma Centrella herself. So, at the moment, diplomacy did not seem very promising.

Until he remembered the reports on the Marian Hegemony's ongoing aggression against the Magistracy of Canopus. That placed Canopus in a position to need help. Also, the Magistracy had been the most vocal of the Periphery states in requesting aid in education and technological advancement, two areas they wanted to desperately upgrade. One last memory surfaced, again of his mother Romano and her standard policies when negotiating a deal of any type.

Offer most of what they want.

Give them some of what they need.

Use them for all they're worth.

Reaching out, Sun-Tzu tapped the glass over the Magistracy of Canopus, marking long seconds as he sat and thought.

BOOK II

Thus, what is of supreme importance in war is to attack the enemy's strategy. Next best is to disrupt his alliances. The next best is to attack his army.

—Sun Tzu, *The Art of War*

Strategy and diplomacy have their place, but do not be afraid to engage with the enemy. A war has yet to be won where men do not die.

—Chancellor Sun-Tzu Liao, in a speech to the graduating officers of Sian Martial Academy, Sian, 30 June 3056

8

DropShip **Heaven Sent**
Zenith Recharge Station, Andurien System
Duchy of Andurien, Free Worlds League
13 April 3058

Marcus gathered his legs up underneath him in the near-zero gravity of the DropShip and then kicked out at a nearby wall, launching himself down one of the *Heaven Sent*'s longer passages. Twisting about until he was headed feet-first toward the DropShip's Number Two 'Mech bay, he then relied on small hand motions and body twists to keep himself on a reasonably level plane. Recessed handholds set into the wall offered the means of either slowing down or even pulling himself along in a more controlled manner, but he saw no harm in a little "flying." His only concern was not drifting too close to the ceiling, where wire-reinforced safety glass surrounding the powerful corridor lights bled a singeing heat. Anyway, just coming off an hour-long workout with Thomas Faber, Marcus welcomed the relaxing sensation of freefall. His muscles throbbed with a dull, weary ache and his sweat-drenched shirt clung with increasing clamminess as his body began to cool down.

Exercise with pulley systems or free weights was virtually worthless in any ship that spent long periods under low-gravity conditions. So Faber had appropriated a ventilated storeroom from Yuri Petrovka and brought in a small assortment of equipment that relied on pneumatic pressure or flexible graphite rods for opposing force.

Marcus spent at least an hour working out with the equipment every other evening, usually in the company of Thomas Faber, though he could never hope to keep up with the big man. Thomas spent at least two hours at it every night, religious in his intention of keeping a rock-hard physique.

Even now, through a bulkhead door and down ten meters of passageway, Marcus thought he could hear the fading grunt-and-hiss of Thomas battling it out with the largest pneumatic press.

And it's not as if there's so much more we could be doing, Marcus thought in irritation. When the *Heaven Sent* and the *Pinhead* had jumped into the Andurien system docked onto the Canopus *Merchant* Class Jump-Ship *Adonis*, they expected to hook up here with a *Tramp* Class Marik freighter for the next leg of their journey.

Floating just under a hard blast of cold air from a nearby vent, Marcus entered a second, shorter corridor that ran at a ninety-degree angle to the first to form a truncated "L." Tumbling against the bulkhead, he bent at knees and waist to absorb the impact until one of his outstretched hands came to rest flat on the cool metal of the hull and the other fastened around the bar-grip of a recessed handhold. With practiced ease he rotated about until his feet drifted only a few centimeters off the floor. This passage ran left five meters to an upper door of 'Mech Bay Number Two. A wheeled hatch hung open to Marcus' right. It led into a large axial trunk extending along the ship's three upper decks to the MechWarrior quarters and then down to the lower levels for the docking assembly, allowing access to each deck in between.

Marcus frowned.

During zero-G or even low-grav conditions, all doors were to be kept closed and tightly dogged down to prevent accidents should the DropShip suddenly need to break away from the JumpShip and begin to move under its own power. DropShip crews obeyed routines like this in their sleep, and the Angels' technicians were equally careful because they'd be the ones who'd have to repair any accidental breakage. Marcus used a reasonably dry spot on the tail of his shirt to dab away the drop of sweat burning at the corner of his left eye. The hatch couldn't have been left unlocked by some careless member of the Angels' families because they were all aboard the *Head of a Pin,* and wouldn't have any business down here anyway.

That left MechWarriors.

Reaching out slowly, Marcus released the metal hook that held the hatch open. He thought he'd just slip through and close it behind him, cutting his Angels some slack, but then steeled himself against becoming too soft. He pushed on the hatch to close it, but just before it shut, a violent rush of air whistled out through the gap between the metal bulkhead and the rubber gasket on the hatch door. That meant another hatch was open somewhere inside the access trunk.

Marcus secured the hatch and dogged it with a quarter-turn of the wheel. A few gliding steps brought him to the door of 'Mech Bay Two. Like all doors leading into a bay, this one had three dogs spaced down each side—metal latches that could seal it even against the pull of vacuum. Because it was the MechWarrior entrance, the door had been fitted with a fast-action lever that operated all six dogs simultaneously.

Marcus paused with one hand on the bright steel lever and almost succeeded in talking himself out of going in. He hated playing mother, reminding children to pick up after themselves. *But it came with the job.* He was betting on Karsskhov or Foley, the two newest Angels. An image of Brent Karsskhov and Charlene taking a stroll through the bay rose unbidden in his mind, and once more he almost turned away. But he steeled himself to behave like a proper commander as he quietly levered open the door. He'd just glance inside. If it looked like he'd be invading someone's privacy, he'd let the reminder wait.

The door opened onto a large, circular grate walkway that circled the 'Mech bay high above the floor, providing access to the head and upper torso area of eight Battle-Mech racks. The acrid scent of 'Mech coolant mixed with the ever-present smell of grease gave the air a familiar tang that was neither pleasant nor unpleasant.

The low-level red lighting often referred to as "night-red"

turned the normally intimidating war machines into ghostly giants. Marcus couldn't see more than the nearest three 'Mechs, the large radar dish of Connor Monroe's *Rifleman* blocking his view into the bay's interior. He launched himself out toward the *Rifleman,* catching one of the rungs welded near the cockpit entry hatch, and hung quietly in the nonexistent gravity as he surveyed the vast, silent bay.

Tiny lights, like those from pocket flashes, played through the cockpit window of Paula Jacobs' *Wasp.*

Marcus tensed, doubt and fear suddenly sending a flush of warmth and tingling over his skin. Someone was torquing with Paula's ride. The *Wasp* occupied a rack not ten meters from the bay doors, which put it about ten meters out and thirty meters left of where Marcus hung from the *Rifleman*'s head. An easy flight, if he decided to go it. The lights flashed again. Definitely two. Marcus thought he'd go and get Faber first before checking things out further. But a noise from behind him never gave him that chance.

It was a rattle of the walkway grating, the sound of someone stepping onto a portion with loose fastenings. Marcus instantly drew his legs up and tucked them beneath him, ready to launch in any direction. The defensive move was quickly justified as he heard the sharp click of a safety being snapped off. Marcus kicked out hard into the middle of the bay as flechettes spanged off the *Rifleman*'s head where he'd been crouched moments before. A sharp sting in Marcus' lower left leg told him that not all the weapons fire had missed.

Damn! A needler. One of the more deadly hand-held weapons invented, a needle gun stripped its ammunition off a block of plastic—shredding the material into thin plastic shards and launching them at high velocity. Entrance wounds tended to be clean, but the plastic quickly fragmented to chew up the inside. Hoping the damage wasn't too severe, Marcus twisted about to ready himself for a hard landing in the middle of the bay.

Voices rose from below him, cursing as at least two men struggled from the *Wasp*'s small cockpit. A soft cough from behind him and another spray of plastic death whispered through the air, missing wide and rattling off into the further reaches of the bay. Marcus knew he couldn't count on such luck forever, but fortunately he'd just slid past the left shoulder of the *Wasp*, into relative safety.

He struck the inner hull of the DropShip with a lot of force. Rather than try to absorb it all, he tucked into a roll that slammed his shoulder and then the small of his back into a firefighting station. Clawing for purchase before he could rebound out into the hidden gunman's line of sight, Marcus was able to grasp the fire station's supply piping and bring himself under control.

The pipes and bundled hose were only vague outlines, but he could see the small green light set over the activation button. Marcus stabbed at it, and was rewarded by the light shifting to red. Besides starting a remote pump, the switch would also trip warning lights on the DropShip bridge. But he knew it would take someone a few solid minutes to get here. He'd just have to buy himself that time. He cursed the lack of an audible alarm, knowing Faber was only thirty seconds away.

Two shadows loomed over him. Three against one, he thought. And me with nothing more damaging than a damp shirt. Using his grip on the pipes for support, Marcus scissored out his legs in an attempt to strike anything vital. He felt his foot come into contact with a leg as he swept the feet out from under one of his attackers. Then hands fastened around his ankle and yanked him free of the fire station.

Marcus curled his legs up into his body, but did not struggle. In the absence of gravity, neither he nor his foe would possess much leverage for throwing a punch, for a body would move backward with the same force as a fist moving forward. His attacker grabbing him was a mistake. All it did was give Marcus the leverage he needed to do some real damage. He speared out with his free leg, catching his assailant in the midsection and throwing himself back and away. The force knocked the other man off his feet, but he did not release his grip, and the two of them bounced and tumbled across the hull. Marcus drew back his leg and kicked out again, and again, relying on the other man's grip for support behind his strikes. If the other man had let go, the kicks wouldn't have done much more than push the two of them apart.

A heavy weight fell against Marcus, pressing him painfully against the hull. The second assailant, back on his feet again, had reentered the fight. *And if the guy with the needler gets down here, I'm history.* Coiling in on himself again, Marcus then thrust out his legs and arms to try and dislodge one or both of his opponents. He heard a grunt as his legs were finally freed, leaving him in a grappling match with the second man. This guy either had a bit more experience in low-G combat or was simply learning fast. Having got his legs wrapped about Marcus, the attacker was trying to squeeze the breath out of him while his hands struggled for purchase at Marcus' throat. Marcus kept his head tucked down, and pummeled the man's kidneys with his fists, all the while the two of them continued to bounce further along the DropShip's inner hull.

The edge of an I-beam stanchion caught Marcus just behind the ear—not enough to put him out but definitely making him see stars. Reaching up over his head, he grasped the I-beam and then jackknifed his body up and over. A grunt of pain and a slackening of pressure around his midriff rewarded the effort as Marcus drove his attacker face-first into the beam. With the man knocked unconscious, Marcus easily kicked him off and worked his own feet back underneath him.

Hanging from the stanchion like some gargoyle, Marcus scanned the shadows for movement. *Now where's your buddy?*

The blow caught Marcus in the right side of the head, rocking him to the left while the heavy sole of the boot raked down the side of his face. His vision blurred, making the shadows and dim lighting run together until the whole scene changed into a giant murky red haze. Somehow he'd managed to hold on to the stanchion, but as another kick caught him in the midsection he slipped free and tumbled across space until he slammed into the wall and then back to the walkway grating.

With one hand gripping a chain-link railing, Marcus

hung in the air and shook his head lightly to clear the pain-shrouded cobwebs that clouded his mind. *He'll be coming after me,* Marcus thought. *Gotta move.*

The shadow came in swift and silent, almost parallel to the ship's hull, with two fists balled up and thrust forward like some kind of battering ram. Marcus leaned away from the impact, one arm looping up to surround the other's arms and keep them pinned to his chest. He tried to wrestle the other man around, perhaps to drive him down onto the grating, but the blow to the head still had Marcus groggy and his assailant managed to get his own feet back under him.

Keeping the man's arms pinned in an arm lock, Marcus struggled to trip up his assailant. The two of them ended up doing a shuffling zero-G dance, each with a hand on the chain railing for support. Then Marcus heard a voice off to the far right.

"Philippe, clear. Get away."

He'd forgotten about the needler! The voice was feminine, but Marcus heard its edge of desperation and knew she was ready to pull the trigger on both friend and foe if necessary. He heard another warning for Philippe to get clear, and by his opponent's sudden, frantic motions Marcus was sure the man heard it too. As the two men struggled to disengage, Marcus was able to finally sweep his attacker's feet up, holding him parallel above the walkway for only a second before hurling him toward where he'd last heard the sound of the voice.

The all-too-familiar cough of the needler gun came from ahead, and razor-sharp flechettes filled the air. Most slammed into the body of Marcus' attacker, jerking it around as the flechettes imparted their own kinetic energy to his still-airborne body. A few made it by, though, zipping past Marcus to shatter against the metal around and behind him. Marcus felt a sharp sting in his left arm and shoulder. Then, with what felt like a bone-shattering blow against his left leg, his feet flew out from under him, cartwheeling him back against the metal hull again.

Marcus ended up adrift and heading much too slowly for the ceiling. Fire arced up his left leg, leaving him breathless and grinding his teeth. Gaining only a slight amount of stability, Marcus looked in what he thought was the general direction of his assailant. He saw her outline where she leaned out from the perch on the *Wasp*'s shoulder, leveling the needler in his direction.

Then a blur of movement arced out from behind the woman holding the needler, an arm hooking her entire head with a violent swinging motion. A deep, dull gong, the sound of a body slamming into the side of the *Wasp*, reached Marcus as his pain-muddled brain pieced together what he was seeing. A large shadow swarmed over the BattleMech's shoulder to grab the falling sniper and keep her from flying off.

"You all right, Marcus?"

The voice was deep and powerful, and Marcus' body went limp in relief. "Thomas? How did you know?"

"Heard the fire station pump start up. It's next door to the workout room. So I swam over to take a look."

And if the pump had been located anywhere else . . . Marcus didn't even want to think about that. "About time," was all he had the strength left to say. Then his left leg hit the ceiling and the lance of pain that shot through him brought with it sweet oblivion.

9

DropShip **Heaven Sent**
Zenith Recharge Station, Andurien
Duchy of Andurien, Free Worlds League
15 April 3058

The *Heaven Sent*'s briefing room wasn't much bigger than the polished metal table and the eight chairs bolted to the deck around it, leaving less than a meter's clearance between chair backs and the gun metal-gray walls. The overhead lights cast a harsh, almost clinical glare over the room, reflecting off the table's dull finish except where the dark glass of a holographic projection screen was set in its center. An auxiliary climate system installed in one of the room's upper corners recycled the air and labored to maintain a comfortable temperature. Without a direct link to the DropShip's ventilation system, the air came out dry and carrying the faint, acrid scent of ozone. The machine's loud hum was easily dismissed, but every few minutes something inside it gave a sharp metallic rattle that broke Marcus' concentration.

Marcus sat at one end of the table, furthest from the door. The three most senior Angels were strapped into the seats nearest him; Charlene Boske to his right, Ki-Lynn Tanaga and Thomas Faber to his left. Jase Torgensson's seat, next to Charlene's, remained vacant. Jericho Ryan and her aide, Shannon Christienson, sat across from each other in the last two seats on either side. In the chair nearest the door sat Flag Captain Drake Montgomery, commander of the Andurien Recharge Station.

The pressure of the pneumo-cast set around Marcus' left leg between ankle and knee distracted him almost as much as the rattle in the climate system. Little more than a plastic sleeve, the device could be quickly inflated into a rigid cast and adjusted for comfort. *Supposedly adjusted,* Marcus thought bitterly. It currently protected a hairline fracture of his left leg, at the mid-humerus. He reached down with his left hand to rub at the cast's upper edge, trying to devote his full attention to Flag Captain Montgomery's report on the event now two days past.

A report that was beginning to raise Marcus' hackles anew.

"That much of her story checks out," Montgomery said, speaking of the female leader of the trio. Montgomery had finally admitted that the three intruders were from the recharge station, a concession he hadn't been willing to make two days before. But the admission came sugar-coated with a story that absolved Andurien of any real responsibility. "Corporal Owens received a personal communiqué aboard the station, which we recovered and examined. It was a coded message instructing her to take action against you, with all the proper authorizations to make it look as if it came from Andurien. We have a record of its receipt, but all the Andurien transmitting stations have been checked and found to be clean. Investigators have concluded that for *reasons unknown* the message either originated aboard the recharge station or, more likely, was sent from a private transmitter up to the relay satellites. Either way, the computer records aboard the station were altered to make it look like a government-sanctioned message."

"And the two men?" Marcus asked.

"Technicians. They're innocent. The corporal commandeered them from the night-shift labor pool. They weren't told what was going on until halfway over on the shuttle."

Marcus let his exasperation bleed into his voice. "I have at least two BattleMechs requiring complete electronic overhaul thanks to their meddling. Those innocents really screwed up the computers on both machines. Not to mention they tried to kill me." He winced at the memory of the needler dart that had struck bone in his left leg. "Who's going to answer for this?"

The flag captain pursed his lips and sighed heavily. "Commander GioAvanti, you have to realize that the authorization was counterfeit. Whoever set this up deceived Corporal Owens, and the rest of the operation was conducted under her authority. She had the clearance to perform such activities only because she is a member of Andurien intelligence." Marcus let that one slide by without comment, and the flag captain continued. "The Duchy of Andurien has issued a formal apology that their representative was used in this way, and is prepared to compensate you for the damage to your machines. If it's any consolation, the corporal's career is over even though it is certainly no fault of hers."

Marcus shook his head lightly in disbelief, though his gaze never broke from Flag Captain Montgomery's. "And that's it? After holding us up for two days, this is the best you can do?"

"Commander GioAvanti, the fact that such an attack was directed specifically at your unit tends to support that it was committed by parties outside normal Andurien channels. Probably someone you dealt with in the past, carrying a grudge. The Duchy of Andurien has no interest in your mercenary company except to bring this regrettable incident to a close." The way Montgomery clipped his words left no doubt that the issue was indeed closed as far as he was concerned.

"If there are no further questions?" Flag Captain Montgomery quickly searched the faces of those gathered around the table while unbuckling himself from his seat. "Then I will return to my recharge station." He rose and drifted from the room with the ease of a man quite used to near-zero gravity.

The dull metallic thud of the closing door suggested to Marcus the closed attitude of the bureaucratic mind. The silence hung heavy in the room, finally broken by a rattle from the climate system. "So, do we believe them?" Marcus asked, his gaze flicking from one face to the next. He could feel the flush of anger still warm on his cheeks, and decided to let the others speak first while he worked to calm himself.

Charlene shrugged. "It could be just as he says. Jase might have been able to turn up more than their *investigation* did, but he isn't here. Given the formal apology and recompense, we really have no grounds to pursue this matter." She shrugged again.

"If whoever came after us knows we're heading into the Periphery," Thomas Faber said, leaning forward, "it might be that they wanted us stopped. If it's the Free Worlds League supplying weapons to the Hegemony, that is."

With a heavy exhale, Marcus shook his head. "Doesn't figure. Andurien has always been a thorn in the side of the League. I can't see the Anduriens taking such strong action on behalf of Thomas Marik, especially against the Magistracy of Canopus."

"That's not as unlikely as it sounds." Jericho Ryan licked at the edge of her lips and frowned, as if trying to decide how much to tell. "Before leaving Canopus IV, I was given access to information showing a possible connection between Andurien and the Capellan Confederation. Nothing major, just some shipping schedules and exchanges of ambassadors and the latest trade agreements. Since House Liao is also suspected of supporting the Hegemony's raids against my people, it isn't inconceivable that Sun-Tzu would use the Duchy to strike at you in advance."

Charlene's voice took on a speculative edge. "Especially after the showing we made against Liao's New Home Regulars."

"Wait a minute," Marcus said, fixing Jericho with a steady gaze. "Didn't the Duchy of Andurien once ally itself with Canopus to invade the Capellan Confederation? Now you think they might have switched allegiance?"

"That was almost thirty years ago, Commander." Jericho's expression was thoughtful. "Things change. Magestrix Emma Centrella cut off ties to Andurien after the failed invasion, going so far as to formally apologize to the Marik family. She also allocated funds to help rebuild facilities on several League worlds that suffered during the war fought to bring the Duchy of Andurien back into the League." She smiled thinly. "Pure survival instinct. The Free Worlds League had to be appeased, and the Magestrix bought them off cheaply."

"And Sun-Tzu Liao?" Charlene asked. "How does he fit into this?"

"The success of the Marik-Liao invasion of the old Sarna March has created some sympathy for him. Word of Blake has capitalized on that, working to reconcile any bitterness left over from the Andurien-Canopus invasion of the Confederation and to restore good diplomatic relations. Much in the same way they're working to strengthen the alliance between Canopus and the Taurian Concordat."

Marcus nodded. "Just like they're trying to do in the Chaos March." He paused to consider. "All right, so we've got a possible connection. Now the question is, what can we do about it?"

"Nothing," Jericho said immediately. "Charlene is correct that the Duchy's apology and compensation, well-meant or not, end the matter. Aggravate the situation now, and it will look like you've got your own political agenda to push." Nods from Faber and Ki-Lynn. "The best you can hope for is to break the supply line flowing into the

Marian Hegemony and then tie it back to the Anduriens. Then you might see some measure of satisfaction."

Marcus could find no fault in her logic. "Agreed," he said.

He unbuckled his restraining strap and stood. Keeping a firm grip on the seat back, he moved around behind his chair and used it to hold himself down against the floor. "Meanwhile we consider the Free Worlds League hostile territory. Charlie, order a double guard at the hatches for both the *Heaven Sent* and the *Pinhead.* Also, two roving patrols in each. Faber, find me Petrovka. Between the technicians and the MechWarriors, we're going to go over both DropShips top to bottom. Make sure Corporal Owens left no other surprises." He paused for a deep breath and glanced with irritation at the climate system, which had begun again with its mechanical rattle. "Anything else?"

Charlene spoke up as she unbuckled her own restraint and levered herself out of her chair. "Buddy system when the JumpShip we're using is at a recharge station or expecting shuttles."

"That one may be hard to enforce," Marcus said. "But we'll make it a strong recommendation."

Jericho rose with a nod to Shannon. "I'll get back to the *Adonis,* then. Captain McFarlaine is ready to jump at our discretion. Shall I give her the word?"

Marcus gave her a quick nod. "The sooner the better." As an afterthought, he asked, "What's our estimated time of arrival in Canopus space?"

"ETA is April twenty-ninth," Jericho said. "That's when we cross the border. But we aren't scheduled to reach the planet Marantha until early May."

With a thin smile set on his face, Marcus drifted around the side of the table, heading for the door. "Never thought I'd say this, but I can't wait until we get into the Periphery."

10

Palace of the Magestrix
Crimson, Canopus IV
Magistracy of Canopus
The Periphery
24 April 3058

Demi-Precentor Jamie Nicholas walked down a wide hall that had obviously been decorated with an eye toward splendor. A plush carpet of dark golds and browns covered its entire length. The walls were decorated with a floral print wall covering and hung with delicately woven tapestries and occasional holograms of the Centrellas—founders and ruling family of the Magistracy of Canopus. Wall sconces of intricately cut crystal provided lighting.

Every ten steps or so a large bay window on the left gave down onto the private gardens one story below, the scene illuminated with beautiful ground-effect lighting now that evening had come to Crimson. Each window also had a window seat covered in dark velvet and cushioned with many pillows. Occasional doorways on the right opened to similarly well-furnished rooms that beckoned warmly, inviting the visitor to be at ease. The place felt more like a private home than a royal palace.

The personal quarters of the Magestrix and her family took up one entire wing of the royal palace here on Canopus IV. Despite Jamie Nicholas's position as Word of Blake representative to the court, she had never been invited here before and likely wouldn't now except for the importance of the package she held tucked under her right arm. But to be sent on without a guard or even the usual perfunctory escort . . . *Ah, Cameron, you knew the Magestrix would come to trust me. Now I only await your order.*

Jamie paused before a tapestry depicting victorious Canopus BattleMechs accepting the surrender of House Liao forces. This must have been early in the invasion, Jamie decided, remembering the reversal of fortune Romano Liao had set in motion as early as 3032. Still, the craftsmanship was not lost on her. The artist had made the ten-meter-tall death machines of Canopus appear somehow more elegant and noble than any 'Mech ever could, while the Liao 'Mechs looked like prowling beasts.

House Liao.

From under her arm she brought out the package and weighed it in upturned palms as if she could divine its contents. Heavy enough, yet not so much it couldn't have been almost anything. The package had been wrapped and sealed with a hologram of the House Liao insignia—a gauntleted arm holding a katana. The hologram had been delicately woven into the fibers of the wrap, much in the same way a verigraphed message was created, making tampering difficult at best. The package also carried full diplomatic markings, putting Word of Blake and especially the Toyama in a bad spot. *Is it enough that I know the contents?* She had delayed its delivery for three days already, hoping for some word from demi-Precentor St. Jamais, before deciding that it could wait no longer.

Another few steps down the hallway and Jamie paused before the door she'd been instructed to look for. Fifth one along the hall, a hologram of the Magestrix' five daughters and one son hanging on the wall just past it. Jamie smiled in amusement. She could still remember the briefing she had received six years ago as a member of ComStar and before being posted to Canopus IV. ROM, ComStar's intelligence branch, had reported the Magestrix having three sons and three daughters. Jamie was four months on Canopus before discovering that ROM had erred.

Emma Centrella had concealed the identities of her two

eldest daughters behind male names for several years. In the early 3040s—after deposing her mother and gaining many enemies—such caution had seemed prudent. The Magistracy of Canopus was a matriarchy, where the Magestrix could nominate the most fit of all her daughters, and Emma Centrella had wanted her potential heirs protected. By 3050 those precautions had been abandoned, but ComStar, grossly ignoring the Periphery in a characteristic lack of vision, had never corrected that mistake in their intelligence reports.

Jamie Nicholas hefted the sealed package again, weighing its importance. *We can only hope that the Word of Blake operates with greater wisdom and foresight.*

The demi-Precentor had already lowered the hood of her robe, and now as she passed through the open door she shook her long red hair out across her shoulders. The Canopus lifestyle favored an informal atmosphere, to say the least, and Jamie Nicholas was always careful to honor those values in whatever small way she could.

The Magestrix' private sitting room was modeled after the formal reception chamber in the residence's main building, but the room's focal point was not the place of the Magestrix. Here the furniture was arranged to give everyone a pleasant view of a large fireplace where a fire crackled merrily, scenting the room with the faint but pleasant aroma of burning cedar logs. The hearth was flanked by beautiful marble statues. From her time in the Magistracy of Canopus, Jamie recognized them easily as images of Adonis and Aphrodite, time-honored representations of beauty and love. Their poses were as natural and sublime as any sculpture of the ancient Greeks.

"Hello, Jamie."

The words rolled smoothly in a rich contralto voice, and Jamie turned toward the room's other door to greet Magestrix Emma Centrella as she entered in the company of her two eldest daughters. The Magestrix wore a formal robe that blended dark blue silks with a molded halter-style chestplate of gold. A golden tiara studded with sapphires held her dark hair back from her face. Dusky complexion, full lips, and large gray eyes gave her something of an exotic look. Even in her late fifties, Emma

Centrella possessed the sensual beauty that reminded others of Canopus' reputation for pleasure. "Wonderful to see you again," she said, her eyes showing both warmth and determination.

The demi-Precentor accepted the sentiment with a smile, reminding herself that Emma Centrella had been a formidable MechWarrior in her younger years. *This is not a woman who practices idle flattery.* "You and your daughters look lovely, Magestrix," she said, taking in the beautiful features Danai and Naomi shared with their mother. Both daughters wore evening dresses, Naomi's of Canopian high fashion, sequined and soft-colored, and Danai's a more daring turquoise and black combination with high leg slits and plunging back. "I am interrupting?"

Emma Centrella waved Jamie to a seat on the overstuffed sofa. "My daughters are going out this evening, but they have a moment or two." She seated herself in a large crescent-shaped chair at the sofa's left, tucking her legs up under her in a decidedly informal post. "And the message did seem to convey some importance."

Seating herself, Jamie placed the Liao package on the small table that separated the sofa from the Magestrix' chair. Danai, Emma's eldest daughter at twenty-one years and the current favorite to succeed her mother, sat to Jamie's right. Naomi, nineteen according to the new Word of Blake profile Jamie had seen, sat furthest removed, kneeling on the floor and leaning back against the sofa's edge.

Jamie frowned ever so slightly at the package, a gesture she knew the Magestrix was sure to pick up. "I believe it is, Magestrix, or I wouldn't have come so late. This package was entrusted to the Word of Blake's care on the Capellan capital of Sian, with instructions to deliver it to you as soon as possible. It is from Sun-Tzu Liao. We have performed the proper scan to ensure its safety, as did your own people when I arrived."

"And what do you think it contains, Jamie?"

Emma Centrella was far too accomplished a diplomat to give anything away by her facial expression, even in such an informal encounter, but Jamie heard the note of curiosity in the other woman's voice. Understandable. Most diplomatic messages were entrusted to ComStar or Word of Blake HPG communication, which could have brought a vid-recorded message from Sian to Canopus IV in five to ten days. Or less than a day at priority classification and rates. But Sun-Tzu had gone to the trouble and greater expense of sending a diplomatic package that had to be carried by courier along a path of DropShips and JumpShips in order to finally reach the Magestrix. Jamie knew it had taken just under a month and had cost the Chancellor nearly a hundred times what it would have taken to send an hour-long holovid by HPG.

And for all that time and expense, we have no idea what it is. And that worries me.

"Word of Blake was not made privy to the contents, Magestrix. Only that it was a gift for you in hopes of improving relations between Canopus and the Capellan Confederation."

Emma Centrella's eyes swept over the package again, her lips pursed in thought. "Childish games," she whispered, shaking her head lightly.

"I do not think that is the case here," Jamie replied, though she did not keep all doubt from her voice. *Play both sides,* the directive from Precentor Aziz had said. Jamie's first impulse had been to destroy the package, worried at Sun-Tzu's sudden interest in Canopus. But Demona Aziz led the Toyama, and Blake's will be done. Jamie believed in her almost as much as did Cameron St. Jamais. "Sun-Tzu also sent verbal instructions. The Word of Blake is to inform you that the Confederation is sending along a new ambassador to the Magistracy of Canopus. With this gift comes a request that you grant him audience."

The previous Liao ambassador had been a belligerent, brusque military man who the Magestrix had finally dismissed from her realm. From the narrowing of Emma Centrella's eyes, Jamie knew that she was not recalling him fondly. *The fools are sending another male,* Jamie thought with some relief. *Praise Blake the Capellans do not learn from their mistakes.* Not that male officials weren't welcome in the Magistracy. Indeed the newest

Taurian Concordat ambassador was a male, but if Sun-Tzu was trying to reconcile with a matriarchal state like the Magistracy of Canopus, where women held the dominant positions, wouldn't it make sense to comply more closely with Canopian custom?

"Turn him back, Mother." Danai Centrella's advice was as sharp as it was abrupt. "It hasn't even been a year yet. I doubt they've had time to learn proper manners, much less respect for you and the Magistracy."

The hard set of Danai's features reminded Jamie of holos she'd seen of Kyalla Centrella, Emma's mother and the previous Magestrix of Canopus. Knowing Danai to be an accomplished MechWarrior and commander of a battalion of Royal Guards, Jamie could understand why the young woman might have little patience in dealing with Liao. Suddenly even Danai's choice of dress made more sense, the turquoise and black of her gown the exact colors of the MAF uniform.

Emma Centrella's face revealed no emotion as she looked at her younger daughter. "What is your opinion, Naomi? Do I receive the new ambassador?"

Naomi shrugged even as she apparently gave the question some thought. Jamie knew that the younger daughter had more skill in public relations than as a warrior, despite her official post as a company commander in the Royal Guards. Would that make her less likely to want to rebuff the Capellans?

"I'd say you should examine your present," Naomi said finally. "If nothing else, it might help you decide firmly against Sun-Tzu Liao."

Jamie tried not to show her relief at these words. Sun-Tzu Liao wasn't known for being particularly subtle. If he didn't trip himself on his own, the Toyama or 6th of June movement could simply throw a few extra vibrabombs in his path.

Emma Centrella reached over and lifted the package onto her lap. She pulled at the tab, a thin wire that sliced through the seam to open easily what could not have been tampered with any other way. Then she lifted the lid of a polished wooden box. "My. How very intriguing."

Fighting against an urge to jump up and peer into the

box, Jamie remained seated as Naomi rose and moved to take the box and wrapping from her mother—leaving in the Magestrix' hands a large, leather-bound book.

Danai was the first to say it. "A book?"

The Magestrix opened the volume and sat quietly thumbing through its pages. The dry whisper of rustling paper nearly drove Jamie mad. *All that effort for a book?* It didn't make sense to her either. The Magistracy of Canopus had one of the poorest educational systems in the Inner Sphere or Periphery. Was this a subtle dig at their efforts to solve that problem? And to send it in this format? Sun-Tzu could have sent a vidbook that would have survived handling better. As it was, the large volume of leather and thick pages looked very delicate even in the Magestrix' fine hands. Better yet, he could have scanned the pages into a file and had Word of Blake transmit the entire text faster and for less money than it took to have the thing carried here.

With a smile of amusement Emma Centrella closed the heavy volume and handed it to Jamie. Though the rough tooling of the soft leather felt strangely pleasant to the touch, she immediately passed it on to Danai at her right. *Don't seem too interested,* she reminded herself. *You're supposed to be a simple messenger.* Watching over Danai's shoulder as the young woman flipped through some pages, Jamie felt a shiver of anger. *Blake's blood! How we underestimated him.*

Page after page was filled with beautifully detailed drawings and color paintings of people engaging in various sexual exploits.

"A book of Chinese erotica," Danai said softly, tracing a finger over the Chinese ideograms running down the page. "But surely the book can't be as old as he made it look."

Jamie felt the flush rise in her cheeks as Danai paused over sketches of erotic devices, though neither of Emma's daughters seemed at all embarrassed.

"Sun-Tzu provided a loose page near the front with a preface in English." The Magestrix' reply was offhand. "The book is an exact replica of a fifteen-century Chinese text on the erotic. This copy happens to be only fifty years old. A well-preserved fifty," she said, voice trailing off in bemusement. Jamie knew the Magestrix was comparing it to her own age, and she felt a well of despair rise within her.

In any Inner Sphere state, and among most Periphery realms, such a gift would be scandalous. That it came from such a repressive state as the Capellan Confederation bordered on the incredible. Jamie still found it hard to credit Sun-Tzu with such bold and insightful move. Only the Magistracy of Canopus, with its emphasis on entertainment and pleasure—a state that supported pleasure circuses throughout the Inner Sphere!—could recognize such a gift for what it was meant to be. Art. A unique treasure that showed an appreciation of the Canopian lifestyle.

Naomi asked the question forming with dread in Jamie's private thoughts. "You will see the Capellan ambassador?"

The Magestrix nodded. "I don't see how I could refuse after this. Chancellor Liao has earned it." Just hearing the Magestrix use Sun-Tzu's title made Jamie's blood run colder. "Perhaps this time he's sent us someone who can be dealt with in a reasonable manner. If not"—her voice took on an icy-cruel edge—"I can always revoke his diplomatic status."

Jamie knew that the Liao ship conducting the ambassador to Canopus IV would arrive in-system in a matter of days. It would then take two weeks for his DropShip to travel from the jump point to the planet. She hoped St. Jamais could respond by then with instructions, but if he were conducting another raid in the guise of Hegemony forces it could be a month before she heard from him.

"In the meantime," Emma Centrella continued in a decidedly more congenial tone, "we must plan a reception to return the courtesy of this gift." She eyed both her daughters meaningfully.

Jamie glanced from one to the other, already guessing who would be put in charge. As she suspected, Danai suddenly found more interest in examining the preface while Naomi brightened at the prospect of arranging a state reception.

There was never a command given, but Naomi knew the duty was hers. "Entertainers as well, Mother?"

The Magestrix nodded. "Make it extravagant. We will invite the other ambassadors, as well as any high-placed corporate interests who we wish to court. You will have this book placed in the gallery hall under glass, but I expect it to be prominently displayed at the reception. I want to see the Capellan ambassador's public reaction to Chancellor Liao's gift." She glanced over at the book. "And I want you to hand-pick a suitable escort beforehand, should the ambassador be unmarried."

Naomi smiled and nodded her understanding of the Magestrix' order.

11

Thistledown Fields Spaceport
Canopus IV, Magistracy of Canopus
The Periphery
9 May 3058

Word of Blake has little to worry about.

Jamie Nicholas stared through the rear window of the hovercar at the *Lung Wang* Class DropShip hovering over Thistledown Fields, Canopus' largest spaceport. It settled onto the assigned ferrocrete pad with a final burst from its landing jets, a great veil of dust swirling up in a tan cloud to blur the lower half of the craft. Emblazoned across the cowling just back of one of the giant air intakes was the brightly painted crest of House Liao's Capellan Confederation. A gauntleted hand reached out from an inverted gold triangle, holding a katana easily half-again the size of a BattleMech, all set against an emerald-green field that seemed to shine as if freshly painted.

Sun-Tzu sends an ambassador in one of the Confederation's newest DropShip designs? If the Chancellor wanted to rub the Magistracy's nose in its lack of technological advancement, Jamie couldn't think of a better way.

Unable to help herself, she opened her door and stepped from the car before the warm air currents had even subsided. The winds tugged at the hem of her robes and the flying dust dimmed their pristine white, but the lure of technology drew her outside. She had seen reports on the newest Capellan DropShip design, but this was her first chance to actually look on one. The *Lung Wang* was classified as a spheroid-type construction, but its elongated body and aft drive thrusters reminded her more of an aerodyne ship like the *Leopard* or even the *Hamilcar*. It boasted an impressive array of weapons for a DropShip of its size, most located in the nose, and she knew it could carry a lance of BattleMechs, plus two aerospace fighters and a platoon of infantry for support. *An aggressive design. I like it.*

As Jamie folded her arms deeper into the opposite sleeves of her white robes, hatches began to open and a team of technicians scurried out to check that the ship had settled evenly on her landing gear. Through the after hatch she could just make out a giant, hulking form back within the shadows. *He's brought his own 'Mech.*

A light smile played at the edge of Jamie's lips as three hovercraft slid out from the same rear bay and formed into a small motorcade, two of the smaller aircars framing a hover-limo. *Ambassador, you make this easy for me.* With the one message she'd received from the Toyama euphemistically placing St. Jamais "in the field," and Precentor Aziz on her way to inspect the Free Worlds League side of the operation, Jamie had worried over how to handle the Capellan emissary to Canopus IV.

It was the reason she'd offered to meet him at the spaceport and escort him to the Palace of the Magestrix— in hopes of finding out something that might help her decide on a course of action. She smiled at the memory of the report that the ComStar chief onplanet had also volunteered, and been refused. Technically ComStar and Word of Blake held near equal status in the Magistracy, competing for all business. It was probably more accurate to say that they were engaged in a subtle war for the

Magistracy, with Word of Blake currently ahead of the game. Jamie possessed a much better rapport with Emma Centrella than stuffy old Precentor Klein—may the heretic suffer his final days in agony. That Sun-Tzu had sent his gift through Word of Blake didn't hurt matters either.

It still bothered her that Sun-Tzu Liao would develop an interest in the Periphery now, with the Toyama's operations proceeding so well. But she didn't let it worry her overmuch. The novelty of the Chancellor's gift would wear off soon enough. And by the way this meeting was shaping up, the ambassador would be ordered off Canopus IV by nightfall.

That thought must have been in the ambassador's mind as well. As of this morning the Capellan JumpShip had remained in position at the nadir jump point. *In case the ambassador isn't staying long.* She was now doubly glad the Magestrix had agreed to let her accompany the ambassador to the royal residence. Seeing his presumptuous arrival, Jamie could now plan on how best to manipulate the man to guarantee his disfavor at court.

All in a day's work.

As the line of hovercars drew nearer, Jamie stepped forward to catch their attention. The first one swung wide to take up a position on the far side of her own car. The hover-limo slowed to a stop just a few steps ahead of her and the third maintained a tight line with the second. The rear gullwing door on the limo hissed as its seal was broken and then swung up. Jamie started forward to greet the Capellan official. Two men immediately stepped out to flank the door, dressed all in black and with machine pistols holstered on their sides. She faltered in mid-stride, then stumbled to a halt as her gaze locked onto the bone-white death's head pins they wore on their collars. *Death Commandos! But that could only mean—*

Her mouth suddenly dry, Jamie bent at the waist, almost mechanically, to carefully peer into the hover-limo's dark interior. All she could think of, staring at the passenger within, was how very stupid she had been.

"You must be demi-Precentor Nicholas," Sun-Tzu Liao said in a mild tone, "my escort. I assume you have no objection to riding in my car to the Palace of the Magestrix?"

Emma Centrella drew in a deep, steadying breath as she gazed into the young Liao's impassive countenance.

She sat on the closest thing the Magistracy had to a throne: a large, rounded chair, well-cushioned and set on a small dais positioned off-center along the wall. A chair on whose edge she could perch comfortably or draw her legs up into a more relaxed position. Right now she sat on its edge. Her left hand relaxed at her side and the right toyed with a marble sphere being held up by a nearby statuette. On the same wall as her small dais, taking up a much larger space, was an indoor waterfall and pool formed from man-made rock. It was in keeping with the Magistracy preference for informal settings that the nature display was the focus of the room.

Though I doubt anyone else besides me has even spared it a thought over the last several minutes.

The tension in the royal hall was beginning to subside after her formal greeting of the Chancellor, though the guards still stood at attention, faces set in hard stares and hands gripping the stocks of their rifles. Sun-Tzu's two Death Commandos looked relaxed but alert, flanking their young lord from two meters behind each shoulder.

Two to her six. And from what she'd heard of the Death Commandos, that was more than sufficient.

The Magestrix was certain of her composure now, though she must certainly have looked at a loss when Sun-Tzu—resplendent in his red silk robes of office— stepped through the door at the end of the hall and announced himself. Her guards had shown more presence of mind, with only a stiffening and slight adjustment of their posture revealing that they but awaited her command. Naomi had not fared quite so well, glancing repeatedly between her mother and the Chancellor of the Capellan Confederation several times before regaining control of herself. Off to one side, behind the line of guards, the young woman Naomi had chosen as escort for the Liao ambassador gasped and looked ready to faint dead away. Fortunately her station was low enough not to reflect on the Magestrix. For once, Emma Centrella was glad for the absence of her eldest daughter. Danai might have reacted badly, especially with the latest evidence of a possible Liao-Andurien alliance aiding the Marian Hegemony.

Sun-Tzu had even managed to use the shock of his arrival to some advantage, dismissing demi-Precentor Jamie Nicholas from the room before Emma was able to collect her thoughts and react. *A minor point, Sun-Tzu. Whatever you wish to conceal from the Word of Blake I can pass along, and you have now used up the capital bought with your surprise arrival.*

"Chancellor Liao," Emma said smoothly, "please forgive the lack of formalities. Had I known about your coming ..." She trailed off, spreading her hands to express her dismay.

Sun-Tzu stood only a few steps away, at the edge of a narrow strip of purple carpet that ran back to the doors. He wore black shirt and pants under the red silk robes. His hands closed in front of him showed off the gold embroidery on his sleeves, a pattern alternating katana swords and crescent moons. Earlier, when he'd turned back to nod his dismissal to Jamie Nicholas, Emma had seen the design of a large zodiacal dial of Chinese origin spread across the back of the robes.

The universe according to Liao, she had thought.

Now the young Chancellor frowned. "I do not understand, Magestrix. Did not Word of Blake carry my words to you along with my gift?"

Emma answered slowly, still not sure of herself. "Well, yes. That you were sending an ambassador, and would I please grant him audience." She smiled in forced mirth. "Surely you are not the new ambassador to the Magistracy."

His answering smile was obviously feigned innocence. "Ah, I see the error. The message should have been that the Chancellor had dispatched a new ambassador to your state. And that he had also forwarded a personal gift, in hopes that you would receive *him.* I'm sure that is how I told it to Word of Blake Precentor Carrington on Sian." He spread his hands in a manner similar to the Magestrix' earlier gesture. "Ambassador Yshigo will not arrive for another two weeks, regrettably. *She* had to finish up business on Capella, and could not take advantage of the command circuit I was using."

You play your little games with a clever hand, Sun-Tzu. But that is all they are. Games. "Had I known, I would have shown honor to an Inner Sphere lord visiting my realm. So let me welcome you again to the Periphery." Only a slight narrowing of his eyes told the Magestrix that Sun-Tzu had not missed her deliberate separation of the Inner Sphere and Periphery. "And now that you are here, what might Canopus offer you?"

If Emma hadn't known better, she might have taken Sun-Tzu's look of confusion at face value. "Magestrix?"

"Your agenda, Chancellor Liao. If there are proposals you wish to make, I may need some time to consult with advisers. But except for matters of state defense, I can promise to clear my schedule for you."

"The Magestrix is most generous, and in fact it is the defense of your state I wish to address. In several ways."

Emma Centrella did not react visibly to Sun-Tzu's words, though she felt her throat suddenly tighten. She heard no hint of challenge in the Liao's tone, but the small fears raised the other evening in her talk with Jamie now came parading forward. *Was Sun-Tzu about to admit his alliance with the Marian Hegemony?* She carefully swallowed against the constriction. "Oh, yes?"

Sun-Tzu nodded. "I know that the Marian Hegemony has been seriously harassing your borders with increased raiding. I would like to offer the assistance of the Capellan Confederation."

Of all things Sun-Tzu Liao might have said or done, Emma Centrella had not expected this and that left her in a dangerous position. She knew it risky to proceed where she did not already know the answers. And she still did not trust Sun-Tzu, nor was it likely she ever would. But she found herself wishing to hear more. "Please continue, Chancellor."

"As I understand it, the main problem is with the Hegemony's acquisition of newer technology. Perhaps they are being supplied, but it would not be unknown if they had located a treasure trove of lostech."

Lostech, the Inner Sphere term for high technology no longer understood because of the ravages of war. There were always rumors of long-forgotten Star League bases still waiting to be found, but Emma Centrella doubted Sun-Tzu believed that was the case here any more than she did. "That is a possibility," she agreed, conceding the point with the right amount of doubt in her voice.

"Well, we can certainly agree that the Hegemony has not developed the technology themselves. Their educational progression is worse even than the Magistracy's."

Naomi's sharp intake of breath drew a disapproving look from Emma, who turned back to Sun-Tzu and smiled humorlessly. Such a blatantly disrespectful comment might have been grounds to expel any lower diplomat from her realm, but she realized that Sun-Tzu was testing, rather clumsily, her commitment to frankness. "It is as you say, Chancellor," she agreed, though a little coldly. "All the Periphery states suffer somewhat in this area. But we are taking steps to improve."

"Of course," Sun-Tzu said, his smile faltering just a bit as if he was realizing his error. "And that is an area where I am willing to help." He took a step forward, and when he spoke again, his voice had dropped to a dramatic whisper that would not carry past his own guards or the two Centrellas.

"Magestrix Centrella, you have been offering good rates to any mercenaries with access to the newer technology of the Inner Sphere or who have been able to appropriate some from the Clans and put it to use. Your problem is that many mercenaries won't travel into the Periphery if they can help it, and your level of technology is lacking in all areas except entertainment and medicine.

"I will bring in technicians and instructors to help you catch up to the new standards faster than you could on your own. The first of these await aboard my JumpShip, the *Celestial Walker,* ready to be brought in on your command. And I will provide you with a steady supply of the new equipment, at a very fair rate of exchange. The same for raw resources. Finally, I offer you immediate and long-term military assistance for relief from the raiders."

Her mind almost swimming with the implications of Sun-Tzu's words, the Magestrix still did not miss the significance of that last remark. "You brought military forces into the Magistracy?" she asked, an edge to her voice.

Sun-Tzu literally shrugged the matter aside. "No more than what would be considered a personal guard. One battalion." His thin-lipped smile and the slight Asian tilt to his eyes gave him a look of craftiness. "But they are veterans all, and they are yours for immediate reassignment."

Too fast, Sun-Tzu. You are impatient, and I can make that cost you. "Brixtana," she said, naming a world on the Magistracy-Concordat border. "You will send them at once? Your battalion can free up Harcourt's Aliens, who I can then shift toward the Hegemony border."

Sun-Tzu was caught, unable to demand a concession from her without losing the good faith he was trying to build. Emma could read it all over his face. He had already offered to send the troops. Then with a shrug he turned and nodded to one of his bodyguards, who trotted back to the door to pass along the order. Turning back to the Centrellas, his face and voice were equally composed. "The word will go up to the *Celestial Walker* tonight. I will remain on the DropShip *Pearl of True Wisdom* until it returns." He smiled. "As easy as that, Magestrix. With the boost I can give your nation, what I ask for will seem like a pittance."

You learn fast, Sun-Tzu. I will grant you that. But now I have removed a potential threat to my world and safety as well as one of your bargaining pieces. "And that is?" she asked, as if planning to immediately grant his request.

"Something that will aid both our realms. Your troops need experience in the new tactics of modern warfare. I need troops to finish retaking what the Federated Commonwealth stole from my realm nearly thirty years ago."

Emma Centrella carefully shielded her thoughts from the young Liao's piercing gaze. *You have the years and bearing of a man, Sun-Tzu. But to me you are still an infant in the politics of the Inner Sphere, regardless of the strength of your Capellan Confederation or any recent accomplishments. You play at games that give you no real advantage, and you too easily give yourself away. Still, you offer what I need—though that alone is enough to make me suspicious of you.*

"There is a reception planned in your honor," she said finally, raising her voice to carry across the hall once more. She enjoyed the quick flash of frustration in Sun-Tzu's eyes without letting on that she'd seen it. "Or, I should say in honor of the Capellan ambassador, but your presence will inspire our entertainers to greater heights."

Almost as if reading her mind, Naomi stood and took a small step forward. Emma smiled at her daughter. "As you seem to be traveling without your betrothed, Isis Marik, my family would be honored if you would allow Naomi to escort you?"

Sun-Tzu's warm smile and bow of respect to Naomi seemed gracious enough, though Emma caught another flash of irritation at the mention of Isis Marik. "I would be honored, Lady Centrella."

Naomi stepped forward immediately, ending Sun-Tzu's audience with the Magestrix. "Chancellor," she said, returning his bow. Sun-Tzu offered her his arm, which she dutifully accepted.

Emma Centrella noticed the look of relief that crossed the face of the courtesan they had chosen for "the Capellan ambassador" as she faded back and then slipped out by a side entrance. While Sun-Tzu escorted Naomi back toward the main doors, Emma Centrella remained seated as if lost in thought. Not until the door finally closed and she was left alone with her guards did she laugh to herself and rise from her chair.

You would hire the Magistracy Armed Forces as you would a mercenary company. A moment of reflection and she amended her thoughts. *No, as one of your Warrior Houses. A bold plan, Sun-Tzu.*

Emma smiled a full, rich smile, then made her way out the same side entrance that would take her to the reception in time to properly announce the Chancellor. *Perhaps one I may even endorse someday. But you are still impatient, and I will make it cost you again before you leave.*

=== 12 ===

The Grand Senate
New Rome, Alphard
Marian Hegemony
The Periphery
11 May 3058

Caesar Sean O'Reilly stormed through the half-open door, then slammed it shut with a shove that set its large glass pane to rattling. Gold lettering on the glass read backward from inside the office, but could easily be distinguished as saying *Office of Communication*. Demi-Precentor Cameron St. Jamais watched as the powerfully built ruler of the Marian Hegemony glanced back through the glass, checking the hallway. Even here in a rear hall of Alphard's Grand Senate, the seat of all legislation for the Marian Hegemony, the Caesar never relaxed.

Satisfied that everyone in the hall had quickly returned to their own business, O'Reilly turned on St. Jamais, his teeth bared and his brilliant green eyes wide with anger. "Sun-Tzu Liao is on Canopus," he said coldly, obviously demanding an explanation.

Dropping his gaze to the Word of Blake reports that he'd been studying a few moments before, St. Jamais finished the section he'd been reading. This was just one of many reports concerning the mercenary units being routed to the Magistracy of Canopus border. *Offense-oriented. Small, but highly mobile. Specialists in infiltration, extended raiding, extraction.* Glancing up again, he took in the Caesar's challenging stance and let how little it impressed him show plainly on his face. "I know," he said simply, then returned his gaze to the briefing that interested him most. *Last assignment, New Home.*

"You know? And what have you done about it?" O'Reilly asked.

St. Jamais pushed the pile of reports to the middle of his desk and leaned back in the office's only chair. Resting one elbow on the chair arm, he rested his chin on the thumb and forefinger of that hand. He toyed briefly with the idea of rising to his feet. It had, after all, been the Caesar who'd provided him with this small office, as St. Jamais' mission precluded him from staying in the Word of Blake HPG compound. Precentor Alphard belonged to the Toyama, but Demona Aziz had ordered St. Jamais to use all possible discretion just in case something went wrong. For the same reason she'd chosen Astrokaszy as the base of their operation instead of a border world under heavy Word of Blake influence.

And if things go bad, I would be her sacrifice to the new First Circuit. St. Jamais held no illusions that, if need be, Demona wouldn't mark him a renegade and have him destroyed—all to protect her own position. That was the game they played. *If not me, it would be another. But I will succeed where another would fail. And when Demona is named Primus, I will be first among her supporters and await the day when she must finally step down.*

And the more he considered both the risks he took and the potential rewards, the less he wanted to put up with Sean O'Reilly. Not only that, he found a certain pleasure in the deference being paid him by the ruler of the Marian Hegemony.

"What would you have me do?" he asked finally, voice calm as he looked O'Reilly in the eye.

O'Reilly shifted uncomfortably, obviously unused to being on this side of such a conversation. He was a man accustomed to the ruthless use of power, and it obviously irritated him that Word of Blake—and St. Jamais in particular—couldn't be cowed.

"Look," he said in a more reasonable tone, "Sun-Tzu Liao has made some big investments in the Hegemony, and so has Thomas Marik. Liao even stands to rule the Free Worlds League, if this marriage to Isis ever happens. I need to know if his visit to Canopus indicates a shift in his allegiance."

St. Jamais' chuckle was ice cold. "Worried about those little pieces of evidence implicating the Capellan Confederation as well as the League that your people left behind after their raids?"

O'Reilly nodded, the humor escaping him. "It would not do if Liao troops suddenly showed up on the Canopus border. Not to mention that the Free Worlds League is our biggest customer of germanium, which is not a luxury item they can afford to suddenly place under embargo. They need it—hell, everyone needs it—for their JumpShips."

"And they might decide that simply taking it away from you would be easier than dealing with a man who would use them in such a manner. You knew the risks," Cameron reminded him. "And it's a bit late to part company now." He smiled at the other's obvious discomfort, then leaned forward, elbows on the desk and hands steepled in front of him. "Don't worry, Caesar O'Reilly. Sun-Tzu Liao's arrival is unexpected, but I doubt it's any cause for concern. In fact, I believe it shows how desperate is the situation of the Magistracy of Canopus. The vultures are starting to circle."

O'Reilly seemed to relax, pacified by the assessment, as St. Jamais had known he would be. He nodded down at the papers St. Jamais had pushed into an awkward pile. "And these reports tell you the purpose for Sun-Tzu's visit?"

A frown. "No." St. Jamais glanced back at the top sheaf, a report on the mercenary companies being hired by Canopus. "Emma Centrella is hiring more mercenaries, just as I warned that she would. They're like most of their kind—most are 'Mech pilots down on their luck and hoping for a quick score that will get them back to Outreach with enough C-bills to pay off their debts."

"Most?"

"There are a few who could mean trouble. The Maginot 'Mechs are a good defensive unit and came at a higher price, so I've given orders to avoid them if possible. Likewise the Griffin's Pride battalion." He reached out to flick the corner of the top page. "Then there's this one—Avanti's Angels."

Caesar O'Reilly leaned over the desk to scan the report. "It says right here that the unit doesn't perform well in defensive situations. What's the problem?"

"Exactly that, Caesar. Why would Canopus hire such a unit, and at a fair price too, unless they planned on offensive action of some type?"

"You must be joking," O'Reilly scoffed. "According to our intelligence, the MAF is in no condition to strike at my worlds. These mercenaries simply bargained better. I'll order a raiding team to destroy them." He waved the matter off as if it could be dismissed with a casual flick of his wrist. "I want to know what Liao is doing on Canopus. You can find that out for me, and you will do so."

St. Jamais heard the arrogance of command seep back into O'Reilly's voice and decided not to test it this time. "I will order a tighter surveillance on the Liao's movements. His meetings with the Magestrix have taken place in secret, but our representative to the court will uncover the reason for his visit." This time St. Jamais' voice lacked the conviction he knew would mollify the Caesar as he wondered again at the Angels' mission. *You can afford to take these mercenaries lightly. I cannot.* Still, the Caesar had at least one good suggestion.

"I notice the Angels are bound for Marantha," he said, checking the report again. "Your military has a pirate point for that system?"

"For all of them," O'Reilly returned. "As I recall, Marantha has several that are in very close. A day, perhaps."

"And Alphard? How close can one of your ships come in?"

"Two days," O'Reilly said immediately. "But why bother? I can divert a raiding team. And you can look into Sun-Tzu's motives."

St. Jamais did some quick calculations. "Because by the time you get word to your raiders, I could be there on the command circuit we worked out for rapid deployment."

Worked out with more Word of Blake JumpShips than you own, St. Jamais thought, and hoped the Caesar was reminded of that fact as well. Command circuits were an established method of bypassing a JumpShip's long recharge time, a prearranged string of starships waiting at jump points along the way to pass the DropShips along in a relay. "And I think these Angels might require my personal attention. Do not worry," he said, raising a hand to forestall another outburst by the Caesar. "I will pass along the orders about Sun-Tzu Liao before I leave. And if he is interfering, *I* will order him eliminated. Having Kali Liao looking toward Canopus to avenge her brother's death would move my plans along that much faster."

O'Reilly's lopsided smile added his silent endorsement of the order. "And these Angels? Do you really think they could be so dangerous?"

"Perhaps not," St. Jamais admitted, rising to his feet and collecting the reports in a neat bundle. "But that no longer matters. I will meet them in a manner of my own choosing and destroy them." He matched gazes with the Caesar, thinking suddenly of preparations he could make to handle Demona the same way. "Before they can use the same tactics to destroy me."

And again, it was not just the Angels he meant.

=== **13** ===

Planetary Administration Building
Jubilee, Marantha
Magistracy of Canopus
The Periphery
18 May 3058

Most mercenary units making planetfall on their employer's world would touch down at a spaceport near a principal city and then be paraded through the streets in a spectacle meant to bolster the spirits of the people. As an offensive unit, the Angels were rarely required to perform such displays. That made it all the more surprising when Marcus was *invited* to shuttle down to the capital to meet with the Marantha planetary defense coordinator as the Angels' pair of DropShips received clearance to ground at a remote facility. Leaving Thomas Faber in charge, he took Charlene Boske and Jericho Ryan with him. Marcus didn't like becoming separated from his people as they made their initial drop onto a new planet, but he thought accepting the invitation might save them all any additional diplomatic nonsense.

Met at the Jubilee Spaceport by some minor official whose name Marcus couldn't even remember now, he and his two companions had been escorted to the planetary administration building in the city of Jubilee. From the third floor of that building Marcus now stood staring out the window as he slipped into a steadily darker mood. He folded his arms across his chest and shook his head to an offered drink after Jericho Ryan decided to raid the office's small liquor cabinet. The clinking of ice being dropped into the bottom of two glasses told him that Charlene had accepted.

Marcus was worried because Jase Torgensson hadn't turned up waiting for them on Marantha. Neither was there any indication that he'd been there nor any message on his whereabouts delivered care of the spaceport. Without Jase's scouting, the Angels would be forced to raid a Hegemony world to try to discover the source of the weapons obviously being supplied to the Marian Hegemony from outside. That would increase the level of opposition set against them. On a more personal level, it also meant Marcus had a lost Angel somewhere inside either the Free Worlds League or out here in the Periphery. Given the sabotage attempt in Andurien, he wondered if Jase would ever be heard from again.

And despite his attempts to remain detached, the loss ate away at Marcus.

The door to the office opened, and he turned to see a woman wearing the turquoise and black uniform of the Magistracy Armed Forces enter the room. Her gloves with spiked wrists and knee-high leather boots, similar to Jericho's, said she was a MechWarrior. A single gold and diamond insignia proclaimed her a major, the Magistracy rank for a senior battalion commander. She shut the door hard behind her. "Stupid, self-important, deluded bureaucrats," she said, almost spitting the words back at the closed door.

Marcus began to feel better.

With an exaggerated exhale, the major turned to the room's occupants and then walked straight to Marcus with hand outstretched. "Commander Avanti, sorry to keep you waiting. Major Judith Wood. Commanding officer of the Second Canopian Highlanders, McGraw's Marauders."

Marcus remembered the unit from the briefing Jericho Ryan had given him on MAF units he was likely to run into. The Canopian Highlanders had started out as two mercenary battalions with a long-term contract to the Magistracy. With the Magistracy's help, they'd expanded over the past thirty years into three short regiments of two battalions each. McGraw's Marauders were the best of the lot, a veteran regiment with several crack lances of the famed *Marauder* BattleMechs. While still technically a mercenary unit, the Highlanders had so adopted Magistracy traditions that the distinction was token at best.

"I asked that you be brought down," she continued, "and some idiotic official decided that you would be more comfortable waiting here." She shrugged and looked around in obvious distaste. "They assigned me this office along with the title of defense coordinator."

Shaking her extended hand, Marcus again marveled at the Magistracy's female orientation. Judith Wood was a handsome woman, with a strong face that he was sure could show both sternness or compassion, depending on which was called for. Her chestnut-brown hair was grayed only slightly at the temples, and the laugh-lines at her eyes made her look more amiable than old.

"Major," Marcus said. "Allow me to present my executive officer, Charlene Boske." Marcus waited while the two women shook hands, and then the major turned to Jericho and returned an old-style salute—fingertips to brow and hand turned inward until the palm almost rested against her cheekbone.

"Now then, Commander GioAvanti, I imagine your first concern is this missing man of yours."

"Yes," Marcus said, silently thanking her for her directness. "I was hoping a message had been left in the care of the MAF ..." He broke off abruptly as Major Wood shook her head.

"Afraid not. And I radioed for a check of passenger lists from all DropShips grounding in the past month. The name Torgensson doesn't appear anywhere." Her eyes narrowed in suspicion, but she kept her voice carefully neutral. "I suppose he could be traveling under another name."

Which would mean false identification and a number of other things you would rather not know about. Marcus appreciated the subtlety of her questioning. "I doubt that," he said, then waited for Charlene, who jumped in perfectly on cue.

"But if you were to run those checks again, Major, could you do the Angels a favor?" She paused to sip at her drink and Marcus let her take over the conversation. "We might have some friends in the neighborhood, so to speak. Dispossessed mercenaries who we might want to sign on. If you could check on the names Jon Howard and Peter Triskalion, we'd appreciate it."

Major Wood nodded. "Of course. But I have to ask you what you plan to do if Mr. Torgensson doesn't show up? According to the dispatch I received, you are acting independently of my command?"

"Yes, Major," Jericho said, stepping forward to answer. "The Angels will be allowed to use Marantha as a base of operations and to leave their civilians here." She had mixed another two drinks, handing one to the major and offering the other to Marcus, which he now accepted.

"And if the raiders attack while they're here?" the elder woman asked.

Marcus reentered the conversation with a shake of his head. "The Angels are not required to serve as garrison troops, Major Wood. We'll only be here long enough to settle in our families and decide on a course of action."

He took a sip of the drink and found it generously laced with the dry taste of good bourbon. "We can't afford to involve ourselves unnecessarily with Marantha's defense."

"I'm afraid that is correct," Jericho backed him up, though a trifle uneasy. "The Angels' contract even specifies the right to abandon any military position assigned them as a base, at the commander's discretion."

Major Wood's brow furrowed and her eyes hardened. "I see. And if I were to offer you an auxiliary contract?"

Both Charlene and Marcus looked up, then glanced at each other in obvious surprise. Auxiliary contracts were not unknown, but they were rare. It could only mean that the raiders were pressing harder than Marcus had thought. Negotiations were usually handled by Charlene and Torgensson. At Marcus' cautioning nod, Charlene asked, "What exactly do you propose?"

"On my authority as planetary defense coordinator, the government of Marantha could offer you recompense for any assistance you would be willing to lend us in a crisis situation. Your contract with the Magistracy taking precedence, of course."

Charlene considered that for a moment, and silence fell over the room as everyone waited. Most of them used the time to sip at their drinks, though Marcus barely wet his lips while he tried to second-guess what Charlene would propose. Finally his executive officer set her glass down on the desk and leaned back against its edge. "The Angels retain full autonomy. You would have to set your forces without us, and then we would decide our own response."

At the slight shake of the major's head, Charlene added, "We're an offensive unit. Within our tactical doctrine, it couldn't work any other way." Another moment's pause. "Full salvage rights. Reimbursement for damages to our equipment. Bounty on each enemy unit, including percentages based on damage we inflict."

Marcus smiled thinly at that last condition. It allowed the Angels to drive off attackers without having to engage hard enough to destroy them. *Not bad, Charlene, but we might be able to do a bit better.* He crossed his arms, resting his drink against the crook of his left elbow. *Let's see how desperate Major Wood really is.* "And half standard garrison pay any time our 'Mechs are on Marantha," he added.

Jericho's eyes widened in shock at such a request, and she stared incredulously at Marcus. Then Major Wood let out a short laugh of admiration. "You certainly know when to press your advantage, Commander." She thought a moment. "Let's say a quarter of standard garrison pay, based on how many 'Mechs are on planet at any given time. I'll still have to run that condition past the new planetary governor, but she seems ready enough to spend the Magestrix' money."

"New governor?" Marcus asked. "Commander Ryan described Sonia Hastings as a safe-seat politician."

"She was," the major said, her tone suddenly solemn. "She fell to an assassin almost two months ago. The new governor then appointed me as defense coordinator."

"And part of your job is to coordinate the defense of the governor's mansion, I'll bet." Marcus smiled and the other two women chuckled when the major rolled her eyes in a look of comical resignation.

The humor had barely run its course when a junior officer entered after a brief knock at the door. He handed a dispatch to Judith Wood and stood by. The major's face clouded over. "How long since contact?" she demanded of the ensign.

"An hour, Major. They swung around the outer moon, decelerating at one point five gravities. No one could locate you." He swallowed hard. "You never come here."

Wood threw up her arms in exasperation and stalked to the middle of the room. She glanced at Jericho and then at Marcus, "Raiders," she announced. "An *Overlord* and three *Union*s coming in under heavy fighter screen. They'll be on the ground any minute."

Up to two full battalions! The mix of anger and disbelief Marcus felt must have showed on his face, because Major Wood was quick to speak. "I know what you're thinking, Commander. I had no idea the raiders were in-system. They came in at a pirate point less than a day out, and sneaked in behind the moon's shadow."

Marcus didn't feel mollified. "Then you won't mind if we sit this one out?" he asked with sarcastic politeness.

"You won't be able to." Judith Wood sounded truly apologetic as she handed him the message. "Unless the *Overlord* changes its trajectory, this one intends to touch down on or near Indian Island. That's where we stationed the Angels." She took a deep breath. "They're dropping right on top of your unit."

14

Marantha Defense Complex
Jubilee, Marantha
Magistracy of Canopus
The Periphery
18 May 3058

"**I** need a map of Indian Island!"

The Planetary Control Station was a part of the Jubilee 'Mech yard, which sat just off the spaceport. Major Wood drove them all there in her personal hovercar, a '56 Canopus Motorworks Highlite that lived up to its advertising—fast in straight-aways and cornering at better than 30 kph with minimal lateral drift. As they made the six-kilometer trip in just over three minutes, Marcus was glad when she finally had to slow for the fist security checkpoint. Then the major dodged between two hangars and plunged down a ramp that led into a large underground bunker with vault-like doors. After parking the civilian vehicle among a row of APCs and jeeps, Major Wood waved Jericho Ryan and the two Angels past four different checkpoints, giving them instant access to her seat of defense.

Marcus watched as the ensign with the wrong map retreated and another ran up with the correct one, a large rolled sheet of colored plastic. The coloration would give him the topographical information he needed to plan

detailed BattleMech movements. Around him the frantic
activity of the room continued—clusters of MAF officers
hovering over maps and around war-boards, enlisted
personnel running the computers and scanners and communications that kept the room tied into all aspects of
Marantha's planetary defense. He unrolled the plastic
over a table-top viewer, clamping it at two edges and
then hitting the light switch. The table surface brightened, back-lighting the map where his Angels had been
dropped.

Indian Island was actually a fat peninsula connected to
the far northwest corner of Marantha's largest continent
by only the thinnest strip of land. Covered with well-
forested hills and a few deep valleys, the terrain lent itself
to stealthy movement by large numbers of BattleMechs.
On the eastern side of the peninsula, right up against the
waters of Freyja Sound, was a large spot of gray that
stood out among the greens and browns. Major Wood had
informed him on the drive over that the only thing beside
hills and trees on Indian Island was an ordnance depot. In
all, it consisted of two DropShip pads, outlying buildings,
and the openings to underground bunkers for the storage
of live ammunition. *And nothing but an infantry platoon
guarding it.* Major Wood had intended the Angels for that
duty, and so had transferred the demi-company there only
this morning.

Will our luck ever change? Marcus wondered.

He grabbed a magnifying screen connected to a tele-
scoping arm and shifted it into place over the ordnance
depot. *Someone had been thinking when they built that
place,* he thought. Except for a few light stands, the trees
had been cleared for over a kilometer both north and
south of the facility and almost as far to the west. A few
hills, and in a few places BattleMech-size breastworks,
provided good covering ground for defending units.

But as commander of a unit that specialized in breaking
the defenses of others, Marcus could already spot several
flaws that a determined force could take advantage of.
There. He stabbed a finger down onto the map, feeling
that heat of the light bleeding through glass tabletop and
thin plastic map. His finger looked huge under the mag-

screen, but it helped him commit the terrain to memory as he traced it alone treelines and hills. *This is where the enemy should make their attempt.*

Directly to the west of the depot the woods ran closer to the installation than anywhere else, less than a quarter-klick. The trees would make approach nearly un-detectable, but the ground leveled out from the edge of the forest into a straight run into the compound. To the north and south of the compound rose two hills that turned the flat terrain into a bottleneck for pouring down a murderous crossfire. But Marcus saw that any unit breaking from the woods could swing north and totally bypass one of those hills, cutting off half the defenders or forcing them to come down and fight it out in open terri-tory. Then the raiders' longer reach could work its devas-tating results.

Marcus glanced up from the map, squinting his eyes as he tried to keep the geography straight in his mind. There were several possibilities, but he would have to orches-trate it in his head first. When he reopened his eyes, he saw that Charlene had appropriated the headset of some communications tech and was busy arguing with someone on the other end. Jericho Ryan stood nearby with Major Wood, the two watching a computer screen and talking in low voices.

"Major, what can I count on for reinforcements? How many and in how long?"

Judith Wood and Jericho both turned. "For *what*?" Wood asked, but as her brain caught up with the questions being asked she quickly answered without need of further explanation. "Nothing."

Marcus shoved himself away from the viewer and approached the major. "Nothing?" He jabbed a finger back at the map, which glowed on the viewer in the greens and browns of its topographical display. "I have an *Overlord* dropping on my people and you can't spare a damn lance?"

"Commander GioAvanti, I don't even know that we can get *you* back to your unit in time, much less route a Drop-Ship out that way." Wood nodded toward the computer screen she'd been observing. "Flight mechanics say that the *Overlord* is coming in light. Maybe twelve hundred tons worth of BattleMechs. That puts them at a very light battalion, or more likely two strong companies. That's the best I can do right now in the way of support."

Waving at the computer, she continued. "We have three *Union*s holding low orbit with their aerospace fighter screen, and ready to drop anywhere. My BattleMech forces are spread thin as it is trying to keep units in position to reinforce each other. These raiders don't mind hitting civilians targets such as transit or industrial centers, and I have to protect all of that. They could hit anywhere, so until they commit themselves I can't promise you reinforcements."

Biting back his anger, Marcus tried to sympathize with Wood. He knew how hard it was to protect against a raiding force. The Angels relied on that same factor of uncertainty. But a full battalion, even a light one, was no small force. "Any chance those infantry troops have some anti-Mech capability?"

"No." Her expression softened then. "I'm sorry, Commander. Pull your people back if you must. But that will force me to pull several companies out of position, and then the *Union* DropShips will have free reign in several areas."

Marcus recognized the desperation in her eyes. Major Woods felt trapped by her responsibility for the people of Marantha. She had counted on the Angels in her defense plans, and pulling his unit out would mean that, somewhere, something else would have to give. *She doesn't want to make that choice, but she's ready to if I force her.*

"Got it, Marc." Charlene walked over, stretching the headset's cord to its maximum and ignoring the impatient gestures of the commtech. "The *Pinhead* spotted the *Overlord* coming down on the peninsula in a safe zone, maybe three hours southwest of the ordnance depot, depending on 'Mech speed. Apparently they didn't want to try slugging it out with our DropShips."

Marcus couldn't blame them there. The *Head of a Pin* was as close as a craft could come to the junkyard and still remains in commission, but it was still a *Fortress* Class ship—well armored and bristling with some heavy weapons. He considered what that might mean as far as the raiders' approach to the depot, then decided that he was still all right. "Does that give us the time to get over there?"

Major Wood started to shake her head, but Charlene jumped back in. "Yes. I have an Ensign Klepper on one channel with a double-lance of *Sparrowhawk*s. He said that each can take one passenger and get us there, if we can handle the Gs."

Before either Angel could make the request, Jericho Ryan snapped to attention before Major Wood. "Ma'am. Auxiliary unit Avanti's Angels requests support by four *Sparrowhawk* aerospace fighters."

Marcus and Judith Wood locked gazes, mentally probing each other's resolve. Jericho's request had reminded them of the verbal agreement reached back at the administrative building. The major would have to abide by the payment terms, and Marcus would have to do his best to defend the installation. The major nodded once and immediately turned to the map Marcus had lit up. "Can you do it?"

Four *Sparrowhawk*s. The Angels didn't have air cover of their own, but knew how to work with it. Marcus looked over the heavy woods covering most approaches to the ordnance depot. The fighters would only be good against 'Mechs once the raiders broke cover, and then only for the short time it took the Hegemony machines to get into the compound and between buildings. *So I have to turn the enemy away from the depot,* Marcus thought. *Keep them in the open.*

And the plan began to come together.

"Okay, Charlie, get Faber back on line. Have him hold back his *Marauder,* Ki's *Archer,* Jericho's *Griffin,* and my *Warhammer.* Also the Savannah Masters." He stepped back over to the map and located the two hills again. *They'll want to swing north,* he thought. "Everything else is to deploy just inside the treeline, northwest of the depot behind hill 15-32. Add Jericho's lancemate, the one with the *Trebuchet,* to the forces being held back." He glanced at Jericho, who nodded acceptance of his deploying her lance into the battle plan. "The deployed units will dampen reactors to minimum power and hold position. Those will be your forces, Charlie. You can get the *Jager-Mech* out there quick enough after we arrive, but I want them in place and cooled down."

Major Wood eyed him with some concern. "In strategic terms, Commander, that's called splitting your forces before a superior enemy."

"Since when are raiders considered superior?" he shot back with a thin, humorless smile. "Charlie, tell Faber to board all noncoms onto the *Heaven Sent*, and pull both DropShips back at low altitude to grid 45-350. That should place them about ten klicks from the depot, across Freyja Sound. They'll bring in the reinforcements."

Charlene finished the message then threw the headset back to the technician. "*Sparrowhawks* are on the pad, waiting for us," she said, already moving for the door.

Jericho caught Marcus by the arm before he could follow. Concern creased her brow, but her voice was only a gentle reminder. "Major Wood can't guarantee reinforcements, Commander."

Marcus smiled. "So she said. But the raiders don't know that, now do they?"

15

Ordnance Depot
Indian Island, Marantha
Magistracy of Canopus
The Periphery
18 May 3058

Demi-Precentor Cameron St. Jamais moved his AWS-9M *Awesome* forward, the 80-ton machine snapping branches off trees like dried twigs as it passed from the woods. After almost four hours of pushing his way through the peninsula's dense forest growth he was glad to see an end to it. The *Overlord* had touched down too far away, he knew that now. Fortunately he'd been able to delay the drop of the *Union* Class vessels appropriately. By now the MAF forces should be too concerned with defense of three major cities to worry about the fate of a few mercenaries. He smiled grimly. Any time now the MAF commander would find out that each city was threatened by only a strengthened lance of six light-to-medium 'Mechs.

Far too late to help the Angels.

Eight hundred meters ahead, across a clearing bounded to the north and south by two low hills, St. Jamais could see a section of fencing and some outer buildings that marked the perimeter of the Indian Island Ordnance Depot. His *Awesome* stood at the edge of the clearing that ran from the edge of the forest toward the depot, bottle-necking between those two hills. To either side of him his Word of Blake raiders were exiting the forest to form a ragged line of battle. Eighteen strong and averaging 60 tons per 'Mech, they were more than enough to take on a mercenary company.

And some of the most advanced designs available, he thought, 'Mechs such as the *Shootist* and the *War Dog* making his *Awesome* seem an old antique. But the *Grand Crusader* he normally piloted was too closely associated with Word of Blake, just as the other new designs were associated either with the Free Worlds League or the Capellan Confederation, in keeping with the cover-up. And the *Awesome* was no 'Mech to be taken lightly. With three extended-range PPCs, it wasn't dependent on ammunition and packed one of the hardest punches on the field.

His sensors had already marked five enemy 'Mechs and painted them on his tactical display as red squares with identifying labels. The most dangerous seemed to be a *Warhammer-Marauder* pair that sat up on the small hill six hundred fifty meters ahead and off-center to the left. An *Archer, Trebuchet,* and *Griffin* sat on a similar hill, slightly closer and off-center-right. All the 'Mechs stood within thin stands of trees, motionless. As if waiting for the raiders to obligingly walk right into a crossfire. It took a few long seconds of silent sensors before St. Jamais realized there were no other 'Mechs than these.

Five against a strengthened company of eighteen?

Cameron St. Jamais felt the first twinge of uncertainty. Where were the Angels? According to the intelligence fed them by Word of Blake personnel on Marantha, the mercenary company should have landed here hours ago. *And what about the DropShips?* Even the nearby hills couldn't have hidden the ten-story height of a *Fortress* Class vessel. Besides that, the *Trebuchet* and *Griffin* didn't fit the BattleMech roster he'd been sent, and both were painted with Magistracy colors.

An old ComStar maxim came to mind as he studied the unexpected situation—*Better to take decisive action quickly than hesitate over the perfect response.* So if he had somehow missed the mercenaries, Word of Blake could still do some damage to Marantha. He was about to order his raiders forward when almost on signal three azure streams of man-made lightning stabbed out from the *Marauder* and *Warhammer* to draw molten lines across Adept-MechWarrior Franklin's *Anvil.*

At over six hundred meters? That matched the reach of his *Awesome!* Franklin's *Anvil* staggered back against a massive elm, which was all that saved him from falling, as the 'Mech's right leg had been neatly cut off at the knee by two of the PPC hits. St. Jamais was familiar with the damage charts for the *Anvil,* and knew such an injury could only be caused by one thing. *Clan tech!* Perhaps not all the Angels had touched down here, but obviously a few of them had.

St. Jamais felt a warm rush of anger as he triggered his own extended-range PPCs at the *Marauder,* two of them slicing across its left torso and arm and the third missing high. Not even the incredible array of new-technology heat sinks his 'Mech carried could shunt away that much output from the 'Mech's fusion generator, and a wave of heat slammed into him with almost physical force.

"All units advance," he ordered as his computer registered the three 'Mechs on the right hill, the trio suddenly firing a combined barrage of eighty long-range missiles.

That kind of firepower, hitting in one area, could cripple a BattleMech; his raiders had to move from under the umbrella of trees.

When his weapons cycled, St. Jamais fired again, risking the heat buildup as all three PPCs hit the *Marauder*. Rivers of molten steel ran to the ground, two of the energy whips laying the bird-like machine's right leg bare to its titanium-steel skeleton. Heat again flooded the cockpit. Sweat ran into St. Jamais' eyes, making his vision swim for the briefest second. To his right and left, his Word of Blake raiders were moving forward, firing flights of LRMs and probing the defenders with light autocannon and extended-range energy weapons.

The first flight of missiles from the defenders all overshot, detonating harmlessly in the woods behind St. Jamais. He laughed, feeling the touch of Blake on him and his unit. Angels or not, the defenders would be easily crushed.

Then a *Rifleman* on the far left took a step forward and disappeared in a series of explosions that threw black-scorched turf up in a veil. It staggered back, missing its left foot, spun and crashed to the ground on its right side.

A *Nightsky,* the smallest 'Mech the raiders fielded, with their light machines busy elsewhere, was not even this lucky. Taking advantage of slightly greater speed, it had tried to angle off to the right in hopes of threatening the missile-launching BattleMechs. Several explosions at ground level made it stumble forward and fall flat on its face, and then another series of explosions took off its head and penetrated to the fusion reactor at its heart. The machine disintegrated in a ball of fusion-heated fire, almost as if it never existed.

Mines! The word screamed out in St. Jamais' mind like a curse. He had walked his unit into a rapidly deployed minefield. That meant Thunder loads—specially designed LRM munitions that detonated before impact to scatter smaller submunitions across the terrain. Though Thunders were normally used to deny an enemy key ground during battle, the Angels must have guessed his approach and used the mines to establish a *line of death.* Even as the thought came, another wave of enemy missiles came pouring at his force. *Trying to cut us off!* At the thought of his unit being pinned between two rows of mines, St. Jamais changed targets in a desperate bid to keep the trap from closing. He twisted the torso of his *Awesome* and floated the targeting crosshairs over the *Archer.* In his haste, only one shot hit.

Knowing how high his heat was running, St. Jamais slapped at the override switch to prevent an automatic shutdown of his fusion engine. Forced into inactivity for a moment, he noticed two new threats blink into existence on his HUD—red squares moving fast along the rear of his battle line. St. Jamais switched over to rearward sensors, which painted the technical profile of two Savannah Masters on his auxiliary screen as they snaked along the edge of the treeline. One of the hovercraft jabbed at the weak back armor of a nearby *Grand Dragon,* while the other ran in complete defensive posture. *A spotter?*

The question seemed to hang in his mind as half a hundred missiles rained down on his machine.

Marcus blinked the sweat from his eyes and gave a shout of defiance inside the *Warhammer*'s cockpit as he and Thomas Faber finished off the *Anvil* with their second concentrated volley as two other raider machines hit one of the Thunder-mined areas below. The enemy 'Mechs were beginning to slow their advance, some already moving back a few steps toward the treeline and apparent safety.

Arriving with only an hour to spare before the raiders attacked, Marcus and his two companions had powered up and moved quickly out of the depot. Charlene moved further afield to take command of the concealed units to the northwest, while Marcus and Jericho joined the other three on the hills. Per his orders, sent in a coded transmission while en route by *Sparrowhawk,* the *Archer, Trebuchet,* and *Griffin* had been loaded half with Thunder rounds and half regular. They used almost every last Thunder missile to blanket the area. After the raiders' engaged, the Angels dropped their last few rounds back behind the attacking forces in an effort to unnerve them.

Then the *Awesome,* the largest raider 'Mech on the

field, disappeared under a deadly hail of LRM fire. Thanks to the C³ unit being carried by one of the Savannah Master hovercraft, Ki's *Archer* accounted for over half of that.

Marcus knew the *Awesome* wasn't out of the fight— that fearsome 'Mech carried somewhere in the range of fifteen tons of armor. But he could hope for a few minutes of inactivity as the pilot recovered from the battering or, better yet, had to pick himself up from a fall. But then the giant war machine began to lumber forward confidently out of the veil of smoke, and Marcus cursed.

He sent twin lances of PPC fire into the forward-most raider 'Mech, a *Shootest* braving the Thunder mines in order to get its autocannon into range. The *Warhammer*'s double heat sinks channeled away most of the heat buildup, and an extra flush of coolant through his vest kept Marcus focused. But if the fighting got much closer, he'd be turning to his medium weapons as well, and the heat would start climbing real fast.

Marcus had fully expected the raiders to fall back in the face of his defense. He'd surprised them with liberal use of Thunder munitions and the long reach and heavy damage of the few Clan-tech weapons the Angels had on the field. Two raider machines were down to stay, several more wounded. But as more raider missile fire and lances of energy swept the two hills on which the Angels stood, his worries returned. The raiders still outmassed his small unit by eleven machines and more than six hundred tons. He had to convince them to turn away, to decide that the potential gain wasn't worth the losses even if they could absorb it all.

As if summoned by divine intervention, a new line of destruction stitched its way along the length of the attackers' line, shredding more armor as laser fire stabbed down from the skies. Marcus nodded to himself as he tightened his grip on the *Hammer*'s control sticks. Ensign Keppler and the *Sparrowhawk*s had joined the battle.

Fall back, he thought, trying to press his will against that of the enemy commander. *You have to fall back.*

Marcus speared the *Shootist* again, lopping off another two tons of armor from across its blocky torso. But instead of falling or even backing off under the damage, the pilot carefully stepped his machine up to a nearby tree and uprooted it. Even as Marcus watched, the 70-ton machine began to literally sweep a path ahead of it—using the tree to detonate the Thunder mines before the 'Mech could step into them. The effort slowed the 'Mech down, and even caused some lower-leg damage, but it also created a path the others could use without paying such a price.

Marcus exhaled noisily, the sound echoing inside his helmet as he thrust the PPC-arms of his 'Mech forward for another brace of shots at the *Shootist. Who were these raiders?*

The second pair of *Sparrowhawk*s began an attacking run on the raiders. They followed in the same line of attack as the first lance, low and straight down the enemy ranks. A mistake, and one the enemy commander made them pay dearly for. As if on cue, almost every missile-carrying raider 'Mech filled the air with long- and short-range missiles. They rose on columns of fire and smoke to throw a screen over the raiders that the light aerospace fighters flew right through.

Ensign Daniels' fighter absorbed the brunt of the attack, a savage brace of LRMs launched by a raider *Apollo* battering the nose of her craft and shredding her right wing to its internal framework. She fought against the damage, and had almost cleared the gauntlet of devastation when a swarm of SRMs punched through her cockpit and sent an explosion into the heart of her craft.

She was dead long before the fusion reactor lost containment and expanded to gobble up whatever fuel it could find.

Ensign Keppler would live to regret his mistake.

Daniels had been on the fast track to advancement, already having amassed the 35,000 C-bills necessary to buy a promotion into the Royal Guards on Canopus. When she pulled ahead of him on the attack run, he didn't rein her back in even though he outranked her. Then, when the missiles spread before them in a lethal curtain, he followed the first course of action his mind frantically suggested and slipped over into Daniels' wake to follow her through the hellstorm.

By the time Daniels' *Sparrowhawk* disintegrated over the far end of the battlefield, Keppler had managed to evade all but the most minor damage to the front and underside of his aerofighter. He never once fired his lasers, too busy performing limited erratic maneuvers— first to throw off the ground fire and then to avoid the pieces flying off the forward *Sparrowhawk*. Flying in and out of Daniel's jet-wash subjected Keppler's *Sparrowhawk* to a beating that made it shimmy so violently it almost tore the control stick from his grasp.

The last hit Keppler took was just after Daniels' craft exploded. A large section of her armor—off the engine cowling, he thought—knifed into his right wing and shattered almost another half-ton of his own armor. As he cleared the debris and rose back up to safer altitudes, he checked his head's-up display. The other two *Sparrowhawk*s were already back on station, holding high cover over the battlefield, and the amber crosses of four raider aerospace fighters were dropping from the upper atmosphere to engage.

A cold rage settled into Ensign Nathaniel Keppler. Rage over the senseless death of Daniels and the very audacity of the Marian Hegemony to raid his world. He pulled his craft around, back toward the battlefield and gaining altitude.

"Skyhook One to Skyhook Three and Four, Daniels is down." He kept his voice calm despite the emotion that threatened to choke off his words. "Incoming hostiles at ten o'clock and very high. Rise up to meet them." Keppler wanted another piece of the raider 'Mechs, but he knew where his skills would best serve the mercenaries fighting down below for his world.

"Keep them off the mudsloggers for as long as you can," he said. "I'm putting up 1,000 C-bills from my own promotion fund for every kill."

"I'm moving in!"

The call came over general frequencies, routed around

Ki-Lynn so all could hear it. Marcus looked at his HUD to see Ensign Tracy Williams move her *Trebuchet* forward from its somewhat protected position. The plan had been to bloody the raiders' noses, forcing them to fall back and regroup. To make them feel defeated. Then the Angels, including those still in hiding, would advance on the offensive. The raiders weren't falling back, though, but responding with greater organization than Marcus would have thought possible. For any of his small force to advance now . . .

Marcus slapped at his communications override. "Williams, remain at your position. Dammit, fall back." She was advancing directly at the *Shootist,* possibly thinking to take it down before it could clear that path through the Thunder mines.

Marcus swore to himself, knowing the *Trebuchet* couldn't hope to last long. All their 'Mechs had taken damage, though it would have been worst if they hadn't been springing first one surprise and then another on the raiders. *Only one more trick left,* Marcus thought, stabbing a button on the comm panel that would relay a signal through Ki-Lynn. *Let's see just how tough the raider commander thinks he is.*

═══════ **16** ═══════

Ordnance Depot
Indian Island, Marantha
Magistracy of Canopus
The Periphery
18 May 3058

From the hills north of the battle, not quite half a kilometer up from where the raiders had emerged, Charlene and the remaining twelve Angel 'Mechs stepped out of hiding at Marcus' signal. Leading the way in her 65-ton

JagerMech, its huge form rocking from side to side with its distinctive swaggering gait, Charlene traversed one of the five safe corridors Faber had scouted after the Thunder minefield had been laid. She hammered at the raider 'Mechs from extreme ranges with her small autocannon, and joined in almost at once with her Mydron Model C mediums. Each depleted-uranium slug shattered armor plates of enemy 'Mechs or flew onward to tear holes out of the trees or the now severely scarred ground.

Two minutes. A digital timer, located on the upper-left corner of her instrument panel, counted down from 120 seconds in bright red numbers. *We've got to press them for two minutes.*

Charlene checked the head's up display. Her *Jager-Mech* and Brent Karrskhov's *Phoenix Hawk* led the charge, though the others weren't far behind. The blue-white lightning of a PPC blast slammed into the *Jag's* torso just beneath the cockpit, its harsh flash forcing her to avert her gaze even as red bolts of coherent light stitched their way up her right leg and probed into the cavity left by the PPC. But her 'Mech weathered the damage. The rough treatment did bounce her around against the restraining straps of her command couch, but with the neurohelmet feeding signals from her inner ear to the 'Mech's huge gyro Charlene kept the *JagerMech* upright and moving forward. The wire-line damage schematic on an auxiliary monitor showed the loss of upwards of two tons of armor, most in her right torso.

Got to watch that, she thought, trying to blink away the blue-black ghost image the PPC had burned across her cornea. She glanced between HUD and the real-life scene outside her viewport, searching for the offending raider as she torso-twisted her 'Mech. As if summoned, the *Awesome* stepped from the knot of BattleMechs that held the center of the clearing and delivered a full barrage of three PPC blasts straight into the *JagerMech.*

They've got to turn, Marcus kept repeating to himself as he walked the *Warhammer* forward and down the hill. *They have to.*

Raiders weren't supposed to have this kind of staying

power. It wasn't worth the damage to stand and slug it out; not when there were easier targets elsewhere. That was the advantage of the raider. That was what the Angels relied on in their own tactics. But here Marcus watched as the enemy force smoothly shifted their focus ninety degrees to meet the challenge of Charlene's command as it moved south to reinforce Marcus' flank. Marcus hadn't seen this kind of relentless grinding since the Clans . . . and that thought raised a dark specter in his mind.

These aren't the Clans, his new mantra began to loop within his mind. *These aren't . . .*

He tightened his white-knuckled grip on the *War-hammer*'s control sticks and fired a brace of shots into the *Shootist.* A moment before, with the aide of a *Tempest* and its Gauss rifle, the *Shootist* had shredded Williams' *Trebuchet* and left it sprawled over the ground with severe internal damage and barely enough armor to protect it from a determined squad of infantry. Now Marcus led the remaining three 'Mechs of his small force forward from their defensive positions, trying to draw fire away from the wounded 'Mech and give Williams a chance to withdraw with her life. This maneuver hadn't been a part of the plan, but the numbers were shot to hell anyway. If the raiders made it out of the Thunder-mined area, the Angels would never turn them away.

Turning back has to look better to them than coming forward, and that's all we've get left. That, and the second half of our reinforcements. He watched the digital timer on his control panel count down past 60 seconds.

Brent Karrskhov watched in growing horror as the *Awesome* unloaded point-blank into Charlene's *Jager-Mech*, a trio of PPCs coring into the *Jag*'s torso followed by a barrage of short-range missiles that left four lines of white smoke connecting the two BattleMechs for an instant. As though shoved by an invisible giant hand, the *JagerMech* fell back, but from the awkward play of its legs Brent knew a gyro hit was the least of Charlene's worries.

With a small jet of released gases and smoke, the upper panels of the *JagerMech*'s domed cockpit blew off and

Charlene's ejection seat shot up through the opening. She rode the ejection blast a good hundred meters into the air, and at the apex deployed the parafoil that would bring her back down.

Would, except for the *Awesome* that was tracking her flight in an obvious effort to finish her off.

Brent quickly activated his jump jets, shoving down on them so hard that his body strained against his restraints. The output of the 'Mech's fusion engine was routed through specially designed exhaust ports mounted externally on the rear of his left and right torso. As the 45-ton *Phoenix Hawk* rose on twin columns of superheated plasma, the jump carried him straight at the *Awesome,* putting his *Hawk* between Charlene's parafoil and the assault 'Mech's single PPC blast.

The young Angel had thoughts of neither glory nor vengeance as the azure stream slammed into the head of his rising BattleMech, the thin armor melting as it ran. And it wasn't even the love he felt for Charlene that kept him fighting the controls, even as he screamed in agony at the intense heat leaking through several rents in his cockpit armor.

The last of his protection fell away in a fog of molten metal, the PPC blast filling his cockpit with hellish energy, and Brent Karrskhov died simply trying to guard the life of another Angel.

Charlene beat against the arms of her command couch and shouted to Brent as the *Phoenix Hawk* began a slow, graceful tumble on unguided jump jets. Her screams echoed sharply inside her neurohelmet as she willed the built-in comm circuit to function even without its tie to the now-dead *JagerMech*. Railing against the straps holding her down almost as if she would fling herself from the descending ejection seat, she watched through tear-blurred eyes as the dying *Phoenix Hawk* began its ungainly descent.

Then as if still guided by live hands, the *Phoenix Hawk* turned again along its original course and fell onto the *Awesome*. The *Hawk*'s right shoulder caved in a portion of the *Awesome*'s left torso. As Brent's headless machine drove in to entangle itself around the legs of the assault machine, the *Awesome* tipped back and fell onto its right side. The right arm snapped off under the huge machine's own weight, but luckily for the raider pilot he hadn't landed on more Thunder mines.

Charlene maneuvered toward an edge of the field where she hoped no mines awaited her landing as the seemingly indestructible *Awesome* extracted itself and rose again to its feet. It stood there for several incredibly long seconds, the battle raging around it but leaving the assault 'Mech untouched.

At that moment a large explosion shattered several trees along the forest edge and tore up a chunk of ground. A second ripped into a *Hunchback* further along the field, taking off its right-side leg and arm. Charlene noted the events mechanically, tears salty on her lips, and stared at the broad-shouldered *Awesome* where it stood majestically over the fallen *Phoenix Hawk*. It was battered and scorched and Charlene doubted it carried more than a fourth of the armor it had walked onto the field with. But somehow the blue-and-black knight symbol of the Marian Hegemony remained intact on the lower-left torso.

With deliberate malice, the assault 'mech positioned itself and delivered several well-placed kicks into the hulk of the downed *Hawk*. Then, turning away from the battle with almost an air of disdain, the large machine began to thread its way back through the minefield. So skillful was the pilot that the *Awesome* barely missed a step where an earlier footprint had not already been stamped into the soft ground.

Charlene watched it go and then looked back at the ruined *Phoenix Hawk*. "Damn you, Brent Karrskhov," she whispered into the insulated privacy of her neurohelmet.

A flight of twelve long-range missiles pounded into Marcus' *Warhammer,* shattering armor plates and driving the machine back. Then came the red staccato darts of pulse lasers biting into the 'Mech, making armor melt and slough off. A grayish-green mist erupted from a right-torso breech as the probing lasers ruptured the coolant chamber of a heat sink.

Sweat ran down Marcus' face and arms as use of both his medium lasers and his PPCs slowly drove the cockpit heat up through the cautionary yellow scale and into the red. The *Trebuchet* he had moved forward to protect lay just behind him, lifeless and discarded like some giant's unstrung metal puppet. Marcus didn't know whether the pilot was still alive; he blocked the bottleneck now for no other reason than to keep the raiders at bay. Ki's *Archer* and Jericho's *Griffin* continued to offer support from the lower reaches of their hill, but Faber's *Marauder* had long since fallen, its gyro spilling out in large chunks from a cavity in his center torso.

And I'm about to join him. Marcus twisted the *Warhammer*'s torso over to the extreme right, trying to keep the raiders from further piercing into the heart of his 'Mech as he snapped off a single PPC blast toward an approaching *Hunchback.*

"Rogue," came Ki-Lynn's whisper through his comm-set, in sharp contrast to the violent explosions of the battlefield. "Rogue, this is Umbrella One. Backboard One is down on the field, Four is down and out. Backboard Two reporting heavy opposition."

An empty, sinking sensation pulled at Marcus' stomach as Ki's words registered. Charlene had been shot out of her 'Mech but remained in danger on the field. Karrskhov was probably dead. Paula Jacobs in her *Valkyrie* was left in command, but her light 'Mech would only last so long in a stand-up fight like this. He swore in frustration. The Thunder minefield hadn't worked. The *Sparrowhawk* strafing run had turned into a disaster. And now the first half of his reinforcement ploy was in danger of total collapse.

The *Warhammer* rocked back a step as a slug from the *Hunchback*'s large autocannon slammed into Marcus dead center. A fresh surge of heat washed over him as his heat scale jumped further into the red. *Engine hit,* he thought, checking the damage schematic of his 'Mech. *I've lost shielding.*

The first blast, shattering a few large pines into match sticks in the backfield, didn't even register with Marcus, whose attention was focused on his tactical display. Then the *Hunchback* that had been closing disappeared from view as the ground next to it erupted in a shower of earth and smoke. When it reappeared, the raider 'Mech was lying on its side missing both right leg and arm. Marcus' first thought was of the Thunder mines they'd laid down. Then he noticed the digital timer reading zeros straight across the display. He checked the HUD for new signals and found what he was looking for in the far-right corner of the compressed 360-degree display. Two new points of light were moving forward, the computer tagging them as the *Heaven Sent* and the *Pinhead*.

The second half of his reinforcements had arrived.

"Turn!" he yelled at the raiders, pumping another lance of blue-white PPC energy into the *Hunchback* to make sure it stayed down as the Angels' *Fortress* Class Drop-Ship hit the battlefield with another volley from its nose-mounted Long Tom artillery cannon. *Now you've got to turn.*

St. Jamais watched as the two DropShips braked hard over the Indian Island facility, thrusters flaring to hold the ships against the pull of gravity. The *Fortress* Class ship pumped out artillery fire onto the rear portions of the battlefield to threaten only his raiders. The *Union* Class began to settle onto the depot's drop pad, vanishing from sight beyond the low hills just as its 'Mech bay doors began to crank open.

Now it was clear. The mercenaries had been playing at delaying tactics while their DropShips had gone for reinforcements. They'd kept his unit off balance and spread out to the point that combined fire had worked only for the mercenaries. He saw that now as the Angels retreated back toward the ordnance facility to regroup with the new arrivals. St. Jamais smashed his gloved right hand into a side panel, shattering the glass cover on the *Awesome*'s magnetic back-up compass.

"All units pull back," he commanded, biting off every word. "Jumpers, straight into the trees. Everyone else follow your original line."

As artillery continued to harass his force, St. Jamais surveyed the battlefield. Eight 'Mechs of his eighteen had fallen, though three were being helped from the field and would return to battle. The Angels had lost only six. In monetary terms the Angels had been hurt deeply. But that they had controlled the battlefield so well, and could inflict so much damage so quickly . . .

Out of sheer frustration, St. Jamais kicked at the nearby hulk of the downed *Phoenix Hawk*, caving in its left torso even more and crushing its engine under the force of his *Awesome*'s 80 tons. "That's one more thing for them to fix," he muttered grimly.

Then he turned and followed his original course off the field. Once safely hidden by the trees, he quickly threw some switches to select his downed 'Mechs. A single stab of a button, and St. Jamais watched as various explosions blossomed out on the field. Fusion engines, their containment ruptured by his transmission, expanded to blow apart three of the five downed 'Mechs; the other two were in engine shutdown and so protected. *But that will limit their precious salvage,* he thought with satisfaction.

It wasn't over yet, he promised himself. Piloting his *Awesome* back toward the pick-up site, he began to formulate plans that would finish the Angels for good. He could learn from his mistakes.

You beat a warrior on the battlefield, he thought. *But you can defeat a mercenary through his purse.*

DOUBLE-BLIND 135

═══ 17 ═══

Ordnance Depot
Indian Island, Marantha
Magistracy of Canopus
The Periphery
19 May 3058

The sun had barely peaked over the mountain range far to the east as Jericho Ryan watched Ensign Keppler's SPR-H5 *Sparrowhawk* nose down through the cloud base at minimum thrust, dropping low to skim over the trees at a hundred meters. *NOE, what they call Nape of the Earth.* Rolling the *Sparrowhawk* over onto its right wing and feathering its engines, Keppler performed a tight, slow turn over the field on which Brent Karrskhov had fought and died, and now the Angels stood in silent contemplation. She couldn't see it, but she knew that a special panel opened in the aerofighter just then, scattering Brent's ashes from the air.

Not exactly Brent's ashes, though. Jericho had been there when Marcus and Charlene first inspected the wreckage of the *Phoenix Hawk*. Not much of its head remained, and the only traces of its pilot were what might have been a few pieces of charred bone. Subjected to the full force of the *Awesome*'s PPC blast, Brent Karrskhov had been caught in a ready-made crematorium. Marcus had pulled a knife from his boot and used it like a small trowel to scoop up ashes and small bits of blackened metal, which he dumped carefully into a satchel Charlene had brought.

The final mix of man and machine.

On the field, the Angels came to attention under Marcus' order and each rendered his own personal salute. Most of the unit's non-combatants wore black, though the occasional uniform stood out. Ki-Lynn was easy to spot, making her bow of respect wearing the white of mourning favored by the Draconis Combine's Japanese culture. A few others of Combine origin also wore white. Thomas Faber and Charlene were dressed in the last uniform each had worn in service to the Successor States; he in the brown and tan field uniform of the DCMS and Charlene in the Federated Commonwealth dress uniform, but minus both rank and unit affiliation insignia. Faber bowed along with Ki, his massive frame slowly tilting downward and then back up. Charlene gave a clenched-fist-over-heart salute.

As always, it was Marcus who puzzled Jericho. The service over, he walked from the field with barely a nod to Charlene, while others stopped for a longer word with her. Jericho knew from talking with other members of the company that Marcus came from the Isle of Skye in the former Federated Commonwealth, and had last served in the DCMS along with Thomas and Charlene. Still he had chosen not to wear any previous uniform, dressed instead in simple black trousers and shirt. Appropriate colors, but the lack of formality also separated him from the others.

But maybe that was what he wanted.

Marcus slowed to a stop as he neared her. "Commander Ryan," he said.

Jericho felt the coolness in his words, and thought she understood. *This is my nation, not his,* she reminded herself. *And contract or not, money or not, we've cost him a comrade and a warrior.* She had stood apart from the service, not wanting to intrude, but close enough to have heard Marcus' words. ". . . who had worked hard to become one of us," he'd said. "Not beholding to nation, world, or even to paymaster, but to the unit. To the Angels."

Is it really so simple, Marcus? Jericho wanted to ask.

Now she merely nodded a greeting. "If this is a bad time, I understand."

He shrugged. "Mercenaries can always make time for business. You need our cost projections and loss-indemnity claims for the battle?"

His tone was almost mechanical, as if the question were part of a litany learned by rote. Jericho searched his face for some clue to his feelings, but found nothing. "I don't need those now," she said. "I know it might take a few days. I do have authorization for you to draw initial supplies from the Indian Island facility, and to move your unit to Jubilee as soon as you can complete your salvage operations. Or before," she quickly added, "if you'd like to begin settling in your families and other field personnel. But that's not really why I came out to meet you."

Marcus' eyes narrowed. "No?"

"I was hoping to talk to you about the battle." She glanced back to where only a few Angels remained. *Or anything else.* "Maybe it's not the best time."

"I sent a report to Major Wood last evening," he said evenly. "It detailed the entire battle and I've already promised her copies of the battle ROMs. If there—"

"Dammit, Commander," she cut him off with a shake of her head. "I don't want to read a report of the action. I was there, remember? I saw it. You bloodied and then turned back a strengthened company with apparent ease." She allowed her voice to soften as a few Angels turned their heads to stare as they passed by. "I also remember you breaking from your plan of battle to save one of my warriors from being stupid. Ensign Williams would have died in her *Trebuchet* otherwise, and I'm grateful. I can examine your tactics all day long, Marcus, but what I want to know is what you were thinking."

She paused, biting on her lower lip and uncertain of how to proceed. Finally, she risked the truth. "Major Wood never allocated reinforcements. Not even when she learned she was facing no more than six medium 'Mechs. She wrote you and the facility off because she never thought you'd be able to hold out long enough for help to arrive. I still can't believe you turned the raiders away—and so quickly—and I was there." She shook her head and turned to leave. "It's just that I don't want to ever make the mistake Major Wood did."

"Jericho."

Marcus' voice was quiet but strong, freezing her in mid-turn. When she looked back, he met her gaze with a reluctant nod and fell into step beside her. "It's not anything special about me," he began, then shrugged. "Not really. You were born and raised in the Periphery, which means you haven't seen quite the variety of tactics I have." He held up his right hand in a quieting manner before she could reply. "And I'm sure there are a few things out here that I've never seen," he said to her unvoiced objection.

After a moment, he continued in a softer tone. "But think about this. The Inner Sphere recently fought the biggest threat it's ever faced when they halted the Clan invasion. Older tactics were swept away in favor of new ones, and these are traveling out to you even slower than the new technology. MechWarriors are afraid of the Periphery." He glanced at some of the Angels who walked nearby, and kept his voice low. "This is Valhalla to them."

"The hall of slain warriors," Jericho said. "I understand. Much of the Periphery was settled by outcasts and rebels and pirates. And it's never been the safest spot to be. But it hasn't been that way for generations. At least not here in the Magistracy."

"Right," Marcus returned. "But a lot of MechWarriors think of the Periphery as the end of the line, a place to hide when on the run or to get banished to when you can no longer compete in the Inner Sphere."

She nodded. "Point taken. So how did that help you yesterday? When they cleared the woods, I figured them to burn us down, mines or not, in a few minutes."

Marcus shoved his hands into his pockets, staring into the distance as if at another place or time. "So did I," he finally admitted. "There were holes in that plan large enough to walk an *Atlas* through. Not the least of which was placing only five BattleMechs between the raiders and the depot."

"Since you mention it, why did you hold some 'Mechs back?"

"Because if things had gone to hell quickly, the five of us presented a strong enough threat to hurt the raiders while the others made their escape." He glanced sidelong at Jericho, as if trying to gage her reaction. "I gambled, Marantha won."

Jericho considered that for a moment before speaking. "Were you so unsure of the plan?"

"Oh, it was a good plan. As good as we could manage under the circumstances. But that doesn't mean a lot on the battlefield." Marcus shrugged. "The raiders could've had the depot at any time."

"So if you'd been the raider commander, how would you have defeated the defense he encountered?"

The ghost of a sad smile played at Marcus' lips. "I wasn't on the defensive. But in answer to your question, I wouldn't have kept my forces bunched up. It should have been obvious that we couldn't afford to saturate the entire area with Thunders. Just a forward line and then spots here and there. So I'd have sent the jumping 'Mechs forward to engage at close range and keep us busy, then have the ground forces move up and finish the job."

"What do you mean, you weren't on the defensive? What do you call it when you're protecting a base?"

Marcus wouldn't meet her gaze. "I wasn't protecting a base, I was staging a battle around it. Make no mistake, Jericho, the Angels would've abandoned the depot in an instant and without a second thought. We were attacking. We drew first blood and continued to hammer at them once they saw they were hemmed in by Thunders. That's why the raiders didn't try any fancy tactics. They *felt* trapped. Then we hit them with the fighters and Charlie's force from the woods to keep them off balance. When the DropShips showed up, they were fooled into thinking reinforcements had come through—and that was the final shove needed to turn them back."

The implications whirled in Jericho's mind. The acrid, gunpowder-stench of the battlefield was suddenly stifling. "You risked our lives, your unit, on a bluff?" Then one of the pieces clicked in with an almost audible sound. "But then you weren't protecting the facility, so you knew the Angels could fall back from the battle."

"Intimidation is a major factor in any engagement. The Angels have been depending on it for years." Marcus let his gaze roam over the battlefield. "The raiders felt harried, so they gave me the initiative. But when the *Shootist* picked up that tree and used it as a giant broom, I thought we were done for." He frowned in remembrance. "Someone had started to think aggressively. Fortunately that warrior was in the minority."

"Was that their commander, do you think?" Jericho sounded hopeful. The ruins of the *Shootist,* and a few pieces of its pilot, were still scattered about on the field.

Marcus shrugged. "Maybe, but I don't think so," he finally said. "I'd bet on that *Awesome.* It was the only assault 'Mech and its pilot was damned good."

"Except that everything he did was in reaction to you." Jericho offered him a thin smile with the praise, trying to draw him out. She definitely wanted to get to know this strange, aloof man, but he definitely wasn't making it easy.

Marcus narrowed his eyes as he continued to sweep the battlefield with his gaze. "But it was *how* he reacted. The raiders never fell back and never seemed at a loss. The *Awesome* even managed to stall Charlene's advance almost single-handedly."

"But he lost sight of his goal," Jericho said, uncomfortable with hearing praise for the enemy, even a defeated one. "There must have been at least ten jump-capable 'Mechs on the field. With that kind of mobility, the raiders could've jumped into close-combat *and* sent a few units on into the ordnance depot."

"The raiders were never after the ordnance depot."

Jericho started as if slapped by Marcus' soft-spoken words. "What do you mean?"

Marcus shook his head. "I didn't really see it till now, but everything points in that direction. For one thing, if you intend to take supplies, you land your DropShip closer. If you intend to destroy them, you assign Battle-Mechs in advance just for that purpose, but not one raider 'Mech ever seemed inclined to do that. The clincher is that they landed only hours after we did, with minimal forces in their DropShip to tie up any support we might hope for from the MAF. They were waiting for us."

"You're saying they had something personal to settle with you?"

Marcus shrugged. "Maybe. Or maybe they know the Angels aren't here for garrison duty and don't want us poking around in the Hegemony. Doesn't matter," he finished, in a tone that made it clear he wouldn't invite further discussion. "They damaged our machines, though probably not as bad as they think—not with the auxiliary contract to support us. But the real hurt has yet to be measured."

Jericho followed his gaze. Back where the Angels had conducted their memorial for Brent Karrskhov, Charlene still stood—alone now—as she gazed up into the brightening sky. Charlene was hurting, that much was obvious. Jericho had heard the teasing talk on the trip from New Home, good-natured kidding about how Brent and Charlie were becoming something of a item.

She wanted to know what this Marcus GioAvanti was thinking right now, suddenly as personally interested in the mercenary commander as she was professionally. But any chance for further talk seemed lost on the cool morning breeze as Marcus let the silence settle uncomfortably between them. So Jericho watched Marcus watching Charlene, who stood on the field in silent contemplation of Marantha's sunrise.

18

Palace of the Magestrix
Crimson, Canopus IV
Magistracy of Canopus
The Periphery
19 May 3058

Sun-Tzu Liao leaned against the balcony railing, tightly
gripping the cool metal to keep his hands from shaking.
He stared at the horizon, his green eyes wide and unblinking. Canopus' sun was just falling below the lip of the
world, turning the clouds a mottled pink and gold. The
light evening breeze felt cool and wonderfully refreshing
against his face, ruffling his hair against his neck. The
sweet fragrances of the royal gardens three stories down
sent up their perfume and he inhaled the scent deeply.

*It is true, what they say. Coming close to death does
sharpen one's senses.*

He stared out past the gardens, where the Thetis River
flowed past the walls of the Magestrix' royal residence. In
the deepening twilight, the river took on a hard, gun-metal
cast. But he could still hear the soothing sound of the
waters as they swirled over a shallows area. *A shallows,
right before the Thetis deepens to more than ten meters.
Perfect for quietly disposing of the demi-Precentor's
body.* It appealed to Sun-Tzu, committing the assassin's
body to the goddess of deep water.

From what his people had been able to uncover in the
last hour, demi-Precentor Nicholas had first shown up at

the *Pearl of True Wisdom,* only to learn that Magestrix Centrella had offered him an entire third floor of the royal residence. In another wing of the residence from her own, of course. Sun-Tzu had carefully *not* noticed the doubling of guards around the Magestrix and her private wing even as he mentally saluted her for it. Giving him these quarters kept him under observation, and he was sure there were more than enough hidden guards to deter his Death Commandos.

But he hadn't worried for his own safety. The last thing the Magistracy of Canopus could afford was to have his sister Kali avenge his death by launching an offensive into their territory. Not that Kali would care whether he died. But it would give her a convenient excuse for trying to take over the Magistracy. No, Emma Centrella needed him alive. Which meant she hadn't been behind this attempt on his life that had so very nearly succeeded.

A soft sound from the room beyond caught his attention, but Sun-Tzu waited while one of the two guards at the balcony door moved inside to check on it. His guess was confirmed when the Death Commando returned to announce Naomi Centrella. Sun-Tzu nodded his assent, never turning away from the view. He felt her quiet presence coming up behind him on the balcony, then her hand close enough to his on the rail that he could feel its warmth though not its touch. He waited quietly for her to speak some inane words of courtesy.

"What a view, Chancellor. A glorious sunset, and the Thetis is always beautiful."

Sun-Tzu smiled, eyes flicking back toward the dark waters of the river. "Yes, I suppose it is." He kept his voice pitched soft and gentle, as if not wanting to disturb the moment. "And your company is always most welcome," he added, wondering if his men were still so on edge that they might have insisted too vehemently on scanning her for weapons.

"You are an important man." Her voice was warm and held no trace of reproach. "Your people are loyal."

At the reception, Sun-Tzu had discovered Naomi to be a charming companion. She seemed able to enjoy the entertainment and other aspects of the reception for their own sake, and never allowed politics to intrude on the evening. In the week since, in between discussions with the Magestrix, Sun-Tzu had grown to welcome her company. As he did now. But as they lapsed back into a comfortable silence, he could not keep his thoughts from returning to the attempt on his life.

Demi-Precentor Nicholas had been visibly nervous upon gaining access to him. He'd put it down to the importance of a message she claimed to bear, but it was enough to put his personal guards on alert. Still, had she not fumbled the needler concealed within her wide sleeves, or had she been smart enough to wear some kind of body armor under those white Word of Blake robes, he would likely be dead. Of all the avenues of approach to his person, he would never have expected the Word of Blake to be a threat.

Thomas Marik? The name rose like a specter within his thoughts. The Captain-General of the Free Worlds League was the Word of Blake's biggest supporter. Had Thomas finally decided to end Sun-Tzu's engagement to Isis in a permanent fashion? It made the most sense in one way, but Sun-Tzu could not imagine Thomas ordering such an underhanded act. Thomas cultivated an air of nobility, of higher morality, ideals, and honor. And unlike most Inner Sphere leaders, the fool actually seemed to mean it. Still, Sun-Tzu could not picture the Captain-General allying himself with the Marian Hegemony either, and Emma Centrella's probing questions over the last few days seemed to indicate that was her opinion also.

The last sliver of Canopus' sun slipped beneath the horizon, though the clouds still reflected its majestic light. Naomi half-turned to him, her voice soft. "What are you thinking, Sun-Tzu?"

The question seemed at once innocent and yet full of hidden import. The hesitant use of his name was not lost on him, either. He shrugged uncomfortably. "That appearances are sometimes deceiving." But often they're not, he suddenly realized. What was the term? Occam's Razor? The simplest solution is usually the correct one.

Naomi Centrella looked back out over the gardens and up into the sky. "Well, the sunset looks beautiful to me.

And it marks the start of Canopus night-life, which can be a most memorable thing."

Thoughts churned within Sun-Tzu's mind, as he barely registered Naomi's words. *A Word of Blake fanatic tried to kill me because Word of Blake wants me dead!* His thoughts turned to other pieces that might fit into place even as he answered Naomi in as calm a voice as he could muster. "But at this moment and maybe under a similar peaceful sky, your people might be fighting for their lives along the border of your realm. Or burying their dead. Or simply watching as the Marian Hegemony destroys a part of their world."

"Or making love," Naomi added, not a trace of shyness in her voice. "I have been trained for war, like my mother and sister, but I prefer to think of the benefits peace brings to our people. Is that wrong?"

Sun-Tzu listened to her with a slight smile, but his mind continued to race with questions. How did Word of Blake profit from the raids on Canopus? He was certain the Blakists were supporting the Hegemony raiders, but reasons—he needed reasons. It would have to be for the same or similar reasons that they wanted him dead. *Because I'm offering Canopus support. They want an unstable Magistracy.* And an unstable Magistracy might lead to stronger ties between Emma Centrella and the Taurian Concordat, or a greater dependence on Word of Blake administration if they could mediate a truce or special alliances the way they'd been trying to do in the Chaos March. Or both. He pondered that even while speaking the answer to Naomi's question.

"Thinking about the benefits of peace is not wrong, unless you are a leader of your people. A leader must always be prepared for war."

Naomi nodded. " 'War is a matter of vital importance to the state,' " she quoted, " 'the province of life or death, the road to survival or ruin.' " At Sun-Tzu's look of surprise, she smiled thinly. "Sun Tzu, the *Art of War.* Your namesake. They made us study his teachings at the Canopus Institute of War." She bit down on her lower lip. "Will war come to my world, Sun-Tzu?"

"War always comes," he said.

"But will you bring it here?"

Sun-Tzu studied Naomi's face for a moment. *I do believe she thinks I would tell her the truth.* "No, Naomi," he said softly, putting as much innocent warmth into her name as he could. "I would not bring war to you." He turned back to his contemplation of the sun setting behind the river and possible Word of Blake motives, allowing her time to consider all possible meanings of his words.

Then her hand slid up against his own on the railing, its touch light and very warm. "My mother believes you might be helping the Hegemony raiders," she warned softly.

He nodded because it was expected of him. *Beautifully done,* he congratulated her silently. *You give nothing away that I don't already suspect from talks with your mother, and you try to gain my confidence.* Perhaps Naomi didn't have the same proclivity for warfare as her sister, but Sun-Tzu could easily see her as a leader of people. "Your mother is very wise," he said carefully, and with the proper amount of regret, "but not always right."

"I do not believe that you make war on us, Sun-Tzu."

"I know." He tried for both sorrow and sympathy in his voice. "I know."

The silence fell again, and Sun-Tzu slowly counted out the seconds until he finally felt the light touch on his arm.

"What are you thinking now, Sun-Tzu Liao?"

He reached over with to take her hand in both of his and give it the smallest squeeze. "How good it is to finally have a friend here," he whispered, gazing up at the first twilight stars so she would not see the smile that must surely be playing in his eyes.

Emma Centrella gazed into the fire, watching the flames dance and crackle. The simple white satin robes she wore threw off the colors of the fire, and contrasted well with her dusky skin. The Magestrix was never one to ignore such details, even in the privacy of her own chambers.

"And he seemed distracted?" She turned her gaze on her daughter. "You believe he has no involvement with these filthy raiders?"

"That I cannot state as fact, Mother." Naomi shuffled from one foot to the other, reminding Emma of her youngest daughter when asked whether she'd finished her school work. "Sun-Tzu might truly be feeling alone and vulnerable here. If so, I am the person closest to him."

And further proof that Sun-Tzu has neither the self-confidence nor self-control required of an Inner Sphere ruler. Yet, she reminded herself, he is not stupid. Inexperienced, perhaps slightly naive. And if he is developing an attachment to Naomi, that could prove useful. After all, Thomas Marik has found cause to postpone his daughter's marriage to the Liao for several years now. Everyone knows that it will only happen as a last resort. Sun-Tzu could be vulnerable.

"Naomi, would it offend you to further this relationship?" Emma's eyes narrowed. "I would like Sun-Tzu to feel at ease with us. With you. Become his friend here."

Naomi kept her eyes downcast. "As the Magestrix desires, of course."

"Thank you, Naomi. We need him friendly to our cause. He is offering us much of what we need to make the Magistracy strong again."

"Then you plan to *lend* troops to the Capellans?"

Emma gazed back into the fire. "That I have not decided. The idea has its merits." She paused. "First we will see what Sun-Tzu gives away for nothing." Was that a catch in her daughter's breathing? "After all, his technical advisors and such are only six days from making planetfall. To retain the goodwill he is trying to foster, wouldn't he have to allow us access to them at once?"

Naomi smiled. "Of course, Mother." She waited a minute or so, then began to withdraw from the room.

"One moment, Naomi." The Magestrix kept her voice carefully neutral, as if the question was not all that important. "You mentioned the sunset, and Sun-Tzu's preoccupation with it. It is far into evening now . . ." She trailed off speculatively.

Emma Centrella couldn't see her daughter's expression, but the caution in the young woman's voice already told her what she wanted to know before two words were spoken. "We watched the stars come out, Mother. And spent some time just . . . talking."

Emma turned to look at her daughter and gave her a warm smile. "Of course. Good night, Naomi."

The smile lasted a second longer than it took Naomi to close the door on her way out. Emma Centrella's smile did not fade to either anger or sadness, but merely settled into a tighter, more speculative one.

19

DropShip **Head of a Pin,** *Jubilee Spaceport*
Jubilee, Marantha
Magistracy of Canopus
The Periphery
22 May 3058

Marcus reached up under his safety glasses to rub one eye free of some dust that had sneaked past the loose seal. The acrid stench of hot-metal work and sweat permeated the *Pinhead*'s 'Mech bay, hanging heavy in the stiflingly warm air. Even the large space-clearing fans set in the open bay door could make little headway, what with the sweltering temperature outside on the landing pad and no breeze to speak of.

The Angels had relocated to Jubilee immediately upon arrival of an MAF garrison force at Indian Island. The *Head of a Pin* had been left behind to complete loading of salvage, then rejoined the unit the previous evening.

Marcus bent back down over the sheet of armor, cutting torch in hand. He was trying to decide the best way to cut armor for the triangular knee cap-guard on Vince Foley's *Enforcer* when Jericho Ryan walked up.

A quick turn of the torch's handle shut off the gas flow. Marcus handed it to one of Petrovka's apprentice technicians and stepped away from the work area. All over the bay Angels were cutting armor and hauling myomer bundles out of their storage containers, everyone working to repair the damage taken on Indian Island. Most of the critical work—the repair or replacement of actuators, gyros, or control circuitry—had already been done. Petrovka had directed the final stages of that aboard the *Heaven Sent*.

"Does your being here mean that I have a full complement of 'Mechs again?" Marcus asked. He spoke loudly—both he and Jericho wore hearing protection in the noisy bay—but still had to repeat himself.

"Sort of," she shouted back with a shrug, but followed it with an impish smile. She beckoned him to follow as she walked back toward the large 'Mech bay doors.

Now what is she up to? Marcus wondered. The Angels had lacked the equipment necessary to repair the cockpit of Karrskhov's *Phoenix Hawk* after the battle, as well as almost everything needed for the *JagerMech*. It had only been sheer luck that they'd picked up the arm Petrovka had worried about while traveling through the Free Worlds League. Now the machine required another arm as well as the complete replacement of its fusion engine and gyro. Jericho had volunteered services and supplies from the Jubilee 'Mech yards at the far end of the spaceport as partial payment for the Angels' services.

Walking down the ramp that led outside from the 'Mech bay, Marcus had to shield his eyes from the bright afternoon sun that beat down on the spaceport from Marantha's clear blue sky. For a moment he thought his vision and the sudden bright light were merely playing tricks on him. When he realized that wasn't it, all he could do was keep following Jericho down the ramp.

Standing there on the ferrocrete pad was Karrskhov's *Phoenix Hawk,* a large, reinforced crate in its massive arms. But it wasn't Charlene's *JagerMech* standing next to it. The other 'Mech had wide shoulders tapering to a narrow waist. Its hips and knees were heavily reinforced, and Marcus didn't need to see the exhaust ports on the backs of them to know the machine was jump-capable. In a variant of normal BattleMech design, medium lasers had been mounted under each forearm instead of on top.

Two more, protruding from the right and left torso, framed the heavy laser in the center torso cavity. Another deviation from standard designs was a head-mounted LRM-5.

"GHR-5H *Grasshopper*," Jericho said, glancing over at Marcus, as if wondering about his reaction. "It's fifty years old, but the owner guarantees me it's a solid machine."

Marcus had recognized it immediately, but he knew the MAF would never turn it over to him in exchange for a *JagerMech*. The *Grasshopper* was designed for infighting. Equipped with energy weapons and carrying almost twice as much armor as the *Jag*, a *Grasshopper* could participate in extended fighting without much worry about ammo. "And the *JagerMech*?" he asked.

Jericho shook her head. "Too much damage. We couldn't adapt a standard Nissan 260 for the engine compartment, not without downgrading the autocannon-5s to older models. And it will take months to get the correct extra-light engine shipped out here. So, consider this on loan until—and if—we get your *JagerMech* put back together." Amusement twinkled in her eyes. "This is Major Wood's backup 'Mech. She thought it might make up for abandoning you." The amusement faded. "She also extends her regrets for Karrskhov."

Send them to Charlie, Marcus thought, frowning at the thought of his exec. After the services for Brent, Charlene had publicly criticized Marcus' tactics as too risky, too flamboyant. She thought he could have provided for a wider margin of safety, and had even argued that a straightforward defense of the ordnance facility would have let the Angels hold off the attackers indefinitely. *Defense!* Marcus couldn't believe she'd said that.

He'd been trying to calm her when she laid the bombshell on him. Not only did she accuse him of not caring for his people, but she said straight out that he was incapable of caring, period. Marcus had put it all down to the loss she'd suffered, but he could tell from the faces of the other Angels present that a problem might be developing. Dark looks directed at Charlene told Marcus that not everyone agreed with her, but there were enough nods and averted gazes to say that some did.

My job is to keep the Angels together and functioning, he'd told himself then and repeated to himself now. *I can't afford to get too close or I'd become as unstrung every time I lose someone as Charlie is now.* How many Brent Karrkhovs had there been in the past? How many in the future? Too many for Marcus to shoulder the emotional baggage of losing them all. *I do what I can,* he wanted to shout.

"Marcus?"

Jericho's look of concern drew him back from the self-recrimination. "Yeah," he said. "Just thinking." He stopped a technician who was boarding the *Pinhead.* "Send Charlie out here," Marcus told him, then picked up the thread of conversation with Jericho. "A -5H? So this is all factory stock?"

"Well, there's an extended-range heavy laser mounted centerline, there." She pointed up to the cavity. "But that hurts it in close combat. Drives the heat up faster, especially when the mediums come on-line." She paused as if considering, and then continued. "What is it? I caught the worried look. Is there something wrong with the 'Mech?"

"No, nothing wrong with it." Marcus rubbed at the side of his face. "It's Charlie," he said, and gave her a brief version of his exec's sudden shift in behavior.

"Marc, one of your people died on the battlefield. And it was someone she cared about deeply. You've got to expect a little frustration, and as the commanding officer you become the target. As for the others"—she shrugged—"no MechWarrior likes being reminded of her mortality." She glanced up at the two 'Mechs towering over them like Olympian immortals. "Piloting these things, we start to believe nothing can touch us. The illusion dies hard when we see what happened to Brent."

It's more than that, Jericho. Charlene's calling into question everything we've become since the Clan invasion. Everything I've become. How can I make any of them understand that I can't afford to get too close, not with the decisions I'm forced to make? But of course he knew they could never understand that.

Seeing him still unconvinced, she pointed to the *Sparrowhawk* grounded fifty meters away from the Drop-Ship. "You command respect from others. Ensign Keppler threatened to resign his commission if not allowed to accompany the Angels." She pulled a folded sheet of flimsy from inside the cuff of her left glove. "Major Wood transferred him to my command, and he'll be coming with us, if that's still all right. I have to tell him it's official, though. Where is he?"

Marcus jerked his head back up toward the DropShip entrance. "Inside, learning how to re-armor a Savannah Master." He shrugged. "Volunteered to help."

"You see? That's what I mean. Your people immediately make Keppler feel a part of the group, and he's ready to follow you into combat. That's quite a compliment."

Is that what you see, Jericho? Marcus stared into her brilliant green eyes. *I see a young man who wants a taste of revenge and I'm convenient transportation.* But whatever the reason, Marcus would be a fool to refuse the air cover. Aloud he simply said, "Maybe you're right. Meanwhile I have to get someone checked out on a *Grasshopper.*"

"More than that," Jericho jerked a thumb back at the box cradled in the *Phoenix Hawk*'s arms. "I'd say you need to find a replacement warrior for a Warhammer as well."

"What do you mean?"

Jericho readjusted the spiked straps belted around her right-hand glove, feigning nonchalance. "I said we couldn't find a Nissan extra-light. However, Major Wood had a new-tech *Cataphract* salvaged from an earlier raid. And it's powered by a—"

"—a General Motors 280 Extralight," Marcus finished, cutting her off. "You mean it? Wood gave that up?" He thought of the *Caesar* walking out of the *Fortress* Class DropShip under its own power, and it sent a chill up his spine. "Jericho, that's great."

"What's great?" It was Charlene Boske coming down the *Pinhead*'s loading ramp.

"Jericho found an engine for the *Caesar*," Marcus said.

"You're checked out on a *Hammer,* but there's a *Grass-hopper* if you'd rather have that."

Charlene looked the *Grasshopper* over with a critical eye. "Tamara Cross would be a better pilot. She likes the larger 'Mechs and she's got a feel for jumping under that much weight." She turned back to Marcus and Jericho. "I want the *Hawk.*"

Should've seen that coming, Marcus thought. He nodded. "You got it. Move Brian Phillips up to my *War-hammer.* That leaves a vacant *Whitworth.*"

Charlene pursed her lips in thought. "What about the MechWarrior who piloted the *Trebuchet*? That 'Mech was scrap metal last we saw."

There was no way to tell who was more surprised at Charlene's words, but Jericho recovered first. "Ensign Williams is available for duty. I was going to have to sideline her. Thank you, Charlene."

The Angels' exec shrugged off the thanks. "The *Whit-worth* and *Trebuchet* are similar designs. And an empty 'Mech doesn't help anyone on the field."

Marcus nodded his own agreement. "Fine. With Jericho's permission concerning Ensign Williams, all three of them run double sim-time until you think they're ready."

"What about you, Commander?"

Marcus stiffened. "If you want to monitor my simulator time, feel free to do so. Warrior readiness is your respon-sibility." He stared at Charlie and silently dared her to make an issue of it. When she didn't, he turned abruptly to go find Petrovka and nearly collided with one of the DropShip crew hurrying down the ramp. The man handed him a slip of paper, which Marcus opened and read quickly, a smile spreading over his face.

"Jase Torgensson just came down at the Freeburg Spaceport on the southern continent," he announced, grin-ning now as he looked up at his companions. "He's catch-ing a military shuttle up here. Arrives in a couple hours."

20

"**I** came through Ryerson, on t'edge of the Duchy of Audurien. Made a friend at the recharge station who had a slight problem over some gambling debts," Jase Torgensson took a healthy pull at his cigarette, politely blowing it toward the ventilation grill set in the wall of Major Judith Wood's office. His gaze shifted between the two MAF officers present, the major seated behind her desk and Jericho Ryan seated next to it. "He gave me a glance at his noteputer, a file on JumpShips passing through Ryerson not required to file manifest information due to diplomatic or military reasons."

From his chair next to the door Marcus nodded encouragement, well-used to Jase's way of glossing over the more delicate points of his work to hit the important facts. If Major Wood or Jericho couldn't figure out for themselves that Jase had bribed the Andurien officer for confidential information, trying to find evidence of arms smuggling, they'd have to settle for what Marcus eventually would put into an official report. Holding the debrief in Major Wood's office was a courtesy, not a classroom.

It had also been an expedient location after Charlene insisted Jase get checked out by the Canopian Highlanders' medical staff. A decision Marcus had fully supported despite Torgensson's assurances that he was all right. His travels hadn't been kind to him, his upper lip still healing from being split open and the flesh surrounding his left eye a bit puffy and bruised yellow-brown. He had also arrived with his left arm in a pneumo-cast, the air-filled pockets keeping it in a stiff brace to allow a hairline fracture to heal. And he carried a set of stitches on his right shoulder from a knife wound. With his deep, soothing voice and the Scandinavian lilt of a Rassalhague native, Jase usually had an air that was cultured and polished. Now he sounded merely exhausted, his normally impeccable appearance ragged and unkempt.

It promised to be an interesting story.

"The 'puter didn't list any JumpShips outside normal traffic except for the Free Worlds League shipping relief foodstuffs to a planet suffering from drought, and the Word of Blake ferrying more of their personnel and equipment to Terra. But it did have an addendum concerning ships to watch for."

"The *Adonis*?" Charlene asked, making Jase raise an eyebrow over his good eye. "Didn't take much to guess," she said. "We passed through the Andurien system, and someone tried to sabotage our 'Mechs."

Marcus leaned forward in his chair, arms resting on knees. "But the question is who did it? Jase?"

"The *Adonis* was flagged for immediate communication of whereabouts, to be transmitted to Precentor Andurien"—Jase paused, eyes finding Major Wood's— "and Precentor Sian."

"To be passed straight to Duchess Humphreys of Andurien and Sun-Tzu Liao," Wood said, looking over at Jericho. "I suppose we should be grateful it didn't go to Thomas Marik on Atreus. In fact"—her eyes narrowed— "if we could get conclusive proof that Liao is behind this, the Free Worlds League would be forced to intervene on our behalf."

"Sorry," Jase said. "I got close, but proof I couldn't get." He brandished his arm in the cast. "A bit too close, you might say."

"Keep going, Jase." Marcus could guess what his

next move would have been. "You tried to send us a message?"

Jase Torgensson nodded, taking another long drag on his cigarette. "*Ja*, soon as I cleared the Duchy. Made another friend at the Granera recharge station, next system along, who sent the message over her name instead of mine. Should've reached you well before the *Adonis* ever left Andurien space."

Charlene shook her head in disbelief. "Would Word of Blake hold us incommunicado? Isn't that dangerous for them, withholding a paid message?"

"No more dangerous a game than the one they're playing with ComStar right now," Jericho said. "About two months ago Word of Blake fanatics shot several ComStar acolytes on Harminous, effectively ending ComStar's presence on that Magistracy world."

"The Magestrix was less than thrilled," Major Wood put in. "But apparently the Blakists voluntarily removed those responsible and made reparations." She hesitated before continuing. "Of course, they still control all the HPG stations on Harminous."

"Word of Blake will do whatever is good for the Word of Blake," Marcus said. "I don't imagine they'd actually withhold the message, but I could see them conveniently misrouting one if Sun-Tzu asked Precentor Sian to do so. It will catch up with us in about a week, along with their regrets and a full refund."

Jase leaned forward and stubbed out his cigarette in an ashtray set on the desk. "I think you've got the size of it, Commander." He resettled himself in his chair. "Anyway, I hit the League-Canopus border at t'Aspropirgos system, and then traveled the Free Worlds League side all the way over to Romita. I made good time, arriving at the Romita recharge station by mid-April. Romita, I'd decided, was the best place to cross into the Marian Hegemony—the nearest point to Alphard, the Hegemony capital."

Torgensson's voice seemed to drag with fatigue. "Along the way I stopped off at a number of recharge stations, checking everything I could, from cargo manifests to message traffic. I was sure I'd find something; arms traffic has to leave a trail if it's being moved in any kind of quantity. The hardest point of concealment should have been at the local-government level, especially where shipping lanes cross a border. Local systems are required to check manifests. But if t'arms are flowing from inside the Free World League, it's well-hidden. I found nothing."

Marcus sat back, rubbing his hands briskly over his face. Then he looked over at the Canopians. "What do you think? Does Sun-Tzu have that kind of influence in the League? Could he hide the shipments?"

Major Wood shook her head emphatically. "I don't think Thomas Marik himself has that kind of influence in the outer reaches of the League. Sun-Tzu has supporters, yes. Short-sighted people who saw his engagement to Isis Marik as a balance to the Steiner-Davion threat. But with the split between Victor Davion and his sister, and Thomas Marik obviously cooling on Liao's marriage to his daughter, that support is limited."

"Sun-Tzu couldn't be shipping directly out from League manufacturers, could he?" Jericho said thoughtfully. "His supply DropShips riding Marik JumpShips back to his border while the weapons and supplies designated for the Capellan Confederation are switched over to an independent?" She noticed a ghost of a smile playing over Jase's lips. "That's it? But you said—"

A raised hand cut Jericho off and kept everyone else silenced. "I don't know this for sure," Jase began, "but it's t'only thing that makes sense. On the way to Romita, I was routed around the world of Campoleone. Didn't think anything of it then. It happens. A DropShip cancels its contract or needs to pick up supplies on a different world . . . any number of reasons.

"Well, I made it to Romita, but I turned up absolutely nothing there. And there wasn't any way I could make it across to Alphard and then back here in time to meet up with you, so I headed back along the same route. And was routed around Campoleone again. T'explantion was plausible, but it started me to wondering. So I stopped over at Gatchina, one jump this side of Campoleone, to catch the next JumpShip normally scheduled to pass through Campoleone. It was rerouted as well, ostensibly for the purpose of picking up a DropShip full of medical supplies and personnel bound for Romita. But that was just too much, so I made a friend in the records department on the Gatchina recharge station."

Major Wood hid a smile behind a raised hand, then managed to regain her composure long enough to say, "Mr. Torgensson, you must be the friendliest person in the Inner Sphere."

"Just doing my part to make the galaxy a better place," Jase said, deadpan. "Except for Campoleone, that is. I couldn't find a way in. As near as I can tell, the system has been isolated from all regular traffic."

Charlene had remained quiet for some time, but now leaned forward with a slight frown of confusion. "I thought you said Romita was the place to cross the border?"

"For direct travel to Alphard, *ja*. You jump into the Niops Association and spend two weeks recharging because they won't let JumpShips wait around as part of a command circuit. Then if the circuit to Alphard is in place, you can be in the Hegemony in a matter of days."

"So, that's the direct route," Marcus said slowly, trying to put it all together. "But what you're saying is that it looks they're stopping somewhere else first?"

Both Jase and Major Wood spoke at the same time. "Astrokaszy."

"What's an Astrokaszy?" Charlene asked.

Jase nodded to Major Wood. "You probably know more than I do. Please."

"Astrokaszy is a planet sitting just off the border of the Free Worlds League, about one jump from Campoleone. It's a harsh world with lots of desert and an Arabic culture. It also has a reputation for being a very dangerous place." Wood smiled humorously. "The MAF fought the Marion Hegemony on Astrokaszy about thirty years ago. Not really for control, just to dispute the Hegemony's claim to it. Before it was over, units from the Free Worlds League and two other Periphery States were involved. They say the place is more barbaric than ever since then—a haven for outlaws and renegades." She winced. "We've also been hearing tales for the past year or so of a lost Star League production facility on Astrokaszy, supported by rumors of new 'Mechs and weapon systems seen on the planet."

"We're just hearing this now?" Marcus said.

Jase rose smoothly to the major's defense. "How many treasure-trove stories have you heard in the past year. Marc? Ten? Twenty?"

"At least that many," Marcus conceded. "But back to the arms smuggling, why would they go to this Astrokaszy?"

"It's a double-blind technique," Jase said. "Astrokaszy already has a thriving black-market operation in place. T'arms and materials are sent there, and the world acts as an isolation and distribution point. If the arms are ever traced, from either direction of the supply flow, there's no solid connection between the Hegemony and their suppliers." He paused. "Wouldn't be surprised if there was a command circuit set up. It would take a longer chain of JumpShips than from the Niops Association—four or five instead of two—all waiting in uninhabited star systems to pass the DropShips along, but if they were placed right . . ."

Jericho caught on to his train of thought fastest. "They would form two-thirds of a command circuit to place raiders right up against our borders. And the materiel wouldn't even have to go back to Alphard. They could resupply raiders right off Astrokaszy. Damn."

"So the only major question left is, who's trafficking through there?" Marcus said.

Jase shook his head. "That I don't know for sure. Somewhere between Romita and my return trip past Campoleone, I asked one too many questions. Or"—he gave Major Wood a slow grin—"I actually made an enemy. When I got jumped on the Gatchina station, I decided I'd worn out my welcome."

"So the final answer may lie on Astrokaszy." Marcus stood. "And even if it doesn't, the planet looks to be the critical link in the supply chain. We can go there and put a serious crimp in their operations—and maybe even find an old Star League depot of weapons and materiel. Jase, how soon till we could hit it?"

"No recharge stations out there," he said. "You're

looking at three jumps through dead systems. Plus Drop-Ship travel time." He fell silent for a bit, frowning in concentration. "Hit the right stars for recharging, we could be on planet in a month and a half."

Marcus grimaced. "Ouch. That's a long walk home." He turned to Major Wood. "I'll have an official report prepared for you by the end of today. Can we arrange for extra equipment—armor, heat sinks, items we'll need for an extended campaign?"

The major nodded. "How soon until you leave?"

"Two days," Marcus said. "We can finish the minor repairs in transit. I'll want to study the charts first, and any information you can feed us on Astrokaszy, but does anyone have questions now?"

Jericho Ryan broke the silence. "Well, nothing extremely important," she said, "but I'm curious." She turned to Jase. "You said you were attacked on the Gatchina station. How did you get out of there, and across Marik space, when somebody must have been looking for you?"

The left side of Jase's mouth turned up in a lopsided grin. "I was traveling under two names at once, paying fares for each, the extra to be assumed only in an emergency such as this. I left t'offender in a locker and arranged passage on a Kline Freighter Company Drop-Ship. Had to take the scenic route back until I could cross into Canopus space."

"And your appearance?" Jericho asked. "That didn't raise any questions?"

The grin widened. "Would you believe the freighter's medical officer was an old friend of mine?"

21

Palace of the Magestrix
Crimson, Canopus IV
Magistracy of Canopus
The Periphery
24 May 3058

The two wings of the royal residence framed a large courtyard garden where hundreds of flowers and non-blooming plants from all across the Magistracy of Canopus grew in elegant profusion. Designed by master gardeners to offer a harmonious blend of color and scent, the spot was a favorite of Emma Centrella's for informal meetings—not so much because she loved the garden but because the surroundings often had a distracting effect on her visitors.

She waited while one of the Royal Guards searched Sun-Tzu Liao for possible weapons before admitting him into her presence. Watching from her seat on a nearby bench, Emma admired the young man's stoic acceptance of what he must surely consider an impertinence. He never once glanced at her daughter Naomi, also standing nearby, though he must certainly suspect that she had reported their conversation of the other night. No one could rule a great state without making such assumptions as a matter of course.

With a curt nod to show that he was satisfied, the guard finally led Sun-Tzu into the garden. Naomi met him first, then escorted him over to where her mother sat. Emma

Centrella rose as he approached, meeting him on equal footing. *A concession I mean to take away very soon.*

"Magestrix," Sun-Tzu said evenly, his lean frame elegant in the drapery of his silken purple robes. Although the three were alone, he kept his hands clasped behind his back in almost military fashion, though the pose was not threatening. "I was pleasantly surprised by the invitation to meet with you here. We have had little time to talk of late."

"I have had pressing matters to attend to." Emma began to lead the way down one of the garden's many cobblestone paths. Sun-Tzu fell into step alongside her, and Naomi followed behind. "Your unscrupulous acts of aggression against my realm for one." She'd insulted him openly, but the only sign was a stiffening of his shoulders and the sudden hard set of his face.

Only in private could the Chancellor of the Capellan Confederation have accepted such an offense and remained in negotiation. But here, the formalities could be dropped with no loss of face—exactly the kind of playing field Emma Centrella preferred. Continuing along the path, breathing in the heady perfume of her realm's rare and beautiful flora, she waited to see if Sun-Tzu would join the game.

When he finally spoke, it was without the slightest pretense of civility. "If I wanted to launch an aggressive campaign against the Magistracy, my forces would right now be landing on Canopus." His voice was pitched low, cold and hard. A proper voice for threats.

But a mistake if he thinks to cow me on my own home ground. Emma naturally assumed the Chancellor's Death Commandos had found their vantage point over the gardens by now, and as much as she respected their talents, they did not much worry her. Danai was safely away from the residence at the moment. *And I have complete faith in my daughter's ability to rule in my place. What about you, Sun-Tzu Liao? Are you ready to hand the Confederation over to your mad sister, Kali?*

"This is not Sarna, Chancellor," she said, alluding to the hostilities between the Capellan Confederation and the tiny alliance of worlds that sat on its border. "The

Magistracy fields a stronger opposition, and we have resources that Sarna does not."

A short pause, then Emma resumed with an icy calmness. "You are funneling weapons into the Marian Hegemony." A full report from Avanti's Angels had come in three days before, with a cover briefing from Major Judith Wood, garrison commander of Marantha. It told her everything they thought or knew, and by now the mercenaries must surely be on their way out of the Marantha system. "To Campoleone, through Astrokaszy, and then on to Alphard. Meanwhile you have the gall to bring military forces into my realm, all the while preaching mutual assistance." The new Word of Blake representative had verified the report with copies of message traffic and JumpShip routes, and even the ComStar officials on Canopus had loosened a bit and were helping her with the investigation.

If her knowledge of the route by which arms and equipment were being smuggled surprised Sun-Tzu, it did not register as anything more than the faintest expression of curiosity. "If you have such detailed knowledge of this conspiracy, I assume you have direct proof with which to condemn me?"

He's amused? "I have enough proof to assure me that you are not trustworthy." Emma slackened her step, then brought the small retinue to a halt. "For instance, what do you have on those DropShips making planetfall tomorrow? My staff has already informed me that their thrust and trajectory indicates a payload in *excess of four hundred tons*! That's about three hundred and fifty more than expected."

Again she had caught him off guard, and it took him a moment to compose his face before speaking. "It was meant to be a surprise gift, Magestrix. Two lances of advanced-tech BattleMechs, including two of the new Inner Sphere OmniMechs. BJ2-O *Blackjack*s. A token of my commitment to bringing the Magistracy up to a higher technological standard."

"Oh, I'm very sure it was meant to be a surprise, Sun-Tzu. But those ships will most definitely not be landing." Her voice never wavered from the calm, commanding

tone with which she'd begun, and she relished his quick
flash of anger over her familiar form of address. Such
things were unimportant, and that they bothered him only
confirmed her initial assessment. He was no more than
a boy playing at being a great ruler. *Now let's see how
desperate you've become.* "You will remove yourself and
your forces from my realm at once."

She could see the calculations shifting into overdrive
behind Sun-Tzu's dark eyes. *Here is where you should
fold your hand, Liao. Like your grandfather, you do not
realize when you've lost. Like your mother, you do not use
well what small victories you gain.*

"Magestrix," Sun-Tzu began, keeping his voice even,
though he seemed obviously concerned. "Let us say that I
will agree to a skeleton crew of your troops taking over
the DropShips, relieving my crew and bringing them
down in a harmless shuttle. You would then be in control
of the materiel and 'Mechs I have brought for you."

You're grasping. Emma steeled herself against the
temptation he offered. "People are working to verify the
connection through Astrokaszy right now. The same
people you ordered sabotaged as they passed through
Andurien."

Sun-Tzu frowned. "I gave no such order."

Naomi quickly drew the Word of Blake and ComStar
documents from a small folder she was carrying and
handed them to her mother. "Here's proof that you did,"
Emma said, brandishing them. "Notification went out to
you on top-priority channels when the Canopus merchant
ship *Adonis* passed through the Duchy of Andurien, a
Free Worlds League state to which you are known to be
strengthening ties."

She handed the Word of Blake report to Sun-Tzu, and
gave him a moment to begin glancing through it. "And
two days ago you sent out requests via ComStar, inquiring
about the production of war materiel in the Free Worlds
League and the ship movements for carrying it."

Sun-Tzu glanced at Naomi, suspicion and astonishment
clearly evident on his lean face, then he clamped back
down into a cold study of both women. Emma spoke
quickly before Naomi could give anything away. "No, it

wasn't my daughter who reported that." Which was half-
true. ComStar had actually turned over that information.
Naomi had simply verified it from conversation she'd
been having with Sun-Tzu over the past few days. "Com-
Star and Word of Blake have both assisted this investigation." Sun-Tzu looked crestfallen, his shoulders
slumped and head shaking lightly. "It's not what you
think. I am merely inquiring on your behalf, trying to confirm or refute your suspicions concerning the League."

"But I do not suspect the Free Worlds League."
Emma's voice was deadly sweet. "I think you are the one
responsible. And not a single HPG in my realm will allow
you to communicate orders to your arms-smuggling network. By the time you can reach your own space, I will
have the proof I need from Astrokaszy." She smiled fully.
"I will then ask Thomas Marik to crush your operation on
Campoleone." *Which he will be happy to do, as your
actions compromise his cherished image as a noble
leader. He may even pay restitution for Canopus losses.*

"May I be allowed one final observation, Magestrix?
Before I am declared persona non grata?"

"Granted."

"If I were behind this, obviously it would be with the
aim of destabilizing the Magistracy as a prelim to an invasion. Yes?" He waited for her curt nod, his smile most
disarming. "Now that you are aware of my heinous plans,
what's to keep me from launching such an attack immediately? Can you recall your forces from the border faster
than mine can strike at Canopus?"

His voice took on a hard edge. "And don't go quoting
me your terms of mutual defense with the Taurian Concordat. For all your mutual defense agreements, how
much have they helped against the Hegemony raids?"

Emma Centrella knew her anger showed, and for the
briefest moment she toyed with the idea of having Sun-
Tzu shot. Yes, Kali Liao would use it as an excuse to
attack the Magistracy, but under her leadership the
Capellan Confederation would suffer. An intense look of
caution in Naomi's eyes stayed her hand, and she nodded
acceptance of her daughter's silent counsel. *I called the*

game, she thought. *I cannot react so strongly because Sun-Tzu has decided to play.*

Without waiting for her answer, Sun-Tzu went on. "Now, if you happen to be wrong . . ." He held up a hand to forestall any immediate defense. "Humor me, please, my lady. As I said, if you happen to be wrong, you lose everything I have promised and you alert those who do work against you."

"And when did you promise the murder of demi-Precentor Jamie Nicholas?"

With senses honed by over twenty years of ruling the Magistracy of Canopus, Emma searched the Liao's face for any reaction. Seeing how little he'd been able to hide his reactions thus far, she expected to glimpse some mix of anger, desperation, and surprise. But it was the complete lack of expression that convinced her of his involvement. That his face could remain so impassive at her accusation also made her question earlier appraisals of his character. "Word of Blake claims to have recovered her body, killed by a needler, and that she was last known to be on her way to visit you with dispatches."

The calm neutrality of Sun-Tzu's expression never wavered. "That would be a matter between the Word of Blake and myself," he said simply, giving nothing away.

"That is the same as admitting to it, Sun-Tzu. Jamie Nicholas was an advisor to my court and under the protection of the Magistracy."

He smiled cruelly. "And the ComStar acolytes that Word of Blake killed on Harminous? Were they any less under your protection? I believe you allowed them to claim—what was it?—internal politics not relating to the Magistracy? Very well. I make the same claim and am willing to pay a similar restitution." His face suddenly recovered its animation, brightening in a parody of a child with a brilliant thought. "In fact, I shall pay you in political coin."

Whatever he is about to propose, deny him. Emma Centrella felt at a loss, suddenly unsure if she was reading Sun-Tzu correctly—or if she ever had. A glance at Naomi convinced Emma that her daughter, too, sensed danger. "And what would that be, Sun-Tzu?" The familiar use of his name didn't seem to carry quite the insult it had at first.

"I shall discover for you exactly who is behind the arms shipments to the Marian Hegemony."

Emma was about to decline angrily when a hand on her arm stopped her. Naomi moved up beside her mother. "How would you propose to do this, Chancellor Liao?"

Despite a slight surge of annoyance at Naomi's sudden entry into the conversation, Emma admired the way her daughter deftly returned the tone to more formal ground. The Magestrix looked to Sun-Tzu, whose gaze had never moved from her face, and nodded once.

"What I propose is to help you invade the Free Worlds League," he said simply.

If not for the gentle pressure of Naomi's hand still on her arm, Emma would have laughed in the young man's face. It seemed that Romano Liao's madness had indeed been passed down to both her children. Seemed. But Emma had learned to trust her daughter's instincts. Naomi might not be much of a warrior, but her political acumen rivaled Emma's own.

Naomi smiled encouragement. "And why would we want to do that, Chancellor?"

"Because the proof you're looking for might not be found on Astrokaszy, but it will be found on Campoleone. Astrokaszy will be the supply point, and you might be able to disrupt the flow of arms into the Hegemony, but there will be little or nothing to connect it back to the source. So the weapons will just be rerouted. At least"— his smile was cunning—"that's how I would do it. Double-blind."

"If we invade Campoleone," Emma said, "Thomas Marik will have to retaliate whether or not he's the one supplying weapons to the Hegemony."

"You're right, he would be forced to retaliate and forced to seek a military solution." Sun-Tzu shrugged, but Emma did not miss his momentary frown. "But against me he could find other means of"—he paused— "reprisal."

Yes, he would finally have a reason to break off your engagement to Isis Marik. That's quite a gamble. Was

Sun-Tzu telling the truth? "So you would take your troops into Campoleone, and we are to trust you to report back what is truly happening?"

"No, I would lend *your* troops to Astrokaszy first. What you need may be there. If not, I will take them over the border to Campoleone under the flag of the Capellan Confederation. Consider this a trial use of Magistracy troops under my command."

Naomi bit down on her lower lip and frowned. "It might work," she said to her mother. "By assigning our troops into his care, the Chancellor would bear responsibility for their actions and conduct. If our troops will follow him, that is."

"They would not have to follow Sun-Tzu," Emma said, correcting the one flaw in Naomi's thought. "They would have to follow their commander, who would report to Chancellor Liao." Emma seemed not to notice her own return to addressing Sun-Tzu by title. *This could amount to political suicide for Sun-Tzu; he must be awfully sure of himself. And it releases me from direct responsibility. How could any Periphery state turn down such an offer?* "That is how your Capellan Warrior Houses work, is it not?"

"Close enough," Sun-Tzu said. He bent his head to breathe in the sweet scent of a blood-red orchid he'd plucked as they walked, then offered the bloom to Naomi before turning again to Emma. "The commander should possess a strong relationship to your house, so your troops will feel they are maintaining ties to their nation. Also, this commander should be capable of taking control of the forces in case it becomes clear that I am acting against the interest of the Magistracy."

Emma smiled thinly. He could have only one person in mind. And though Naomi's qualifications as a warrior were borderline-average, her daughter could indeed retain some amount of independence and make the decision to break off from San-Tzu's plans. "I am not approving this mission yet, Chancellor. But I would be interested in hearing which Canopus officer you would have at your side."

But Sun-Tzu surprised her again. With a quick look of

regret at Naomi, he said, "I would think Danai Centrella the only logical choice. She could command a battalion, which is more than large enough and she is a skilled warrior. She would not be dependent on me and my command lance for direction."

And you deprive me of my heir-apparent. Not a bad play. Emma ignored the pained expression on Naomi's face and mentally organized her conditions. *You are once again reaching too far, Sun-Tzu Liao. I promised I would make you pay again for your presumption.* "You will use Magistracy JumpShip and DropShip assets, except for your own *Lung Wang* Class DropShip, of course. Danai is to retain complete autonomy." She smiled, remembering that thorny clause in the contract with Avanti's Angels. "Your command lance will be further augmented by a liaison officer and her lance." *And with that many applying a direct brake on you, your command of the unit is honorary only. We will use your authority to get over the border if necessary, but there will be no illusion that anyone besides Danai is in command of the Magistracy troops.*

Sun-Tzu nodded reluctantly. "I would suggest one minor alteration, Magestrix."

"And that is, Chancellor?"

"That we still use the *Celestial Walker*. Its lithium-fusion batteries give it twice the range of your normal JumpShips. I believe you have several recharge stations that would allow us to proceed to the border of the Magistracy rather quickly. By then, you could have two MAF JumpShips in place that would get us to Astrokaszy in an abbreviated command circuit."

Emma Centrella considered the wisdom of rapid movement against allowing Sun-Tzu access to his people for any longer than necessary. "Agreed," she finally said. "Provided you take up a Canopus crew that verifies all ship movements."

"Why, Magestrix, one would think you did not trust me." Sun-Tzu chuckled dryly. "And who is my liaison officer to be? I would like to meet her as soon as possible."

"You have already met her, Chancellor," Emma said with a smile. "Naomi will also accompany this expedition."

Sun-Tzu visibly balked, but then recovered. "As you desire, of course."

Yes, Sun-Tzu. I place my two eldest daughters in your care. Both serve to benefit. Naomi is an accomplished diplomat, but she may learn more of the ways of command. Danai would just as soon spit in your face, but perhaps even she will learn something of politics. Meanwhile, both of them can serve as your keepers. And if harm were to befall either one, you would bear responsibility for that as well. Meanwhile, I will have your technicians and your trainers and your "gift" of Inner Sphere OmniMechs—and several months to learn what I can at no further cost to my realm.

And that is the proper way to conduct business.

BOOK III

"One who has few must prepare against the enemy; one who has many makes the enemy prepare against him."
— Sun Tzu, *The Art of War*

"I go to war only when I am ready."
— from an interview with Chancellor Sun-Tzu Liao, Sian University Press, 7 October 3057

=== 22 ===

DropShip *Heaven Sent*
Shervanis Spaceport, Shervanis Caliphate
Astrokaszy
The Periphery
28 June 3058

The loading ramp began to lower from the *Heaven Sent*'s main 'Mech bay down onto the pale golden sand of the Shervanis Spaceport. Marcus stood just inside the bay doors, out of the harsh sunlight but still awash in the heat that rose off the sand like a never-ending power spike from a 'Mech's fusion engine. Sweat beaded over his skin and soaked his clothing. *And I thought the Marantha tarmac was hot?*

Half a kilometer to the east, directly opposite where he stood, the city of Shervanis sat squat and ugly. It was Astrokaszy's largest city, but looked like little more than a kilometers-wide sprawl of light-colored adobe buildings and dark, narrow streets. To the south, just visible past the edge of the bay doors, Marcus could see the barren foothills that he knew from maps would turn quickly into the badlands. A five-kilometer wide strip of broken rock and treacherous ravines, the badlands were all that separated the sandy plains of the Shervanis Caliphate from the actual Shaharazad Desert.

Halfway between the outskirts of the city and the Drop-Ship a small caravan approached, dozens of dark-skinned servants stooping under the weight of six canopied litters.

Marcus divided his attention between gazing out over the city and watching the caravan as he formed his first impressions of Astrokaszy.

Desolate, devastated, and dismal were the words that leapt to mind.

The trip from Marantha to Astrokaszy had come off almost without a hitch. Dorian Anastius, captain of the Canopus *Merchant* Class JumpShip *Marathon,* knew his trade. Or, better said, knew his trade routes. Even with such a remote destination as Astrokaszy, the seasoned spacer knew just how far to reach in a single hyperspace jump and what star systems offered the fastest recharge times along the way. Preparing to jump from the Marantha system with both the *Heaven Sent* and the *Head of a Pin* in tow on the twenty-ninth of May, Captain Anastius had promised Marcus a trip of four weeks, no more. And that would include the eight days it would take the DropShips to travel insystem from jump point to the actual surface of Astrokaszy.

If not for an unexpected glitch, the *Marathon* would have made it on the nose. As it was, she only missed it by two days.

Preparing for the third and final jump, the *Marathon* had developed a problem with the equipment used to reel in the ship's enormous jump sail. A JumpShip unfurled its sail to collect the solar energy needed to recharge the Kearny-Fuchida jump drive, and no captain would simply abandon a sail without very good cause. It had cost them four days of station-keeping to repair the equipment and untangle the sail's fouled lines. Hoping to redeem himself, Captain Anastius then jumped into the Astrokaszy system at a pirate point that shaved two days off the usual eight for the inbound trip.

The power wielded by a MechWarrior vanished during space transport, when he or she had to place life and equipment in the hands of others. *MechWarriors prefer fast transport,* Marcus thought, staring out at the inhospitable landscape, *even to a place as desolate as this.*

From orbit Jericho had pointed out the Shaharazad Desert, a dry ocean of sun-blasted plains, badlands, and rolling dunes that ringed the planet's equator and stretched over five thousand kilometers wide north-to-south at any point. It seemed no life could hope to survive in this dun-yellow wasteland. But here, as on hundreds of worlds throughout the Inner Sphere and Periphery, humans had made their niche. Cities and villages existed along the northern and southern borders of the Shaharazad, where the *mean* temperature was bearable and the world's scarce fresh-water resources surfaced in oasis-like pools and a few pitiful rivers. The two dozen or so larger cities, those with ample fresh water even in times of drought elsewhere, were seats of power and each was governed by a caliph—a self-styled supreme ruler.

According to MAF information, these petty tyrants laid claim to nearby villages and large sections of desert, calling them *caliphates.* But their true power usually stopped at the city's edge. Villagers paid tribute and token allegiance to whichever caliph currently had warriors stationed in their village, subject to constant change as the caliphs raided each other's realms and conducted sporadic invasions that actually did little in the way of changing borders. It reminded Marcus of the disputes between the Great Houses of the Inner Sphere. Though they'd been warring for supremacy for almost three hundred years, their borders had remained fundamentally unchanged until the recent Clan invasion and the troubles in the Chaos March.

As for the desert, if anyone truly ruled the Shaharazad it was the sheiks and their nomadic tribes.

The caravan Marcus had been watching halted now at the foot of the DropShip ramp. Six canopy-covered litters were carried by eight slaves each, five empty and one with a single occupant. Two guards armed with automatic rifles flanked each litter. The guards wore caftans, flowing light-colored robes that helped protect them from the sun. The slaves wore only simple gray cotton shifts, their dark skin blistered along shoulders and arms and feet. They were fettered to one another about the ankles. A revulsion gnawed at Marcus' insides, and the sound of rattling chains grated against his nerves.

"Remember, we aren't here to buck the local customs," Jericho said in a stage-whisper as she moved up alongside him. With her were Ki-Lynn Tanaga and Thomas Faber. Jase Torgensson, fully recovered from his ordeal in the Free Worlds League and looking as polished as ever, hung back from the others, as always preferring his own bit of personal space.

Marcus nodded once as he watched a lone figure dismount the litter and approach the ship. Jericho had warned them to expect slavery, among other barbaric practices. Now was not the time to begin a crusade. "But it does make me question accepting this Shervanis' hospitality," he whispered back.

Caliph Malachye Shervanis had transmitted his greetings as the Angels' DropShips entered orbit, extending an invitation to visit his grand city that they might pay their respects. It surprised everyone, mercenary and MAF alike, as no one had suspected that anyone on Astrokaszy possessed technology advanced enough for ground-to-ship communications. For a moment Marcus had wondered if this was their quarry giving itself away through the use of advanced equipment, but the another dozen such invitations from rival caliphs quickly followed. One of them, from a Caliph Rashier, had even included a thinly disguised bribe, an offer of a "one-day garrison fee" if the Angels would join him for dinner and discussion.

The Angels also learned that Word of Blake operated a small communications facility on the outskirts of Shervanis. "Why not? They're everywhere else these days," had been Jericho's comment. Marcus noted silently that Word of Blake seemed to be showing a lot more interest in the Periphery than ComStar ever had.

The Shervanis family, descendants of the planet's earliest settlers, had traditionally wielded much power on Astrokaszy. The Angels had to begin somewhere with their search for evidence of weapons smuggling and a possible raider staging area, and so they decided that meeting Malachye Shervanis was a good place to start. His caliphate was supposed to be one of the more enlightened ones on Astrokaszy. Besides that, the Word of Blake presence in his city would give the mercenaries immediate communication back to the Magistracy and, if necessary, the Blakists could mediate between the Angels and Shervanis.

But Marcus had also been warned that no caliph could be wholly trusted. They continually fought one another and occasionally the desert sheiks for dominance, quick to exploit any advantage. With the arrival of a strengthened mercenary company on the planet, Jericho had predicted that Marcus would receive offers of employment from every caliph and, failing that, threats. Marcus had brought Jericho, Ki-Lynn, Jase, and Thomas down with him in the *Heaven Sent*; while Jericho's lance and the rest of the Angels transferred to the *Pinhead* and remained in orbit as a deterrent under the command of Charlene Boske. The MAF reports provided by Major Wood numbered Caliph Shervanis' personal army at two lances of poorly equipped BattleMechs. No matter how beaten up the *Pinhead* was, a Fortress Class DropShip could level the caliph's entire city. So, with Jericho abandoning her MAF uniform for more appropriate mercenary dress, the five accepted an invitation into what could be the enemy's den.

Marcus stepped out into the sunlight to greet Caliph Shervanis' representative. The man was dressed in formal robes, heavy silks and other weaves Marcus couldn't identify, all elaborately embroidered with golden thread. As if in defiance of the world's harsh sun, the man wore no headdress and had his head shaved smooth. His dark brown skin glistened under a thin layer of sweat. He stopped several paces short of Marcus and bowed slightly, hands held in front of him and touching fingertip to fingertip. Uncertain, Marcus imitated the gesture.

"I am Arch Vizier Ji-Drohmien," the man said, his accent heavily rolling the r's, "the Exalted One's personal advisor and"—he smiled thinly—"right hand."

Wondering at the hidden humor in those last words, Marcus ushered the man up into the shade of the 'Mech bay. "Marcus GioAvanti, commander of Avanti's Angels."

The other man's sharp eyes swept the bay, pausing only an instant over each of the five BattleMechs. "Beautiful machines, Commander. And the rest of your company?"

"They remain in orbit, Arch Vizier. I would not wish to appear threatening to our host by bringing down more BattleMechs than he has at his command." Marcus watched for any sign on Ji-Drohmien's face that perhaps Shervanis might have more than two lances of 'Mechs nearby.

The other man's expression remained respectfully neutral. "A wise decision," he said, gesturing back to the waiting litters. "My master has sent convenient transport. If you are ready."

"No," Marcus said, a note of finality in his voice. He saw Jericho tense, but wasn't about to board a slave-carried litter. "That is, we would prefer to furnish our own transportation." He glanced over at Torgensson. "Jase, go get one of our hovercars. The large touring coach." He turned back to Ji-Drohmien. "Perhaps you would ride with us, Arch Vizier?"

The other man's crafty smile worried Marcus, making him wonder if he had somehow made a mistake. "A wonderful gesture," Ji-Drohmien said. "In the name of our enlightened leader, Caliph Malachye Shervanis, I welcome you to Astrokaszy."

Jericho did not miss the troubled look that crossed Ki-Lynn Tanaga's face as Marcus sent Jase for the hovercar. But with Ji-Drohmien standing so near, she had no chance to voice her concern. *Whatever it is, we'll find out soon enough,* she thought, climbing into the vehicle. The car's top had been removed to let them ride in the open air, a good thing since it was unlikely any air cooling unit could match the desert heat. Jase drove, and within minutes they were moving through the narrow streets of the city of Shervanis.

Some of the buildings were constructed of wood and quarried stone, but most were the dun-colored adobe structures typical of desert terrain. Along the outskirts of the city Marcus noticed more than one area that was little more than organized piles of rubble, remnants of the latest round of war between Shervanis and who knew what other caliph. People were apparently living there in rickety lean-to structures while attempting to rebuild homes of marginally better quality. Passing out of the war-torn areas, the hovercar skirted a large industrial center that seemed to consist mainly of burned-out buildings and abandoned warehouses. Then they were into a crowded residential area that smelled of urine and sun-rotted refuse.

People on the street dressed mostly in homespun garments, the adults in long flowing caftans and children in shapeless tunics. Some wore clothing dyed in bright colors, garments of somewhat better quality, but little else seemed to separate the prosperous from the destitute. Even as the little group neared the inner city, the only signs of prosperity were the rough white stucco coating a house or the presence of the occasional slave some households could afford. All stared openly at the novelty of the hovercar, until they recognized the arch vizier sitting in front and quickly returned to their own business.

Besides the looks of fear and hate, Jericho also saw many pistols and rifles and wondered that Ji-Drohmien would travel the streets so unprotected and unconcerned for his life. As she studied the people more closely, though, she saw that the dominant expression was indeed fear. And apparently not of the arch vizier.

They might hate this man, but they fear Shervanis. The caliph could turn his BattleMechs against them, and who could stop him? They have nowhere else to go, except into the desert.

The Caliph's palatial dwelling, set in the center of the city, was surrounded by a defensive wall of reinforced ferrocrete. Twenty meters high and nearly ten meters thick, the wall would be a formidable obstacle to any attacker not equipped with jumping 'Mechs. It also told Jericho that Malachye Shervanis considered it of greater importance to build a solid defense for himself even as the city outside his walls fell into decay. And at the main gate she caught another glimpse of Shervanis' *enlightened* rule—a dozen heads set on poles, rotting in the hot, dry atmosphere.

Ji-Drohmien dismissed the sight with an imperious wave of a hand. "An example," he said, not bothering to mention of what. As a warm desert breeze brought the stench of rotting flesh to her, Jericho swallowed hard to keep her gorge down.

The caliph's palace was an amazing contrast to the city. A good half a kilometer square, the grounds included several groves of fruit trees being tended by slaves. A large two-story palace sat at the center, its squat, onion-shaped domes of gold and red topped with spires. The walls were a smooth and pristine white. Two BattleMechs, an ancient *Quickdraw* and a *Clint* in not much better condition, patrolled the grounds. The place spoke of wealth and power, an impression that only intensified once inside.

Floors were tiled with pink marble, and everywhere slaves were cleaning and polishing. Ji-Drohmien led them down several narrow corridors, past doorways curtained in heavy silks or hanging beads and guarded by the occasional turbaned Bedouin carrying a large scimitar. He finally instructed them to wait in a small anteroom while he announced their presence. Female slaves descended on them with jars of wine, platters of dates and nuts, and shallow bowls of water for washing the dust from their hands. Nausea still clutched at Jericho's stomach at the memory of the impaled heads, and she was glad when Marcus waved the platters away.

Not until they were finally left alone did Ki-Lynn finally speak up. "The litters were a courtesy," she said to Marcus. "A gift from Caliph Shervanis."

"And he will be insulted that I refused them."

"No. Unless the caliph presents you with something personally, you may refuse. That is your right as the guest. But then you brought out a superior method of transportation. A pasha could and will interpret this as an insult."

Jericho caught the underlying hint of a possible exception. It seemed that Marcus did too. "Unless?" he asked.

"Unless you now present the hovercar as a gift to the caliph."

Jericho caught the look of exasperation stealing over Marcus' face. "That's why Ji-Drohmien appeared so pleased with my suggestion." At Ki's light nod, he exhaled in one sharp, short breath. "Nothing to be done about it now. Next time, Ki, please warn me."

"I'll try. But it would be almost as insulting if a woman spoke out in a place like this."

How did she know so much about Arab culture? Jericho wondered. The Angels' comm officer always seemed to be full of such useful information. Didn't matter now, though. And though it galled her, Jericho filed the information concerning "a woman's place" away for future reference. This wasn't Magistracy. Exercising her rights would only make trouble for the Angels and jeopardize this mission for her people.

Marcus was having none of that, though. "Ki, you're a warrior. These people will respect that." He paused, then seemed to reconsider. "But, next time, manufacture some pretext to pull me aside and then tell me. That goes for everyone," he said, glancing over at the others. Jericho thought his eyes might have rested on her a few seconds longer, but their gray depths were unfathomable.

"You called Shervanis a pasha," Jase said. "I thought he was a caliph?"

Ki nodded. "Pasha is a title of honor, not rulership. Much like the Combine way of using *san* and *sama*. Its correct use would be to call him Malachye-*pasha*."

The talk died away as Ji-Drohmien returned with a rustling of his long silk robes. "His Highness will receive you now," he said, leading the Angels down another short stretch of hall and through a set of brilliant red and gold beaded curtains. It occurred to Jericho that the very layout of the palace, with its narrow corridors and many turns, was meant to be confusing as well as intimidating. One could never be sure if a curtained doorway gave into a new hall or a room full of guards.

This time it opened into a circular room. Lounging on a dais littered with pillows, clad only in a small purple vest and full white trousers was the man she assumed was Caliph Malachye Shervanis. Behind the dais was a thick wall of copper, on which beasts that resembled giant jungle cats spun and danced in a huge bas-relief. At the dais' edge a burning censor let off the strong scent of aromatic incense, while on a nearby table an arrangement of tobaccos and various illicit drugs had been set out next to a large water pipe.

Shervanis studied his visitors, his eyes so dark they seemed black. They reminded Jericho of pictures she had seen once of an old Terran aquatic terror called a shark. Though desert-born, the caliph seemed just as deadly.

Said to be nearing sixty, Shervanis was slender and still showed the wiry strength he must have possessed all his life. Two scantily clad female salves catered to him, one feeding him from a bowl of fruit while the other merely knelt nearby. A single male guard stood off to one side, holding a large fan made of huge feathers that he waved lazily through the air to generate a breeze inside the stuffy room.

"Highness," Ji-Drohmien called from the door as he let the Angles enter first, "Commander GioAvanti and four of his warriors."

"Ah, excellent." The pasha's voice was quiet and heavily accented, almost impossible to understand. "My arch vizier informs me of your generous loan of a hover-car to speed your trip along." His dark eyes watched Marcus expectantly.

Marcus didn't hesitate. "With the full intent of presenting the vehicle to Your Highness, of course, Caliph Shervanis."

The black eyes blinked once, slowly. "Very generous, Commander," he finally said. "Much appreciated. But we cannot accept." He spoke carefully, so no meaning would be lost. "As your host it would be discourteous to take advantage of your misfortune."

"Misfortune, Caliph?" Marcus looked appropriately concerned, though Jericho knew it was all a part of the act. Any moment Marcus would admit to being in financial trouble, and that the Angels were on Astrokaszy to recoup recent losses by searching for the rumored Star League-era base. They had decided on the cover story before leaving Marantha. It was one the caliph was not likely to question.

But Malachye Shervanis was not waiting for that explanation. He spread his arms in a wide shrug, his right arm sliding out from where it had been hidden among the pillows. His hand had been cut off at the wrist, and not evenly. Scar tissue ran down the inside of his forearm, though the stump had been mercifully capped with a silver guard. "An HPG message arrived today, alerting all Periphery states and independent worlds to watch for your arrival. It appears that your debts have been called into immediate account on Outreach. Your creditors have declared you insolvent, and any planetary militia is charged with seizing your 'Mechs and returning them to your creditors as collateral."

The caliph accepted a grape from his slave and smiled cruelly as he chewed and then swallowed it. "It appears, Commander, that you shall not be returning to the Inner Sphere any time soon."

23

Palatial Estates
City of Shervanis, Shervanis Caliphate
Astrokaszy
The Periphery
28 June 3058

You shall not be returning to the Inner Sphere any time soon.

The words still echoed in Marcus' mind as he traversed the narrow corridors of the palace. His boot heels clicked against the marble floor, the sound creating hollow echoes as he went, chased by the soft whisper of sandals constantly reminding him of the "escort" that followed.

Arch Vizier Ji-Drohmien had appointed a turbaned warrior to each of the other four Angels also, saying these would take them to their rooms and guide them about the palace later. *To keep us under guard and threatened until the caliph can press his desires*, Marcus translated. He had remained behind to speak a few final words with Shervanis, and upon his dismissal found two such escorts awaiting him.

"As befitting your stature of most honored guest," Ji-Drohmien told him with a thin smile. Marcus had let that pass, wishing he could step outside the palace's confining walls and walk off the frustration he felt. The two guards corrected his path only once when he made a wrong turn, and soon he was striding across the wide entrance hall and through the doors that opened onto the grounds.

Someone was waiting for him at one end of the covered entrance. The figure had its back to him, and Marcus thought for a moment it was Jericho Ryan. But this person did not have Jericho's height or full figure, and her hair was much too long and straight. No, it was Ki-Lynn. Marcus was surprised at his error, but then realized sheepishly that it was because he'd been hoping to run into Jericho all along. As an outsider, she seemed easier to talk to somehow. Until now at least. With her and her lance now attached to his Angels, he'd become as responsible for them as any other of his people. And the idea that she might be becoming special to him was suddenly disturbing. So much so that he almost forgot Ki-Lynn was standing there waiting.

"*Konnichi-wa*, Marcus," she said. *Good afternoon.*

The calm patience in her voice told Marcus she'd already spoken the greeting once, and would likely do so again with the same neutrality until answered. "*Konnichi-wa*, Ki-*san*." His Japanese was nowhere near perfect, but several years in the Draconis Combine had made it adequate for simple conversation. "*Gomen-nasai.*" *Sorry.* "I was distracted."

"*Wakarimasu.* Understandable, considering the length of your talk with Caliph Shervanis."

As always, Marcus paid more attention to the way Ki said a thing, or sometimes how she didn't say it. The art of discussion among the people of the Combine often made subtlety and vague allusions the only way to approach even the most ordinary matters. Ki-Lynn was masterful. Marcus guessed she wanted to talk about the meeting. "Walk with me, Ki," he said.

He also did not miss the slight shift in her gaze that drew attention to her own escort, a large Bedouin who waited impassively on the other side of a pillar. Marcus led the way out onto the grounds, following a flagstone path that seemed to circle the palace. Ki-Lynn walked beside him in gracefully measured paces, and three of the caliph's warriors trailed them by a few steps. *Let them,* Marcus thought.

"We have close company," he said, speaking to Ki in Japanese. He was aware that if what she had in mind held no particular importance, she would steer the conversation into English. He was not surprised when she responded in kind.

"Did the oyabun threaten you?"

Oyabun. That, of course, was Japanese for the leader of a yakuza crime organization. Marcus smiled at Ki tagging Shervanis with a name the guards weren't likely to connect with him. "No. Just some not-so-subtle blackmail. He knows the best he can do is place the five of us under arrest. But then he'd have to turn us and our 'Mechs over to Word of Blake for immediate transfer back to Outreach. Meanwhile Charlie's up there hanging over his precious realm with a full company of BattleMechs."

"Then we are truly declared bankrupt?"

Marcus shrugged uneasily. "You know our financial situation as well as anyone. According to the oyabun, somebody bought up our notes, and our new creditors are calling the loans due. I guess it's possible we overlooked some little clause in our agreements, but the only way we can hope to resolve the matter is to get ourselves back to Outreach. And regardless of whether or not we work it out, we'd be violating our contract with the Magistracy by leaving now—not to mention that the backlog of operating expenses alone would bury us in debt." *Again,* Marcus thought, but didn't have to say aloud.

Ki-Lynn let the silence drag out a moment. "Do we have any options?"

Meaning what does Shervanis want from us? They'd circled around to one side of the palace now, coming up on a grove of citrus trees whose aroma of tangy fruit wafted toward them on the warm breeze. Marcus lifted his right hand to shade his eyes from the late afternoon sun and watched as slaves searched the whip-like grass under the trees for fallen fruit. Turbaned guards carrying scimitars and a few automatic rifles covered them, and a 40-ton dilapidated *Clint* stood high-guard over the entire grove.

"He mentioned a neighboring oyabun, Rashier—the one who offered that pitiful bribe to get our attention. He described the man as a violent terrorist committing unspeakable crimes against the population of his own realm as well as others. Our host would like us to stage a humanitarian effort to rid Astrokaszy of this creature."

"Do you believe him?"

"That Rashier might be a monster?" Marcus shrugged. "Why not? That the oyabun is any better? No. He merely wants something for nothing. Can't afford to hire us, so he'll try to pressure us. I imagine he thinks to hold us hostage and force Charlie to attack his rival in exchange for our release."

Out in the grove, a slave ran up to a guard with a piece of fruit. Perhaps it was bruised or otherwise damaged, for the guard inspected it, then threw it away with a cuff at the slave and a muttered curse. The slave stood there gaping pitifully while the other guards shared a good laugh. *I hate this place,* Marcus thought. As if reading his mind, the *Clint* twisted its upper torso just far enough to bring the small party into the forward arc of its weapons. Marcus felt his hands itch for his own 'Mech controls so that he could blow the arrogant Shervanis guard into scrap metal.

"He will try to coerce you only so long," Ki said as they continued on. "If you do not agree soon, he will resort to threats."

"You seem to know a lot about these people," Marcus said, fishing. Ki was usually close-mouthed about her past, but now that it impinged on business he wanted to know what her sources were.

"The Dragon once had to deal with similar warriors," she said, and Marcus knew *the Dragon* referred to the Combine as a whole and the Coordinator as its worldly manifestation. "They were a proud and fanatical people."

Understanding dawned like a light switch being thrown. "The Arkab Legions. Of course." Marcus remembered hearing about them in various DCMS briefings, though he'd never met any. The Arkab Legions were descendants of Moslems who'd left Terra to colonize desert-like worlds in the Draconis Combine. Arkab was an Oriental bastardization of the word "Arab." "You see a lot of similarity?"

"Some," Ki said. "This world is more barbaric and primitive, but the people seem to share some of the same protocols. Foremost among those is that a person in power is entitled to tribute from the weaker. After that, they may deal as equals, but if you happen to start in debt . . ." She shrugged, trailing off.

Marcus understood. Starting in debt was a loss of more than money or face, it meant a loss of psychological advantage that was hard to regain. "So the question is, can our host get around the legalities by claiming personal rights to us and our equipment?"

Ki-Lynn stopped walking and stared into her commander's eyes. "You ask the wrong question, Marcus. It should not be, if he can, but *when* he *will*? And that is as soon as he sees no further chance of obtaining your assistance through easier means."

From an upper-floor balcony, two men looked down on the mercenary commander and his communications officer as they rounded a corner toward the rear of the palace. Both men held cups filled with deep purple wine that had been served chilled but was rapidly warming.

Demi-Precentor Cameron St. Jamais watched his companion carefully. "You are sure, Arch Vizier? Caliph Shervanis will deliver them into my hands with their 'Mechs?"

The dark-skinned man ran a large hand back over his smooth-shaven pate. "You can see that we already have their leader and four of his MechWarriors as our"—he smiled—"guests."

St. Jamais waved that aside imperiously. "But the machines. They are worth millions of C-bills each, and that is where the Angels can best be hurt. They can refill empty cockpits with new warriors. Perhaps from another caliphate."

"We had hoped they would parade their 'Mechs into the

city, which would get them away from their DropShip. Caliph Shervanis is now attempting to convince them to bring the machines out under the ruse of a mission."

The demi-Precentor stared at Ji-Drohmien over the rim of his cup as he took a healthy drink of the sweet cool wine to hide his anger. "Do not ever consider me a fool," he said, keeping his voice low and even. "Shervanis hopes to pressure the mercenaries into attacking Caliph Rashier or possibly Caliph Zander."

Ji-Drohmien's smile was wide and full of strong white teeth. "You promised us the machines. What does it matter if we put them to use before or after we acquire them?"

"It pushes back my time table. I'm not sure how much GioAvanti knows, but if he and his people are here, then the Magistracy Armed Forces might not be far behind. I showed you the dispatches. Emma Centrella is up to something, playing with JumpShip schedules and shuffling her troops. The Angels must be dealt with and my forces removed from Astrokaszy before MAF JumpShips begin arriving." Not for the first time St. Jamais cursed the loss of demi-Precentor Nicholas. She had been an important cog in his intelligence machine, and now he felt as if he was stumbling about half-blind. "Do you have any good news to report?"

"The commander, this GioAvanti, he is disturbed by the news that his force is under a seizure edict."

St. Jamais nodded. It was just as he knew it would be. "A ploy that will only work for as long as we can keep the Angels isolated. But if we deny them use of the HPG facility for too long, they will grow suspicious. Malachye-*pasha* had better act fast."

"Do not worry, my friend. His Highness has kept every promise so far, and will deliver on this one as well. You will have the mercenaries and we shall have their machines."

St. Jamais spun on his heel, the cape of his Word of Blake uniform flaring out behind him as he passed through the open balcony doors. "Soon, Ji-Drohmien," he said over his shoulder. "Just make it soon."

=== 24 ===

Grand Pavilion, Palatial Estates
City of Shervanis, Shervanis Caliphate
Astrokaszy
The Periphery
28 June 3058

"**N**ot quite the place for a private meeting," Jericho
Ryan half-yelled.

The music thrilled around them, the deep rolling bass of
a dozen drums underscoring the higher-pitched crash of
cymbals and tambourines. It washed through the high-
vaulted pavilion in waves, sensual and wild. Dark-
skinned dancing girls moved about the floor with erotic
abandon, hips gyrating and arms and legs trailing long
ribbons of colorful silk that swirled and snapped behind
them. Others moved about bearing huge platters of
steaming food and ice-cooled fruit or large jars of wine
that they would slosh into any proffered glass. The scent
of cooked meat and the musky fusion of perfume,
incense, and sweat hung over the room.

Thomas Faber skewered a hunk of charred flesh from
the tray of a passing servant and added it to the growing
pile on his plate. "Maybe not private, but it's well
catered," he said, drawing a flash of annoyance from
Jericho.

"You must not have walked around much this afternoon." Jase Torgensson sipped from the pewter cup he'd
been given upon entering the ballroom. "I saw the caravan

of slaves delivering this feast. An old woman dropped a basket of oranges." His soft voice carried only far enough to reach the rest of the group. "They beat her to death."

Faber looked at the orange slices balanced on his plate and suddenly stopped chewing and spit out the fruit. "Sorry," he said, looking embarrassed.

Marcus paused to let the awkwardness of the moment pass before speaking. "Find anything else out, Jase?" His voice was dead and flat, about the way he'd felt since his second meeting with Shervanis. He kept a smile painted on his face for the benefit of their host, who now and then glanced over as if to reassure himself that the Angels were still present. Catching the Caliph's eye, Marcus raised his glass in a silent toast. "Serpent," Marcus muttered into his glass as he forced himself to take a swallow.

"My watchdog scares away anyone who might talk with me," Jase said, referring to the guard assigned to follow him around. "Hard to make friends. But I did get in touch with a Word of Blake acolyte. He happily informed me that ComStar no longer maintains the facility here and that it was Shervanis who invited in the Blakists. I asked about sending out some priority messages t'Outreach, but all I got was a run-around. Apparently I have to speak with the demi-Precentor—who was unavailable." He shook his head. "Seems like they're trying to keep us incommunicado. Can't say for sure that it's Shervanis, but I'll know before tomorrow is over."

Ki-Lynn's voice was soft, but she could still be heard over the commotion of music and revelry all around them. "I managed to speak with Arch Vizier Ji-Drohmien after our talk, Marcus. As your comm officer, I was allowed limited access to Malachye-*pasha's* communication room." Marcus knew it went without saying that she'd been well-guarded the whole time and her communications monitored.

"I spoke to the *Heaven Sent,* and they've received only a single communiqué from Charlene. The *Head of a Pin* acquired visual on some BattleMechs operating in the Shaharazad south and west of here. Older machines. Poor repair."

That meant those couldn't be the Hegemony raiders.

And if the *Pinhead* had spotted any newer 'Mechs in the city of Shervanis, Ki would have mentioned it. Marcus lowered his voice as the music began to fade. "Tomorrow the *Heaven Sent* will report an ammunition explosion in the 'Mech bay." He saw the look of surprise on all but Ki-Lynn's face. "It's something I arranged before we left the ship, just in case. It should be enough for Shervanis to let us return to the DropShip. We'll be under heavy guard, that we can count on. Our host won't want us lifting off without paying a tribute of some type, but I have no intention of playing into his greedy hands." He grimaced under the amused stares of Faber and Jericho. "All right— greedy hand. Jase, you've got until mid-afternoon tomorrow to find out what you can."

"Got it."

"They'll be wanting to keep us away from our 'Mechs, but a tech will be sitting in each one and the machines'll be in maintenance mode. Not much they can do but move the arms, but from our guards' standpoint it should be intimidating enough."

There were nods all around. Then Jericho frowned and tipped her head toward the main floor of the pavilion. "What's going on out there?"

The music had died to just the low rumbling of drums as the dancing girls escorted the guests off to one side, creating a large open circle in the center of the room. Two of the caliph's men entered the open area, both wearing only flaring black trousers and each carrying two scimitar-style blades in one hand. The men were large and well-muscled, one with dark olive skin and the other black as polished ebony. The olive-skinned man wore his hair cropped close to the scalp and his upper chest was tattooed with a large flaming sword. The black warrior wore his hair long and plaited, almost like a horse with a braided mane.

"Bloodsport," Ki-Lynn whispered.

Bloodsport. Marcus watched with morbid fascination as the two warriors saluted the caliph, each touching his free hand to his chest and then his forehead. Then they turned to each other and transferred one of the blades they carried to the other hand as they struck classic defensive

poses. Marcus knew bloodsport had once been a form of
entertainment in the Draconis Combine, and he'd heard
that it was still practiced in some areas. But to watch
these two face off with such casual disregard for what
they were about to enact sent chills up his spine.

Caliph Shervanis rose from his pillows, holding his
arms up for attention. The drummers quieted down, so as
not to compete with their master. "This day a group of
warriors came to Astrokaszy and courteously paid their
respects to me before others. Now, I return that gift with a
demonstration of the prowess of two of our warriors." He
reached down with his good hand and helped a dancing
girl to her feet, both her hands held high to show a beautifully jeweled dagger. "To the winner," he proclaimed.

Marcus thought the caliph might be referring to more
than just the jeweled blade. And the noticeable tightening
around the dancer's eyes told him he wasn't the only one
who thought so.

As the caliph sat down, the drums rose in a crescendo
that was capped with a loud crash of cymbals. As if
transformed, the two big men moved toward each other,
masks of hate suddenly contorting their faces as the
blades whirled in front of and around their bodies in an
incredible display of technique. They met with a ringing
of steel against steel as each made and quickly deflected a
good dozen slashing strokes from the other. It seemed as
if it could go on forever in an endless chain of slash and
parry when the olive-skinned warrior suddenly kicked the
other man in the chest hard enough to send him stumbling
backward a good three meters.

But the ebony warrior rose smoothly to his feet, and they
were at each other again. Now it was the olive-skinned man
who went tumbling away, this time from a kick to his
shoulder that was also beginning to leak blood from a cut.

The ebony-skinned man tossed his head back to flip the
long braids back over his shoulders and charged in. Again
the clanging of steel on steel. Each man tried to kick the
other way, and both pulled back under a sudden flurry of
whirling blades. Then the olive-skinned man tried to press
in past the other's defenses, but was just as suddenly sent
reeling with his left foot neatly severed at the ankle and a

second cut opening a red line across the tattoo on his chest. Even with the fight clearly over, the ebony-skinned warrior offered no respite and drove in to impale his opponent on the end of his left-hand blade.

The sound of the drums and crashing cymbals echoed hollowly in Marcus' ears as the wet choking of the dying man reached him. Had Shervanis offered this display in some attempt to win him over, he wondered. Was Marcus supposed to be impressed by how little the caliph valued the lives of those he ruled? That thought made him remember Charlene's accusations. He'd never sacrifice any of his people in some kind of game or amusement, but he hadn't been able to shake his doubts ever since she'd confronted him.

The drums had died away under the cheers and shouts of the dark-skinned Astrokaszy natives. Standing up, Caliph Shervanis shouted over the din toward the Angels. "Commander GioAvanti, what did you think?"

For a moment it occurred to Marcus to pretend not to hear, but he changed his mind as the dark-skinned warriors nearest the Angels turned expectantly toward him. He took a healthy drink from his cup, buying himself a few extra seconds as he swallowed the sweet wine. "A remarkable display of skill," he finally called back to the Caliph. "A fearsome warrior."

Caliph Shervanis smiled, his lips skinning back from his teeth in an almost feral grin. "Fearsome. A fine quality in a warrior. But the greatest quality? What do you say, Commander GioAvanti? What is the greatest quality to be found in a warrior?" His spoke the words in an obvious challenge, then calmly picked up the stem of a large hookah and sucked in a lungful of whatever drug they smoked here on Astrokaszy.

Marcus stood staring at the caliph for a moment before replying. He knew he must choose his words carefully. "A belief in his cause," he said. "A righteousness that always leads to victory, even when the battle is lost."

Shervanis exhaled noisily. "An interesting thought, Commander. And most appropriate coming from a man who commands a military unit known as the Angels." He sat up straighter. "I would like to test this. You will fight

Kabahstalla," he said, nodding toward the black man, who had remained in the circle formed by the crowd of spectators. "No," he corrected himself, "one of your warriors should fight him. A test of belief in his or her commander."

Marcus stared at the caliph, eyes wide with astonishment. Shervanis expected him to let one of his warriors fight against that—he reached for the words—whirling dervish? It would only be a death sentence. "Caliph—" Marcus began what he hoped was a polite refusal, but was cut off.

"That one," Shervanis said, pointing his stump of a right hand at Faber. "He looks like a good match."

Think fast, Marcus chided himself. *Stall.* Then he thought of how a superior Clan force would bid away some of its strength for the honor of being allowed to participate in combat. Could Marcus work a similar deal here? *Try to bargain.*

"He might be," he said, then paused to let the Caliph recognize the reluctance in his voice. He felt the warning pressure of Ki-Lynn nudging him in the back. "Thomas is a fine warrior. I suppose it would depend on the terms."

"Terms?" The black, soulless eyes of the caliph narrowed, and his tone was sharp. "What do you mean by terms, Commander?"

Thomas Faber rose from the cushions to stand next to Marcus, his large frame dwarfing his commander's. Before Marcus could speak, Thomas answered for him.

"Terms are always the most important question, Caliph Shervanis," he said, shrugging as though it was obvious. "I am a mercenary. What am I fighting for?"

Thomas Faber had watched the bloodsport event with the critical eye of a professional warrior. As a young man he'd participated in such contests back in the Draconis Combine. His size and temperament made him a natural for it, even when still in his teens. Born to the lower class, Thomas had viewed it as his one way off the world of Bjarred. He'd worked hard, risen up through the ranks until finally attracting the direct notice of the planetary governor, who asked Thomas to fight for him against champions of neighboring worlds. In return the man promised Thomas admission to a minor MechWarrior academy; all Thomas had to do was survive one year of fighting.

In the years since, the big man had tried to forget that year of fighting and blood, though it still showed in his slugging-match style of BattleMech combat. Now the memories boiled to the surface, and Thomas hated Caliph Malachye Shervanis for bringing it all back.

He had recognized immediately that the dark-skinned man held the advantage in the first fight. His opponent had feared him. He'd also seen the naked hunger for the dancing girl in the black man's eyes, almost like a trained dog being offered a slab of meat as a reward for work. Through the entire contest Thomas studied each move by both combatants, muscles tense when he spotted a slight opening the olive-skinned man could have exploited but didn't. Then it was over, and Thomas ground his teeth together as the final bubbling gasp of the dying man reached him.

When Caliph Shervanis suggested a match against one of the Angels, Thomas knew he would be the one. The women would be exempt here, prizes only, and Thomas was not about to let either Jase or Marcus step into the arena against this Kabahstalla. So as Shervanis asked about the terms, Thomas rose to his feet to bargain for himself.

His words seemed to amuse Shervanis, who laughed full and rich for several seconds before answering. "A mercenary indeed," the caliph said, rubbing his good hand against his side. "What would you have?" he finally asked.

The question echoed in the recesses of Thomas' mind. *What would you have?* The very question posed him by the governor back on Bjarred so long ago. Those words had set him on the path to becoming a MechWarrior, a station far above what he could otherwise have hoped to achieve. Thomas doubted he could push Shervanis quite that far. He pointed to the dancing girl standing at the edge of the dais and still holding the prize dagger across unturned palms. "Her. You would release her completely to my"—he paused—"care." He grinned wolfishly, trying to look every ounce the crude warrior.

Thomas had never been heavily trained in the warrior arts of sensing out another person's *wa* or *ki* or whatever they called it, but he could still feel the sudden hostility in Jericho Ryan and the astonishment in both Jase and Marcus. *I know what I'm doing,* he wanted to tell them as Shervanis' feral grin grew even wider. "Done," the caliph said, slapping the silver cap on his right arm into the palm of his left hand.

"Then we shall need two neural whips," Thomas said simply, catching Shervanis just as he settled back against the cushions again.

"Two *what?*" the caliph asked, decidedly less delighted than he'd been a moment before.

"Neural whips. They are the personal weapon of choice in the Draconis Combine," Thomas lied. Neural whips were a sadistic weapon, causing extreme pain with the disruption of the neural system wherever it struck an opponent. They were banned throughout most of the Inner Sphere, though the Combine still allowed their use in certain agencies.

Thomas looked surprised by the Caliph's sudden silence. "Forgive my presumption, Highness, but I thought it was custom for the challenged to choose the weapon. I'm afraid all I know is the whip and regular hand-to-hand." *And there would be no way you could make me pick up a blade again, not unless it was to slice your head off your shoulders.*

Thomas kept his eyes locked to the caliph's. Again, he wished he'd been trained more as Ki-Lynn had, able to sense another's internal energies and overwhelm them with your own. Instead he could only wait calmly for the caliph's decision.

"Of course, we would not expect you to demand a weapon with which Kabahstalla had no prior experience," Shervanis finally said, his dark eyes reminding Thomas of a hooded cobra's. "I thought you two could engage without weapons. A match of skill and—how did your commander put it?—belief."

Thomas exhaled slowly, moving forward. *That removes the blades. Now all I have to do is win.*

The body of the olive-skinned man was dragged from the cleared space, trailing a bloody smear across the floor. Thomas stepped from between a pair of guests and into the circle, removing his shirt. He kicked his shoes off and to one side, throwing his socks after them. Kabahstalla handed his blades to a nearby guard, then waited calmly for his opponent to ready himself. A few stretches to loosen the muscles, and Thomas nodded toward the other dark-skinned man.

While Kabahstalla saluted Shervanis, Thomas bowed in Kurita fashion to the caliph and then slightly deeper to Marcus. Perhaps it wasn't quite proper, but it demonstrated where his loyalties lay and that was enough for him. The drums rolled up to a violent level, and with the crash of cymbals both men moved toward each other.

Kabahstalla came in fast and aggressive, trying to overwhelm Thomas in a style similar to his swordplay. *Mistake,* Thomas thought. He crouched to keep his center of mass low, bare feet planted wide apart and arms held ready before him. As he expected, Kabahstalla tried for a kick at his conveniently lowered head. Thomas ducked under the kick, sweeping back with his right leg to connect with the other man's ankle. Kabahstalla fell awkwardly, and Thomas sprang back to a defensive posture. *Keep him mad and I own the fight.*

The two men circled each other, Kabahstalla favoring his right ankle only slightly. Wary now, the black man did not attempt another reckless charge. He struck out with hands and feet, probing Faber's defenses. For his part Thomas concentrated on blocks and dodges, all the while smiling at Kabahstalla as if the other man's attacks meant nothing. The black man stepped up his attacks, and Thomas parried each successive strike a bit closer, drawing in his opponent under the guise of wearing down.

And, now! Thomas left himself open for another blow to the head, then ducked under the punch and struck out open-palmed to stiff-arm Kabahstalla in the lower chest. He felt at least two ribs break under the blow as

Kabahstalla's feet left the floor and the man flew back two meters to land hard on his back.

The fight's over. He can't continue. Thomas heard the voices in his head as he watched Kabahstalla try to roll back onto his feet. But the memory of Kabahstalla's last opponent was still too fresh in Thomas' mind. As the black man managed to get his right leg underneath him, Thomas sprang forward in a low sidekick that caught him in the knee and folded Kabahstalla's leg unnaturally inward. *That ends your fighting days,* Thomas thought as a shriek of agony escaped the other man's lips. He snapped another kick alongside Kabahstalla's head, rendering him mercifully unconscious.

With a deliberate slowness, Thomas walked over to the caliph's dais. Many guests moved out of his way, giving him a clear path, but others among the sharp-eyed natives glared at him with a prideful malevolence. Too late he wished he'd waited for his opponent's capitulation, and he cursed himself for letting anger rule those last few strikes.

At the edge of the dais, Thomas accepted the jeweled dagger, which he thrust into his belt. Then he took the dancer's hand and helped her down to the floor. She stared at him with wide, soft brown eyes. Her eyes were beautiful, but also filled with fear of what was essentially her new owner.

Thomas knew that Shervanis would be studying him, trying to decide whether or not to take offense. To let the man see the anger still smoldering behind his own eyes could only work against the Angels. So he kept his gaze firmly locked on that of his "prize" and willed himself to not even glance at the Caliph.

"My thanks, Malachye-*pasha*." He tried to smile in a close approximation of lust, hating himself for the intensified fear in the young woman's eyes. "A truly lovely reward."

=== 25 ===

A small unit such as the Angels survived by relying on the strengths of each member. As much as Thomas Faber's calm acceptance of the challenge had first surprised Marcus, he quickly recognized the big man's control over the situation and backed off. He would trust Thomas to know what he was doing, even if it looked as if he was about to throw his life away in an effort to save the others.

As Karrskhov had.

The thought that he could leave such a choice up to a single member of his command startled Marcus. Charlene's accusations came back to haunt him; did he really care about his people? *Yes. Dammit, yes.* He didn't take unnecessary risks with either their lives or equipment, and he would never sacrifice the life of another Angel, no matter how many others it would save. *Unless the life was my own,* he thought. *Maybe I do distance myself from the others, Charlie, but that doesn't mean I don't care.* He watched Thomas thread his way through the guests. *And I respect them enough to honor their personal decisions.*

Still, Marcus remained on edge throughout the fight, teeth clenched so tight his jaw hurt. He shrugged

Jericho's hand off his shoulder, even though he realized she was only trying to offer some silent support. He didn't rejoice or even relax when Faber won, either. *Victories must be defended,* he reminded himself. And Shervanis' darkening mood warned Marcus that the defense had better come quickly.

"A truly lovely reward," Faber said, leering at the dancing girl.

Marcus knew Thomas could be boisterous and rash one minute, taciturn the next. Not mood swings, but as if saving up strength in the lulls between his more energetic moments. But he had never seen Thomas act any way but respectful to women, and so easily recognized the sudden rakish attitude for the act it was. From Jericho's reactions, though, Marcus knew she'd bought into the routine and maybe that meant Shervanis had as well.

"Your Excellency," Marcus called out loudly, drawing Shervanis' attention away from Thomas. "I appreciate your instruction. You have proven me completely in error."

The caliph frowned, a guarded expression in his black eyes. "How is that, Commander GioAvanti? Your mercenary defeated one of my best warriors."

And quite adroitly too. Marcus glanced at his man. Thomas was moving back to rejoin the other Angels, his *prize* in tow. *This would be easier if you hadn't crippled Kaba-whatever-his-name-was,* he thought, but found himself unable to hold it against Thomas. He'd seen something in the big man's eyes that said he'd acted in the only way he knew how.

"As you just said, Caliph Shervanis, Thomas is a mercenary. He wasn't fighting for me or the Angels." He tried to look disgusted. "He fought for *her.*" *And there's your way to save face, Caliph. Unless you're ready to slaughter us now and take your chances with the Angels' vengeance.*

"Are you saying that lust defeated Kabahstalla's belief in me?" The pasha sounded dubious, and still dangerous.

Careful, Marcus. "Surrounded by all this?" he said, gesturing around at the revelers and entertainers who had quieted to a hush. "How could anyone deny the power of desire, Malachye-*pasha*. You have proven its lure to all of us tonight." Marcus smiled, as if half-joking but still partly serious. Then he sobered. "To be fair to Kabah-stalla"—he stumbled over the name—"Thomas also loves to fight. It's a toss-up which he likes to do more," he finished, eyeing the dancer in an exaggerated manner.

Caliph Shervanis smiled wide and full, then erupted into laughter. The tension in the room eased as others also began to laugh or merely turned back to earlier conversations. At a signal from Shervanis, the musicians struck up a spirited tune that soon had the dancing girls once more moving about the hall in a swirl of flesh and multicolored ribbons. The caliph raised a large cup filled with the purple wine in salute to the Angels, which Marcus returned before shifting his attention back to his comrades.

"Thank you, Marc." Thomas rejoined the small group, still leading the dancer by the hand. She looked defeated, having moved past fear to simple resignation. Jericho glanced from Marcus to Thomas, as if she couldn't decide who to take issue with first.

"So what do we do with her?" Marcus asked, nodding toward the scantily clad woman.

"She's away from him," Thomas said with a shrug, "and that's the important thing." He gave the young woman an apologetic smile. "I'll get you off Astrokaszy," he promised, keeping his voice low. "Then you're free to go." Turning to Jericho, Thomas smiled. "She could get employment in the Magistracy, couldn't she? Maybe as a dancer?"

A look of surprise mixed with relief washed over Jericho's face. "Yes. Yes, of course."

Ki-Lynn raised her own cup to her lips, using it to hide her warning. "Do not look." She paused, making sure everyone had time to steel themselves against the natural compulsion to glance around, "The Caliph is heading this way."

Jase was the fastest, changing the subject by loudly speculating on where the Angels should start looking for the rumored Star League facility. Marcus started to make suggestions when the caliph interrupted. "Commander, I do not intrude?"

"Of course not, Caliph Shervanis." Marcus smiled thinly, as if nervous at the caliph's attention. Not a difficult feat. "The Angels would always make time for you." Marcus looked past the older man at the two hulking guards who had followed him from the dais and two more dancers Shervanis had apparently commandeered in route.

"Excellent," the caliph said. The man swayed a bit on his feet, his indulgence in wine and hashish revealed in his posture as well as on his breath. "Commander, I wish to compliment you again on your warriors. I may have been too surprised at Kabahstalla's defeat to properly congratulate MechWarrior Faber."

What are you up to, Shervanis? Marcus kept a grin plastered on his face, but inwardly his mind raced to second-guess the wily pasha. Half-drugged or not, Shervanis would be a man best not taken lightly. "His Excellency is most kind."

"Actually, I have been most delinquent in my manners as a host." Shervanis waved the two dancers forward. "I suddenly realized I had not thought to arrange"—he smiled, teeth large and wolfish as he gestured to the dancing girls—"pleasant companionship."

"Ah, Caliph Shervanis," Marcus paused, at a loss. What had Ki told him earlier? To refuse a direct gift would be taken as a personal insult? But if the caliph insisted on providing companions it would separate the Angels from each other. "Most generous," he said, stalling. He wished he could consult with Ki-Lynn, but there didn't seem to be any way. Marcus would have to stumble along on his own. "Too generous, in fact. I could not accept."

Shervanis' dark eyes narrowed. "And why not?" His voice was hard and dangerously cold.

"Well," Marcus began, but let it trail off. *Think.* "If I were to accept—"

Marcus hadn't really thought it all out, but was relying on bluff to get him through. Fortunately, Jericho stepped in smoothly. "If he were to accept," she said, moving forward and taking Marcus by the arm, "he would find himself in very hot water. Might make even the Astrokaszy deserts look inviting." Her voice was at once playful and disarming.

The caliph blinked his surprise. "I didn't know. That is, Arch Vizier Ji-Drohmien never told me you two were . . ." He trailed off, glancing from one to the other.

"Involved?" Marcus finished for him, hoping the pasha's apparent surprise wasn't mirrored on his own face. He was all too conscious of Jericho's touch, a warm flush spreading up his arm. He swallowed hard, but made an effort not to squirm under her grip. "Well, the arch vizier never asked. And we do not flaunt the relationship in public. You understand, of course." He lowered his voice, as if speaking only to the caliph. "As commander of a unit, I have to remain," he paused as if searching for the word, "morally superior. No fraternization during a mission."

He felt the stiffness in Jericho's grip, but she quickly covered her discomfort to continue the charade. "Typical," she complained with a smile. "All work and no play." She leaned in to nip Marcus playfully on the ear and then retreated back to her earlier position.

Shervanis looked from one to the other, his face once more masked in politic neutrality. "Indeed," he muttered. "And the other two?"

"The same," Jase Torgensson was quick to respond, all smiles and happiness as he glanced at Ki-Lynn, then back at the pasha. "We don't suffer the command stigma, but there is a little matter of Combine etiquette while in public."

"Faber is one of the few eligible bachelors in the Angels," Marcus lied. "But he has found himself a diversion."

Shervanis let nothing show, either in his face or tone. "Of course," he said simply, then waved off the two dancers, who melted quickly into the background as they returned to their duties. "Well, then, enjoy yourselves, my guests. Sample what Shervanis can offer you. And, Commander, tomorrow I hope to discuss again what your Angels can offer me."

"At your disposal, Caliph Shervanis," Marcus said as

the pasha turned back toward his dais. He waited in silence until he could be sure that the trailing guards couldn't overhear them even without the music. Faber sat the dancing girl off to one side, where she could be excluded from the conversation.

"I don't think he bought it," Marcus finally said. "But he won't push the matter. I'm sure he's got other plans for us." He chewed his lower lip and thought. "I don't know about anyone else, but I've had enough *fun* for one night. We'll start leaving here; two by two, over the next hour. We keep to the new story, too, so we stay in pairs. That means one person can sleep while the other keeps watch." He swallowed hard. "Jericho—"

She interrupted him with a teasing smile. "It's you and me. I can handle it, Marcus." She paused, head cocked to one side as if deliberating. When she continued, her voice was playful. "I made the bed, now I have to sleep in it?"

Jase hid his smile diplomatically behind a raised hand, and though Ki-Lynn kept strict control of her expression Marcus read the amusement in her eyes. Thomas didn't even try to hide his. "Thomas," Marcus said with a trace of annoyance, "you're out of here in ten minutes. Then Ki and Jase."

"I have a better idea, Marc." Jase glanced around the room. "This is the first time today I haven't had a watchdog. I want to hang around a little longer, maybe make a few friends." He glanced at Ki-Lynn. "And no offense, but—"

"But you work better alone," Marcus finished. "Okay, Jericho and I in thirty minutes. Ki, you head to your room in about fifty. Make a small show of saying goodnight to Jase." Ki nodded, which was enough of a guarantee for Marcus. "Jase, don't stay here much longer. This trip into Shervanis was worth a shot, but I don't like the look of things.

"We play it safe until tomorrow, then we get out."

Lounging against the wall not ten meters from the Angels, Cameron St. Jamais watched as the mercenaries rebuffed Malachye Shervanis and then talked briefly among themselves. He wore a sand-colored caftan, his dark skin making him blend in easily among the Astrokaszy natives.

He stroked the shoulder of a courtesan provided him earlier by Arch Vizier Ji-Drohmien, the woman's unruly hair and unnaturally light skin reminding him of Demona Aziz. The music might have diverted his attention toward baser thoughts, but his Word of Blake training gave him clarity of mind as he caressed the young woman's shoulder and continued to spy on the Angles.

St. Jamais watched as first Thomas Faber left with the dancing girl, and then not thirty minutes later Marcus GioAvanti followed with his Canopian bitch. *Sleep well, Commander,* St. Jamais thought, bidding the mercenary commander a silent good-night. *Tomorrow you and your Angels die.*

26

Palatial Estates
City of Shervanis, Shervanis Caliphate
Astrokaszy
The Periphery
29 June 3058

Whoever they were, they took few chances.

Marcus heard the scuffle in the hall, where the guards assigned to him and Jericho had apparently been overcome. Grabbing weapons for them both, he woke her and they took up station behind an overturned table that might serve as a shield against anyone coming through the door. Four shadowy figures entered, dressed in the usual flowing caftans but dark-colored instead of white or tan. Two of them carried submachine guns and moved immediately for the window. The third used a needler rifle to loosely cover Marcus and Jericho. The last figure stopped to fasten the doors behind them, but carried only a pair of falchion-style swords, curved and flaring out near the end in a wide tip.

Assassins don't stop to lock the door behind them, Marcus thought, holding Jericho in check while the figures busied themselves about the room.

The man with the swords approached. Only his eyes were visible above the cloth masking the lower half of his face, and they showed his surprise at finding the two of them together. Carrying both swords in his left hand, he gestured to them with his right. "Come. We get you out of here now." His accent was thick and he spoke much too fast. It took a few repeats before Marcus understood what he was trying to say.

One of the men used a special cutter to get through the room's single large window, which Marcus had noticed on earlier inspection couldn't be opened or easily smashed. Ropes gave them access to the ground, and then the six of them were sprinting for the walls, where other men with ropes waited to move them along faster. Marcus' concern at that time had been for the other three members of his unit, but the swords-carrier promised that other teams were getting the others safely away.

Obviously in charge of the team sent to retrieve Marcus, the swords-carrier introduced himself on the run as Nihail Sallahan and explained that he and his men were from Caliph Rashier, sent to rescue the Angels from the evil and unholy Shervanis. As widespread machine gun fire and several explosions ripped through the night stillness, he also assured them that it was all part of the diversion meant to cover their escape. If all went well, he would get the Angels to the *Heaven Sent,* which could carry them all to safety.

It wasn't until the small team reached the outskirts of Shervanis that the holes began appearing in their plan.

The five teams rendezvoused inside a half-collapsed and abandoned adobe building. Several horses and a single, battered jeep stood outside, all a part of the escape plan. Sallahan's group was second to arrive, preceded by the team sent after Jase Torgensson.

Marcus stopped Nihail when he tried to explain that Jase wasn't in his room. "He wouldn't have been,"

Marcus said. "He'd be with Ki-Lynn." That involved a little more explanation, but Nihail seemed satisfied and lapsed into a determined silence.

The team sent after Jericho came in next, missing two of their four people. "Ran into patrol of the *jinn*," Nihail said. When Marcus asked, he learned that *jinn* was apparently the Arabic term for minions of the devil, al Shaitan. *Shervanis doesn't get good press in the Rashier Caliphate,* he thought, and settled down to wait for the other Angels.

A fourth team finally brought in Ki-Lynn Tanaga at gun point.

She bowed formally to Marcus. Not that he would ever require it, but he knew that it mattered to her. "*Gomen nasi,* Commander. Jase had not yet returned from the feast. I could not convince them to wait while I retrieved him."

Marcus looked over to where the four-man team talked in hurried Arabic to Nihail. One man held a compress to his face, and when he removed it to speak Marcus could tell by the swelling and angle that his nose was broken. A dark glance toward Ki-Lynn told him what his comm officer wouldn't. "S'all right, Ki. They had a separate team for each of us because of our scattered locations. Just bad luck is all." He doubted that Ki took much comfort from the words. Inwardly he railed against the fates and tried to come up with some plan to return and rescue Jase.

He completely forgot to worry about Thomas, until a lone warrior rushed in to speak with Nihail. The team leader dragged the man over to Marcus. Deciding that Thomas, too, was now a prisoner of Shervanis, Marcus thought he'd already imagined the worst. So when Nihail said, "Your ship is attacked," without preamble, it hit him like a PPC blast. "Many machines." The other man said something else and Nihail translated. "Unable to take off. Most of crew escaped in flying vehicles and are safe. Second ship down in foothills to south."

The information all swam about in Marcus' head until one statement surfaced above the others. *Second ship? No!* Marcus shouldered his way past Nihail and several other Astrokaszy warriors and rushed outside. From the roof of the jeep, he jumped up onto the small adobe structure and stared off to the southwest.

The telltale flare of the *Fortress* Class DropShip burned bright and steady several kilometers off. It held position at what Marcus estimated at some three hundred meters off the ground, while every few seconds he caught the quick flash of light from a hull-mounted PPC as it stabbed down at the desert below. Marcus felt frustration welling up inside him. Charlene wasn't supposed to attack unless sent for. Or until such time she could assume him incapacitated. Even an attack on the *Heaven Sent* should have been verified by him first. Only one other possibility, in Marcus' mind, could have brought her down.

He spun on Nihail, who had climbed up with a few of his men and Jericho. "Who are they fighting?"

"They fight the cursed Shervanis. He who would enslave our world to his—"

Marcus cut him off with a wave. "Yes, but what forces? What BattleMechs? How many?"

Nihail spoke with the messenger who'd remained on the ground. "Many, he says. Several dozen. Machines with Shervanis' unholy dark sun insignia and others bearing the mark of al Zaitan's henchman—a dark and armored figure."

The Marian Hegemony raiders! "No," Marcus yelled at the skyline. "Dammit Charlene, no!" Nihail's man had said the second ship had grounded in the southern foothills, but the *Pinhead* now flew a supporting high-cover, which meant the BattleMechs were already on the ground and engaged.

"Nihail, I need that jeep and a radio. One that can broadcast in the upper bands for combat. I've got to get out there."

The dark-robed warrior shook his head. "Not possible. We fall back to second plan. Head north and make it to hidden landing area for helicopter." Marcus started to turn away, but the other man grabbed the front of his uniform and hauled him back around. "Listen to me, sahib. Caliph Rashier will help you. He is only man can help you now. I will take you to him."

Marcus swept up his left arm and broke the man's grip, face flushed warm in the cool desert night air. "Because of your caliph's help I have two people still unaccounted for in the palace. I'd go back for them except right now the ones out on the desert need me more. I'm going out there." He glanced toward the distant fighting. "Those ships hold everyone and everything that makes the Angels what we are. I will not abandon them."

Not abandon them. Marcus' last words echoed harshly in his mind. Was he more afraid of losing his people, or losing his DropShips and the equipment they contained? Whatever the truth of the matter, he was too close to things to know the answer right now. Either way, he had to get out to that battlefield.

"You serve your friends best by coming with me," Nihail said. "If your people live through the night, Caliph Rashier can help them."

"It's that *if* that worries me. I'm going out there, Nihail. Did your Caliph give you orders to shoot me if I resisted?" Marcus matched gazes with the other man until Nihail's dark eyes dropped. "Didn't think so."

Marcus walked across the flat roof, moving past the other two Astrokaszy warriors who had come up after Nihail. He caught the movement in his peripheral vision, just a fraction of a second too late to avoid the majority of force behind the blow. The rifle stock caught him just above the ear, knocking him to his knees as the blackness swirled around him in sickening waves.

The second blow brought the darkness down on him with smothering force.

27

City of Shervanis, Shervanis Caliphate
Astrokaszy
The Periphery
29 June 3058

Thomas Faber fought his own battle with consciousness as feedback through the neurohelmet he wore spiked pain deep into his brain. The *Clint*'s control sticks trembled with violent force as he waded through another single-story building, the 'Mech swaggering drunkenly from side to side. Then he broke free, leaving behind a pile of collapsed rubble to stand between him and the pursuing *Dervish*. A single long-range missile clipped him in the right shoulder, barely enough to give the medium 'Mech a shove. Amaáli, the dancing girl he'd won from Shervanis, whimpered with fright where she crouched in the tight space behind his command couch. Thomas set his teeth against the pain from the neurohelmet and coaxed the *Clint* to better speeds.

Thomas never learned exactly who the people were who'd helped them escape from the palace, except that they were from Caliph Rashier and they had weapons to back up their orders. They'd led him and the girl down a series of narrow palace corridors and straight into a small cluster of Shervanis' guards. Relieving one of the robed warriors of his Rorynex submachine gun, Thomas whisked Amaáli away and through another series of twisting passages and turns until they were far from the site and just as thoroughly lost.

Then the shouting and alarms had started to sound.

Thomas had waylaid the next guard they came across. By luck they'd somehow taken a turn that was only a short passage from a small 'Mech park holding two of Shervanis' BattleMechs. Thomas had tackled one of the guards, whose tolerance for pain was far weaker than his desire to become a martyr. After assuring Thomas that the voice-recognition program had long since ceased to function and the *Clint* could be started up with its code phrase alone, Thomas had left the man unconscious and bound.

For as long as BattleMechs had been around, there had been means to prevent their theft. Voiceprint identification and "key" code phrases had been the standard methods for decades, ever since neurohelmet technology had been refined. Before that, neurohelmets had been so fine-tuned to the individual's brain waves that no one but the regular pilot could use a particular helmet without suffering from painful feedback.

Just Thomas' luck that the *Clint*'s neurohelmet and control circuitry dated back that far and then some.

The *Clint* stumbled as a salvo of eight LRMs slammed into its rear-left torso, chewing through to the foamed-titanium bones of the machine's internal skeleton. The 'Mech dropped to its knees as Thomas used the *Clint*'s left hand to steady it against the wall of a nearby warehouse. A wave of static washed through his mind, followed by throbbing pulses behind his eyes.

He was trying to make it to the outskirts of the city. *Almost there,* he thought, wrestling the 40-ton machine back to its feet. The larger buildings of Shervanis' abandoned industrial district rose just ahead, the two- and three-story warehouses promising some protection from the trailing *Dervish* of Shervanis. A few hundred meters beyond that would be the edge of the city and freedom. *Hold it together a few more minutes, Thomas. Almost home.*

Not that he really knew what to expect once he cleared the city. His sensors had already identified a *Fortress* Class DropShip pulling back from a high-cover position near the city's edge, heading south into the badlands. It had to be the *Pinhead*, but did that mean the Angels were in retreat? The unit's BattleMechs were riding on different frequencies than he could monitor, and neither DropShip had answered him on the general bands.

I've got to get out there, Thomas thought. Get out there and into his 'Mech. With feedback from the helmet making his vision swim, he doubted he could even hit the *Dervish* except at point-blank range. Now was not the time for heroics, not when the Angels might need him. He swiveled the *Clint*'s torso and snapped off one shot with the AC/5 that was its right hand—not really trying to hit but hopefully keeping the *Dervish* from thinking him totally helpless.

As if in response, another flight of LRMs hit the *Clint*. Five missiles gouged more internal framework from his left torso, knocking out the medium laser there. Six others speared him in the center back and drilled in to tear away at the shielding to the fusion engine. Thomas kept control of the ungainly 'Mech, but the sudden spike on the 'Mech's heat scale told him he was in trouble unless he did something right away.

Thomas quickly brought the jump jets on line. The *Clint* rose into the air, venting plasma through the jump-jet exhaust ports in its rear torso and legs as Thomas angled for the city gates in the distance. Amaáli screamed, but Thomas couldn't do much about that right now. Trying to fly forty tons of metal through the air was trouble enough. Compounding the problem was the neurohelmet feedback and the fact that he wasn't used to piloting a jumping 'Mech. It wasn't even that he hoped to bring the huge battle machine down on its feet; he'd be happy just finding a way to soften the landing.

Plunging down into a two-story warehouse wasn't quite what he'd call a soft landing, but to a BattleMech it offered two separate barriers of resistance before coming into contact with unyielding ground. The roof caved in under forty tons of BattleMech belly-flopping into a pool of brick and cement.

Even though it threw him against the restraining straps hard enough to bruise, the final jarring of the *Clint* hitting solid ground was much lighter than Thomas would have expected His primary display showed black so he switched over to thermal and then magscan. *I'm in a basement.* That explained the softer landing; three floors had worked to absorb the impact, not two. Still, his damage schematic showed a shoulder actuator out in the *Clint*'s left arm and a few tons of armor shattered across its entire body. Thomas tried to get the 'Mech to its feet, but he was apparently buried under fallen rubble.

With the 'Mech lying face down, Thomas actually hung suspended over his control panel by the seat's restraining straps. He pulled the heavy neurohelmet off his head, and turned to check on his passenger. Amaáli was sobbing hysterically, obviously shaken and nursing a small cut on her chin from having been thrown against the control panel, but seemed mostly fit. He started to hit switches, damping the fusion engine as fast as he could. Separated from the pursing *Dervish* by several hundred meters and at least two buildings, he knew the *Clint* would no longer register on sensors. With the 'Mech now buried within the warehouse debris, the only thing that could give him away was the magnetic field that help contain the fusion engine at his BattleMech's heart. He couldn't help thinking that he'd landed in a perfect hiding place.

Thomas hated the idea of being out of the action, but he just couldn't see trying to reach the outer wall now. The *Dervish* would be on top of him before he could extricate himself, and the neural feedback was coming dangerously close to impairing his judgment. Maybe it would be best to lay low here for a while, then make his run when it was least expected. All that was left to do now was the thing he would find hardest.

Waiting.

Fleeing through the hills south and west of Shervanis City, Charlene Boske's demi-company of Angel 'Mechs skirted the edge of the badlands as they fought to swing around the main force of Hegemony raiders and regain the flatlands to the north. Charlene Boske, her *Phoenix Hawk* one of the faster machines, brought up the rear. She swung wide around each hill, constantly breaking away and merging with the others as she drew the pursuing raiders off first to the right and then the left.

She was buying time, though for what Charlene no longer knew. All that could save them now was a miracle, she thought as Paula Jacobs' voice bled through the background noise again, accompanied by another light wash of static.

"Repeat, I've lost Flanker Two and Three," said Paula from her *Valkyrie*. "They blew the leg clean off Kelsey's *Jenner*, but I think she punched out. Geoff is gone. That damn *Awesome* tore his *Panther* apart and then deliberately kicked in its head."

Charlene bit down on her lower lip as she listened to the report on Flanker lance. The warm, salty taste of blood started to leak into her mouth. She pivoted the *Hawk* on its right foot, spinning nearly a hundred and eighty degrees with almost reckless ease, to fire her large laser at the pursuing *Lynx*. The emerald beam of coherent light cut a molten swath across the raider 'Mech's upper chest and head. It wasn't enough to penetrate, but she knew the *Lynx* pilot would be momentarily shaken. Riding out her momentum, Charlene leaned her *Hawk* forward into a run and slid in between a pair of hills. That bought her a moment's respite. Nothing more.

Charlene and the rest of the Angels had stayed behind in the *Pinhead* while Marcus and his team went down to the surface of Astrokaszy in the *Heaven Sent*. When the other DropShip had reported unknown forces attacking the city, she'd expected some order from Marcus to support one side or the other. The Angels would either topple Shervanis if he was working with the raiders, or they would assist him and gain his favor. She'd ordered the *Pinhead* down, holding off at two kilometers until the word was given. Then came word from the *Heaven Sent* that it was under attack by a company of Hegemony raiders who'd emerged from the city. Charlene had immediately ordered Captain Stanislaus to land the *Pinhead* south of the *Heaven Sent*'s position, and then she led the other eight Angels and three MAF MechWarriors out to lend immediate assistance.

Don't kid yourself, she thought now as she worked her

way around a new hill to link back up with her unit. *You didn't think of anything but avenging Brent, and now it's cost the life of another Angel.* An image of Geoff Vanderhaven's warm smile rose unbidden from her memories, and she dismissed it with a violent shake of her head. She still had eleven lives depending on her; she could grieve later.

Charlene knew Marcus would never have committed the Angels so rashly. Even before the *Pinhead* had landed, the *Heaven Sent* reported itself airborne but with heavy damage to thrusters—they hoped to clear the area, but couldn't be sure. The raider company had moved off to meet the *Pinhead,* and another six raider 'Mechs had emerged from the city to support them. Charlene had kept half her twelve 'Mechs at the edge of the hills, supported by the *Pinhead* now flying low-altitude cover, sniping at the approaching raiders. Then Paula—in command of the other six BattleMechs left her by Marcus—reported another company of raiders pushing in from the north. Paula had been trying to get in behind the raiders, and now found herself being viciously shoved back.

Charlene's vengeance-inspired offensive had turned into a game of strike-and-fade among the low hills southwest of Shervanis. The raiders pressed them from two sides, and then three. They controlled the higher ground and methodically herded the Angels in front of them. Charlene managed to keep the Angels from being forced into the broken rock and ravines of the badlands, worried about such treacherous and unfamiliar terrain, but was unable to otherwise regain the initiative. She lacked Marcus' intuitive grasp of the battlefield. There were too many factors to juggle.

The absence of raider aerospace support, for one. It bothered her, but she wasn't about to complain. Ensign Keppler, the MAF fighter pilot who'd accompanied them to Astrokaszy, was flying reconnaissance in his *Sparrowhawk* and occasionally dipped in for a strafing run, but it wasn't enough to turn the tide of battle. That much Charlene knew. She also knew she'd better do something—and now.

She opened the commline. "Flanker Lance, fall back at

top speed. Regroup." She gave the order even knowing it could be a problem. Flanker Lance was a bit more north of the badlands than Charlene's force. If they couldn't break away and regroup fast enough, they'd get caught between the raiders engaging them and the ones following Charlene. "We'll hold the door open as long as we can," she promised.

"Hawk One, please repeat." The radio stripped most of the emotion from Paula's voice, but Charlene could still hear the confusion. "I said that Kelsey might have punched out. Repeat, Kelsey still alive. I need support to push the raiders back and extract her." Toward the last, Paula's voice edged into high-pitched tones that worried Charlene. The one thing she didn't need was for her flanking commander to get rattled. *But I can't make her understand because normally I wouldn't agree with leaving an Angel behind either. Damn you, Marcus. Damn you for not being here.* "Flanker One, we can't afford an extraction at this time. We've got to pull back now. Rendezvous at once. Hawk One out." She hit the switch for private communication with the DropShip. "*Pinhead,* we need immediate pick-up. Find the nearest area to land and beam the recall signal to everyone."

Even as she switched back over to regular comm channels, her sensors were screaming at her, and Charlene checked the head's-up display floating just above her normal level of vision. With three hundred-sixty degrees of data compacted into one hundred-twenty degrees of vision, it took her a few seconds to locate and identify the enemy 'Mech sighting in on her. It was the *Lynx,* coming up over the top of a nearby rise.

"That's one mistake you won't live to regret," she muttered to the enemy pilot, though of course he couldn't hear her. The HUD showed another Angel and an MAF warrior nearby. Almost as if on cue, all three 'Mechs twisted about, and a flurry of laser and missiles struck out at the raider 'Mech just as it launched a spread of LRMs at Charlene's *Phoenix Hawk.* She rode out the light buffeting as seven of the missiles hit her in the torso, shattering nearly half a ton of armor plating. The *Lynx* paid a heavy price for its audacity, though. Standing on top of a hill made it an easy target, and Charlene's return fire savaged its front armor. She thought the *Lynx* might weather the damage, but then a medium laser from one of her other 'Mechs scored the *Lynx*'s head, slicing off the last of its armor as several AC/2 shells slammed into and through the cockpit.

Its cockpit a tangle of molten steel and crushed armor plating, the *Lynx* slowly toppled forward and fell head-first from the small rise. It slid to a stop not far from the feet of Charlene's *Phoenix Hawk*. She trembled as she watched, the destruction of the *Lynx*'s cockpit reminding her of Brent Karrskhov's fiery death. "Thanks," she said mechanically. "Whoever did that."

"My pleasure, Hawk One."

Charlene hadn't noticed that she'd keyed open her commline, but the solemn tones that made it through the radio filters shocked her back into action. Checking the auxiliary monitor tied to her rear sensors, she saw the 'Mech that had taken down the *Lynx*. Those arms ending in barrel-like appendages and the forward-thrusting spherical cockpit could only be a *Vulcan*; one of the MAF BattleMechs and piloted by the only male MechWarrior among them. She couldn't remember his name, so she only repeated her thanks as she stood over the fallen raider.

Even in retreat, she thought, *we never miss a chance for salvage.* She grabbed hold of the *Lynx*'s right arm with the *Hawk*'s left hand and wrenched it upward, using the large laser on her right arm to sever it at the shoulder. A medium laser, a couple of actuators, and some armor; that's what she'd traded for two BattleMechs and the life of an Angel. She almost threw the arm back down, but the mercenary in her would never allow it. *Marcus would be so proud,* she thought, and immediately hated herself.

"Hawk One, this is *Head of a Pin*." The radio filtered out most of the emotion, but a note of frantic urgency still managed to get through. "We're down. Repeat, we're down. A kilometer west of your position with a lance of Hegemony raiders moving in on us."

We're down could mean a lot of things, but from the frantic tone Charlene realized which it was. The *Pinhead* had touched down? "Easy there," she said. "Who is this, and what is your status exactly?"

"Right. Sorry, Lieutenant Boske." There was a pause, and when he continued his voice sounded stronger. "This is Second Mate Davis. The Captain is unconscious and the First Mate was helping man the Long Tom artillery so I don't know how he is. We landed in a minefield. Severe damage to landing gear and main drive. Hull breaches all along our port and aft quarter. We're going nowhere, Hawk One. And damn fast."

And from our last option, I'm left with none. Charlene checked the topographical map loaded onto one of her auxiliary monitors. *They herded us in this direction,* she realized. The terrain here became very uncertain, full of narrow valleys and sharp-ridged hills and a few cleared spots such as the one the *Pinhead* must have found. *Perfect area to mine, since they can bet exactly where we're going to travel. The raiders learned too well from our use of Thunder munitions against them.*

We can't stand. We can't escape. Not as a unit. Charlene opened communications to the Angels, feeling cold even in the *Phoenix Hawk*'s steamy cockpit. *I have to save what lives I can.* "All units, this is Hawk One. The code is Lucifer Seven."

Her voice sounded weak and her throat felt dry and constricted as she gave them their final orders. A Lucifer code meant a no-hope scenario; one that hadn't been used since the Angels were last routed by Clan Smoke Jaguar on Labrea over seven years before. Lucifer Seven meant no reliable extraction either, so every Angel was on his or her own. They would flee by any available path, with the hope of regrouping later. Charlene knew it was necessary, but that didn't make it any easier.

"Repeat," she said, "Lucifer Seven. The *Pinhead* is down and the *Heaven Sent* is unreliable. Southern hills bordering the badlands may be mined. The badlands too, for that matter. Use your own judgment."

There had to be more she could do. Such a situation was hard to plan for, so the contingencies always had to be invented on the spot. Charlene thought fast and furious, her grip on the *Phoenix Hawk*'s controls knuckle-whitening. "*Pinhead* crew abandon station using all available vehicles. Take everything you can easily grab, but don't wait around long enough for those raiders to take you apart. All BattleMechs pair up where possible. Try to stay in two-unit elements. Cut and run for the desert, but don't head directly south. And don't try to stay in contact with anyone else! If we cluster together, the raiders can take us all. If we fragment . . ." She trailed off. *If we fragment, some—a few—will fall through the cracks,* she finished silently. "Avoid raiders at all costs." *What else?*

"Keppler, recon for any unit that requests it. Then get your ass back to the JumpShip if you can. Get a report back to the Magistracy."

She tried to force some strength back into her voice. *Give them some hope.* "We aren't finished for good, Angels. Get clear. Wait a few days and then try to find help. The nomad warrior tribes might take us in, they might not. The *Heaven Sent* might be able to make pickup. Lay low and quiet until then."

"We've fallen from grace," she whispered to herself. "But there is always redemption."

28

'Mech Staging Area
City of Rashier, Rashier Caliphate
Astrokaszy
The Periphery
29 June 3058

Marcus jumped to the ground, the long blades of the helicopter still cutting the air with a vicious slashing sound. He ducked instinctively as he followed Nihail Sallahan off the tarmac of the aerodrome, and then straightened while they crossed hard-packed dirt to a large old hangar. Jericho and Ki-Lynn followed immediately behind him.

The black-robed warrior hadn't done much more than nod a curt apology when Marcus regained consciousness in the helicopter. Marcus would have liked to throw Nihail out the open door, but he quickly realized that the man had been right. About all he might have accomplished in a battered old jeep in the middle of 'Mech combat was get himself killed. It was just that realizing it didn't make him feel any better.

The hangar was constructed of mud and stone over a frame of rough-hewn timbers and milled planks. It sat just within the walls of another caliph city-stronghold, one much smaller than Shervanis but still impressive for its more heavily built defenses. Marcus had seen from the air that less of this city had fallen to rubble, and on the ground the buildings looked much better constructed. It spoke well of the ruler, this Caliph Rashier.

Nihail waved aside the guards at the open hangar doors, passing the three MechWarriors straight through. Two aging BattleMechs stood inside the makeshift 'Mech bay, whether all or only part of the Caliph's forces Marcus had no way of guessing. They were a *Spider* and a *Centurion*—both looking much-abused. A few support vehicles were parked around the feet of the two 'Mechs, like the toy cars of two giant children. An old Rommel and a beat-up pair of Striker light tanks were the best of the lot. Nihail led them toward the vehicles and a line of guards that ringed the foot of the *Spider*.

The guards looked no less threatening than Shervanis' had, chosen for size and armed with large scimitars that would require both hands to wield. They wore the closest thing Marcus had yet seen to an Astrokaszy uniform: loose, blood-red pants and full shirt cuffed tightly at ankles and wrists, short black vests, and on their heads the *kaffiych*, a piece of cloth held in place by a rope-band, instead of turbans.

Marcus also thought he saw more than deference in the way they stood aside for Nihail. Something more akin to fear. Marcus puzzled over this Nihail as they passed through the line of warrior-guards toward another man waiting for them. He was so lost in thought that Jericho had to nudge him when he missed the first comment by their host.

"Commander GioAvanti?" The dark-skinned man smiled when he gained Marcus' attention. "Ah, good. I am Caliph Srin Obbaka Rashier. Nihail radioed ahead his report. I am sorry we were unable to extract all your people."

After Shervanis, Marcus thought he knew what to expect of a caliph, but Rashier surprised him. Leaning casually against the *Spider*'s foot, the man wore nothing more elegant than loose black cotton trousers and a white shirt with full sleeves. His skin was dark, nearly as dark as Thomas Faber's, and his hair cascaded down his back in oily black ringlets. His expression was animated, but Marcus noted that his smile did not touch his cruel, dark eyes.

"Caliph Rashier," Marcus said, bowing his head only slightly. "Can you tell me the outcome of the battle? Do you know what's happened to the Angels?"

"Not much goes on in the Shervanis caliphate that I do not know, Commander. If not for the support of those accursed warriors with their technological god, Shervanis would have been brought to his knees years ago."

Marcus did not miss the fanatical gleam in Rashier's dark eyes, and so dismissed the religious reference as an allusion to the new Hegemony equipment. "And what do you know of the battle?" he asked again, trying to control his patience.

The caliph's smile was not a pleasant one. "Your mercenaries were beaten back into the desert within an hour of their landing. The minions of al Zaitan pursue them. And what they overlook, the desert is likely to claim. The Shaharazad is not a place to inspire tales of hope, Commander. It is treacherous, and where the land isn't hostile, the nomadic warriors hold dominion. They will swallow up what is left of your unit."

As simple as that. Marcus could feel the tension in the muscles of his chest and arms as he clenched his fists so tight that the fingernails dug painfully into his palms. *No, I refuse to believe it. The Angels are survivors.* He couldn't accept the possibility that the battle had been so disastrous that the Angels might have been smashed beyond his ability to ever bring them back.

"What was lost can always be regained," the caliph said as if echoing Marcus' thoughts. "I need warriors, battle commanders, instructors. Together we can bring down the unholy Shervanis."

Marcus shook his head. "I appreciate the effort you made to rescue us, but right now I have more pressing concerns. Perhaps after I locate my people we could discuss this. If you would lend me—"

"I have already given you the gift of your lives," Rashier said, cutting Marcus off, face suddenly darker. "Shervanis never had any intention of letting you go. He would have turned you over to the raiders and kept your BattleMechs. I risked my network of agents to assist your escape. I spent incredible resources and lost fifty-two of my finest warriors. Perhaps, Commander, you should reevaluate your position."

Marcus bristled under the rebuke. He noticed Nihail's hand slip back within the folds of his dark robes, a gesture Marcus was sure he was meant to see and take as a warning. But his anger and grief over the possible loss of his company far outweighed any caution about paying proper respects to another tyrant of Astrokaszy. Courtesy be damned.

But before he could say a word, Ki-Lynn stepped forward. "Commander GioAvanti meant no disrespect, Srin-*pasha*. Having lost warriors of your own, perhaps you can understand his concern for members of the Angels who might still be alive and in need of assistance." She turned to partially face Marcus. "Just as he understands the need to somehow reimburse you for your losses in retrieving us."

You don't make this easy, Ki-Lynn. She had explained before that acknowledging the superior position, and the use of bribes in the form of gifts, were all part of the game. *Again we are starting seriously in debt, and this time with less to offer.* Then Marcus remembered that these people also believed strongly in the eye-for-an-eye philosophy. "I can't promise you much, Caliph Rashier. But I guarantee you the heads of one hundred and four of

Shervanis' warriors in retribution for your own losses." *Twice what you lost, and easily guaranteed in any war between the two of you.*

"A respectful offer, Commander. But her"—Rashier nodded to Ki-Lynn—"do you always let a woman speak for you?"

"The women of my force are warriors, Caliph Rashier. If you want our help, they will be treated as such." Marcus matched gazes with Rashier, determined to win this point.

"Warriors?" he asked. "This is not Canopus. Here warriors prove themselves."

Marcus heard it happen, and by the time he turned it was all over. Jericho Ryan had almost instantly disarmed one of Rashier's guards, who now lay unconscious on the ground at her feet, scimitar planted point-first into the hard-packed dirt. Marcus turned back to the caliph, and found Nihail holding back another guard with his sword extended out like a gate. Everyone waited tensely until the caliph managed a thin smile and a nod. "As you say. They will be treated as warriors."

"Then you have my pledge, Caliph Rashier. And if I can salvage anything of the Angels, I will give you every assistance against Shervanis. My word."

Caliph Rashier let the offer hang there for a moment. Nihail took the moment to prod Rashier's guard back into place with the flat of his falchion, then returned the blade to the folds of his cloak. *Rashier isn't afraid to surround himself with competent men,* Marcus noted. He was just as dangerous as Shervanis, but perhaps he might be easier to deal with.

"Do you remember what you told that devil, Shervanis?" the caliph finally asked. "About a warrior's belief, his faith, being able to carry him through?" He waited for Marcus' careful nod. "I look forward to seeing how much faith your Angels truly have. My people are in contact with your DropShip *Heaven Sent.* It did manage to lift off, though it was forced to land in the deep Shaharazad. A captain . . . Cliffy? He reports that the ship should be ready to rendezvous in three days."

Marcus felt a surge of elation that not all the Angels'

assets were lost. It was short-lived, however, as the caliph's expectant look sobered him. "It appears, Srin-*pasha*, that we are again in your debt."

Rashier's answering smile, thin and cold, told Marcus that the debt would not be forgotten.

 29

Badlands, Shaharazad Desert
Astrokaszy
The Periphery
29 June 3058

Sunset over the Shaharazad Desert was supposed to be a beautiful thing; pale golds and reds spreading over the normally washed-out blue of the Astrokaszy sky. The sand and rock of the desert lost the harsh glare they gave off during the day, and the light wind that habitually blew in from the east carried with it the first touch of night's chill.

To Cameron St. Jamais, watching the play of color through the viewport of his *Awesome*'s cockpit, the entire scene lacked glory.

He would have preferred a dark blue fighting against bold red and gold and purple streams. Maybe a low-lying cloud cover on the horizon that would seem to boil in a blood-red froth as the sun dipped toward it. Such were the sunsets he'd seen on Campoleone. Violent, passionate moments. Moments rare in the calling of the Word of Blake.

But times were changing. The Inner Sphere lay on the cusp of a new era, one of chaos and madness from which it could be led to the proper order. It was the Word of Blake's solemn task to ensure that this was so. Not as the puppet of Thomas Marik and his Free Worlds League nor in a return to the old ComStar methods of waiting and watching. No. St. Jamais knew he would be the instrument of chaos, and if Demona Aziz did not interfere he would let her begin the task of illuminating the path to Blake's vision. Then, sooner or later, he would ascend to the coveted place of Primus of a new order. The fall of the Angels heralded his eventual rise to power.

He scanned the horizon, as if he might catch a glimpse of BattleMechs on the move, though he knew the remnants of Avanti's Angels to be almost a full day's travel off in various directions. He had smashed them, driven them into a trap reminiscent of the one they'd used against him on Marantha. St. Jamais was grateful for Caliph Rashier's timely attack. It had cost him a few more lives and an extra BattleMech perhaps, but in the end it provided an opportunity Shervanis never would have.

What was now left of the Angels could only be a few scattered BattleMechs separated from their sources of supply and extraction. His aerospace forces, waiting all this time at a pirate point above Astrokaszy, had forced their JumpShip from the system by now, cutting off any hope of retreat. The Magistracy would know the raiders had staged off Astrokaszy, but by the time they could investigate in force, his people would be gone and the only evidence remaining would point back to Sun-Tzu Liao. That was the purpose of a double-blind, after all. Isolation. Protection.

No, the Angels were beaten and any mercenary who survived the units he had out roaming the edge of the desert wouldn't last long out there. There would be no major outcry at their loss; just one more mercenary unit that never returned from the Periphery. Meanwhile he had better things to do making sure that security held up around the hidden distribution center in the city of Shervanis. The three lances he'd detached were more than enough to clean up the mercenaries.

Only one Angel had ever held much of his interest anyway. GioAvanti. St. Jamais had often imagined the battle between him and the mercenary commander who had so cleverly thwarted him on Marantha. But Shervanis reported GioAvanti killed along with three others while trying to escape the palace. Two female MechWarriors were now being held prisoner at the distribution center, but they meant nothing to St. Jamais. Perhaps he would simply turn them over to Malachye—the caliph had expressed special interest in the two women, and perhaps it would quiet the petty tyrant's insistence that St. Jamais use the Word of Blake forces stationed on Astrokaszy to strike back at Rashier. But Cameron St. Jamais did not relish the thought of turning former MechWarriors into slaves, or worse. Better to die on the field of battle. Perhaps he would merely execute the prisoners once he was sure they had no further value as bargaining pieces.

He turned his *Awesome* around and began to head toward the distant glow of Shervanis. All the way back he fought in his imagination a glorious one-on-one battle against Marcus GioAvanti—blow by blow, and as always, the victory went to Cameron St. Jamais.

30

Badlands, Shaharazad Desert
Astrokaszy
The Periphery
1 July 3058

Charlene's sensors screamed for attention, piercing tones that warned of inbound missiles. A second later a flight of long-range missiles slammed into a nearby standing column of striated sandstone. Large shards of the pink-and-yellow-streaked rock rained down around her *Phoenix Hawk,* clattering off the cockpit and upper torso. Twisting the upper half of her 'Mech back along the missile's flight path, she dropped her cross hairs over the distant image of a target her computer tagged as an *Assassin* BattleMech, then cut loose with the emerald beam of her large laser. Her targeting systems registered the shot as a glancing blow off the *Assassin*'s right arm, and then the raider 'Mech dropped from sight among the jagged hills and standing columns of rock that surrounded them.

They're pressing again. Trying to drive us into the open desert. The heat level in the cockpit spiked briefly as the *Hawk*'s heat sinks tried to cope with the desert heat and the large laser output, but the automatic increase to flow to her cooling vest adjusted for it well enough. *If things get heavy, though, we're going to bake.*

After the order went out for the Angels to flee into the desert, she had paired off with Chris Jenkins—the MAF officer piloting the *Vulcan*. They'd passed into the badlands and then skirted the edge of the open desert, heading west and pausing only for a few hours' rest that first night. Thinking themselves safe, they'd stopped early the night before and slept in turns: two shifts of three hours each.

And early this morning a medium lance of raider BattleMechs had run across them.

Chris' *Vulcan* led the flight through the steep, winding canyons, sharp-edged hills, and standing columns of rock that butted up against the Shaharazad. The badland. Though both their 'Mechs were jump-capable, they kept to the ground to save reaction mass and in hopes of losing their pursuers. The *Phoenix Hawk* brought up the rear because it packed the bigger long-range punch.

Charlene maneuvered around a large outcropping of orange sandstone and stepped up her speed as she and Chris entered a small straight-away. *We've got to lose them.* Within the first hour of flight this morning, the sensors in Chris' *Vulcan* had picked up another pair of 'Mechs pacing them from the desert. The same readings had popped up several times since, usually to the south as they edged closer to the desert but occasionally more to the front. They weren't more of the Angels; at least, no answer had come in response to their comm signals. *If these are more raiders trying to set up for an ambush, we'll have to hit them hard and get past them before the rest can catch up.*

The *Hawk*'s computer suddenly painted two targets on the HUD: the *Assassin,* joined by a *Vindicator.* Another flight of LRMs streaked toward the back of the *Phoenix*

Hawk, followed almost immediately by a stream of blue-white energy as the *Vindicator* fired its PPC. Charlene had already turned the *Hawk,* preferring to take the damage against her right flank than against the weaker rear armor. The five LRMs peppered her 'Mech's right leg, gouging small craters in the armor. The PPC missed high, exploding the top of a nearby standing column of stone. Counting herself fortunate, Charlene fired off a single return shot from her large laser and then slipped around the next turn even before her computer could register whether or not she'd hit.

A shallow valley spread out before her, widening as it opened out toward the other end, where Chris Jenkins' *Vulcan* stood. Several small hills of broken rock dotted the valley floor. The wind swept fine sand across the ground like a pale, swirling mist breaking against the hills and the legs of the other BattleMech. Beyond the *Vulcan,* Charlene could see the dunes that marked the beginning of open desert.

"Hawk One, we have a problem." Chris' voice sounded weary as it came over the commline, even through the electronic filtering.

"Head north, Ensign. We'll go deeper into the badlands."

The *Vulcan* began to reposition until it faced the approaching *Phoenix Hawk.* "Not a good idea, Hawk. There's desert to the north. We'll be running out onto a spur, with nothing but sand and space on three sides. We'd be looking at five to ten klicks of open desert until we could get back to badlands."

Charlene slammed her palm angrily against the arm of her command couch. *Damn.* "Got any good news?"

"My flamer still works."

And there it was. Take their chances in the desert or stand and fight here, where they could still expect to find some cover. Chris voted to fight here, where his 'Mech could come in close and use its fusion-powered flame weapon to drive up their opponents' heat. Charlene had to admit she was tired of running. She dropped the arm of the *Lynx,* which she still carried from that on-the-spot salvage two days prior. "We hit them as they come around that last corner," she said, "then jump for that small hill to the left. With luck, we get off two salvos before they can respond."

Here's where I atone for bringing down the Angels, she thought, training all her weapons on the entrance to the valley. She would sell herself as dearly as she could, buying Chris Jenkins an opportunity to escape just as she would any Angel. *Just as Brent did for me.*

The *Vindicator* was unlucky enough to be the first 'Mech to round the outcropping of rock that guarded the valley entrance. The *Phoenix Hawk*'s emerald beam slammed into it, followed by a flurry of ruby darts as both 'Mechs unleashed their medium lasers. Unprepared, the raider 'Mech rocked backward as it lost over a ton and a half of armor from its front side. It fell from their line of sight, back behind the outcropping from which it had come.

That puts it out for a moment, Charlene thought, already skimming the *Hawk* toward the small hill she'd pointed out before, and readying her weapons for another strike at the *Assassin*. The heat in her cockpit was riding high after that initial exchange, and sweat streamed down her face and gathered on her exposed arms. No matter. Unless they could bring down the raiders fast, they'd be in trouble.

But the *Assassin* did not round the bend as she'd expected. Riding in on its own jump jets, the 40-ton 'Mech coasted over the low rise on Charlene's left to threaten their flank. At almost the same time, a *Hermes II* and a *Centurion* stepped out into the valley mouth.

All older designs, Charlene recognized, thanking the raiders for the small favor. She cut loose with two of her medium lasers only, giving her heat buildup time to dissipate to reasonable levels. By chance she happened to fire at the same raider that Chris did, both of them scoring against the *Centurion*. Then Chris stepped his *Vulcan* out from protective cover and ran toward the *Assassin,* drawing its fire and leaving Charlene in her protected position to hold the entrance.

Sitting behind partial cover, forcing the other two raiders to come at her across basically flat ground,

Charlene held a slight advantage that she put to good use. The autocannons mounted by the *Centurion* tore large chunks out of the hillside in front of her. Only one of the depleted-uranium slugs made it past from the *Centurion*, but it shattered nearly a ton of armor from her center torso. The laser fire was slightly more intense, carving another ton from her right torso and savaging her right arm until she began to fear for her large laser. Then the *Vindicator* reentered the battle, and one blast of man-made lightning from its PPC flayed off every last ounce of armor from her left arm, laying it open to the titanium-steel skeleton.

With a quick turn and two long strides, Charlene brought the *Phoenix Hawk* fully behind the hill. That bought her a few seconds at best, and in the time she had, she took quick stock of Chris' fight. The *Vulcan* and *Assassin* were engaged in a close-quarters dance at the wider end of the valley—the *Assassin* leery of Chris' flamer and Chris just as worried over the other's SRM system and medium laser. *Come on, Charlie, use your head. You're not tired of living yet.*

Then, just as the raider *Assassin* had before, two new 'Mechs sailed over the valley's lip on jets of superheated plasma. Their low-altitude jumps kept them hidden until the last possible moment when they were suddenly clear of the rim and dropping back to the ground. They landed behind Charlene, leaving her bracketed between the three raiders. A *Shadow Hawk* and an *Enforcer*, both raising arm-mounted weapons in her direction. Charlene brought up her *Phoenix Hawk*'s right arm, struggling to get a lock, but knowing she would never make it in time. Both 'Mechs fired in a release of energy and autocannon rounds that Charlene knew would scour her *Hawk* clean of armor in the best case, and would more likely leave her piloting forty-five tons of scrap.

Except both of the new BattleMechs missed her altogether.

It only took a second for Charlene to finally order the scene in her mind, though it seemed like several long minutes. These new 'Mechs did not bear the Marian Hegemony's dark knight insignia. They both had the slap-dash look of machines repaired in the field with armor plates scavenged from other 'Mechs and applied in patchwork design. The *Shadow Hawk*'s AC/5 looked as if it had been ruined long ago and never repaired.

These weren't raiders, Charlene realized, but members of the nomadic warrior tribes that inhabited Astrokaszy's deserts! And despite Jericho Ryan's warnings about the nomads' tendency to prey on any who where not of their own tribe, they were attacking the raiders and that made them allies. Even if only temporarily.

As the nomads broke off, one to either side, Charlene stepped her *Hawk* out from behind the hill and found the *Vindicator* rounding it from the other side. *Too late for you,* she thought, thumbing the master triggers on both control sticks. Her large laser speared the raider in the left torso, while a medium laser and machine gun on each arm dug further into the armor along the BattleMech's entire front. Its return PPC shot boiled away most of the armor on her right leg, and Charlene knew a moment of fear before the *Enforcer* spat out a one hundred millimeter slug of depleted uranium that also smashed into and through the *Vindicator*'s left torso.

A cloud of debris seemed to blow out the back of the raider 'Mech as it pitched forward violently in a spinning fall. *Ammo explosion,* Charlene thought. *Its LRM magazine ruptured.* The 'Mech's CASE system had channeled all that potentially destructive energy out specially designed blow-out panels in the back of the 'Mech, but such concentrated force was still more than the pilot could handle and the 45-ton machine plowed into the ground, left shoulder first. Before it could try to rise again, the *Enforcer* pumped two more slugs into its back, both penetrating the weaker back armor and smashing into the gyro housing.

He knew the best place to hit it for a quick disable. Charlene turned her weapons toward the *Assassin,* ready to assist Chris and glad the nomads weren't firing at her. Yet.

But just as quickly as the nomadic warriors had arrived, the *Assassin* decided that it had had enough and suddenly rose into the air on twin columns of plasma, quickly disappearing over the valley rim. Charlene knew that chasing the smaller 'Mech would do no good. With its top speed of over 110 kilometers per hour, she could never catch it. What didn't make sense was its sudden departure. *Even at three to four odds, the raiders had superior weapons and armor, and once they'd gotten around that hill and into a slugging match there was little doubt they would have won. Almost as if—*

She broke off from her train of thought as new contacts appeared on her head's-up display. *Almost as if they'd seen something she hadn't.* Two more BattleMechs ran into the valley from the open desert. They were lights, a *Panther* and a *Stinger*. Easing back on the foot pedals, Charlene throttled down until the *Hawk* came alongside Chris' *Vulcan*. The new 'Mechs were of the same general condition as the first two, with the patched-over armor and lack of any identifying marks. Awaiting their approach, she checked the *Hawk*'s damage display for armor and weapons availability, and discovered that her armor was basically nonexistent.

Two-to-one odds again. At least with the raiders, I knew where I stood.

31

'Mech Staging Area
City of Rashier, Rashier Caliphate,
Astrokaszy
The Periphery
3 July 3058

Marcus grimaced as the *Heaven Sent* barely cleared the high walls around the city of Rashier and hovered awkwardly over the cleared landing area near the hangar. It was obviously showing the effects of the damage it had taken.

As the craft slowly settled down toward the hard-packed ground, Marcus squinted against the cloud of dust thrown up by the blast of the fusion drive, taking note of the severe armor damage and the gaping hole blown in the aft-port side. Several raider 'Mechs had concentrated fire there, weakening the number-two landing gear, gutting the aft-port weapons platform, penetrating the fighter bay, and finally damaging the fusion plant at the heart of the DropShip. He couldn't see how Captain Clifford Mattila had managed to take off, much less move the DropShip a good five hundred kilometers along the edge of the desert.

The screech of bent hydraulic components and metal under stress set Marcus' teeth on edge. For a moment he thought the number-two gear would collapse. The stress-bearing joint buckled visibly under its share of almost four thousand tons, but held. Then the wash of fusion-warmed air subsided as the drives cycled down from a roar to a low rumble and finally silence.

Caliph Rashier, who'd been watching the event from a slightly safer distance, now moved forward. His retinue of guards enveloped Marcus, then moved on past him to form a protective circle in which the two men could talk. Rashier seemed almost too security-conscious, but Marcus knew the caliph also spent a great deal of time away from the safety of his own palace as he actively participated in preparing for war against Shervanis.

"A fine display of skill, Commander. Seeing your ship like this, I would not have thought it capable of take-off."

The damage to the *Heaven Sent* hurt Marcus almost physically. Not that he cared more for it than the lives of his people, but this ship was their only way off planet. "I'm sure Captain Mattila will be happy to hear that," Marcus said dryly. He watched as the ramp extended down from the lower 'Mech bay, and Ki-Lynn jumped up onto it and entered the ship. "He always claims the ability to do the impossible." *We'll fix it,* he promised. *The Angels, whatever was left of them, would not be stranded on Astrokaszy.*

If the caliph noticed the sarcasm, it was ignored. "You requested an interview, Commander. Is there something I can do for you?"

"Actually, I wanted to present you with a more physical token of my appreciation, Caliph Rashier." The words were spoken through clenched teeth, but amiably enough. He watched as Ki-Lynn appeared at the head of the ramp again and waved two hovercraft from the bay. Painted a desert camouflage of tan and yellow, the vehicles rode on a cushion of air with large fans at their rear for propulsion. They weren't armed with much more than a medium laser apiece, but they were damned fast.

"Savannah Master hovercraft," Marcus told Rashier. "They can fly across semi-level ground at better than two hundred klicks per hour, perfect for desert warfare. Lightly armored, but the idea is for them not to be there when the enemy starts shooting back."

The caliph seemed suitably impressed, eyes wide with greed as he studied every aspect of the hover vehicles driving past him toward the hangar. Once they were out of sight, he carefully blanked his face of emotion and returned his attention to Marcus. "A wonderful gift, Commander. But perhaps a bit too much for what I have done for you."

And you want to know what I'd like to buy with them. I have to admit, Caliph, your system cuts out a lot of the politics. "Well, there is something else, if the Caliph could spare the resources." Marcus waited for Rashier's nod. "I would like to contact the desert warrior tribes. Try to locate some of my people and see if any of them would join us against Shervanis."

"Desert trash," Rashier said, a sneer twisting his face. "We are better off without them."

The sudden anger in the caliph's voice gave Marcus pause to think. *Tried to recruit them before, Rashier?* "They have BattleMechs. Perhaps not as well-kept as yours, but I've heard that some of the larger tribes have just as many."

"I have five 'Mechs, all in good condition, fully armed and armored. You have as many, and are pledged to assist me against Shervanis."

"And we could destroy Shervanis if all he had were his two lances of older machines. But that isn't so. He has nearly a full battalion of newer BattleMechs with weapons that could destroy us at ranges your 'Mechs cannot reach."

The caliph seemed reluctant to consider that argument. "The desert warriors pilot garbage that would not last a minute against Shervanis' minions." His tone suggested that the argument was closed.

Marcus wasn't about to give up. "That's a minute that Shervanis and the raiders will not be shooting at us, Highness. Surely you can see their use as a diversion, if nothing else." He thought he saw a gleam come to Rashier's dark eyes and pressed the advantage. "And besides, seeking their aid is only secondary. I wish to locate my warriors, and the desert nomads may know something of their whereabouts. What if the Angels weren't destroyed? If I could raise another lance of them, we would stand a far better chance." *A strengthened company versus a battalion. I must be crazy.* He changed his mind. *No, Rashier is crazy and I am desperate.*

"I would have thought, Commander, that your ship could have been used to contact your warriors if any survived." The caliph's expression was hooded again, and he watched Marcus carefully.

"Normally it could. But when the raiders took the *Head of a Pin* they must have found our logs for frequencies and codes. What channels aren't being jammed they're using to try and contact the Angels and lure them into traps." Marcus nodded toward Ki-Lynn, who was descending the ramp with Clifford Mattila, the *Heaven Sent*'s captain. "Fortunately Ki-Lynn had started to routinely change all codes between battles, and when Charlie called a Lucifer Code, the battle codes were then considered void. Contact has to be made through other means now."

Rashier nodded. "I see."

The caliph seemed to be considering the request now, but Marcus was certain it had more to do with how much more Srin-*pasha* could get out of this. "I understand that there might be additional expenses in contacting the various desert tribes. Also that the practice of ransoming is common with them. I cannot promise much more at this time, but I will repay you however I can."

"Of course," Rashier said smoothly. "After all, the equipment you have aboard the *Heaven Sent* is necessary to maintain your own machines." He waited for Marcus, who nodded in relief. "But we might regain your other ship once we defeat the dog Shervanis, yes?"

Even under the hot afternoon sun, Marcus felt a cold chill as Rashier mentioned the *Pinhead* with so little regard. *Does he want the DropShip?* A more worrisome question surfaced. *If he does, what is there I could do about it?* "Yes, Caliph Rashier, we might." He swallowed hard. "But right now such material thoughts are of secondary importance to locating my people."

Caliph Rashier smiled broadly. "We shall see what we can do."

Marcus nodded his thanks and turned away before Rashier could read his thoughts from his face. *I would give up the* Pinhead *to save even one life, Caliph, and if that is the price to pay for dealing with the devil, then so be it. But never forget, Lucifer was a fallen angel who rose to power again in hell.*

He glanced around at the hot, dry land his Angels had come to. *And by now we're halfway there.*

32

"The Nook" Oasis
Shaharazad Desert, Astrokaszy
The Periphery
1 July 3058

Steep, sheer walls of rock rose up on three sides, the rim of a box canyon cutting into the clear night sky above the Shaharazad Desert. The cliffs looked gray-black under the thin sliver of Astrokaszy's only moon, which hung above them with its mocking Cheshire grin. Just as the high walls provided shade during the sunlit hours, now they held in some of the daytime heat to ward against the serious chill of a north-desert night.

The dying embers of what had been a huge bonfire threw a reddish cast over the faces of those sitting around it. Against the dark skin of the Astrokaszy natives, it lent an almost golden hue. *And it probably makes me look beet red.* Charlene set her plate aside, only half finished. The spiciness of the curried meat burned her mouth too much to continue.

A veiled woman quietly stepped forward out of the darkness to remove the plate while another one refilled Charlene's cup with fermented goat's milk. Charlene felt uncomfortable, surrounded by men who looked at her with disquieting expressions. The suspicion and the hostility she could deal with, but the more important warriors viewed her with amusement. As they might a child playing at adult games. She wasn't sure how to handle that, except to match it with constant reminders that she was a warrior as well.

Twisting around—slowly, to attract the attention of every man seated about the fire—she waved twice toward the *Vulcan* 'Mech standing at the outskirts of the camp like some silent sentinel. Just back from it stood the shadow-giant forms of Charlene's *Phoenix Hawk* and three of the desert warrior 'Mechs. The fourth machine in the lance she'd met earlier that day stood guard at the canyon entrance. Chris stood a similar guard here, ensuring her safety against all others in the camp. Even if set upon by another BattleMech, one blast from Chris' fusion-powered flamer and the camp and all its inhabitants would be cinders. But rather than take offense at her indirect threat, several of the desert warriors nodded their approval of her caution.

Aidar Sildig leaned forward over the glowing coals, his face lit up like some kind of solemn jack-o-lantern. He'd led the lance that had first run off the raiders and then brought her here, to the camp of the Desert Wind warrior tribe. "Charlene, what do you think of our home?"

Charlene glanced around at the seated men, many of whom wore mustaches and long beards. She knew the bearded man seated directly across from her on an enormous pillow was the sheik—their ruler. Aidar had not given his leader's name during introductions, and the man had said maybe three words to her since her arrival. *You are welcome,* as she recalled, which could be taken any of several ways.

Aidar had carried on most of the conversations since her arrival, and earlier had shown her around the camp. The desert warrior's skin had tanned to the point that he looked like a native, but his speech gave him away as not being of Astrokaszy. He admitted to having been a member of a mercenary company that had come to Astrokaszy ten years ago in search of the rumored Star League-era base. They had never left. Caught up in the wars between caliphs, the unit was ground down until a fortunate few managed to escape into the desert. He'd eventually been adopted by the Desert Wind tribe.

His story still sent a chill racing along Charlene's spine, hitting a little too close to home. "Surprising," she said, finally answering his question about what she thought of their home. "And efficient." She glanced out into the darkness, where the first circle of tents were barely visible in the fire's glow. Further back she knew would be a slap-dash corral that held goats, sheep, and horses.

"You are well-protected in here," she continued. "But you're ready to move as needed. I've seen nothing that couldn't be relocated rather easily, especially with the carriers you've rigged up for your BattleMechs."

The compliment was deserved, and the men knew it. The carriers were giant metal baskets that could be fixed to the back of a 'Mech like a backpack and others that were meant to be carried by either hand grips or cradled in a BattleMech's arms. As Aidar explained it, the entire camp, livestock included, could actually be loaded onto the four aging BattleMechs and relocated faster than any other method. A few of the more hostile gazes softened a bit with Charlene's acknowledgment, but the suspicion and the amusement remained.

"And our machines? What about them?"

Charlene pursed her lips, considering her next few words carefully. "I am impressed with how you've managed to keep them up." And that much was true. On returning to the oasis, nestled within this canyon on the outskirts of the badlands, the desert people had begun to tear down the *Vindicator* for salvage. Tools were carefully handled, as their replacement would be difficult at best. Others began to work on the light armor damage done to the *Shadow Hawk*. The *Enforcer* acted as a gantry, lifting a platform to the level so that the nomads' technical people could work. Another of the desert Battle-Mechs, the *Panther*, had held up a winch and boom assembly that could be used as a crane to bring in and hold armor plates and the like in place for welding. Efficient and totally self-reliant. *But* . . . "But they're falling apart. Without the kind of major overhaul they could only get in a 'Mech yard, natural systems failure will claim them eventually. And if the raiders had put up any kind of fight, I doubt you could have escaped today without one 'Mech being reduced to walking scrap."

One of the MechWarriors jumped up at her blunt words and was prevented from leaping over the coals only by Aidar's restraining hand. Most of the men began to refute her claim, their voices clamoring with one another in an attempt to be heard. Then the sheik leaned forward and slashed the air with an imperious gesture and a shout of "Enough!"

The clamor died away quickly. "What the woman says is true," he said, then lapsed back into silence.

Aidar picked up the conversation from there. "We do what we can. We raid other desert tribes, and when the caliphs are foolish enough to send a patrol into the desert we raid them. But it is not enough. That is why we always look for those who might wish to join our family. Just as a family needs new blood, it also needs new machines."

They mean me. "No offense, Aidar, but I don't plan to stay. I need to locate what I can of my own people and try to find a way off Astrokaszy." She paused, then addressed the circle of men. "I would think you would all be doing the same thing. You are MechWarriors. From what Aidar has explained, there are at least thirty men in this camp able to pilot all four of your BattleMechs. If you could get back to the Inner Sphere, or even out into another

Periphery state, you might be offered the chance to pilot a 'Mech again."

"In service to someone else and for their cause," said a man Charlene had not heard speak before. "That is no future."

Charlene frowned. "And this is?"

"This is a hard land." Aidar gazed down into the fire. His voice lowered to almost reverent tones. "It tests us. But somewhere there is the promised treasure that will deliver to us the power to bring down the caliphs and their petty kingdoms."

You've been here far too long, Aidar Sildig. "You're talking about the rumors of a Star League base?"

Aidar nodded.

Charlene shook her head sadly. "Almost every planet I've ever been to has a similar legend. Chances are it doesn't exist."

Aidar said nothing, and so the sheik answered for him. "It exists. And until it is found we grow stronger in our purpose."

It all sounded to Charlene like pseudo-religious babble that the Astrokaszy natives used to entrap mercenaries like Aidar. *Help us find the treasure, and we shall all have our reward.* She held back any sharp retort, however. *If it gives them something to believe in, I have no right to ridicule it. It's only because I believe in the Angels that I have no other need of a religion.* Then the humor of the thought struck her and Charlene grinned, wondering if Marcus had intentionally chosen the name of the Angels for any similar reasons.

Aidar mistook the sudden shift in her mood for agreement with the sheik. "You would consider it?"

"Hmm? Oh, no. Aidar, I'm sorry, but I have responsibilities to my people. If any of them survive, they'll be waiting for me to contact them."

Aidar glanced toward his sheik, who stared back with impassive eyes. "Some of your mercenaries have been taken in by another tribe. Three, possibly four."

Charlene jumped up, fists clenched, then quickly turned to wave an *everything's all right* to Chris in his *Vulcan* before returning an angry glare at Aidar and then the Desert Wind sheik. "Why didn't you mention this earlier?"

The old man held out a hand to silence Aidar, and turned his gaze on Charlene. The embers of the fire danced in his eyes, giving them almost demonic light. "Because I know what it is to find yourself abandoned on this planet. I was left here thirty years ago, part of a mercenary force the Free Worlds League abandoned when its peace-keeping mission failed. A rival tribe has just added three BattleMechs to their strength, and it is my duty to increase my own strength accordingly. If not for your warrior's instinct that left a man on guard, I would have killed you both just for your machines."

The depth of the man's feeling came through in his words and sent a thrill through Charlene. Brutal honesty could be very effective. But instead of being intimidated, she felt pity for the aging warrior. "Why fight with other tribes? Have you never thought that by allying yourself with them you could actually rival one of the caliphs?"

"One, yes." Aidar reentered the conversation at a nod from his ruler. "Not Shervanis, but perhaps any of the others. But to do so means to trust the other tribes, which we do not. And we would also have to gather our forces together, which would make us vulnerable. Out here in the desert, we can survive."

"You mean you can hide." Charlene was being deliberately inflammatory now, but she wanted these people's attention. "The caliphs obviously get first shot at anything landing on Astrokaszy, and that's not counting the raiders currently helping Shervanis. They'll always be ahead of you in this race. If you don't take more direct action, they'll always be the stronger."

"You think this?" The sheik lounged back on his giant cushion. "Perhaps you are right. But you do not know all our resources, warrior Charlene."

Charlene sat back down, keeping the sheik's attention with a level gaze. "Maybe not. But I can offer you something you seem unable to reach on your own. If you help me contact the Angels, I guarantee you they will not remain with your rivals. That solves one of your problems. And if you allow me to regroup here, in the safety of this canyon, I will do you two more services."

"You have my attention."

"We still have one DropShip out in the desert somewhere. The *Heaven Sent.* I don't think Shervanis got it because the raiders are still jamming the frequencies it would use to contact us. It can provide you with the facilities needed to overhaul your machines. Then, once we report back, I think I can promise you that other forces will be following us to put an end to Shervanis and his allies."

The sheik sounded amused. "So the *Angels* promise us succor against our rivals, the use of a ship known as the *Heaven Sent,* and eventual deliverance." He smiled and then laughed, a full and rich baritone. "Perhaps our time is indeed at hand."

Growing serious then, he sat up and fixed Charlene with a thoughtful look. "Word shall go out tomorrow," he promised. "And in the meantime, I think it would be good for you to see something of our true strength."

Charlene nodded carefully, unsure of what she might be getting into, but glad to have some amount of support. "I would be honored." *I think.*

"Good. Aidar will organize a raid, and you will participate. I shall order your 'Mech rearmored. If what Aidar told me is true about these new machines of Shervanis out in the desert, then it is time to remind him of why he has walls about his palace."

33

City of Rashier, Rashier Caliphate,
Astrokaszy
The Periphery
4 July 3058

The square was noisy with the hawking cries of vendors as they held up their produce for general inspection. Most of them worked out of wheelbarrows or carts, with only one or two of the nearby buildings used in any manner of organized commerce. A few merchants sold dry goods such as whole cloth or ready-made garments, but most of the trade was in the food staples people needed to simply live from day to day on Astrokaszy. None of it looked well-kept, the heat of the day browning leaves and sucking the moisture out of anything not kept carefully shaded. The sweet fragrance of ripe fruit hung over the market square, teasing passersby and promising relief from thirst or hunger. But underlying that was the acrid scent of sweat and the sickly sweet odor of overripened and spoiled produce.

Marcus paused over a bin of blood-oranges. *Like everything else on Astrokaszy, even what looks promising has the stink of decay not far beneath the surface.* He picked carefully, digging under the first layer of softer fruit to grab a firm blood-orange that had been protected from the sun. He handed it to Jericho and dug for another. The owner of the cart didn't object, but the slight scowl on her dark face showed that she wasn't thrilled over Marcus' careful shopping either. Not until he pulled out a C-bill and offered it to her. She snatched it from him, giving him a thin, yellow-toothed grin as she dug into a change purse for Astrokaszy coin. Marcus didn't give her the chance to cheat him on local currency values. "Keep it." That seemed to soften her hard expression, though he couldn't be sure.

"You're generous," Jericho said, peeling her fruit with the benefit of slightly longer fingernails. Some juice shot out from beneath her fingers, drawing a dark line across the front of the coveralls she'd borrowed from a technician aboard the *Heaven Sent*. Marcus had opted for simple trousers and a loose shirt, but he wore his white neo-leather jacket draped across his shoulders like a cape, protecting his neck and arms from the sun's burning rays.

He shrugged, quartering his own orange with a pocket-knife. "I've lost people who can never be replaced and machines worth millions of C-bills each. When I get off this dustball—if I ever do get off it—whatever's left of the Angels will be facing bankruptcy. A few C-bills hardly matter."

Jericho still winced. "I'm sorry," she said quietly, then walked along for a moment in silence. She watched as Marcus bought a handful of dates from a vendor, again paying with a C-bill and then handing half of them to her. "I haven't seen a lot of scrip changing hands here. I'd have thought that off-planet currency wouldn't be worth as much, but these people treat it like gold."

"Well, I doubt Canopian dollars would spend well here, or even League Eagles. The caliphs control currency flow, so they underrate money that's hard for them to spend."

Jericho nodded. "And C-bills are easily spent at an HPG station."

C-bills, or ComStar-bills as they were originally called, were the one common medium of exchange throughout the Inner Sphere and Periphery. They weren't backed by precious metals, but instead were promissory notes for time in hyperpulse generator communications. The faster-than-light communications administered by ComStar and Word of Blake was all that kept a civilization spanning thousands of settled worlds from fragmenting beyond repair. *Even an isolated world like Astrokaszy maintained some ties to other worlds,* Marcus thought. And while the presence of a Word of Blake HPG station—even a minor one—had surprised him, he could see that the stronger caliphs did have need of it. *But she doesn't really understand.*

"Partly." Marcus bit into a segment of the reddish-orange fruit. It was sweet and quenched his thirst even better than water. He strained the juice out, then bit the pulp from the rind to finish eating it. "Let's say you rule a caliphate," he said. "If there are C-bills circulating in your caliphate, how do you work the exchange so you get the best deal at both ends? You need to get them from your people, but you don't want to give Word of Blake a high margin in the exchange rate."

"You couldn't do that. Get the best from both ends. Unless . . ." she trailed off.

"Unless you coined the local currency," Marcus reminded her.

Jericho stopped walking, holding a section of blood-orange halfway to her mouth but apparently forgotten. "The caliphs just coin some extra money and buy the bills from their people? But that further undervalues their own system."

Marcus shrugged, looking around at the Astrokaszy natives in their sun-shielding robes or extremely light cotton clothing. "As long as it affects the masses and not you, why would you care?" He started walking again.

Remembering the fruit, Jericho popped the segment into her mouth and then moved to catch up. "It's irresponsible," she said, sounding frustrated.

"And every Great House has probably done the same thing. Not to the same extent, though. Only in times of dire need. That's one of the reasons why House Bills are almost always rated under C-bills."

The two paused in the shade of a two-story adobe shop. The owners sold baskets and pottery out of the lower story. All useful items; Marcus saw nothing just for decoration. Laundry hanging out of a second-story window said that the owners lived above the shop. "Astrokaszy isn't so different from the rest of the Inner Sphere or the Periphery. There are always those who want supreme power and are willing to hire or threaten others into helping them get what they want." *And maybe that's why I'm feeling particularly fatalistic. Feeling used, Marcus?*

"Meanwhile they trade off ownership of villages the way the Successor Houses trade planets," Jericho finished the thought.

Marcus leaned back against the adobe wall, its rough surface grabbing at the leather jacket and pulling it off one shoulder. "It's just a bit more brutal," he said, then lapsed into silence while he finished off his fruit.

It was interesting to stand there watching the faces of those passing by, but it was hard to tell what they were thinking or feeling. Most wore expressions that were either unreadable or simply drained of all emotion by the struggle to survive. The few who seemed to take notice of the two outsiders gave them glances or stares in various mixtures of curiosity, fear, and a good dose of hatred. Sidearms were common, slug-throwers mostly, and Marcus began to feel naked without his Sunbeam laser. No one stopped to harass them, though, and thinking about it now, it seemed strange that no one had asked for handouts after the way he'd spent money on some simple fruit.

Then he remembered the looks of fear. *Word has gotten around that Caliph Rashier guarantees my safety. Nihail promised me I wouldn't need my weapons, and I don't.* He thought about the caliph's dark-robed advisor, still intrigued by the enigmatic man even after several days in the city, but then a hand on his arm drew his attention back to the here and now.

Jericho had turned so that she could face him, her left shoulder still up against the light-colored adobe wall. "Marcus, what are you going to do?"

It was the start of a conversation he'd dreaded ever since she invited herself along on this walk through the city. He could hear the real question lingering behind her words, *what are WE going to do?* Not the hardest question to answer, except that he felt sure she was speaking

in terms beyond the end of their walk and maybe beyond
Astrokaszy.

So keep it in terms you can deal with. "I'm going to pull
what I can of the Angels together, assuming there's anything left. Then I'll work on how to get us off this world."

"And if there's nothing to pull together?"

Her hand remained on his arm, and Marcus tried to
ignore the flush of warmth spreading slowly up toward
his shoulder. "I started the Angels with nothing more than
four 'Mechs, a beat-up DropShip, and a small pile of salvaged armor," he said, his tone more brusque than he'd
intended. "That's about what I have now. I can resurrect
the unit if I have to." He glanced down the bare-earth
street. "I won't let it die here."

"The *Marathon* will bring back the Magistracy Armed
Forces. You know that, don't you? We'll have help."

Marcus shook his head, refusing to meet her stare,
afraid of what he might see behind her eyes. "I can't
count on that, Jericho. Keppler reported that the
Marathon had escaped by the time he got there to warn
her, but that doesn't mean they'll be back in time to do us
any good. We're looking at months of round-trip time."

The hand fell away. "So you plan to be gone before
then?"

A single nod. "But first"—and now his head came back
up, though he still wouldn't meet her gaze—"I plan to
hurt Shervanis as deeply as possible."

"An avenging Angel?" she asked without a trace of
humor.

"Sure, if you like. Some religions say the Archangel
controls the gates of heaven," he said. "If Shervanis and
Rashier want to start a holy war, I'll happily kick those
gates wide open."

Jericho smiled, though sadness still showed in her
green eyes. "So that's how I'll picture the pearly gates
from now on. Heavily fortified and with a big BattleMech
guarding the entrance."

Marcus smiled at the image she'd painted, but shook
his head. "Ready to lead you into paradise or blow you
into oblivion," he said, the whisper of laughter in his

voice. "I suppose some people look at BattleMechs exactly that way."

She smiled in return, letting a comfortable silence exist between them for a few moments. "How can you expect to hurt Shervanis?" she asked after a moment. "Even with some losses the other night, his Hegemony friends must still have nearly two full companies."

"I don't know. Divide and conquer, I suppose. But that's going to be hard to do with the kind of numbers we're working with. Unless I can come up with some mighty clever strategy."

Jericho's eyes narrowed in concentration. "One who has few must prepare against the enemy," she quoted. "One who has many makes the enemy prepare against him."

Marcus nodded, recognizing the lines immediately. "They teach *The Art of War* in the MAF too?" Then he remembered another favorite maxim of his own. "The strong dictate, the weak posture. When my enemy cannot tell the difference, I have already won." He shrugged. "Or something like that."

"Can't place it," Jericho said, with a light shake of her head.

"Shiro Kurita. Twenty-three hundred and, well, a long time ago."

Jericho settled back against the wall, staring out into the crowd. "So you'll find a way to fulfill your contract, and then get away. Hopefully before Rashier finds another way to extort equipment from you. Then you collect the balance of your pay with the Magistracy and you go back to the Inner Sphere."

Again, Marcus heard the unspoken question behind her words and it tore at him. He knew she was fishing, hoping to find out if he cared, maybe even that he'd admit to it. But no matter how much he did care, he'd never tell her. There was a battle coming, and that meant he could lose her as he had so many others. Perhaps it was better to think only of what might have been. He reached over, enfolding her hand in his and holding it loosely. *Leave it at that, Jericho.*

"Marcus, what are you going to do?" The same question as before. The same pleading. Whispered so that he barely heard it.

"I'm going to head back to the hangar," he said, voice calm. He shoved himself away from the wall with a quick thrust of his shoulders, but did not release her hand. With his other hand, he pulled his jacket squarely over his shoulders again. "On the way I'm going to buy a whole bag of those expensive oranges. And then later I plan to sit down with some of my officers and try to come up with a plan."

He released her hand. "And I'm not looking beyond that. Not now."

34

Palatial Estates, City of Shervanis
Shervanis Caliphate, Astrokaszy
The Periphery
5 July 3058

Cameron St. Jamais paused just outside the doorway, his face almost pressing against the strings of heavy wooden beads that served as a partial curtain. The guards had passed him through automatically, and now he eavesdropped on Caliph Shervanis and Arch Vizier Ji-Drohmien as the latter reported on the defensive measures of the City of Rashier to his master. St. Jamais supposed it was considered an honor to be one of two men with unrestricted access to Shervanis, but all he felt was loathing and disdain for the caliph.

The Arch Vizier was a different story, however. Something about the man bothered St. Jamais. He was clever, possibly even as crafty as Shervanis. On Astrokaszy that could make a man powerful. But Ji-Drohmien also seemed to have a firm sense of proportion and, from what St. Jamais had seen, a nearly inexhaustible supply of patience. A rare thing on this barbaric world, and a quality that could make any man dangerous. Just now the Arch Vizier was trying patiently to explain why Shervanis should not order an all-out attack on the Rashier Caliphate.

"Even with the loss of the *Clint*," Shervanis was saying. "I still outnumber Rashier in 'Mechs. How can you say I don't?"

"Highness, we have intelligence sources in the Rashier Caliphate. We know the *Heaven Sent* has landed within the city walls, and that it must carry at least five Battle-Mechs of finer quality than our own."

Shervanis slashed the air with the stump of his right wrist. "Damn the mercenaries and their 'Mechs. St. Jamais can give me one of his lances to match them. Or a company to crush them."

"St. Jamais will do nothing of the kind," the demi-Precentor said calmly, pushing his way through the curtain of beads, which rattled as they fell into place behind him. "My troops stay where they are until I'm sure the Angels are neutralized."

"Rashier invaded my city. That demands a response."

St. Jamais shrugged. "Then go light some fires in his city and steal some of his prisoners. I see no reason to commit BattleMechs for no gain of my own."

"Do not mock me, Blakist. You made certain agreements and you will honor them."

"What my master means to say," Ji-Drohmien said, stepped forward, "is that he wonders about your promise to help him gain dominance over the other caliphates."

St. Jamais looked at Shervanis, who stood glowering near a small table set with wine and fruits. "Our agreement specified that we would assist as our forces permitted. There was never a time frame set. Just now I am content to guard the distribution point against any Angels still left. I'm down a full company of BattleMechs, and expect no replacements until the next ship from Campoleone. I will not waste more of the Word of Blake's resources chasing desert riffraff or pursuing your personal vendettas. My patrols will return within a few days, and will remain in the city."

"Perhaps I would not have need of your forces if I could have overhauled my machines with the materiel you took from the other DropShip. Our agreement was that the mercenary machines and materiel would be mine if I neutralized their commander. Which I did."

"Only after my forces were indemnified for actual battle losses. I lost three 'Mechs against the mercenaries because of that damnable *Fortress* DropShip. Then two more trying to track the Angels into the desert." St. Jamais paused. "And you did *not* neutralize Marcus GioAvanti. In fact, you let him escape, and then tried to lie and cover up your blunder when I could have detached a few 'Mechs to make sure he didn't make it out of the city."

"So I am to receive nothing out of our agreement?"

"I leave you the DropShip."

"Which I have no means to repair," Shervanis said with a snarl. At St. Jamais' shrug he crossed his arms and sneered. "And what of the prisoners? You took two MechWarriors and some others. Or do you plan to recruit them as replacements for your own warriors?"

"The prisoners are my concern only as long as I think they have information or any other use against what may remain of the Angels. Once I'm done with them, you may have the women."

"I also turned over the other Angel to you. The man."

"Let's not kid each other, Malachye. You don't care a fig about him. In the condition you handed him over to me, he's lucky to be alive."

"My father would have sent them all out into the desert tied to some horses to let the sun devour them slowly." Shervanis smiled thinly. "At least I can find proper uses for two of them." A pause. "You find something amusing?"

"Just thinking, Malachye-*pasha*. You have given me an interesting idea that I may find use for in the future."

"Good. Then in return you will lend me a single lance of machines with which to punish Rashier."

He does not give up. Perhaps he needs another reminder. "And if I do not?" St. Jamais asked softly.

Shervanis shook off a restraining hand laid on his

shoulder by Arch Vizier Ji-Drohmien. "You might find my caliphate less friendly to your cause."

"There are several dozen caliphates on Astrokaszy large enough to suit our purposes. I would imagine that the just stipend alone that we pay you for use of a few empty warehouses would be enough to purchase Rashier's loyalty."

Shervanis' grin turned wicked. "But you do not want it widely known that the Word of Blake is behind this operation. After all that evidence we have so carefully planted leading back to the Capellan Confederation . . . it would be a shame for the effort to go to waste."

St. Jamais shook his head sadly. "Then you leave me little choice."

Shervanis clapped the stump of his right wrist down into his left palm. "Good, then we will expect—"

"No, no choice at all," St. Jamais interrupted. "After all, there are currently more Word of Blake 'Mechs in your city than there are Astrokaszy 'Mechs."

This time Ji-Drohmien physically imposed himself between his caliph and St. Jamais. "Of course there are," he said smoothly. "And we know there is nothing to fear because the Word of Blake is a friend of Astrokaszy and therefore a friend of Caliph Shervanis. My master was about to suggest that you thoroughly inspect the planted evidence that links us with House Liao. Especially that which proves we had no choice but to comply or face an assault by his Death Commandos."

St. Jamais crossed his arms over his wide chest. "Is that so, Caliph?" He waited for Shervanis' curt nod. *Well, you don't get off that easily.* "Then we're still friends, aren't we? And I would be happy to inspect the evidence. But my schedule is so tight, Caliph. You understand that over-seeing our mutual concerns takes precious time." *You acknowledge me as the stronger, so now it is time to pay for my services. These are your own rules, learn to play by them.*

Ji-Drohmien never so much as batted an eye, though St. Jamais did notice a stiffening of Shervanis' posture beyond the Arch-Vizier's shoulder. "If my master would be so gracious as to allow it, I would like to honor your patience and generosity with a gift. Taken from my own estates, of course. A half dozen of the finest Arabian horses in my stable. Transported off-planet, they would fetch a nice sum. And of course for all your men a steady supply of fresh fruit for your tables."

And everyone saves face, eh? St. Jamais nodded to the Arch Vizier. *Such a waste, this man serving Shervanis. Perhaps I shall do him a favor and remove Shervanis from his path before I leave. The 6th of June can apply its proven methods in any environment, even a place as pitiful as Astrokaszy.*

35

Shaharazad Desert, Astrokaszy
The Periphery
7 July 3058

A wall of heat slammed into Charlene as the continual firing of her large and medium lasers spiked the cockpit temperature first into the yellow zone and then into the red. Fans did their best to remove the lung-scorching air, but in the meantime she gasped for breath as sweat poured down her face and arms and beaded on her legs. The cooling vest was all that was keeping her conscious at this point—that and a stubborn resistance to anything smacking of submission, even if to her own body.

The large rolling dunes of the Shaharazad Desert spread out on all sides, rising and falling like some enormous dun-colored sea. Dark, glassy patches where BattleMech lasers had fused the sand threw back sparks of sunlight. The only orientation points were those pre-programmed into the BattleMech computers. After several days of this, Charlene was beginning to think she could spot the telltale differences between dunes, but knew better than to trust such impressions yet.

The *Phoenix Hawk* rocked backward as a full flight of ten LRMs from the raider *Grand Dragon* she faced chewed into her left torso. A blue-white lance from its right-arm PPC followed, flaying away more of the Durallex plating as her armor there became more memory than fact. She carefully walked the *Phoenix Hawk* backward and around the slipface of the dune her HUD registered as point A-1. Sixty meters back she halted the giant battle machine, dividing her attention between the HUD and the true-life scene outside her viewport while the heat buildup in her cockpit slowly dropped back toward reasonable levels.

Now I'm supposed to wait.

Her targeting and tracking system had already lost its fix on one of the desert warriors and the raider he fought. The raider 'Mech was an *Assassin*; though she had no way of telling if it was the same one she'd seen before. Aidar Sildig in his *Enforcer* registered only intermittently, a good three hundred meters to her left and engaged in a vicious game of cat-and-mouse, with two heavy raider 'Mechs playing the cats. She had done her job, pulling the *Dragon* out of formation by pretending to give ground to the heavier machine. Not that it took much pretending. The *Dragon*'s pilot was damn good and held a 15-ton advantage. Most of the armor replaced by Aidar's people had already been scoured off or burned away by his LRMs and PPC.

The *Grand Dragon* rounded the dune, its splayed feet kicking up large sprays of sand. It twisted heavily to the left to engage Charlene, belching a tongue of flame and smoke as another set of LRMs shot from the protruding launcher. Charlene quickly engaged the *Hawk*'s jump jets and eased into a short backward hop. Only two of the missiles caught her, barely making a dent in her right-leg armor, and sixty meters further back she settled into partial cover behind the tailing of another dune. *Just a few steps,* she cajoled silently, intentionally firing her two medium lasers high of the mark. *Just to let you know I'm still interested.*

The *Dragon* gave her three more steps, scoring again with both PPC and LRMs. The stream of man-made lightning took her *Hawk* high in the center torso but failed to penetrate. Fortunately the entire flight of LRMs slammed into the dune guarding her *Hawk*'s lower half, throwing a sheet of sand high into the air like a curtain. The wave broke over her, and when her monitor cleared it was as if she'd been transported to a scene from some holovid drama.

A dozen magnificent horses were converging on the *Grand Dragon,* racing down the dunes on either side of it and a few galloping up from the rear. Graceful and strong, the animals had long silky manes and tails that streamed as they ran. They bore their riders toward the raider machine, whose pilot seemed unaware of their approach. With the high background heat of the desert, that didn't surprise Charlene.

But as the first grappling hooks flew up to snag the raider 'Mech's arms and shoulder ridges and the main communication antennas, the pilot must have finally noticed something amiss. His 'Mech took a lumbering step backward, and the PPC barrel of its right arm tracked around, trying to lock on to a target.

Charlene had been told what to expect, but it was still a sight to watch eight riders suddenly abandon their mounts to scale the sides of the giant war machine using their ropes and grappling hooks. Four others who had missed their initial throws galloped around in confusing patterns, trying to draw attention from their brother warriors, who were involved in a rite of ascent. When a shot from the *Grand Dragon*'s left-arm medium laser vaporized one rider and half his horse, no one but Charlene seemed to pay any heed.

It amazed her that the abandoned horses never bolted or seemed to panic in the slightest. They waited patiently where they'd been left, heads held high and noble as they awaited the return of their riders. *Some of them won't be coming back,* Charlene thought as the *Grand Dragon* lurched to the right and threw off one of those warriors climbing up its side. One warrior had slipped partially into the 'Mech's knee joint, and as the *Dragon* now straightened, the man was torn in half by the pivoting metal. Another was caught against the monster's hip,

smashed flat by the BattleMech's blocky lower-left arm.
And a fourth fell when he tried to slide around the
Dragon's hunched shoulders to get at the cockpit hatch—
the 'Mech's deliberate step to the side burying the man
under sixty tons of metal.

What a waste of fine warriors, Charlene thought. She
stood forgotten by the *Grand Dragon* as it battled with the
desert warriors clinging to its frame. Four of them had
reached the cockpit hatch, where they clung to hand grips
normally reserved for technicians and the 'Mech pilot
himself. Charlene knew each man carried a small shaped-
charge explosive. One of them must enter the cockpit and
dispose of the MechWarrior inside, allowing the machine
to be taken almost perfectly intact. When the *Dragon*'s
head bobbed forward, a small puff of white smoke rising
from behind it, she knew the cockpit had been breached.

Aidar Sildig had explained the ritual to her, but she'd
barely been able to conceive of it, much less believe he
was telling the truth. Horse-mounted warriors against a
BattleMech? Using grapples and rope instead of the usual
grapple-rod and anti-Mech infantry? Not to mention the
fact that their only weapons were knives. It was suicidal
at best, but the finest warriors of Aidar's tribe clamored
for position among the twelve. Four were dead, four had
merely failed, and four more now rode atop the *Grand
Dragon*. Even as Charlene watched, dumbfounded at the
waste of lives, one warrior made it through the hatch,
knife in hand.

The shape-charges that had breached the cockpit were
intentionally under-powered so as not to damage important control components. It wasn't because the desert warriors cared about the life of the pilot, but only that they
wanted to take the 'Mech nearly intact. The raider pilot
was almost certain to have a weapon stashed in his
cockpit, something that would be more than a match for a
single warrior with a knife. But being under-armed was
part of the glory of the ritual. The other three waited for
the first warrior to succeed or fail.

He apparently failed. The next warrior, knife clamped
between teeth, dove through the hatch.

Charlene felt her gorge rise, but swallowed it back

down. The ritual seemed barbaric in its simplicity, in its tragic cheapening of life, she thought, as the next warrior climbed through the *Grand Dragon*'s cockpit. She could admire their raw courage and dedication to tradition, but their indifference to death made her shiver with dread.

It made her suddenly realize how wrong she'd been about Marcus, criticizing him for taking risks that unnecessarily endangered the lives of the unit. How could she have been so unfair to him? It must have been her grief over Brent that had made her thinking go astray. Just because Marcus tried to maintain some emotional detachment didn't mean he didn't care about his people at all.

Then the *Grand Dragon* suddenly moved forward again, but in an ungainly fashion, and the fourth warrior slid down his rope and back to his horse. *They've got it.* She'd watched the whole thing—knife-wielding warriors capturing a BattleMech—and still found it difficult to believe what she'd seen. The surviving warriors were riding off, each leading at least one other horse whose ride would not be going back. *They'll regroup an hour's ride from here where Aidar and I will meet up with the carriers that brought them out here. Until then I have to help the others break off and evade pursuit.*

And if I'm lucky, I'll get the chance to apologize to Marcus someday.

=== 36 ===

'Mech Staging Area
City of Rashier, Rashier Caliphate
Astrokaszy
The Periphery
8 July 3058

Hooks sailed up the side of the *Spider,* two out of five catching one of the back "wings" that acted as cooling fins and helped stabilize the light recon 'Mech in its longer jumps. Two of Rashier's men clambered up the ropes, one fumbling his first few swinging grasps and only making it about two meters off the ground before the high-pitched shrill of The General's whistle stopped the whole exercise.

Marcus watched as The General contemplated the sorry trainees from his perch atop a packing crate labeled: *Dangerous! Explosive! MG Ammunition.* Hanford Lee was commander of the Angels' ground forces, all fourteen of them. They'd made it away from the downed *Head of a Pin* in the Savannah Masters, and had managed to reach the *Heaven Sent* before running into raider patrols or the roving packs of desert warriors. The Angels rarely employed ground troops except for sentry duty or clean-up detail, as on New Home. But from forty years with the DCMS and then the Rasalhague Drakøns, Lee knew how to train and command and keep troops ready. Everyone called him The General, but despite his age and battlefield experience he had no problem deferring to Marcus as his superior officer.

Lee opened his mouth to let the whistle fall to the end of its lanyard. "You call that an assault?" His voice was strong and powerful, accustomed to calling out orders across a hot battle zone. He jumped down from the crate and walked over to the group of Astrokaszy warriors. He limped only slightly, favoring the right leg with its artificial knee.

The two men still hung onto the rope, dangling above the floor as their muscles strained. The other three stayed frozen at attention. They'd learned not to move without orders on the very first day, when one of them had let go his rope and then argued his point with The General. After the man had picked himself up off the floor, Nihail Sallahan had walked over and knocked him down again for insubordination.

"Why are these two the only ones hangin' off the ground?" The General asked. He jerked a thumb toward a long, heavy bar set across two ladders at a height of about three meters off the floor. All three of the men who'd missed their throws moved, jumping up to hang from half-flexed arms. The General turned his attention toward the uppermost man, who hung just above the *Spider*'s knee.

"Going for the hip, weren't you, Flash?" He waited for the dark-skinned man to nod, responding to the nickname given him by The General. "You got maybe ten seconds when these babies pause in combat. If your charges ain't planted, they're off like rockets again and there ain't a lot you can do trailin' behind them like a banner. Until you *know* you can make it, don't get greedy. Take it in the knee." Another nod. "Get down."

"Speed Bump," Lee called out loudly, turning to the man who was barely two meters up. "Ankles don't count. You need to swing up that rope. Never lose your momentum. There's no reason why you can't get a meter with every pull. You're gettin' only thirty centimeters, if that. If you weren't so damn good with the hooks I'd bounce you outta the squad. Then again, if you had grapple-rods you'd probably never miss." He sighed heavily. "Get down."

"As for the rest of you, hang there awhile and think about how you'll hit the target next time."

Marcus hid his grin behind a cough. He had voluntarily sat in on such training in the past, and his muscles remembered the torture of hanging there. Then he swallowed his mirth and broke the silence with some of his own observations.

"MechWarriors will tend to ignore you," he said. "Until those hooks start flying. You can't do enough damage with portable weapons unless there are a lot of you with really heavy equipment. They'll underestimate you. Use that! And don't count on ten seconds. We may be slow sometimes, but that doesn't mean we're stupid. Hooks and ropes mean explosive charges, and any MechWarrior who's had to limp back to his DropShip with a ruined knee actuator won't want it to happen twice."

Lee nodded his agreement, then had a comment of his own. "And don't get cocky if you happen to knock a tin can over. Even lyin' on the ground with a bad gyro and bleedin' heat out the fusion reactor a 'Mech is a dangerous thing. It can still fire and thrash about. If you catch one prone, great. Give it an enema. In fact, one of the best things you can do for your MechWarriors is to swarm a 'Mech they've downed and turned their backs on. Right, Commander?"

Marcus winced at the memory. "Hey, he was powering down."

"Yeah. But he powered right back up again, didn't he?" The General glowered and Marcus held up his hands in surrender. "Never trust a MechWarrior," he said, emphasizing each word as if it was the greatest advice he could give.

Then The General let the other men climb down, and after giving them a moment to rub life back into their arms, he ran them through the drill again. Four of the five connected with their hooks. Marcus saw a look of desperation cross the fifth man's face, and wondered at how The General could inspire such terror in what had been a belligerent and hostile trainee three days ago. He wouldn't get to see this round, though. Even as the whistle shrilled out again, Marcus noticed Caliph Rashier and his island of guards crossing the old hangar toward him. He jumped down, preferring not to have The General interrupted since he couldn't guarantee what the man might say in front of the caliph.

Or even *to* the caliph.

Nihail slid out from between two of the advancing guards and parted the way for Marcus to directly approach Rashier. Their eyes met for a moment, and as always Marcus felt as if the other man was trying to tell him something he simply could not understand. It was irritating that Nihail was still such a mystery, but not in an unpleasant way. More like a puzzle you had to admit you had yet to solve.

Marcus considered what he knew about him. Nihail Sallahan held a high position in the caliph's circle of advisors, and also seemed closer to understanding the common people in a way the caliph could never hope to. Nihail had been the one to suggest that Marcus leave his personal weapons aboard the *Heaven Sent*.

The Caliph's protection is all you will need in the city, Nihail promised. He'd been right. Marcus had never seen the man dressed in anything other than the flowing black robes of a desert warrior, belted with a red sash and sometimes with a red cord holding his *kaffiych* in place. He didn't seem to carry any weapons but the two swords that sometimes appeared from the folds of his robes, though he seemed able to hide almost anything under there. *But what does all this tell me about the man?*

And then Marcus knew what it was about Nihail that made him stand out, and it had nothing to do with the garments he wore. *The people support Rashier because he has power and they fear him. The warriors fight for him for much the same reason.* But it was not fear with Nihail. He served Rashier out of respect and loyalty, Marcus felt sure.

And maybe that's another reason why I dislike the caliph; he doesn't seem to deserve the loyalty of a man like Nihail, who seems to have the makings of a much better ruler. He remembered thinking the same thing about Shervanis' Arch Vizier, Ji-Drohmien. *Is it a rule of Astrokaszy that superior men must serve under tyrants or religious fanatics?* Then Marcus considered the alternative—being the caliph with a dozen other powerful leaders drawing a bull's-eye on your head—and wondered if Ji-Drohmien and Nihail might not both be smarter than he gave them credit for.

"Commander GioAvanti," Caliph Rashier said in greeting. "Forgive any interruption to your training schedule."

Marcus wondered what the man wanted to extort from him this time, but of course he didn't say that. "No interruption, Srin-*pasha*. I've finished with your Mech-Warriors for today, but The General could continue working even if the hangar was burning to the ground around him."

Rashier's eyes flicked to the walls of the old building with concern. "Yes, well, I would hope such things could not happen in my city."

For some reason Marcus was reminded of the tales he'd heard of Romano Liao and her bloody purges all in the name of personal security. He thought that could easily happen here if Nihail were not around as the voice of sanity. "What can I do for His Highness today?"

"I want to know if your warriors could be ready to move against the cur Shervanis within three days."

Three days! Marcus had been thinking maybe three weeks, to give him enough time to locate more of the Angels. "Why so quickly? Has something happened?"

Rashier nodded to Nihail, who picked up the explanation in his patient manner of speaking. "The evil Shervanis is trying to convince the heretic commander to join him in an attack on Caliph Rashier's holdings. We wish to strike first."

"I can understand that. But there is such a thing as striking before you're ready. We couldn't hope to take the city."

Nihail shook his head. "We think we could. But we probably couldn't hold it. The attack would be intended to deeply wound Shervanis' forces, as you have suggested before. Then we could hope to win in the next attack. Or possibly the next."

Rashier finally being reasonable? Marcus was astonished. "We try to lure off a heavy or assault lance and then destroy them with little damage to ourselves. That kind of loss would hurt him."

"No," the caliph said. "We must be ambitious. You will lead your entire force from the open desert, directly south of the city, through the badlands, and then draw out these men who fight under false colors. These offworlders. After the battle is joined, my machines and two hundred of my finest warriors will hit them in the flank, from the northwest, and together we will destroy them. Then Shervanis is left with only his own machines."

"Shervanis expects reinforcements," Nihail said. "More of these godless minions."

Marcus started. "You're sure?"

Caliph Rashier looked insulted. "I told you. Nothing goes on in Shervanis' realm that does reach my ears. Now, can you do it?"

Marcus shook his head. "Five BattleMechs against two companies of improved 'Mechs? We couldn't hold out long enough for your troops to show up." He wasn't about to let Rashier use the last of the Angels as mere bait. "Even then we'd still face two to one odds."

"But if *you* had double that?" The caliph's voice was almost a silky purr.

"With your machines in the main strike force? That would leave us nothing substantial to use in a hit from the flank." Marcus paused, Rashier's emphasis on "you" catching up. "The Angels?"

Nihail produced a sheet of rough paper from the folds of his black robes and handed it to Marcus. As Marcus opened and scanned it, Nihail informed him of the exact contents. "Your unit co-commander, your exec, she says she has recovered five of your people, plus one other. Only five machines, though, and not all in good repair. They wait in the care of the Desert Wind tribe."

Five Angels! And the sixth had to be a member of Jericho's lance. The Angels were hurt, but now he saw the possibility of their resurrection as much more than a promise made to Jericho. His mind worked in overdrive, calculating time for travel and rearmor of the damaged machines. "This Desert Wind tribe. Where are they?"

A shrug from Rashier. "No one knows, and they wouldn't say if they did. Somewhere between here and the black city of Shervanis."

"So within a five hundred kilometer-stretch east of here, and probably closer, or the *Heaven Sent*'s radio couldn't have picked them up in the condition it's in. We could force-march to meet up with them in a day. I'm sure. Give me a day to rearm and armor with the last of our reserve materials, and yes, we could be attacking in three days." Marcus could hardly believe the Angels would be back together again. "Can you guarantee the timing of your arrival, though? I can hold if we keep on the move, but without your flanking attack to throw them into some confusion, I couldn't hope to win. These raiders are good."

Rashier waved Marcus' concern aside as if it bore little consequence. "Your approach is well-concealed. You can make it all the way through the badlands into the region we call The Fringes, an area of rough and broken ground leading into the flatlands. By taking the northern route, my smaller force should be hiding in place before you reach that position. And if not, there is a maze of arroyos just to the east, where you could effectively tie up these raiders for perhaps an hour, with only acceptable losses."

How many lives in an acceptable loss, Rashier? Marcus wanted to ask, but didn't.

"In the meantime," Rashier continued, "I will order my agents in the city to stage minor raids and other disturbances. This will guarantee that a few of these heretic warriors will be left behind in the city, along with all of Shervanis' machines. That will cut your odds down further."

"We have trained for some time for this attack," Nihail said. "We know the terrain and a dozen ways to approach any area around the city." He glanced meaningfully at the *Centurion,* the other 'Mech stationed in the hangar, giving Marcus his first clue that the man was also a Mech-Warrior. Somehow it didn't surprise him. "We can be there," he promised. "And Shervanis' minions shall be driven before us."

Marcus nodded, comforted more by Nihail's simple words than any of Rashier's promises. "That's good enough for me," he said directly to Nihail, then returned to more general address. "The plan sounds workable. I'll want to see maps and perhaps make some minor adjustments. To start with, Caliph Rashier, I'll need two of your MechWarrior trainees to move the extra BattleMechs aboard our DropShip to the warrior camp. I can move our ground infantry in conventional hovercars, but I'd like to borrow your Savannah Masters as escorts until we're set up for our final run toward Shervanis." *You owe me for a change,* Marcus thought, *and you'd damn well better pay up.*

Caliph Rashier didn't hesitate, giving Marcus a firm nod and a grin. "Of course, Commander. Anything you need."

37

"The Nook" Oasis
Shaharazad Desert, Astrokaszy
The Periphery
10 July 3058

The Desert Wind camp was a beehive of activity. Some still worked to repair what damage they could to the more battered of the Angels' BattleMechs, a task the technicians Marcus had brought with him were trying to assist. The rest of the tribe swarmed about in nervous clusters, wary of the newcomers. Charlene doubted any of them had ever seen so many 'Mechs gathered together at once, and they probably felt more than a little threatened.

The Angels' *BattleMaster* and *Archer* loomed at the canyon entrance like two giant sentinels, standing a silent vigil as they faced out toward the open desert. Six more BattleMechs stood nearby along the canyon walls, towering above the camp and the clumps of palm trees. The last two 'Mechs were the ones under repair, which included a desperate attempt to reattach the left PPC-arm to Brian Phillips' *Warhammer*.

Charlene wiped sweat from her brow with the back of one hand. Even at ninety degrees in the shade of the canyon walls, she knew it wasn't all from the heat. She only hoped she didn't look as nervous as she felt. She planned to resign her post as exec, unless Marcus beat her to it by dismissing her. Her stomach churned at the thought. *The Angels are my life. But I acted recklessly*

*and with the same disregard for lives I accused Marcus
of. Because of that, they were almost destroyed.*

Before she could speak, Marcus had moved past her to
where the rest of the Angels were gathered. She watched
as he personally greeted each one and asked after their
health. Though he did it casually, and always with an eye
toward their battle readiness, she could sense the relief in
his voice, and once she saw it in his slate-gray eyes when
her gaze briefly met his. The others seemed to sense a
slight change as well and responded to it. Marcus didn't
shy away even when Paula planted a kiss on his cheek.

Then he turned back to Charlene and she snapped to
attention, giving Marcus a salute straight out of the old
Federated Commonwealth handbook. "Returning your
command," she said.

Marcus gave her the sharp—almost curt—bow and
click of his heels that she knew were a holdover from his
upbringing as a member of the wealthy GioAvanti family.
Then he looked around at the Angels, who were relaxing
to more typical attitudes. "Five?" he asked, counting
heads. "Your message said five plus one. I thought that
meant one of Jericho's."

"It did. Chris Jenkins is helping out on Paula's *Valkyrie*."
She nodded toward Connor Monroe. "Connor came in only
this morning, minus his *Rifleman* unfortunately."

"My ransom," the young man said, clearly upset. "They
tore it apart for salvage, which is pretty much all it was
good for anymore. The nomads practically gutted her
when they ambushed me. Still, it was ours."

"Damn paper-thin armor anyway," Marcus said. "The
configuration of Faber's *Marauder* isn't too dissimilar.
Think you could handle it?" He waited for Monroe's
startled nod. "Who else is without a ride?"

Brandon Corbett shrugged uneasily. "That would be
me, Marc. Almost the same deal. My *Hunchback* got
chewed to pieces at long range by the desert warriors.
Gave it up to win free passage for Tamara and her
'Mech."

"Which is in almost perfect condition," Charlene
added. "The *Grasshopper* was the best of our lot until you
showed up."

Marcus nodded. "I already have Jericho checked out on the *BattleMaster*," he told Corbett. "So you pilot her *Griffin*. It's closer to your old weight anyway. The *Griffin* and *Marauder* have already been blanked, so the two of you can go set up security programs and get used to the machines. Take 'em into the desert if you want, but no further out than a kilometer. Go."

Both men moved at once, trotting toward the line of BattleMechs. Charlene didn't miss the solemn looks on their faces, and knew they mirrored her own. She still didn't know for certain who'd made it out of the city. "Jase and Thomas?" she asked, just to be sure.

"Never made it out of Shervanis," Marcus told her, then briefly recounted the events of the last week. "What do we know of the others?" he asked when finished.

Charlene swallowed hard. "Geoff is dead. We're sure of that. So's one of Jericho's people. We think Kelsey Chase might have made it out of her *Jenner,* and we don't know what happened to the fourth Magistracy warrior, Shannon Christienson." She smiled tightly. "We do know that Vince Foley is alive. He and his *Enforcer* are being held for ransom by another tribe. No time to get him even if we had the equipment they want."

"And everyone else? How'd you get them here?"

"Well, we owe two tribes some time in our 'Mech bays if we make it through this. They were taking promissory notes so I did what I could."

Marcus shrugged at her concerned tone. "I can live with that." He nodded a dismissal to everyone else. "Let's take a walk."

Charlene had no idea what was on Marcus' mind, and every time she thought she might bring up her resignation, there was always another question to be answered. She showed him around the camp, introducing him to warriors she knew. Both Aidar Sildig and Sheik Carrington—she'd finally learned his name—were in consultation. Marcus didn't seem surprised at Aidar's status. "It seems to be a rule that competent men rise to the position of number two on this world. What I don't understand is why they won't help against Shervanis."

"Carrington has them all wrapped up in a religious

quest for mythical treasure," Charlene said. "Aidar plans to shadow us in toward the city with a few of his warriors. But all they'll do is pick off any stragglers that wander too far out. They won't risk their people in an operation that benefits a caliph."

Marcus frowned. "Damn. We could've used them. Right now I'm predicting no better than a twenty-minute opportunity for Caliph Rashier to drive in from the flank, regardless of his optimistic estimate of an hour. Four more 'Mechs could've upped that time to thirty or even forty minutes."

The way these people fight, it could've meant we wouldn't need Rashier at all, Charlene thought. "I've looked over the basic plan you sent, and I think we can extend that time by ourselves. It depends on how you want to divide our forces." She paused a moment in thought. "How close do you plan to get to the city?"

"Rashier guarantees we can approach up to five klicks. I'm personally counting on only ten."

Charlene glanced over at the line of BattleMechs. "Anyone ever tell you that white and gray aren't desert camouflage colors?" she asked, unable to completely restrain a touch of humor in her voice. Four of the five 'Mechs Marcus had brought in were painted exactly that scheme.

Marcus smiled thinly. "We'll be skylining it anyway once we get that close. Paint won't matter. And I want them to know exactly who we are."

"I think you solved that problem easily enough." She looked over the fifth 'Mech, Marcus' *Caesar*. It had been given a shiny white base coat, then a special clear-coat that gave it an iridescence almost like mother-of-pearl. As if that wouldn't garner enough attention, dark reds and browns had been used to paint flames that licked up the outside of both legs. Across the *Caesar*'s chest in an off-center crescent was the name "Archangel" painted in brilliant gold.

"Jericho did that after a"—he paused—"talk we had."

The two stood there a moment, gazing at the 'Mech. Finally Charlene decided the time had come. The icy tightness twisted deeper as she first cleared her throat. "Permission to fulfill personal obligation?"

"Granted," Marcus said, sounding almost amused.

Her voice lowered, and she spoke as if he weren't there. "I'm sorry," she said simply. "I was wrong to criticize you back on New Home, wrong to accuse you of unnecessarily risking the lives of the unit. And I'm ready to make recommendations for a new exec, Marc." She glanced toward her commander. Marcus pursed his lips as if considering the idea. She steeled herself against a show of emotion as he began to speak.

"There is someone I have in mind," he said, rubbing at the side of his face with one palm. "I hear she's piloting a *Phoenix Hawk* these days."

The tightness loosened as Charlene saw that he meant it. "I believe you can count on her," was all she said. That was enough. *Maybe everything isn't right between us, not yet. But I'll make it right.*

38

Industrial Sector
City of Shervanis, Shervanis Caliphate
Astrokaszy
The Periphery
11 July 3058

With the late-morning sun already beating down outside, on the way to normal high temperatures, the interior of the adobe warehouse felt relatively cool. Inside, two companies of Word of Blake BattleMechs stood in close-quarter ranks. MechWarriors were in various stages of climbing up to their cockpits or already mounted and beginning their startup sequences.

Cameron St. Jamais paused, halfway through his cockpit hatch, to watch a *Quickdraw* near the large warehouse doors take its first few ponderous steps. In all his years of ComStar and then Word of Blake training, with all the plans and intrigue of the Toyama and the 6th of June movement, this was the one sight that never failed to impress.

BattleMechs on the move, preparing for battle.

He ducked through the hatch, closing and fastening it down behind him with a violent twist of the locking mechanism. The battle was about to be joined.

Already this morning, Rashier's warriors had carried out several attacks in the city. Sniper fire against palace guard-posts. A few commando teams had made it onto the palace grounds, and at least one team was still engaged in a firefight within the palace itself. Then came reports through Ji-Drohmien's intelligence network of increased DropShip activity in the Rashier Caliphate. St. Jamais still remembered his frustration with Ji-Drohmien at the lack of further details. *DropShip activity* could mean a lot of things, including the landing of Magistracy reinforcements. He'd been forced to send his remaining aerospace fighters to check it out.

Finally, Shervanis' desert watch stations reported signs of nearly a full company of Angel BattleMechs moving in from the desert far south of the city. *So the mercenaries aren't as finished as I thought.* The reports about Drop-Ship activity could be a ruse. In fact, it felt like just the kind of ploy Marcus GioAvanti would use. Still, it was better to be sure that Canopian reinforcements hadn't somehow miraculously arrived weeks before they should have.

So, Commander GioAvanti. We get our time on the field after all.

St. Jamais slid into his command couch, fingers stabbing a series of buttons that would bring his *Awesome*'s fusion reactor on line. A low rumble, like the growl of some caged beast, sounded from under his seat. Pulling the seat's harness over his head, he fastened all the straps into the quick-release buckle that pressed against his chest, and snugged them down. Next was the line to his cooling vest. It plugged into a snap-fit socket on his left side, and he shivered as the first slug of coolant sped through the tubes woven into the ballistic cloth of the vest.

His neurohelmet rested on a shelf above his head. He drew it down and put it on, the padded shoulders of his vest helping to support its heavy weight. Four sensor leads hung from the helmet's chin, and these he attached to biomed patches. Stripping the backing off each patch, he stuck them to his upper arms and thighs, melding man and machine. St. Jamais felt an initial rush of adrenaline that set his muscles trembling with pent-up energy.

The Angels can't be in very good shape, he thought. *I'll meet them at the edge of the badlands before they can disappear among the gullies and washouts, and I'll crush them for good.* They were proving to be a persistent threat, and St. Jamais wanted to see them destroyed.

Apparently, so did Shervanis and Ji-Drohmien. Even with heavy Rashier activity within his own walls, the caliph had ordered four of his seven functional 'Mechs to accompany the Word of Black forces. Ji-Drohmien had assured the caliph that three 'Mechs were sufficient to put down any Rashier infantry assault here in the city, especially since their intelligence net reported all of Rashier's machines still in the Rashier Caliphate.

St. Jamais was not so arrogant as to pass up the support, especially after underestimating the Angels twice already. *Perhaps I will step on Rashier after this as a lesson to others about defiance to Blake's divine will. And as a favor to Shervanis.* With two companies of his "raiders," augmented by a lance of Shervanis' 'Mechs, he should be able to overcome anything the Angels could throw at him.

Then a remark made days before by Shervanis returned to mind, and St. Jamais nodded grimly. Yes, that would work nicely. *Just in case.* A small measure of resistance to the idea gnawed at him. *They're MechWarriors,* it argued, but he quashed it. Hadn't he decided the other day that the principles of the 6th of June could be applied against anyone?

As the cockpit screens winked to life around him, feeding him information on the status of his weapons and other systems, a digitized voice spoke into his ear. "Identify," was all it said.

"Cameron St. Jamais." He waited a moment while the computer compared his voiceprint with the one buried deep within its security system. But because voice patterns could be faked by recordings, the 'Mech would not turn control over to anyone without the code phrase that was also programmed in and known only by the machine's authorized pilot.

"I am my brother's keeper," St. Jamais said, vowing silently that the Angels had caused him trouble for the last time.

Thomas Faber resisted the urge to power up the *Clint*.

The call ordering Shervanis' First Lance to report to someone named St. Jamais outside the southeast gate had just come over the radio. Thomas had no idea who this St. Jamais was, but bet on him being the Capellan commander in charge of the bogus Hegemony raiders. And the two forces were meeting up not two hundred meters from his position, which placed a lot of 'Mechs a lot closer to him than he liked.

Twelve days in hiding had taken their toll on the big MechWarrior. The warehouse he'd crashed into sat on the edge of what Shervanis probably called his industrial area. Most of the nearby buildings stood abandoned except for the occasional patrol, which had made the job of foraging for food and water more difficult. Still, on the second night he'd managed to sneak Amaáli out and into one of the safer residential areas where she could hide. Then he'd sat out the days trying to adjust the stolen BattleMech's neuro-feedback without the proper tools.

Nights, though, were another matter. Nights were for scouting.

On the eighth night he'd located the three warehouses being used as the weapons distribution point out to the Marian Hegemony. They were deeper into the industrial area. It surprised him that security wasn't tighter, with only routine patrols on guard in the area. Apparently the Capellans had no fear of discovery. Two nights ago he'd finally managed to get inside one of the buildings, where he found crates stenciled with the Capellan Confederation's gauntlet-and-katana insignia. He wrote down parcel numbers, shipping routes, anything he could find that might later serve as evidence. Almost too easy, he'd thought, but put it down to the recent defeat of the Angels and the lax discipline that often accompanied assignment to backwater worlds.

Thomas had decided to give the Angels a few more days to make some kind of move. His position, in partial control of a stolen 'Mech, might have been worth some tactical advantage. Now it seemed as if the fight would take place outside the city. As soon as the raider 'Mechs were well on their way, he could wade out of here and try to catch up.

He snapped on a cockpit light, staring into it for a long moment to readjust his eyes from the gloom. It wouldn't be long now, and he'd better be ready for the harsh glare. *Thirty seconds to work my lower half out from under the rubble,* he calculated. *Another minute to clear the city's edge and be free of Shervanis' enlightened rule once and for all. Even if they detect me, I don't think Shervanis can get any of his 'Mechs out here fast enough to stop me.*

"Raiders, this is St. Jamais." The words leaked out of the near-muted radio, and Thomas was quick to increase the volume. He caught the trace of an accent through the filtered sound, but couldn't place it. With the thousands of possible dialects in the Inner Sphere and Periphery, that wasn't surprising. "Point lances continue forward and deploy five hundred meters into the hills ahead. Assault and striker lances deploy at the edge of the hills. Wait for my signal to advance. Raymond and Terrence, hold back with me a moment."

What were they waiting for? Thomas assumed they must be at the city gate if deployment orders were going out, but why the wait? His answer came a moment later as St. Jamais spoke again, and it sent chills racing through him.

"Bring the prisoners up now," the voice said. "The two women to Terrence and Raymond, but bring that Torgensson fellow to me."

Thomas' hand hovered over the switch that would power his 'Mech to life. "No," he whispered to himself inside the silent cockpit. "Not yet. Stick to the original plan or you'll die here."

It was only through great force of will that he managed to pull his hand back from the panel, but he promised himself he wouldn't wait long. *Whatever he wants the prisoners for, it can't be anything good.*

===== **39** =====

Badlands
Shaharazad Desert, Astrokaszy
The Periphery
11 July 3058

Marcus crested a low, rocky hill in his *Caesar,* then walked his war machine down into a large, dry basin. The red rock of this area of the badlands filled Marcus' windscreen and primary monitor, the stone all around him carved into insane patterns by wind and the occasional desert flash flood. Even the rare flat surfaces like those his 'Mech now traversed were streaked with treacherous narrow gullies and sinkholes that could snap a Battle-Mech's leg off if the pilot wasn't careful.

"Initial contact. Vanguard reports one lance of mediums." Pause. "Make that two."

Damn. So much for Rashier's guarantees. Marcus swallowed dryly, the ozone scent and acrid taste of warm circuits scratching at the back of his throat as Ki-Lynn calmly informed him of the presence of raider forces forty minutes sooner than expected. Not good.

Already the output of his fusion engine, combined with the natural heat of the day, had driven up the temperatures of his cockpit. The Angels had reconfigured the cycling time on all weapons to compensate somewhat for slower heat dissipation, but it wouldn't take more than a few minutes of hard action to spike heat levels into the red.

Marcus tightened his hold on the *Caesar*'s control sticks, their neoleather grips chafing under his grasp. *And we've got to draw this out long enough for Rashier to join up with us.* He expertly sidestepped a cleft that might have trapped The Archangel's foot. *Think,* he commanded himself, *and quickly.*

Paula Jacobs and Brandon Corbett comprised the two-'Mech Vanguard element. Jericho Ryan and Chris Jenkins, the last MAF warriors, made up Visitors, a second two-Mech element running parallel to Vanguard out in front, though not swinging out as wide. Both elements were operating as advance scouts, running a few minutes ahead of the Angels' main force on a north-by-northeastern track that was supposed to lead them all up to the border of the city of Shervanis.

Marcus commanded the main force, a lance of their heaviest BattleMechs already deployed in a ragged line of battle. Ki's *Archer,* his *Caesar,* Connor Monroe in Faber's *Marauder,* and Brian Phillips anchoring the west flank in Marcus' old *Warhammer.* They made for a solid anchor on which the outriding elements could depend.

The last two BattleMechs were Charlene's *Hawk* and Tamara Cross in the *Grasshopper.* Escorted by The General and his ground troops in three civilian hovercars, they made up the Reserves element running a few kilometers behind. Holding these forces back had been Charlene's addition to the general plan, setting up another delaying action. It seemed now as if they would need it.

Another twenty klicks further along, according to the plan Marcus and Caliph Rashier had originally worked out, Vanguard could have pulled at least one lance of raiders off to the east to tie up the enemy forces in a game of hide and seek among the maze of narrow arroyos and washouts. If they did that now, it would bog the Angels down here, in the middle of the badlands, with Rashier's forces at least an hour distant north and west—and probably closer to ninety minutes.

And that was just too far away.

Marcus opened communications with Ki-Lynn. "Have Vanguard slide off to the west. Repeat, west." It made sense to him. *When the reinforcements can't reach you*

in time, move the fight closer to the reinforcements.
"They're to switch to a running game. Swing them toward
the rendezvous." Marcus wanted to ask Ki to break radio
silence and check on Rashier, but knew that would be
risky. *Ki's good, but that's still some distance through
difficult terrain, and Rashier probably wouldn't break the
silence anyway.*

Forty minutes early. The time hung over his thoughts
like a specter, and Marcus fought an urge to kick his
'Mech up into a run. The early appearance of the enemy
upset him. What happened? Patrols they didn't know
about? Rashier had guaranteed Marcus a close approach.
Right about now the caliph's warriors should be making
their first diversionary attacks on the city of Shervanis,
attacks intended to keep some of the enemy forces tied
up. Now Marcus couldn't even count on that.

It was every commander's nightmare that no plan sur-
vives contact with the enemy.

Make them react to you. The thought cut through all the
useless ruminating. It was a military tactic dating back
thousands of years, and basically amounted to making the
enemy *think* you were defeating him. The Angels knew
how to do that. Marcus also knew that somewhere far off
on either flank were supposed to be the MechWarriors of
the Desert Wind tribe and possibly others. They weren't
going to interfere, but they might pick off stragglers.

"Drake, this is Lyre," he said, calling Ki-Lynn. As
usual Ki acted as his filter, though one of his channels
was a general frequency that anyone could use to radio
him. Marcus referred to it as the panic channel, and voices
coming over it heralded bad tidings. "Tell Vanguard to
swing a bit wider than planned, and don't be afraid to
pour on speed. If they can make any of the raiders fall
behind, the tribes might lend us a hand after all." *If they
actually followed us into the badlands,* Marcus thought.
And not stayed out in the desert.

"Copy, Lyre," Ki said, the radio filters stripping away
any emotion her naturally calm voice might have allowed.
A few seconds later, just as calmly, she said, "The
Visitors are falling back, reporting contact with heavy
BattleMechs."

Jericho Ryan and Chris Jenkins. They would fall back on the four-Mech lance Marcus headed, trying to pull faster raiders after them that could then be quickly put down by their six machines. "Call up the Reserves," he ordered. "Place them on hot standby." One of the options the Reserve element gave them was the ability to act in minor what Rashier would do seriously—hitting after the initial engagement to promote confusion. *All our players are accounted for,* Marcus thought, *and our grace-time is all used up.*

The *Caesar* managed less than two dozen steps before Jericho's BattleMaster and Chris Jenkins' *Vulcan* swung out of an arroyo not three hundred meters ahead and to the right, running back toward Marcus' lance, which was spread out in a line across the dry basin. After a hundred meters the *BattleMaster* pivoted back. Marcus leveled the *Caesar*'s right-arm PPC at the arroyo, easing into the shot just as a raider *Ostsol* ran onto the basin and a *Quickdraw* skimmed a low rock formation in cover of it. On the far left another pair of raider 'Mechs swung out from behind standing rock columns, trying to engage Brian Phillips in his *Warhammer* at extreme ranges.

The computer was busy painting the raider 'Mechs as red squares on the *Caesar*'s tactical screen, as opposed to the blue circles of the Angels, when Marcus identified the greater threat. Triggering his PPC he sent a lance of azure energy streaming at the *Quickdraw*. In a high-heat environment, missile boats and autocannon had the advantage. The *Ostsol* depended on lasers, which would run up the raider's heat quickly and ruin its effectiveness.

With the odds at four against two—or five against two, if he counted Connor Monroe's *Marauder* traveling at the outer edge of its range against either pair of raiders—one would think the fight a quick one. Marcus knew better. BattleMechs could soak up a lot of damage, which gave the raiders a chance to withdraw or inflict some good damage of their own. Either way, the bulk of the raider force would not be far behind, and the Angels couldn't afford to slug it out, no matter how well they could divide up the enemy.

The first exchange of heavy fire proved the point well.

Jericho had also scored against the *Quickdraw* with a full brace of four medium lasers and her SRMs. Another two hundred meters off to Marcus' left, Connor Monroe had also blasted it with the *Marauder*'s twin PPCs. Ten years ago such a shot would have been impossible for the *Marauder*; almost six hundred meters distant. Rediscovered technology had extended weapon ranges, though, and the C^3 computers slaving the *Marauder* fire control to Jericho's BattleMaster improved targeting by almost fifty percent.

Their combined fire slammed into the *Quickdraw* just as it touched down, vaporizing armor and raising a cloud of molten particles around the raider 'Mech. Unable to keep his balance under the barrage, the raider pilot released a full spread of long- and short-range missiles into the back of Jenkins' still-fleeing *Vulcan* before falling.

Even a few missiles could have penetrated the weaker back armor of the *Vulcan*. And as the *Quickdraw* lost its footing under the heavy fire, the *Vulcan*'s entire body shuddered and stumbled first to its knees and then went prone. *Gyro hit,* Marcus thought, his jaw clenched tight enough to ache. *The* Quickdraw *would probably regain its feet faster than Jenkins.*

Marcus swore softly under his breath, then stabbed at the comm switch, opening a line to Visitor element only. "Jenkins, your weapons are in the front of your 'Mech. So's your stronger armor. Get up, dammit."

The *Ostsol* caused almost as much damage to Marcus' team. The pilot chose Ki's nearby *Archer* as his target, chewing into her right torso with both large pulse lasers, carving away almost every last ounce of armor protecting her ammunition storage. Ki kept her 'Mech standing and launched a full spread of forty missiles in response. Only a third of them hit, with fully half the missiles detonating prematurely. The effect looked quite minimal.

Until the *Ostsol* took another step.

The premature detonation had littered the ground with Thunder submunitions, effectively mining almost nine hundred square meters of terrain just in front of the *Ostsol*. The ground itself seemed to explode around the raider 'Mech, hiding it in a veil of smoke and flying dirt. For a moment Marcus dared hope that both raider 'Mechs were down and could be finished off quickly, but then the *Ostsol* was past the cloud of smoke and debris and still racing on into point-blank range with Ki-Lynn's *Archer*. The armor on its right leg had been shredded—stripped right down to the ferro-titanium bones of its framework—but it still came.

Sweat ran down Marcus' face, burning his lips with the taste of salt. He couldn't afford to push his heat so early, and he couldn't squander ammunition for his torso-mounted Gauss rifle. *Only sixteen shots,* he reminded himself, taking extra time to lock on to the threatening *Ostsol. Make each one count.*

The *Ostsol* pilot wasn't foolish enough to run at high heat before he could close to a range where his medium lasers could tear into his opponent. Marcus counted on that, though Ki-Lynn let fly with another full spread of missiles as soon as possible. This time all forty were the real thing, and over half of them peppered the *Ostsol.* Armor plates shattered across its entire front, a few missiles digging deeper into its already ruined right leg, though apparently not hitting anything vital. Like a determined juggernaut, the raider 'Mech raced forward.

In the lower half of the *Caesar*'s left torso, power was pulled into the Gauss rifle capacitors, which would eventually discharge at a much higher rate of energy release than the fusion engine was capable of providing. At full charge, enough power trickled out and to the coils that lined the long barrel to generate a small electromagnetic field. It grabbed onto the nickel-ferrous metal slug loaded into the rifle's breech, polarizing it. Then the capacitors dumped energy into each set of coils successively, accelerating the slug along the barrel and finally forcing it out at a muzzle velocity approaching one thousand meters per second.

The slug—slightly oblong and given an almost perfect spin from riffling in the barrel—weighed over one hundred kilos and took less than half a second to make contact with the *Ostsol*'s left torso. There it impacted with a force rivaling the largest of BattleMech autocannons, shattering armor like glass and then punching through several internal supports. It ricocheted off the engine's physical shielding, tearing a gash along it that allowed excess heat to bleed through. Finally, its energy nearly spent, it rammed into the *Ostsol*'s anti-missile system ammunition, which exploded with enough force to finish the job of gutting the *Ostsol*'s left torso.

Marcus never saw the *Ostsol* hit the ground, for he was already twisting his *Caesar*'s torso back to the left as soon as he saw the AMS ammo cooking off in secondary explosions. The *Quickdraw* pilot had decided to remain prone, bracing his 'Mech's left against the ground while firing his missiles and right-arm mounted medium laser. Both Jericho and Connor Monroe pumped megajoules of energy into it, with Jericho bearing up under the return fire as she finally backed out of range of its medium weapons. Over the crest of a hill maybe eight hundred meters distant, Marcus counted another three 'Mechs skylining through the air to enter the battle on the basin. On the left flank Brian Phillips was getting desperate as his *Warhammer* fell back under concentrated fire from four more medium and heavy raider 'Mechs.

"We need the Reserves up here now," Marcus said. Tying in through the *BattleMaster*'s targeting and tracking system, he was able to get a hard lock onto the *Quickdraw* and adding to the raider pilot's misery with a new blast of blue-white PPC energy. Ki's acknowledgment of the order came a moment later as she finished off the *Ostsol*, aided by Chris Jenkins, who'd finally got the Vulcan back on its feet.

"Have Monroe break off and assist Phillips on the left flank. To all warriors, we're going to pull off toward the west and then swing north, following Vanguard." That put the *Warhammer* and the *Marauder,* machines that preferred long-range jousting, to opening the hole they would need. Marcus could see the plan in its overall shape, the tactical implications all worked out in his mind. But each minor aspect worried him as he committed people and machines on little more than gut instinct.

"This is the commander of the Marian Hegemony forces."

The voice was low and sinister, even through the electronic filtering, and Marcus instinctively knew it was one practiced for dealing with the enemy on the battlefield. The emotion came through in the pitch and rhythm. *Probably has a gentle and soothing voice ready for his own people,* Marcus thought.

"We will accept the surrender of any member of Avanti's Angels. Those who cease fire now will be relocated off-planet with their 'Mechs and allowed to return to Outreach. This is the only offer we will make."

And extremely generous, Marcus thought as he maneuvered over to support Phillips and Monroe. He didn't believe the man for an instant. It was more than the cultivated voice. The raiders had gone out of their way twice now to bring overwhelming force against the Angels, and been thwarted. *They want us dead and buried. The better to keep their secret.* He found it difficult to believe the raider commander would make the offer, much less expect the Angels to trust them.

Made it sound like we have no choice.

"Marcus." Jericho's voice was disembodied and stripped of most feeling, but he could still hear the distress. Besides Charlie and Ki, she was the only other person with a private channel to him, "Marcus, check out the advancing 'Mechs. The *Awesome*."

The *Awesome* would be the raider commander; Marcus had felt sure of that on Marantha. Why it would bother Jericho he didn't understand, but if the Angels could bring that 'Mech down, it might throw the raiders into disarray. On his HUD Marcus found the *Awesome*, one of the three 'Mechs approaching from over the hill dead ahead, and punched in a tight visual on his primary monitor. In his mind he was already directing a thrust to bring the assault 'Mech down.

Those plans died in a wave of horror and shock as the image resolved into the *Awesome*'s broad-shouldered visage.

Just below the cockpit window was a narrow lip of metal. A deflection plate. In case of catastrophic failure of the fusion-reactor shielding, the plate would direct the blast away from the air immediately over the 'Mech so as not to injure the pilot who might be ejecting. A person stood on that lip, ropes around arms, legs and torso holding him in place. Marcus zoomed in again, losing some definition but still able to recognize the build and general features.

Jase Torgensson.

A quick check showed two more warriors tied just below the cockpits of the 'Mechs flanking the *Awesome*. Kelsey Chase, and possibly Shannon Christienson, one of Jericho's MechWarriors. Marcus' numb brain supplied her name as he let the *Caesar* slow to a halt. He was barely able to comprehend what he was seeing.

Whoever the raider commander was, he would make sure that at least three MechWarriors died before any of these 'Mechs were fired on at all.

40

The Fringes
Shaharazad Desert, Astrokaszy
The Periphery
11 July 3058

Heat washed through the cockpit, turning it into a sauna. The air stank of sweat and the acrid ozone-scent of warm electronics. Pulling the *Caesar*'s upper torso around in a violent twist that strained its turret-assembly waist, Marcus scanned the path behind him for any sign of the *Orion* that had chased him into this maze of standing rock columns and narrow passages.

The sweeping end-run Marcus organized on first contact with the raiders had allowed the Angels to break away initially. Drawing the raiders after them in a running fight that pulled them all north and west—always north and west—the Angels had fought to link up with Caliph Rashier. It had gained them nearly forty minutes. Now, having nearly run out of the badlands and the cover they provided, into what Rashier had called The Fringes, Marcus also felt himself running out of options.

Around him other members of the Angels fought and ducked among the stone labyrinth, sometimes matched against two raider opponents. Where Marcus could get a target lock he added his assistance with all the hellish blue-white energy from his extended-range PPC. Every few moments his heat buildup forced him to alternate to a trio of medium lasers, as he carefully rode the edge of the yellow band, teetering on the red. He switched just before the heat buildup could begin to seriously hamper his targeting effectiveness.

The *Orion* that hunted him labored under no such penalty. Leaning out from behind a wide rock column, it cut loose with its LB-X autocannon again, the round breaking up into smaller fragments that struck The Archangel and scoured armor off like some giant shotgun. One or two plates clanged off the side of the *Caesar*'s protruding head, throwing Marcus against his restraint straps too violently for him to return fire.

He opened communication with Ki-Lynn. "Where the hell are the Reserves? I wanted them to close up with us ten minutes ago. This *Orion* is taking me a bite at a time."

Where the hell was Rashier, for that matter? Marcus wondered again. Ki had been trying to contact the caliph for a good quarter-hour. By now the man should have realized that their plan had been shot to hell by the early arrival of raider forces. Or at least, Marcus trusted that Nihail could puzzle that out.

As if sensing his thoughts, Ki-Lynn replied to both questions. "Raiders slipped their second lance of light-mediums in behind us," she said, sounding unflappable as ever. "Reserves have reported two *Blackjack*s causing trouble with Streak-variant short-range missile systems. Still no answer from Rashier."

Marcus checked the nightmare that had settled over his tactical screen. The passages were so narrow and the rock thick enough to shield magscan that he had only a rough idea of where any of his forces were. Half had been forced out the far northern side of the maze, up onto a plateau—part of an area known as The Fringes. These Fringes might still offer the Angels some basic cover, but beyond them were the flat desert plains where sat Shervanis' city and a few of his *protected* villages. From what Marcus could tell, maybe only four of the Angels remained in this tight area of the badlands. The battle raged all around him, but far out of his control for the moment.

Then force it back under your control, he commanded himself, hands knuckle-white on the control grips.

"Send them some indirect fire, Ki. Thunder munitions. Have Charlie pull back and spot for you so you can drop the mines out of sight of the *Blackjack*s and whatever the hell else might be back in there. Then Tamara can lead them into the mines. Thunders'll rip the legs off those lighter 'Mechs." Marcus leaned too far out in taking the next corner, and scraped against a wall of striated pink and red rock. He fought for a few seconds against gravity, the signals from his own inner ear transmitting to the *Caesar*'s gyro via neurohelmet. "I know you're getting low on Thunder ammo. Send no more than two flights, and tell Charlie she's got to do the best she can with it."

Three 'Mechs left in this maze, bottling it up against a full company of raiders. Four to five more Angels scrapping it out on the plateau against another company. It couldn't go on much longer. The delaying tactics his people had been using were working, to a point. The battle had drawn out for almost an hour, but while it kept the Angels functional, it also meant the raiders weren't taking the critical damage necessary to knock them out of the fight. There had been no repeat of that first engagement, the quick deaths of the *Quickdraw* and *Ostsol*. With their commander on the field, the raiders had fought a much more cautious battle, wearing at the Angels' strength.

And it will work. The certainty hung over Marcus like a guillotine ready to drop. Half the Angels had come into the fight already battered from the previous engagement, and at least one lance of Shervanis' BattleMechs were acting in support of the raiders. Another guarantee by Rashier shot to hell, Marcus thought. Shervanis couldn't have much left protecting his city, and Marcus hoped the diversionary attacks by Rashier's men had laid his city in ruins. Marcus had given orders to take down the caliph's 'Mechs by concentrated fire whenever possible, those machines being not as well equipped as the raiders' and easier to remove from the fight. But the numbers were still against the Angels, and it was only a matter of time now.

If we could take out their commander, we might have a chance. But even as the thought suggested itself again, Marcus banished it. Not at the cost of Torgensson's life! It would demoralize the Angels to so coldly sacrifice one of their own, a fact the raider commander was counting on. Marcus had given strict orders against firing on those particular three raider 'Mechs, but he knew the longer the battle drew out the harder that choice would be to maintain.

Stepping out from between two high walls, Marcus found himself standing in a shallow washout along the southern edge of the plateau. Out among craters and a few rock formations, half of his Anglers were playing a deadly game of tag with the raider 'Mechs that had already made it through. *And more will be coming right behind me. Where the hell is Rashier?* Then two more 'Mechs ran down into the washout from further along; Jericho, now piloting a very beat-up and limping *Battle-Master,* being chased by a *Caesar* twin to Marcus' own. At two hundred fifty meters the raider stood outside optimum range, but Marcus had it by the back and the *BattleMaster* carried the Angels' C^3 master computer.

He tied in through Jericho's targeting and tracking system, able to lock on as if the raider were a hundred meters closer. The *Caesar's* Gauss rifle spat out a silvery ball of ferro-nickel alloy that slammed dead-center into the raider *Caesar's* back. Marcus couldn't help but wince in sympathetic response, knowing the light armor carried there.

The Gauss slug cracked through the armor plating as if it didn't exist, then tore through the internal skeleton with incredible fury. The entrance scar glowed a brilliant red for a moment, almost as if the 'Mech was bleeding. Then the fusion engine, released from captivity, expanded to consume all available material. The enemy *Caesar* exploded with enough force to shake rocks loose from the walls around them and collapse a standing column of stone to seal the passage Marcus had just exited.

Whipping his 'Mech into a run, Marcus swore under his breath and made for a shallow crater where he could hope for some amount of cover. *Caught in the open, just like the other* Caesar. The thought was hardly complete before his sensors screamed at him in warning and the computer painted a red square on his HUD. *Behind me!* Marcus turned The Archangel hard left, straight into a steep rock formation, but the quickest way to deny any raider a shot into his rear armor. Red stone filled his cockpit window, and he felt the urge to grab sky. *Why didn't you install jump jets instead of those extra mediums,* he berated himself, then positioned his arms to absorb most of the impact and push himself back off.

The missiles slammed into his left arm and torso just as he rebounded and pivoted to keep The Archangel from damaging itself against the steep wall. Marcus immediately began to walk backward, wanting to get moving more than he worried about returning fire. Then the *Orion* stepped from a passage further along, launching a new wave of long-range missiles and spitting out a burst of rounds from its autocannon. This time Marcus did return fire with his PPC. The azure whip traced a line in the rock, just to the *Orion*'s right, leaving a molten scar behind. Fortunately the *Orion*'s aim wasn't much better, the autocannons burst missing high and only a quarter of the missiles striking the *Caesar*'s right leg.

Marcus took stock of his Gauss ammunition, noting that less than a ton remained. *Run the heat then,* he thought, firing off his PPC again, this time tagging the *Orion* square in the center torso.

As he weathered the return fire, he glanced at his display and for the first time noticed a green circle racing toward the engagement. *A vehicle?* Then it was joined by a second and then a third. For a moment Marcus hoped that Rashier had finally arrived, and scanned the HUD for approaching BattleMechs. Nothing. Then *Caesar's* computer tagged each vehicle as non-combatant hovercraft, and Marcus understood what was happening. The General and his small band of infantry had finally caught up and were trying to distract the *Orion*. Marcus admired the bravado, but thought it matched by stupidity. Those vehicles weren't armored and didn't have the performance value of Savannah Masters. *Machine-gun fire will rip them apart.*

But the *Orion* quickly found itself facing a bigger problem than infantry driving civilian hovercars. Two 'Mechs suddenly emerged from the badlands and were racing against its rear. As if on prearranged signal, both BattleMechs took to the air on jets of plasma, separating into a triangle with Marcus that would force the *Orion* to let one of them at its rear armor. The Reserve element, Marcus realized, and none too soon.

Beset on all sides, the *Orion* abandoned its weaker spot to the *Phoenix Hawk* and concentrated on the *Caesar*. *Must be my paint job,* Marcus thought and smiled grimly. He missed with his Gauss rifle, the silvery ball ricocheting off the cliff face rising up in the background, but he did manage to catch it again with his PPC. Both Charlene and Tamara Cross added to its misfortune with a barrage of laser fire, though Tamara missed with her *Grasshopper's* single large. It showed the poor judgment of the *Orion* MechWarrior, to assume the lightest 'Mech posed the least threat.

Charlene's *Hawk* cut loose with its large and two medium lasers, coring into the *Orion's* back and carving at its gyro housing. The *Orion* dropped like an unstrung puppet, arms and legs splayed wide. Down but not out.

But now more raider 'Mechs were beginning to emerge from the stone labyrinth, including a *Tempest* chasing Ki-Lynn's *Archer* before it. The *Tempest's* slow gait and pronounced limp told of a run-in with Ki's Thunder munitions, but it was still coming. Tamara and Charlene both jetted back toward Marcus' position, covering Ki as best they could while putting distance between them and the hard-hitting raiders.

We've lost the initiative, Marcus thought. There wasn't more than the occasional request for support over the panic channel, but he could feel it in his soul. He began to back The Archangel toward the crater he'd been making for earlier. *Dammit, we've hurt them, and from my count the Angels can't have lost more than three 'Mechs so far. But Rashier isn't going to make it in time and we're tiring.* Marcus could tell by their movements that a few of his 'Mechs had suffered gyro damage while machines such as Jericho's *BattleMaster* and now Ki's *Archer* were practically walking skeletons devoid of armor.

"All units," Marcus called out, overriding his link to Ki and transmitting on one of the general frequencies he reserved for such occasions. "Angels fall back from the badlands. Establish a defensive line on the plateau. Reserves and Visitor One form on Lyre." He could tell by the HUD that Chris Jenkins had never made it out of the badlands. *So Jericho is alone now, except for one of her warriors strapped to the face of a raider War Dog.* "Be ready to turn and hit the raiders already on the plateau. If we get the chance, we'll clear a path to the west."

The *Awesome* and its two flanking 'Mechs, their human shields still tied in place, held the center of the raider line that formed in the shadow of the badlands and now moved forward with deliberate purpose. Most of these Battle-Mechs were still fresh, except for one or two like the *Orion,* which crawled slowly to unsteady feet and took a place along the raider's left flank. *We can't beat them and we can't hold.* The *Awesome* was the key, just as the raiders knew that destroying his *Caesar* would secure a victory over the Angels. *But not at the cost of Torgensson's life, dammit.* Marcus pounded the arm of his command couch at the unfairness. *But it's that or flee back into the desert, and next time we'll have only half as many 'Mechs able for the attack.*

And there it was, all laid out before him. Three lives for ten. Not just Torgensson, but all three captive warriors. This was no longer about fulfilling a contract. From now on it was strictly personal. The Angels had gone through too much, and to run now would destroy them. On Marantha or New Home or anywhere before that, yes, they would have run to cut their losses. But Marcus didn't have the stomach for it anymore. His people were suffering because they believed in him. He owed them more than a few words and a shrug over somebody's grave. And he couldn't run when he knew it meant abandoning three of his MechWarriors to an enemy who would use them so cheaply.

He swallowed hard against a suddenly constricted throat and then opened communications with the entire unit again. "Angels, prepare to turn back and engage raider line. Concentrate on its left flank. Reserve element, you two are hitting the *Awesome* and his two partners. Free the hostages if you can. You have one pass to do it, because then Visitor One and I hit the *Awesome* with everything we've got left. On my mark." The tension pulled every muscle in Marcus' body taught. "Now! At them, Angels!"

If the Angels had any doubts, it didn't show as every unit broke away from the few raider 'Mechs holding the middle of the plateau to suddenly come around on the main raider line. The raiders had lagged over six hundred meters back while forming, but now numbered better than a full company, and half of these as yet untouched by battle. Some long-range fire was exchanged, with lucky shots from both sides. Connor Monroe in the *Marauder* stabbed a stream of PPC energy into the head of the already hurting *Orion* Marcus had tangled with, taking it out of the fight. But the *Awesome* managed to strike back, with two of its three blue-white PPC beams fusing together into one heavy stream that drilled through the remaining torso armor on Brandon Corbett's *Griffin,* completely destroying the gyro and fusion engine. The young MechWarrior rocketed out of the cockpit as his ejection system threw him a hundred meters up and back.

Marcus felt cold, detached even as he watched. Both lines were breaking apart now, though they still worked their way closer to each other. His *Caesar* rocked under light autocannon fire but held its footing. He kicked the 'Mech up into a run, preparing for his chance at the *Awesome,* and then quickly throttled back into a walk as the scene through his cockpit window suddenly took on aspects of the surreal.

The Angels' infantry, momentarily forgotten while the hovercars had hidden down in the shallow crater near the plateau, now came flying out to streak toward lead elements in the raider line. Not too surprising that Hanford Lee would choose to join the Angels in their desperate bid for victory. What surprised Marcus was that The General had recruited help—and what help he had recruited.

Horses and a few old desert-style jeeps also came pouring out of the crater, fanning out into their own line of battle only fifty meters distant from the advancing raiders. Large, beautiful animals with wild manes and tails and each one ridden by a caftan-robed warrior. Thirty of them at least. The jeeps also carried desert warriors, but these were armed with laser rifles and SRM packs, as were Lee and his infantry.

Marcus couldn't see what they hoped to accomplish, except that they were drawing fire from the raiders that would have been meant for his 'Mechs. "Flank speed," he called out over the battle frequencies. "Now, while we can." The cold dread of a moment ago was forgotten as he watched thirty horsemen, a few battered jeeps, and three civilian hovercars spend themselves against the raider line. *A few seconds is all we'll get,* Marcus thought. *The raiders will move past the line and only the hovercraft have any hope of keeping up.*

Then the first ropes sailed into the air from the horsemen, grapples locking into the 'Mechs' shoulder joints and communication antennae. At least half the black-robed warriors rose from their mounts and began to clamber up the sides of the raider 'Mechs, and Marcus experienced the same stunned reaction that Charlene had at the same sight. A bolt of electrical current thrilled through his body and lent him a sudden burst of strength.

Courage and spirit against a thousand tons of technology. If nothing else, Marcus knew it was a sight he would likely never see again.

41

The Fringes
Shaharazad Desert, Astrokaszy
The Periphery
11 July 3058

And then all hell broke lose.

Charlene couldn't shake that ancient line from Milton's *Paradise Lost* as she watched the scene unfold before her. The desert warriors swarmed up the side of a half-dozen raider BattleMechs, throwing the entire enemy line into disarray. As the Angels heavily engaged the raiders' left flank, careful to avoid any 'Mechs with people on them, four new 'Mechs designated as gold triangles on her HUD suddenly appeared behind the raider line. Two came in on low-altitude jumps that barely cleared the jagged rock formations along the edge of the badlands, and two more bolted from the badlands to strike at the center of the raider forces. Charlene recognized Aidar's *Enforcer,* as well as the *Shadow Hawk* and recently captured *Grand Dragon.* The Desert Wind tribe was making a grand play. One that had just as much chance of destroying the tribe as it did of increasing their strength.

All along the raiders' left flank the Angels drew strength from the desert warriors. Two of the Mech-Warriors being held hostage had been cut free by the nomads; Kelsey Chase had already mounted an abandoned horse and was riding after a rope trailing from the *Orion* she'd been tied to. The MAF MechWarrior, Shannon

Christienson, had been picked up by The General in his hovercar as he continued to join in with the infantry's harassment.

That left Torgensson.

Charlene in her *Hawk* and Tamara in the *Grasshopper* held the middle of the field for the Angels. They had tried to avoid pushing through the mounted desert warriors, but it was beginning to look as if they'd have to. The *Awesome* unleashed its PPCs against anyone who tried to get close, whether horseman or BattleMech. The raider commander had burned out the *Shadow Hawk*'s center torso in one concentrated barrage and driven back the *Grand Dragon*. The charred flesh and ashes of several horses and their riders littered the ground around it, testimony to the *Awesome*'s destructive firepower against an unarmored foe.

Charlene thumbed the trigger for her large laser, burning a scar across the shoulder of a raider *Guillotine* on the right flank. Only the desert warriors' *Grand Dragon* and *Enforcer* held that part of the field, and were about to be crushed. If that wasn't enough, another 'Mech moved from the badlands to join up with the raiders, designated on her HUD with the red squares of raider/Shervanis forces. It was a *Clint* running with a peculiar gait akin to gyro trouble, but it still could augment the raiders with another A/C 5.

"Reserve Two, prepare to jump on my command. Jump in behind the *Awesome*. Hit it from behind, and maybe we can shut it down before Torgensson buys it." It wasn't the best plan, but it was all Charlene could think of in the scant seconds left before Marcus ordered the concentrated-fire barrage.

Then the *Clint* beat her to it.

Fighting the neural feedback, Thomas Faber concentrated on remaining upright as the 40-ton *Clint* lumbered forward with all the grace of a one-legged *Goliath*. His recirc fans had quit an hour ago, and now the desert heat had turned his cockpit into an oven—baking him at over forty-three degrees Centigrade. Only the cooling vest kept him conscious. That and the knowledge that the Angels needed him.

He'd made it from the city and all the way here before encountering any of Shervanis' BattleMechs. While trying to catch up to the raiders he'd heard some radio traffic about diversionary strikes against the city, but he knew that where the raiders went he would find the Angels. He'd tracked the enemy along their near-circular path, and while paused at the edge of The Fringes, he'd seen the way things were unfolding and what exactly this St. Jamais had done. Watching the raider line fall back in the middle, their 'Mechs trying to shake loose the persistent desert warriors, he decided that his one goal here would be to help remove the leverage the raiders held over the Angels' heads. To rescue Torgensson.

Approaching the *Awesome,* his only concerns were remaining upright and hoping not to catch stray PPC fire from his own comrades.

A new group of riders were making a dash at the *Awesome,* trying to get under the reach of its PPCs. Thomas stepped up from behind and to the *Awesome*'s right, grasping the assault 'Mech's right-arm PPC with his *Clint*'s left hand and pulling it around.

In any other circumstances, two BattleMechs would rarely get so close. But the *Awesome* had no reason to suspect Thomas and it was far to late to react as Thomas eased his autocannon up to the *Awesome*'s torso-mounted PPC and sent a fifty-millimeter slug straight down the barrel. The *Awesome* had been building for another blast, and now that energy spilled out through breeches in the barrel, wasted. But it didn't wash over Torgensson, who Thomas could see was still alive, though looking half-dead. And it ruined a third of the assault machine's firepower.

That was the opening the desert warriors had been waiting for. Three of them latched onto the *Awesome* and began to ascend quickly up the side and back. One swung around to the front, slashing at Torgensson's bonds with a wicked-looking curved knife that went right back between the warrior's teeth as soon as the hostage started to slip free. Faber managed to get his 'Mech's left hand under the near-conscious MechWarrior, who slid into the cupped palm of the *Clint*.

Good enough. Faber backpedaled the 'Mech, disengaging from the *Awesome,* whose pilot was suddenly more worried about the black-robed warriors crawling over it. Torgensson's savior never made it away from the *Awesome*'s chest as the 'Mech's block-like left hand came up and smeared the warrior against its armor.

The *Awesome* wasn't done with Faber, though. Unable to reach another of the warriors working his way up its back, it turned and fired off its two remaining PPCs and some laser and short-range missiles into the already-awkward *Clint*. One PPC bolt amputated the *Clint*'s right leg at the knee, while the second evaporated armor from the chest area and cut deep into the internal structure. Rather than fight the inevitable, Thomas abandoned himself to gravity and worked to protect the delicate cargo still cupped protectively in his left hand.

It wasn't the support Marcus had expected, but he and his Angels made the most of it. The left flank of the raider line shattered under their determined assault of point-blank combined fire, which was now degenerating into individual shooting matches. But then the raiders' right flank closed in, threatening to use similar patterns of combined fire to finish off the Angels.

Marcus pumped his next-to-last Gauss slug into the left arm of a *Guillotine,* shattering the last of its armor and punching through myomer bundles and ferro-titanium skeleton to lodge somewhere near its shoulder actuator. The arm dropped to the 'Mech's side, lifeless, but the *Guillotine* managed to return fire with three of four medium lasers and a flight of six short-range missiles. The ruby laser darts chewed into the *Caesar*'s right leg and center torso, stripping off more armor. Four of the missiles hit home but scattered enough that no armor was breeched.

I can't take much more of this, Marcus thought, fighting to control his 'Mech under so much damage. *None of us can.*

The heat in his cockpit had dropped back to tolerable

levels ever since the destruction of the *Caesar*'s Clan-tech extended-range PPC meant the 'Mech couldn't generate as much heat. *Gauss rifle almost out of ammo, all I've got left are the medium lasers.*

Trying to tell anything from his HUD was almost useless, with so many 'Mechs mixing it up at close range. From what he could make out, the desert warriors had created havoc at the center of the raider line, trading two of their beat-up 'Mechs for the raider *War Dog.* The horsemen had actually caused the more serious damage, apparently capturing three raider 'Mechs, though only one, the second *Orion,* had started to move as yet. Through his viewport Marcus saw Charlene's *Phoenix Hawk* stumble to the ground on the far side of the *Guillotine,* its right arm amputated at the shoulder and the right leg dangling from the hip by only a few strands of myomer.

That brings us down to five 'Mechs still on their feet. And two desert warriors, though the Enforcer's *main weapon is ruined, and it doesn't look like much more than a walking scrap yard.* Marcus traded medium laser shots with the *Guillotine,* ruby and emerald light spears crisscrossing between them and making more armor melt and run to the ground in red-hot streams. *One last Gauss shot, but not for him.* Marcus swung away, ready to plow onward and after the *Awesome.*

Take down the raider commander and force him to surrender; that's all we've got left. That or retreat. And to pull out now, after losing so many lives and 'Mechs, would spell the end of the Angels as an effective fighting force.

"DropShip!" a voice yelled over the panic channel. "*Overlord* coming down hard at half a klick north-northwest. Hegemony insignia."

No, dammit, no. An *Overlord* could bring massive weaponry to bear, smashing the Angels like a giant hammer against the anvil formed by raider 'Mechs. Marcus stabbed at his comm panel, unit-wide frequency. "Confirm that," he commanded.

"Confirmed, Lyre." It was Jericho's voice, resignation bleeding through the airwaves as her borrowed

BattleMaster pulled back into a crater for some protection against the advancing right flank of the raiders. "It's being buzzed by a couple of aerospace fighters, but it's Hegemony no doubt."

Marcus backed the *Caesar* up as he fought the control sticks to swing his torso around on the *Awesome*. *One shot. It had to come down now, or the Angels would be forced to flee into the badlands if they were to have any hope of eluding the raiders.*

Aerospace fighters?

The question hit Marcus' mind as he also realized he hadn't taken any recent hits from the *Guillotine*. The answer was apparent once he'd checked the HUD and then followed it up with a stare of disbelief through his viewport. The raiders were pulling back! A few remained behind, tying up Angels who were still up and active, but the *Guillotine* was already a good hundred meters away and moving into a run, and beyond it another five hundred meters was the retreating form of the still-intact *Awesome*.

Now the rear guard turned and fled, no longer bothering to trade shots but trying to close the distance to their DropShip as fast as possible. Marcus didn't understand, but as the *Guillotine* passed within two hundred meters of the *BattleMaster*, Marcus tied through to Jericho's targeting and tracking system and let fly with his last slug of Gauss ammunition. The silvery ball tagged the heavy 'Mech square in its rear-right torso, cracking through the thinner armor and spinning the 70-ton machine forward and into the ground.

Then some newly arrived BattleMechs appeared from the edge of the badlands, running forward onto the battlefield and deploying into a line separating the Angels from the raiders. A lance, then a company. Each 'Mech bore the insignia of the Magistracy Armed Forces; the three stars over a green closed-crescent field. They seemed content to let the raiders retreat, not wanting to tangle with an *Overlord*, but they did shield the Angels from any further damage.

Marcus turned the *Caesar* in a slow circle and surveyed what was left of his unit. Jericho Ryan in the *Battle-*

Master. Tamara Cross in the *Grasshopper.* Ki's *Archer* helping the *Marauder* piloted by Connor Monroe back onto its feet. And him. Five 'Mechs, presiding over a battlefield of smoking rock and twisted metal.

More 'Mechs kept pouring from the badlands. Two companies. A full battalion. All bore the colors of the MAF. Not Major Wood's unit, but at this point Marcus wasn't about to be choosy. *We're alive, and the Angels can rebuild.*

Then the final lance cleared the rugged twists of the badlands. Four black-painted 'Mechs, three of them with a large death's head standard painted on their upper-right torsos. *Death Commandos.* Marcus felt a chill at the sight of these infamous warriors and could think of no scenario that would let them show up as part of Canopus forces.

The final 'Mech was impressive indeed, stately as it moved onto the plateau as if the MechWarrior had not a care in the world. A 90-ton *Emperor,* broad-shouldered and with giant LB-X barrels in place of lower arms, the machine looked both imperious and deadly. It was not painted with the death's head, but instead its broad chest displayed the gauntlet-and-katana insignia of the Capellan Confederation.

Marcus stood his ground as the assault 'Mech moved slowly up and past his *Caesar.* It was as though the other pilot felt firmly in control of the battlefield. *Arrogant son of a bitch,* Marcus thought, then decided to ignore it for now. He twisted The Archangel around to watch the *Overlord* DropShip take back to the air in a cloud of dust and sand.

This isn't over, Marcus promised silently. *He wasn't sure how, or when, but the Angels would meet up with these raiders again. I'll find you,* he promised the raider commander. *I'll find you, and then I'll follow you and destroy you.* He breathed out in a heavy exhale, tension flowing out of his muscles and ordinary exhaustion moving into its place. *But not today.*

Now he had warriors—friends—to see to and a unit—his home—to rebuild.

BOOK IV

And therefore only the enlightened sovereign and the worthy general who are able to use the most intelligent people as agents are certain to achieve great things. Secret operations are essential in war; upon them the army relies to make its every move.

—Sun Tzu, *The Art of War*

Never place too much trust, power, or confidence in any one person. Too often he will end up failing you.

—Sun-Tzu Liao, journal entry, 24 June 3045

42

The Angels met in the shade cast by Sun-Tzu Liao's *Lung Wang* DropShip. The *Pearl of True Wisdom* had landed soon after the *Overlord*'s ascent, and now rested peacefully in the open area not far from where the battle had taken place. Jericho Ryan mixed in easily with the Angels, and was now talking with Paula Jacobs. Adair Sildig stood slightly apart to represent the Desert Wind tribe, with the rest of his warriors fanned out alongside the DropShip in various states of repose.

Most of Marcus' people still wore the sweat-drenched shorts and T-shirts of their 'Mech cockpits, and one or two still had on their cooling vests. The desert warriors all wore their long caftans, reminding Marcus of Nihail, though these robes were light-colored to better protect against the sun. Everyone looked exhausted, even hardened desert-dwellers such as Adair. Marcus could see in their eyes and their weary smiles that they all knew how close they'd come to defeat.

Only to be rescued by Sun-Tzu Liao.

Marcus shook his head. He still found it hard to believe, especially in light of Thomas Faber's report on the arms warehouses he discovered in Shervanis. Could Sun-Tzu be trying to play a third aspect of the Astrokaszy double-blind? One Marcus couldn't grasp? He knew it was possible, but somehow it just didn't sit right.

He took a long pull from a plastic liter bottle of Vita-Orange, a sports drink favored by MechWarriors for replacing the electrolytes lost in the intense heat of Battle-Mech cockpits. The weak orange flavoring rolled quickly past his tongue as he swallowed, the beverage cool and soothing to his throat. More of Sun-Tzu's generosity. Besides offering the use of his DropShip's medical facilities to all the injured, Astrokaszy native or not, the Chancellor of the Capellan Confederation had supplied the Angels and their associates with food and drink. Marcus had to admit that he was beginning to come down on the side of Sun-Tzu Liao.

"Torgensson's going to live," Marcus said, pacing along the front row of the gathered warriors and rubbing at the soreness left by his 'Mech seat restraints digging too tightly against his right shoulder. "He's got a broken leg and is suffering from time spent in the company of Malachye Shervanis—not to mention being tied to the front of a 'Mech in combat—but he's basically all right. I think he's already making friends with the Capellan doctor."

That drew a number of smiles, though Marcus caught several apprehensive glances up toward the large Capellan Confederation symbol painted on the side of the DropShip above them. He couldn't blame his people for being nervous. House Liao wasn't known for its generosity, much less acts of humanitarian aid. So far Marcus had met with Sun-Tzu for only a moment, when he'd asked for an opportunity to speak with him after he'd had a chance to rack his *Emperor* in the *Lung Wang*'s 'Mech bay. Even in that brief exchange Marcus shivered under the gaze of the young Capellan ruler.

"Shannon Christiensen and Kelsey Chase are suffering a bit from the long exposure to the sun," Marcus continued. "But they're both all right, and Kelsey will be released from the sick bay after a full night's rest. And before any of you start worrying about that, let me tell you it was my idea for her to stay there." Marcus knew his people, and Kelsey would push herself too hard too fast.

Case in point being that she had scaled the *Orion* 'Mech she'd been tied to and taken it over when the desert warriors had failed.

Charlene spoke up from where she sat on a patch of sun-baked red clay. "Aidar, someone is supposed to be out here to talk to you as soon as possible about your wounded."

The dark-skinned native nodded. "I am more concerned with the BattleMechs our warriors captured."

As Charlie said, more concerned with equipment than lives. Marcus thought of the Angels he wouldn't be seeing again, those who'd fallen and would remain forever in the Periphery so far from home. Brent Karsskhov, Geoff Vanderhaven, and most recently Brandon Corbett. Each left a hole inside him that would be a long time healing. "I'll bring that up to the Chancellor when I talk with him," Marcus promised. "As well as a fair share of salvage from this battle."

Thomas cleared his throat meaningfully. "We aren't going back in to hand Shervanis his head on a plate?"

"I'd like to," Marcus said, a touch more vehemence in his voice that he'd intended, "but we'll be sitting this one out. Danai Centrella is claiming that privilege for her MechWarriors." Marcus finished off his drink in a long swallow. "Too bad, because we could've used that stockpile to rebuild."

Charlene nodded. "And our contract?"

"Closed out," Marcus said. "Our contract ended here, this battle. This shipment of arms and supplies have been disrupted to the Hegemony, and with my report to Danai Centrella the Magistracy forces have been duly alerted to the exact location of remaining stockpiles. And"— Marcus smiled fully—"Danai assured me that no letter of indebtedness ever reached the Magistracy. And even if it has by now, the Magistracy of Canopus takes care of its own—whether regular forces or mercenary. They'll make good our loans, and we'll in turn pay them back. We're covered."

He let the whistles and exclamations of relief play out before continuing. "I don't know how well or how fast we can re-man or re-equip. We lost good people here, and that will hurt us for a long while." He glanced self-consciously at Jericho. "But we can also hope that some of those who fought with us will remain. As for material resources"—he shrugged as if that was not so important—"right now we're looking at five to eight functioning or repairable machines. That includes ransoming Vince and his *Enforcer* from the other desert tribe. With decent salvage from the field, we'll soon be back on our feet.

"The Angels are survivors." He let his pride in them show in his voice and face. "No one can take that away from us."

A comfortable silence descended over the gathering of warriors then, broken only when Charlene reached out with her foot to nudge Marcus' boot. She nodded toward the main 'Mech bay door. "Marc, they're coming down. You should go meet them."

The mercenary commander glanced to where Sun-Tzu Liao and two MAF officers were strolling down the ramp in the company of a squad of guards. "Guess I should," he said. "Coming with?" he asked Charlene.

She shook her head. "Sun-Tzu brought his Magistracy liaisons. You better take yours."

Steeling himself against a show of nervousness, Marcus offered Jericho a hand up from the ground. He caught the look of surprise on her face when he didn't let go of her hand right away, but walked partway to the meeting with her alongside. He had also caught several half-amused glances among his Angels, including a nod of approval from Paula Jacobs. It would take time for him to grow comfortable with such public displays, but Marcus promised himself he'd try. He was glad Jericho didn't say anything, seeming to understand his need to keep this light. She only gave his hand one quick squeeze as they dropped hands in the last few steps of the approach to Sun-Tzu Liao.

If the Capellan Chancellor noticed anything of their relationship, he didn't show it. He stood at the center of his retinue of guards, reminding Marcus of the way Rashier like to do the same thing. Sun-Tzu was lithe and looked even younger than his years, which Marcus knew were all of twenty-six or twenty-seven. There was no sign of madness or rage, two traits so often associated with the Liao ruling family. As earlier, Marcus found the Liao even of both voice and expression.

"Commander GioAvanti," Sun-Tzu said in greeting. He was dressed in his red silk robes of state, though he still wore the black sweatband from earlier in his 'Mech.

Practical, Marcus thought, blinking away the tears of sweat that burned at the corners of his own eyes. "Chancellor. Please allow me to introduce Commander Jericho Ryan, my Magistracy liaison."

Sun-Tzu waved off Jericho's salute an unnecessary. "Of course." He then introduced her to the two daughters of Emma Centrella, though Danai excused herself curtly to see after her troops.

"You will have to excuse my sister," Naomi Centrella said, giving Marcus a disarming smile. "Recent events have left her rather frustrated."

Marcus had caught the venomous look Danai gave Sun-Tzu in parting and decided he didn't really want to know why. Trying to deal with Sun-Tzu, and now yet another daughter of the Magestrix, seemed more than enough for anyone in a single day.

Sun-Tzu studied the painted nails of one hand. In true Liao fashion the last three fingernails on both hands were grown extra long. It didn't seem feminine in the least. The nails looked razor-sharp, and he examined them with the same critical eye a samurai Combine warrior might have used on one of his swords. "Now, Commander, there were some points you wished to discuss?"

Marcus nodded, trying to ignore the cold stares of the four Death Commando guards. "The field salvage first of all. More than half of the Angels' BattleMechs are still out there. And over a company's worth of raider machines."

"Yes." Sun-Tzu trailed the flat of the nail of his little finger along his jaw. "But it was our arrival that sent them into retreat. I would be delinquent in my responsibilities as leader of this force if I did not insist on something."

And you have the upper hand with nearly a full battalion at your disposal. So now we're back to the Astrokaszy rules of bargaining? "Of course," Marcus said aloud. "I would not offend you by suggesting otherwise." *Just once in the near future, I'd like to be able to come right out and say what I think without worrying about whose toes I'm stepping on. But the Chancellor of the Capellan Confederation isn't the person to start with.*

"Good. Then you will first split the salvage with the Astrokaszy natives as you see fit. Afterward, I will accept ten percent of the salvage from both parties, according to what each claims." Sun-Tzu paused. "I will not expect you to count the three 'Mechs captured intact in these figures."

Ten percent? That's it? "The Chancellor is most fair." And that made Marcus uneasy. "And the supply depot in the City of Shervanis? Our contract specified a one-tenth share in captured stockpiles." *Though, technically, you could keep us from that by attacking the city yourself.*

Sun-Tzu smiled thinly, as if amused by some private joke. "Let us return to that. From Danai I understand that you will be forced to remain here some time still. You have two DropShips to repair? I will leave behind one lance of BattleMechs, no more. They will augment your forces until I return."

"You're going on to Campoleone?" Marcus asked carefully. Leading Magistracy troops across the Free Worlds League border, even under the flag of the Capellan Confederation, could be interpreted as an act of aggression. He had no desire to anger Sun-Tzu by pressing for details, but the Hegemony raiders were a matter that affected the Angels as well. "My Angels would be interested in accompanying you, if it meant another go at the raiders."

"The raiders are not heading for Campoleone," Naomi informed Marcus in a carefully neutral tone. She glanced at the Chancellor.

"I vowed to see that raider commander destroyed," Marcus said. "There's a chance he's heading—"

"He's not going either to Campoleone or back into the Hegemony," Sun-Tzu interrupted. "He was allowed to withdraw only because of an agreement we struck at the time of his boarding the *Overlord*. You will not see him again."

Marcus did not insist further. He could hear the note of finality in the Chancellor's voice. He wondered, of course. All prisoners from the battle had been claimed by Sun-Tzu in the name of the Magistracy of Canopus, and now came news of private negotiations and a proposed action against Campoleone. *Politics,* he thought. *The Angels don't need them.* "And the other point? The warehouse in the city of Shervanis?"

Sun-Tzu shrugged, the hard set of his features softening and a thin smile playing at one corner of his mouth. "Technically, the warehouse has already been captured."

"What?"

The Chancellor's voice was cold and serious, belying his look of amusement. "While you spent yourselves in the desert, Caliph Rashier attacked the city of Shervanis. Apparently he defeated the BattleMech force left to guard it, and a traitor within the palace murdered the caliph. Rashier now owns the city."

Marcus could feel the rage building inside him, but he held it in check while his mind worked feverishly. *Rashier betrayed us?* Then Marcus remembered a talk he'd had with the caliph about using a diverting force to lure away some enemy forces.

Sun-Tzu continued. "I have no reason to attack Rashier. And it would be bad politics for the Magistracy to turn on a leader who'd just defeated an enemy of their realm."

Rashier left us to be torn to bits. Would he have then made a deal with the returning raiders? Probably. So it would only be good Astrokaszy custom to pay him back for his treachery. He considered Sun-Tzu's words carefully, and then understood the amused expression. Apparently he and Marcus were thinking along the same lines.

"That's all right, Chancellor Liao. I think we can work out some kind of understanding." Marcus smiled. *He may not have a legitimate reason to order an attack, but the Angels do.* "How much would it cost me to hire your battalion for some easy work? Say about nine-tenths of the raider supply stockpile?"

Naomi Centrella hid her feelings behind a mask of neutrality, but Sun-Tzu returned Marcus' smile. "I think something can be arranged, Commander," was all he said.

43

Freedom City (formerly City of Shervanis)
Rashier Caliphate
Astrokaszy
The Periphery
13 July 3058

Marcus noticed that not one guard would meet his gaze. They searched him at the door, another fact not lost on him, and then passed him into the warehouse. The sound of nails being ripped from wood and the drone of moving equipment greeted him as he walked across the spacious but busy floor. Caliph Rashier and a few others stood near the center of the large building as workers broke open crate after crate of military supplies, cataloguing them and displaying the contents to the delighted caliph.

"Commander," Rashier greeted him as if the two were old friends. On a leash he held two huge spotted cats that resembled Terran leopards—the former pets of Caliph Shervanis. Nihail Sallahan hovered off to one side, eyes watchful, and Arch Vizier Ji-Drohmien stood nearby with a basket of fresh meat from which he occasionally drew bits to throw to the large cats. Rashier gestured about him. "See what we have wrought? An end to the devil Shervanis and the discovery of a treasure trove of arms and equipment."

Marcus smiled in apparent good humor. "I must have missed this part of the mission briefing."

Did doubt flicker for a moment in Rashier's eyes?

"Yes, well. Ji-Drohmien sent us word that only a medium lance would be guarding the city. I had no choice but to strike, or lose a great opportunity. Sorry there was no way to contact you, but everything worked out."

Marcus sought out the eyes of Nihail, whose dark eyes met his impassively for a moment before he let his gaze drop to the floor. Marcus had no doubt that the man had intentionally broke eye contact. *So he used you as well.*

"And of course we will help you repair both of your DropShips. I would even like to reward you from out of this stockpile. Good equipment for your Angels."

"The caliph is too kind."

Rashier grinned expansively. "And why not? You held up your end of the bargain. You saw our display?"

Marcus had indeed. Lining the road up to the city's main gate was a line of severed heads set on poles and still dripping gore onto the sand. The stench of the fresh killing was near intolerable, and Marcus knew from his first visit within the city walls that it would soon give way to the more pleasant odor of sun-rotted flesh. He'd counted the heads, already knowing but wanting to make sure. *One hundred and four; just what I promised you, Rashier.* And the head of Malachye Shervanis on the very last pole.

"Ji-Drohmien arranged it," the caliph continued. "Thought it would ease your mind about any further obligation to me."

Glancing at Shervanis' arch vizier, Marcus suddenly knew where the flesh meat had come from and felt a little sick to his stomach over the whole affair. *You mean you wanted to remind me of what I owed you. But it doesn't work, Rashier.* Marcus felt the vibration of heavy footsteps in the soles of his feet and knew that the time had come.

You're about to learn the full price of treachery.

Shouts coming from the warehouse main doors drew the attention of everyone but Marcus. Then a few scattered shots rang out as some of Rashier's guards fired on the approaching BattleMech out of reflex. The large and powerful fists of a *Grasshopper* came crashing through the ceiling, collapsing the entrance over Rashier's guards and tearing out a hole in the roof and wall big enough that almost all of the twelve-meter-tall machine could be seen by those inside. Workers bolted and ran for the rear doors as its right arm came up and leveled its medium laser at a nearby crate marked clearly as explosive ammunition.

"What? What is the meaning of this?" Rashier stammered.

"Divine retribution," Marcus said coldly, folding his arms across his chest. "The Angels have come for you."

Hot fury burned in the caliph's eyes. "Kill him," he commanded Nihail, stabbing a finger at Marcus. "No, wait. Take him alive. They will bargain for their precious commander."

"No, they won't, Rashier. Sun-Tzu Liao is in charge of the Angels in my absence. I think he would rather see this city razed to the ground."

The mention of Sun-Tzu spiked fear in the other man's eyes, though it was quickly replaced with hatred. "Then you are a dead man as well." He turned to Nihail. "Kill him now."

So here's where I find out if I ever read you correctly, Marcus thought, and again matched gazes with Nihail. Those dark unfathomable eyes stared back unblinking. *I'm ready to die for my people,* Marcus told him silently. *Are you still ready to give your life for this man?*

Nihail's speed was impressive. Reaching quickly inside his robes, he pulled out his two scimitars in one hand and an old needler in the other. Then he tossed the needler to Marcus, took his swords into two hands, and in the next moment he had Ji-Drohmien by the throat, with one of the swords threatening to slice him from ear to ear if he made a wrong move.

Catching the weapon, Marcus nodded to Nihail. "Welcome to the unit." He leveled the gun at Rashier. "You broke faith with the Angels, and it has cost you everything, Rashier. Even the loyalty of your own people."

To the caliph's credit, he was determined to meet any end with whatever dignity he could. "Kill me, Commander. Shoot me in cold blood." He glowered. "My people will avenge me."

"Don't be too sure. A company of Canopian 'Mechs under Naomi Centrella have secured this city by now. Probably without a fight. All military equipment will be confiscated by the Magistracy forces. Danai Centrella is moving against your city to the south, under orders to strip it of any defensive ability. And the transmissions have already gone out to the neighboring caliphates and all desert warrior tribes that both cities will be left standing defenseless. They will pick your bones clean, in good Astrokaszy fashion.

"But kill you?" Marcus said. "No, Rashier. The Desert Wind tribe has volunteered to take you and Ji-Drohmien into their fold. You will become true warriors, or die in the attempt. So I leave your life to Astrokaszy and the desert.

"You earned it."

44

Word of Blake HPG Station
Ausapolis, Campoleone
Rim Commonality
Free Worlds League
2 August 3058

The atmosphere in the HPG station main control room was tense, uneasy. Alpha Adepts hurried about the room or sat at consoles, some concentrating on the normal operations of the station, but most helping to coordinate with military forces. The white jumpsuits of these Word of Blake communication technicians were disheveled from a long night at their posts, and most had cast off their white and gold shoulder wraps in favor of comfort.

Precentor Demona Aziz commanded the center of the room, hood of her pristine white robes thrown back to reveal her face and dark wiry hair. She paced around the huge Word of Blake insignia emblazoned on the tile floor, walking just outside the outermost ring, careful not to step on the broadsword that pointed in the direction of the hyperpulse generator. Now she stopped as one of the technicians approached her with an update.

"What do you mean, they just took off again?" Her eyes were wide with anger and more than a little fear. *This is their third aborted attempt at landing. What game is Liao playing at?*

The adept would not meet her stare. "I only know what was reported, Precentor. The Canopian *Overlord* landed. This time they began to deploy BattleMechs, enough for our aerospace assets to identify at least two companies bearing the Magistracy of Canopus insignia. When our *own* ships landed within five kilometers, the *Overlord* loaded up and took off again under maximum thrust."

Keeping my people up all night chasing you, Sun-Tzu? Well, my troops have remained rested aboard their Drop-Ship and I could bring fresh adepts into the control room, so go ahead and make your grand play. What I field here are vintage Star League-era machines as well as some of Word of Blake's newest designs. "Recall DropShips and order our fighters to stand down," she ordered. Then, "What is the word from jump point sensors?"

"No other JumpShips beside the Canopian vessel," a technician on a far console answered back.

In his last message out of Astrokaszy before ordering the HPG station destroyed, Cameron St. Jamais had informed her of the inopportune arrival of Magistracy Armed Forces, most certainly led by Sun-Tzu Liao. *But he should have reached his JumpShip days before Sun-Tzu left the planet. Cameron, where are you?*

Demona continued her pacing like some caged animal. The Astrokaszy operation had folded, and while the planted evidence should cover Word of Blake's tracks well enough, there would be no fooling Sun-Tzu Liao about where to lay the blame. She had never believed the Liao would bring foreign troops into Marik space, in itself a hostile act. But then she would not have thought her plans could be so totally ruined by some small mercenary unit and the machinations of the Inner Sphere's weakest leader.

No, not weak. She realized that she'd underestimated him, a grave error. She wished for St. Jamais' presence, that she could order him to assassinate Sun-Tzu Liao to completely obliterate her mistake. Another part of her burned with cold fury that he'd already attempted and failed at that thing—and against her orders. Still another part longed for even his briefest touch.

Mostly, I want him here to take the blame.

Her most able lieutenant had failed her, and now he wasn't even present to act the part of a martyr to the cause. *My own personal double-blind missing. How selfish of him.* She laughed softly, a sound more of frustration than humor.

And then, as if in response to her laughter, came the distinct sound of gunfire and several small explosions. She barely had time to spin around before the two doors leading into the main control room slid open, and four small olive green objects came streaking through. There was the sound of metal objects bouncing across the tiled floor and then an eruption of thunder-claps that buffeted her senses and knocked her unconscious.

Naomi Centrella walked beside Sun-Tzu Liao. His stride was direct and full of purpose, and she couldn't help but admire the Chancellor's poise as they followed a pair of Death Commandos down the hall and into the main control room of the Campoleone HPG station.

The room had been cleared of all Word of Blake personnel except one. Precentor Demona Aziz stood in the center of the room, having been revived from the effects of the stun grenade and properly searched. She kept her back straight and head high and regal, but Naomi—with the benefit of years studying people at court—recognized the haunted look of a cornered animal in her eyes and drawn face.

"Chancellor Liao," Aziz said, her voice not so much as a tremor off of a properly respectful tone. "I hope you appreciate the delicacy of your position."

Sun-Tzu and Naomi stood at the lower tip of the

broadsword in the Word of Blake insignia, separated from the precentor by few mere footsteps. He crossed his arms over his chest and regarded her stoically. "What position is that?"

"You have brought foreign troops into the Free Worlds League and there attacked a Word of Blake hyperpulse generator station. The Captain-General will not be pleased."

"He will have no cause to complain. My troops never touched Campoleone until I received permission to land from the planetary governor, who was more than happy to sell you out. He didn't like the way his future looked, tied to your falling star, until I agreed to keep his name out of any official reports."

Naomi studied Sun-Tzu, noting the absence of dissimulation or verbal fencing. He went straight to the heart of the matter, his presence commanding in the knowledge of who was truly in control of the situation. In every new set of circumstances she'd been shown another new face, and always what Sun-Tzu wanted her to see. But not this time. There would be no false fronts put up here except by Precentor Aziz. And if Danai were present she would no longer consider Sun-Tzu someone to be casually dismissed. Naomi had no doubt that was the reason Danai was in command of the diversionary force that had drawn off the bulk of the station's defenders.

But if that is so, then why am I here? Naomi felt as if cold hands brushed the nape of her neck and she shivered. It was a question she no longer felt impartial enough to answer.

Precentor Aziz nodded, as a gamesman acknowledging a good move by an opponent. "Governor Searcy always was a weak man. That might win you some clemency for bringing MAF troops here, but not against attacking us unprovoked. You can prove nothing."

Sun-Tzu shrugged. "That doesn't matter anymore. The Marian Hegemony has lost its supplier, and without you their stockpile of new technology will steadily decrease. Canopus, on the other hand, is learning the fundamentals behind recent technological gains and will soon be able to hold its own." A thin smile eased over the Chancellor's mouth, but did not reach his eyes. "Thomas can be handled."

Doubt clouded the eyes of Demona Aziz for a brief moment, but she did not drop her calculated geniality. "You know, I do believe that you can handle Thomas Marik. Certainly you have proved yourself more resourceful than I would ever have thought."

"My thanks for your vote of confidence." Sun-Tzu's voice was ice.

"But we can now help each other," the precentor said quickly. "The Toyama can provide you with more leverage in the affairs of House Marik, and with your direct support I could challenge Blane for leadership of the Word of Blake. I would make concessions to you, of course, for the Toyama's earlier poor judgment."

Cocking his head to one side, as if considering the offer, Sun-Tzu asked, "But what of Astrokaszy? The news will spread."

"Lay it on the doorstep of Thomas Marik. Or threaten to. At the very least you could force the issue of your wedding to Isis."

Naomi stiffened involuntarily. She knew that Sun-Tzu's engagement shouldn't mean anything to her personally, and it suddenly worried her that it did.

"Word of Blake certainly knows how to find advantage in events, don't they?" Sun-Tzu asked. "Even their failures."

Demona seemed to read some degree of acceptance in Sun-Tzu's voice and relaxed marginally. When she spoke, it was with great conviction. "We are great survivors, Sun-Tzu Liao. The Word of Blake could serve you well."

Before Naomi could react, Sun-Tzu Liao pulled a needler pistol from the wide sleeves of his red robes of office and leveled it at Demona Aziz. The first wave of needles shredded her shoulder and cut into her neck. He pulled the trigger twice more, sending further bursts directly into her chest. She fell heavily to the floor as Sun-Tzu handed the pistol to a nearby Death Commando. "This is how you will serve me best," he said, looking down at her corpse.

The blood-spattered face of Demona Aziz stared up at

Naomi Centrella. Naomi had never seen death so up close and personal before. She was shocked and baffled, for it had come when the precentor had virtually capitulated to Sun-Tzu. "I don't understand," she said.

Sun-Tzu Liao placed a gentle hand on her arm and turned her from the sight. "You will," he said softly, leading her from the room. "I will teach you."

Epilogue

Word of Blake Central Chambers
Geneva
New Switzerland, Terra
27 August 3058

The boardroom of what had once been the flag building for a multiplanetary corporation was well-lit and comfortable. Word of Blake had renovated it, removing the old conference table and installing a full circle of translucent podiums. Missing were the slightly raised podium at which the Primus would stand and the soft spotlights that should fall over each podium. In fact, to demi-Precentor Cameron St. Jamais, the room's sole occupant at the moment, the chamber reminded him of a cheap copy of the old Hilton Head First Circuit Compound. But that, of course, had been nearly destroyed in Operation Odysseus.

If it were me, I would build completely from scratch and raise a magnificent cathedral-style compound. Our strength should come from our history, and this room reminds me too much of ComStar's secular philosophies.

Cameron had always seen the split between ComStar and Word of Blake as an almost personal affront. He was one of the divine instruments of Jerome Blake's will. *The sword of righteousness.* He glanced down at the floor in front of the podium where he stood, studying the broadsword-insignia of the Word of Blake. *My idea,*

*Demona—which you stole quick enough. But that doesn't
matter because you are finally gone and out of my way.*

Word of Precentor Aziz' death had preceded his arrival,
reaching Terra by hyperpulse communication over a week
ago. *Sun-Tzu made good his threat then.* At the moment,
all anyone on Terra really knew was that Demona's death
was somehow connected to reports of a Liao-Canopus
task force entering Marik space. Details were sketchy,
and Cameron St. Jamais knew more than anyone else ever
would. Not for the first time he gave thanks to the Blessed
Blake that he had held fast against the strong desire to
return to Campoleone despite the Liao's warning. Had he
not, it might have been his head up on a pole.

Doors off to the right swung open and Precentor Blane
walked into the room, the elder man's gold-embroidered
robes and the thin gold torque and headpiece he wore pro-
nouncing his status as Primus. St. Jamais wondered at
how a man with such a plain face could ever hope to
inspire the Word of Blake to anything. *You are a great
arbitrator, Blane, and little else. And now I will rely on
your mediating nature to help achieve my own ends.*

"Demi-Precentor," Blane said, once the outside guards
had closed the doors behind him. "Sorry to have kept you
waiting."

St. Jamais nodded solemnly. "Precentor Blane."

The precentor stepped up to the next podium over from
Cameron's. Not his normal position, but with just the two
of them the formalities didn't matter so much. "I wanted
to talk with you before the formal meeting of our First
Circuit. I have read your report of the situation and admit
to being distressed."

Our First Circuit? St. Jamais bit his lip to keep from
uttering a sharp response. In his opinion, it should be *The*
First Circuit. But apparently Blane still considered Com-
Star to be misguided rather than the heretics they were.
*We will never reconcile with them, but Blane refuses to
see that.* "Yes, Precentor, it is unfortunate. I had hoped to
present you with greater evidence of Demona Aziz'
treachery, but she cunningly kept me between her and any
official tie to the operation. Now it appears my efforts are
in vain. Precentor Aziz had been murdered, the Toyama is

without leadership, and I will bear the brunt of the criticism by the First Circuit." St. Jamais frowned in a perfect display of dismay and then waited for Blane's reaction.

It was not what he expected.

"You misunderstand, Cameron. I am distressed because the plan fell apart when it had every possibility of succeeding."

St. Jamais did not need to fake his surprise at Blane's words. "But, Demona worked to undermine you." Then he quickly added a, "Sir." St. Jamais watched as a tight smile turned up one corner of Blane's mouth. A cold empty feeling rose inside him. "You knew? All this time, you knew?"

The amusement in Blane's voice was evident. "Did you actually believe I would allow Precentor Aziz such room for potential gain, without having a way to keep an eye on her?"

"Then why didn't you stop her?" St. Jamais forced himself to calm down, placing his hands flat on the podium to keep them still. He had almost said *us* instead of *her*. "With support I could have ended the operation smoothly." Then the light dawned and St. Jamais felt suddenly out of his league for the first time in years. *Blane had known and silently approved!* "You used her. Used all of us." He was shocked, yet he couldn't keep a trace of admiration from his own voice.

Precentor Blane smiled fully and in apparent good humor. "Demona Aziz was a brilliant woman, but too impatient. Too fanatical. I allowed her to play her game. Had it succeeded, I would have hailed it as a great victory to the others, an example of my own ability to assign the right person to the task, then given her another assignment to keep her occupied. I think you know as well as I that she would not have had the temperament to maintain good relations with Canopus for long."

Actually I know she could be very patient, Blane. When she had to be. St. Jamais' discomfort was quickly dissipating. "And if she had failed?"

"Then I would have publicly condemned her and used the excuse to break up the Toyama. Classic double-blind strategy, Precentor St. Jamais. Demona Aziz was my safeguard, the more so since she never realized it." Blane tugged at the collar of his white and gold robes, adjusting the high-built shoulders.

No-lose scenario. Blane rose another notch in St. Jamais' opinion. *Very neat and—had he said Precentor?*

Blane apparently read the question in his eyes. "Demona failed and now she's gone. Because of Sun-Tzu Liao's involvement, the whole affair is being swept under the rug so I will not have the public outcry that will demand sacrifice. And as you pointed out, the Toyama is without a leader."

St. Jamais wanted to shout for joy, but he kept his face like stone. "What do you wish of me, Precentor Blane?"

Serious now, Blane folded his arms across his chest and studied St. Jamais as he spoke. "You will support my policies so long as they do not conflict directly with the Toyama faction. Step out of line, and I will bury you." He paused, as if to make sure the warning sank in. "The first order of the day is that you personally clean up the mess you left behind in the Periphery."

"And what has happened since my departure?"

"Well, Sun-Tzu Liao is on his way to Atreus and then on to the big summit on Tharkad. I imagine you've heard about the Jade Falcon attack on Coventry by now. He'll have his hands full playing politician, but I imagine we shall hear of his demands soon enough. However, Naomi Centrella, who is still traveling with the Liao, is already demanding large concessions on behalf of the Magistracy."

"Naomi? Not Emma Centrella?" *Curious.*

Blane nodded solemnly. "I estimate we have less than two weeks before Danai returns to Canopus with the full report and the Magestrix is in position to make the demands herself. You will make reparations to the Magistracy of Canopus before then, through Naomi. That will place her on our side *before* Emma Centrella announces us persona non grata. You will make the reparations from Toyama resources, and lay all blame at Demona's feet."

Blane fell silent, and Cameron considered everything being offered. *So I rise to the next step, but with Blane's assistance, rather than in spite of him. And I am to accept a weakening of the Toyama as we make full reparations. But what is lost can always be regained.* "Accepted, Precentor Blane." *As if there was ever any choice.*

St. Jamais returned Blane's parting nod and then stood there as the Primus walked silently from the room. He then moved around to the podium's front, over to the insignia on the floor, and walked a slow circuit of the rings and then down the length of the blade. At its tip, he stared back up along its length.

Precentor St. Jamais. The entire Toyama was his to control, and with that the 6th of June movement would rise to greater influence than ever before. Fledgling plans on how to deal with first the Magistracy and then later the Capellan Confederation were already forming. And somewhere along his rise to greater power, Cameron St. Jamais promised himself to take care of one other small matter still left unfinished from the Periphery.

Someday I will find Avanti's Angels again. And when I do, they all will fall, burning star by burning star.

ABOUT THE AUTHOR

Loren L. Coleman has lived most of his life in the Pacific Northwest, an on-again off-again resident of Longview, Washington. He started writing as a hobby in his high school days, but it was during his five years as a member of the United States Navy, nuclear power field, that he began to write seriously.

His first year out of the military, Loren joined the Eugene Professional Writer's Workshop, and within a few months sold his first fiction story to *Pulphouse, A Fiction Magazine*. He was then introduced to the game-writing field, where he spent the next two years as a professional freelancer, writing source material for game companies such as FASA, TSR, and Mayfair Games. For FASA, he has written material for both the BattleTech® and Earthdawn® games. When the opportunity arose to write a novel set in the BattleTech® universe, he eagerly accepted. *Double-Blind* is Loren's first novel. His second BattleTech® novel, *Binding Force*, will soon follow.

Loren L. Coleman is currently back in Longview, Washington. He has a wife, Heather Joy, and two sons, Talon LaRon and Conner Rhys Monroe.

House Hiritsu Stronghold, Randar
Sian Commonality, Capellan Confederation
24 April 3047

A sharp kick just behind his right knee caused the leg to buckle. Aris Sung fell heavily to both knees just as the main doors were swung open by muscular guards who must have heard their House Master approaching. The bright steel of two katana blades pressed down hard from behind him, one on each shoulder, to keep him from any attempt to rise. The wielder of the blade pressing down on his right shoulder sawed with his weapon, ever so slightly, to cut through Aris' tight-fitting black shirt and into the flesh beneath. Aris clenched his jaw against the pain and kept his eyes focused on the doors, waiting to see the person he had gambled his life to meet.

A woman entered, dressed in dark green silk robes that were almost black. She walked with strength and purpose to her step. Her hair was dark with a touch of iron gray at each temple, but the cheekbones were high and wide, and the tilt of her eyes spoke of Oriental ancestry. Late thirties, he judged, only because he knew how to look: This woman had the agelessness common to many women of her race, though Aris thought it more a result of her uncompromising will than something genetic. Not even time dared presume too much in her presence.

The room was simply constructed and furnished, an oddity in one of the largest strongholds on Randar. Aris could still remember the effort of scaling the outer walls, made of steel-reinforced ferrocrete and designed to keep out BattleMechs. Avoiding patrols. Passing through armored doors. Now here he was surrounded by hardwoods polished to such a high shine that the grains seemed to dance under the flickering lamps. Mats of woven rushes. Against the near wall was a low platform, too modest to be called a dais, but what sat on it could definitely be construed as a throne. A bench seat that Aris guessed to be constructed from dark maple. Hand-carved and padded with simple pillows of green satin.

And on the wall above the seat, an empty sword rack.

The woman stepped onto the platform and quietly stared up at the empty rack for a long moment. Aris Sung counted thirteen drops of blood that seeped past the dark cloth of his shirt and trickled down his side. A good omen, he decided. He had just turned thirteen years of age.

The woman settled herself on the bench seat, arranging her robes about her as if by afterthought. Not a word had yet been spoken by anyone. Aris felt sure that were he to try, his throat would be cut before he could utter two words. So he waited, meeting her icy blue eyes with a determined gaze of his own. He willed himself not to blink, carefully widening and relaxing his eyelids.

Neither one of them moved for half a minute, and then Aris took his first calculated risk. He straightened his back, slowly so as not to invite a deeper cut into his right shoulder. Then he rocked back, jaw set against the pain as he risked a deeper cut, until resting comfortably against his own calves. Adjusting his posture from defeated slump to comfortable meditation.

She blinked.

"Lance-leader Non." She turned her gaze to stare over Aris' right shoulder. "How does Crescent Moon happen to be missing?"

"House Master, we caught this thief in the outer chambers." The answering voice was proud and firm. An accomplishment under her direct observation, Aris thought.

Her gaze took on an inscrutable aspect, but her tone became almost playful. "Then why didn't I see Crescent Moon lying on the floor where it would have fallen, Ty?"

The pressure eased against Aris' shoulder as the sword-wielder considered this riddle. According to information bought at a high price by Aris, the katana sword Crescent Moon had originally been given to the first Master of House Hiritsu by Dainmar Liao, twenty-third Chancellor of the Capellan Confederation, at the time of House Hiritsu's formation almost two centuries before. Only the current House Master was allowed to touch the artifact. For almost a year and a half, ever since his initial rejection by House Hiritsu, Aris had been planning its theft. Always enforcing patience upon himself until he knew he would succeed. If he were caught too soon, any Hiritsu warrior would have cut him down on the spot. But to steal the sword would demand the immediate attention of the House Master.

Apparently Lance-leader Non had finally come up with an answer that satisfied his inner doubts. "We searched the outer chambers. He must have cached it somewhere else within the stronghold. Or possibly outside the walls, before returning to steal again."

Time to turn the conversation, Aris decided. If the House Master passed sentence now . . . He kept his voice even and relaxed. "And how many times would you say I walked through Hiritsu security, Ty?"

As expected, the familiar use of the warrior's name infuriated the man. In one fluid motion the lance-leader laid his blade flat against Aris' shoulder and then slid it forward to rest its point just under Aris' chin and tilt his head back. "No one gave you leave to speak, carrion."

"It is a fair question, Lance-leader." Was that the trace of a smile tugging at the right corner of the House Master's mouth? Aris couldn't be sure.

The lance-leader read it as a challenge. "We will find it, House Master York."

"Like hell." The point pressed up harder, breaking the

skin, but that was only pain, and Aris felt confident now that this man was too well-disciplined to kill him without the order from his House Master. That was the way of things. The will of the House Master *is* the will of the House. "You will never find Crescent Moon without my help."

Now there was no trace of amusement in her face or tone. Stone-faced and icy-voiced, she asked, "Do you really think so little of us?"

Careful, Aris warned himself. He bit back on the response that leapt to mind, boasting of his own abilities. That was not the way. "I think that highly of House Hiritsu," he finally said. "I spent sixteen months getting ready for this night. I left nothing to chance."

House Master York's eyes narrowed to sapphire splinters as she studied him. "You are willing to wager your life on that?"

"Will you put up a position in House Hiritsu against it?"

The moment the words left his mouth, Aris knew he had made his first real mistake. Over his left shoulder he heard a female voice whisper, "Impudent bastard," and there were several more oaths from the far background at his presumption, but those did not concern him. What did was the way House Master York's eyes suddenly widened and glanced toward the ceiling in thought. Her fingers rubbing together in anticipation. If the streets had taught Aris anything, it was body language. He had just given the House Master his motivation, his goal, and now she was puzzling it through with the relish of a master gamesplayer. Putting herself in his place.

When her eyes started to roam the room slowly, searching, he knew she almost had it. "You're not going to find it sitting on your ass," he said, deliberating forcing some scorn into his voice and trying hard to keep his own fear from showing.

The point disappeared from under his throat and a sharp pain bit into the side of his head, making his ears ring. For a moment Aris thought he was dead, but then realized that Lance-leader Non must have hit him with the flat of his blade. That, more than anything else so far, had actually scared him. He had been a quarter-turn of the wrist away from death.

The gamble had paid off, though. House Master York was no longer searching the room. Her piercing gaze was fastened intently on him. "What is your name?" she asked.

"Aris Sung." He thought about adding more, his home city or name of his father, but then decided it wiser to leave his answer at that. There might yet be a limit to the House Master's patience.

"Aris Sung. I welcome you into House Hiritsu." The blades fell away from his shoulders with the House Master's announcement, though Lance-leader Non at his right shoulder seemed to hesitate ever so slightly. "Does this make you happy?" she asked pleasantly.

You mean, can I die happy? Aris translated. That thought had to be foremost on the House Master's mind. She could order the death of a House Hiritsu member as easily as she could order the death of a thief. The door was cracked open, and it was now up to him to make sure it was not slammed in his face. So he leaned forward and bowed his head in shame. "No, House Master York," he said.

"And why not?"

It was time to make amends. "Because this unworthy one has spoken rudely to a highly placed House warrior, to the House Master herself, and dared to lay hands on Crescent Moon, which is taped to the underside of your seat. I expect and await punishment. I regret that you will have to stoop over in order to retrieve the blade." Was that enough?

"I won't have to stoop at all, Aris Sung. After I leave, you will return Crescent Moon to its place of rest, voluntarily, and suffer twice the punishment."

Aris felt his hopes rise slightly. He could die only once, so perhaps House Master York had other plans in mind.

"Lance-leader Ty Wu Non. You are recognized as this child's Mentor. He is now your responsibility. I want him trained against the day such audacity might actually be of use. Start with fifteen lashes for touching Crescent Moon, another fifteen for his insult to me, and five for the insult to yourself. Then run him for eight kilometers. If he falls, shoot him."

"Yes, House Master."

Aris looked up, not wanting to speak out of turn, but realizing he had to make sure his debt was fully repaid to the satisfaction of the House Master. "Yes, Aris Sung," she recognized him. "You have something to say?"

He nodded, and met her gaze. "The House Master has not sentenced me for the second offense of touching Crescent Moon."

Her gaze was cold and appraising, as if wondering just how much a thirteen-year-old child would take upon himself and could hope to stand up to. Finally she nodded to Aris' new House Mentor. "If he lasts the run, another twenty lashes." Then she gathered her robes about her and left the room with the same forceful stride she had entered with.

Aris smiled grimly. He was right where he wanted to be. Now he had to survive it.

Awesome

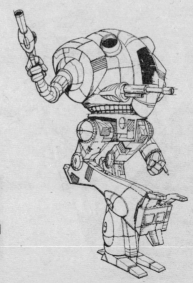

Caesar

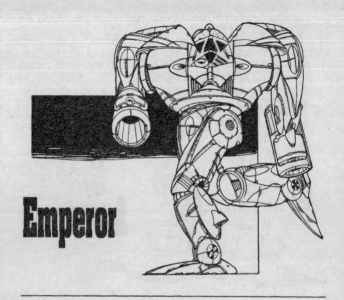

Emperor

**Falcon
Hawk**

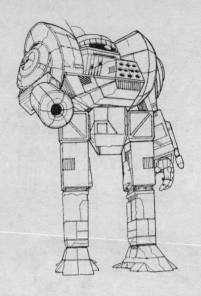

Grand
Dragon

Grasshopper

Shootist

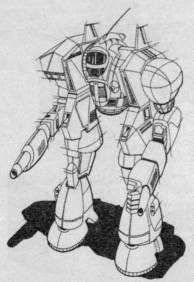

War Dog

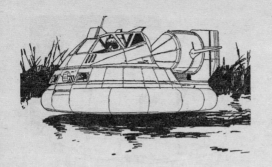

Savannah Master

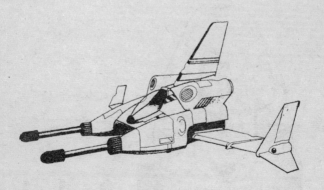

Sparrowhawk

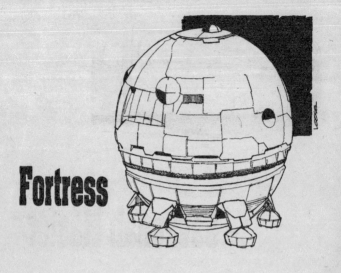

Fortress

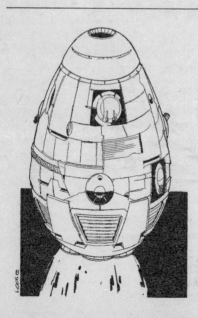

Overlord